Edit

The author did an awesome job of telling this story. His descriptions were so vivid that I felt like I was right there with the characters, feeling what they were feeling, seeing what they were seeing, I felt the love they felt for one another or the disgust they felt for another. I found myself rooting for the success of some characters or side-eyeing others. All in all this was a five star read from the beginning to the very end. It was hard to put it down even after I had finished! Great job Asani Bandz! I would definitely pick up anything else that he writes in the future!

BABE ST
ASANI BANDZ

Rarri

Written by Asani Bandz

Dedication

I would like to dedicate this book to my sons Kevin & Nike. You two are my pride and joy. I love you both more than words can explain. I am more than grateful that God blessed me with the opportunity to be your father because the day you were born was the moment that I found my purpose in life. I promise to continue to make y'all proud. Akins boys are forever, Love dad.

Acknowledgments

First & foremost I would like to thank God for blessing me with a gift I never knew I had, until now. Secondly, I would like to thank the lyin' ass bitches who put me in jail because without y'all I don't believe this book would exist. It is what it is, I can't even be mad. I also want to wish y'all the best and I truly hope y'all are OK out there. Ain't no point in crying over spilled milk especially when it's spoiled.

I would like to thank Precious for helping me with the original version, even though we went our separate ways I will always love you for that and so much more. You still my boos.

I want to thank my moms & pops for everything they taught me. Even though y'all are not together that never stopped me from admiring the relationship the two of you share. Pumpkin heads (Jackie & Destiny) I love y'all, big bro tryna get it together. I miss y'all so much & I'm proud of both of y'all. Granny, I love you leave them cigarettes alone lol

To the rest of the family, I love y'all too & will see y'all soon

Fa'sho I want to thank everybody who kept me writing from the beginning. If it wasn't for Y'all niggas I wouldn't have kept goin. Doody, Voodoo, T-bird, Albert, Beyon, Lavish, Tug5, Poetry, Cocaine, Erin, Malcolm, NBA, V-Boy, Zeus, Frosty, Buccy Blue, E-rocc, Ricc rocc, loony, Taboo, T.O, Dus Locc, Crash, Nation, TJ, 4-Fingers, Fab & Dre… it's long list I know I forgot a lot of people but y'all know who y'all are good looking, cuh. I really appreciate all the positive feedback from everybody.

Prologue

"Puff, puff, pass," Pretty Me da P said to Trouble from the back seat with his hand extended reaching for the blunt.

"Shut yo ass up nigga. Ain't nobody tryna' smoke all yo shit cuz," Trouble scolded before passing the blunt to Lil Trouble in the passenger seat.

"Shid! I am," Lil Trouble replied before taking a big ass hit of the blunt, damn near making it half the size it was before he got it. "Neighbor Hood, stupid," he added, and they both began to laugh almost into tears.

Trouble and Lil Trouble were brothers both from Neighbor Hood Sixty Crip. Trouble was known to be laid back and about his money but would bust his if he even thought you tried to cross him. Lil Trouble was the wild card that niggas hated to be around cause all he liked to do was bully and punk muthafuckas every chance he got.

"Stop playin'. You always on that bullshit," Pretty Me da P said from the backseat.

"*You always on some punk shit*", Lil Trouble thought before taking another hit of the blunt.

"Give cuz his shit back before he start cryin'," Trouble told his little brother.

"Ain't nobody bout to start cryin'. Matter fact, y'all keep that. I'm already rollin' another one. I need to stop smokin' after niggas anyway. Ain't no tellin' where yall lips done been," Pretty Me da P joked and started laughing.

“That’s funny comin’ from the nigga who be fuckin’ on prostitutes. I’m pretty sure you be kissin’ them bitches. Probably eatin’ they pussies too,” Lil Trouble said, and on cue, they both added “on Hood,” giving each other dap and laughing their asses off.

“Fuck y’all,” Pretty Me da P said, knowing that what was said was true.

All the gangsters knew he was soft, and all the pimps knew he was fake. The only people who seemed to not notice was the girls who fell for his spell, but that would shortly come to an end.

“What type of nigga names himself, *Pretty Me,* anyway?” Lil Trouble scolded.

“A nigga who get bad bitches,” Pretty Me da P shot back.

“Nigga, the last bitch I seen you with looked like a straight smoker,” Trouble teased. “Hold on, that bitch *IS* a smoker!” he said in a matter of fact tone and laughed.

By this time, Pretty Me da P was quiet. With his ego bruised and something to prove he said, “Y'all know Trina?”

“What Trina?” Lil Trouble asked, looking back at him curiously.

“Trina, Trina!” Pretty Me da P said smoothly while finishing rolling up the blunt.

Trouble looked back surprised and stunned like he couldn’t believe what he was hearing and asked, “Bino sister, Trina?”

Knowing he had the brother's most undivided attention, he felt like the man. He lit the blunt, inhaled the smoke, blew it out and said "yup," seemingly more fly than intended.

Trouble looked at Lil Trouble in disbelief. Lil Trouble kept his eyes on Pretty Me da P looking for any sign of bullshit. He had been trying to get with Trina ever since Middle school but to no avail, so to hear that Pretty Me da P snatched her up, left a foul taste in his mouth.

"Cuz lyin'," Lil Trouble said before he turned around and lit the Newport that was in the ashtray.

"If I'm lyin', I'm dyin'. She been on my team for about three months now," Pretty Me da P assured.

He could practically see the steam coming off of Lil Trouble. He decided to put the fork in his back and kill him off with the last bite.

Pretty Me da P leaned forward putting himself in the middle of the brothers, but keeping his focus on Lil Trouble and said, "she told me you been tryna hook up with her on some square ass shit. Talkin' bout *I wanna marry you* and all that. Hahaha," Pretty Me da P chuckled. "She even showed me that text message you sent with a picture of you holdin' yo lil ass dick talkin' bout *this could be all you*. We was dyin' laughin'. You lucky I stopped her from postin' that shit on Facebook. On God, that shit would of went viral," he said laughing, then leaned back and took a pull of the blunt.

"Matter of fact, watch this," he said pulling out his phone.

“Cuz if you post a picture of me, I’m knockin’ you out on Neighbor Hood Crip,” Lil Trouble barked while smacking his fist into his palm hard as hell, almost after every word he said.

“Calm down killa, I wouldn’t even play you like that,” Pretty Me da P replied before hitting the call button on his phone and placing it on speaker as it rang.

“Hello?” A female voice answered on the other end of the phone.

“Say, bitch! If you really bout yo ho’n, step out the room and let me see what you got goin’,” Pretty Me da P said, then hit the end button before she could even respond and stepped out the car.

Not even 10 seconds later, there was Trina stepping out of the room with her long curly hair, caramel complexion, phat ass, and what seemed to be the world’s smallest dress, but still fit her so perfectly.

She turned around, popped her ass and twerked exposing her cheeks, then walked back into the room and closed the door, leaving Trouble and Lil Trouble with instant hard-ons.

“I’ll see you niggas later,” Pretty Me da P said, flipping a quarter through the passenger window making sure it landed in lil Trouble’s lap. He gave him a wink and added, “get like me,” then walked off.

“It’s always the bitch ass niggas who get the baddest bitches. That shit crazy cuz, on Neighbor Hood,” Lil Trouble said angrily, but more butt-hurt than anything.

“Shid. Bino bout to get out the Pen. Last I heard, cuz was on S-time. That nigga gon go crazy when he find out cuz puttin’ his sister down. Cuz name gon be Ugly Me da P when Bino done with him,” Trouble said before starting the car and leaving the hotel parking lot.

Pretty Me da P put his key in the door and walked into the hotel room. Trina was in the bathroom with the door cracked getting dolled up and playing *‘Patty Cake’* by YG on her phone.

“Damn bitch! You still ain't done gettin’ dressed?” he said, pushing the bathroom door open.

“I was just about to text you and tell you don’t come up cause I got a date on the way for $800. Put that weed out. I don’t know if he gon be trippin’ off the smell. Plus, I told him, I don’t smoke,” Trina replied reaching for the blunt.

“Trippin’? Bitch, I run this shit! I don’t give a fuck about no trick trippin’. You need to be worried about if I’m trippin’,” Pretty Me da P gamed and hit the blunt, then blew the smoke in her face. “Worried about a trick trippin’,” he added and shook his head in disgust.

“I’m not worried bout him trippin’ daddy, I just wanna get this money off him so I could pay you. Don’t you want me to pay you?” she asked grabbing his dick the way he liked.

“What you think bitch?” he countered, hitting the blunt again.

“Mmm, I love when you talk to me like that,” she moaned.

"I asked you what you think, not what you love, bitch," he said.

"I thin—"

"KNOCK, KNOCK, KNOCK, KNOCK."

"Fuck, that's him," she said. "You gon have to hide under the bed daddy."

"I ain't hidin' under no fuckin' bed," he whispered.

"Well you gon miss out on this fuckin' money," she spat back, foldin' her arms.

"KNOCK, KNOCK, KNOCK, KNOCK."

"Bitch hurry up!" he said and put the blunt out then got under the bed.

Trina grabbed her perfume and sprayed the room trying to cover the weed smell as much as possible.

"KNOCK, KNOCK, KNOCK, KNOCK."

"Comin'," she said and gave the room a look over before opening the door.

" Damn Trina, You look even better in person " he said looking down at her.

"Thank you," Trina replied blushing. "Shawn, right?"

"The one and only," he replied walking into the room. Do you mind if I use the restroom? It was a long drive here"

"Not at all. It's right there," Trina said, pointing to the door to the restroom and got on the bed.

For some reason, she had butterflies. She didn't know if it was because her pimp was in the same room or because she was attracted to Shawn. In all, she didn't expect him to look the way he did. He was average height with a fit body and handsome face. He didn't look like the type to pay for pussy. At that thought she cursed herself. "Damn, I forgot to get the money," she mumbled.

"Dumb ass bitch," Pretty Me da P said to himself, hearing what she said.

As soon as Shawn closed the bathroom door, he pulled the shower curtain back to make sure nobody was in there. Then he flushed the toilet and turned on the sink as if he was actually using the restroom. When he looked in the mirror, the warm face he used at the door was replaced with a devilish grin and menacing eyes as he thought about what was about to happen.

Trina was just about to ask was he okay in there, but the bathroom door opened as soon as her mouth did, and he was stepping out.

"Not to sound rude but I forgot to get the money from you when you came in," Trina said shyly.

"Oh yeah, it's right here," Shawn said, reaching into his jacket pocket, but instead of pulling out the money he smacked the shit out of Trina, almost snapping her neck and sending her flying on the bed. Before she could even react to the first blow, he punched her so hard that it immediately knocked her out. Then he began to rape her.

She woke up to him on top of her missionary dripping sweat and grinding her like a wild animal.

"No! Get off of me! Stop!" Trina tried crying, but that only aroused him more.

"Daddy help me! Please! Daddy, please help me!" Trina tried pleading.

Pretty Me da P was under the bed with both hands covering his mouth so Shawn wouldn't hear him crying like a little bitch. He shed more tears than Trina just at the thought of being found under the bed and of what might happen to him.

"Get the fuck off of me. Daddy help! Get him off of me! Daddy, please! Help me!" Trina cried.

Pretty Me da P didn't move. He just kept his hands over his mouth, closed his eyes and cried harder. Quietly!

By this time, Trina was desperate. "Get the fuck off me!" she screamed, clawing at his eyes drawing blood, and leaving four big ass scratches on each side of his face.

"Argh, you bitch!" he screamed and threw punch after punch, knocking her back out. He was so angry he continued to hit her while she was unconscious. To say he beat her is an understatement.

After he felt satisfied, he put on his clothes, lit the half blunt he saw in the ashtray and left.

Pretty Me da P was so scared he didn't move just in case Shawn came back.

"Cough, cough… agh…agh…" Trina moaned, waking back up, but not able to move. She heard noise and felt the bed slightly move and began to cry again, "No, please don't," she thought it was Shawn again, but it wasn't. It was Pretty Me da P looking at her like a scared child with a face full of tears.

He couldn't even recognize her. One of her eyes was black and completely closed shut, while the other one was barely open to the point where he didn't know if she could see him or not, and her face was almost covered entirely in blood.

He wiped the tears from his eyes and grabbed his car keys from one of the drawers. The whole time, Trina watched him with her one eye.

"Daddy, why you ain't help me… daddy help me… please, daddy help me," Trina cried.

Pretty Me da P back stepped toward the front door, tripping and falling to the floor with tears in his eyes again. He got up and ran to the door. He was so shook up, he couldn't even open it.

"You ain't no pimp. You a lil bitch!" Trina said, loud enough for him to hear as he finally got the door open and ran out, leaving her alone.

Chapter 1

"You drivin'," Trigg told Spank.

"I ain't drivin'… I drove last time. Today, I'm bout to do my thang," Spank said aiming the gun, pretending to shoot imaginary targets in the house.

"You drove last time cause the time before that, you ran up on a nigga and ain't hit shit," Trigg said, taking the gun from Spank.

"See, that's why I need to get craccin' right now, cause you ain't gon never let me hear the end of that shit. Let me just—"

"You drivin' cuz," Rarri cut Spank off as he walked back into the room. He was holding an AK-47 with a hundred round drum.

"Here, Trigg," Rarri said, handing him the choppa.

"Hop through the window and put the burners in the car… g-mom's in the livin' room. Me and Spank gon go through the front."

"Fa'sho," Trigg said and went out the window.

Rarri and Spank walked to the kitchen, got three sodas, and headed through the living room towards the front door. Rarri's grandmother was sitting on the couch laughing at the T.V.

"I'll be back granny," he said, giving her a kiss on the cheek.

"Where you goin' boy?" she asked.

"To Spank house for a lil bit," he lied.

"Good," she said digging in her purse, pulling out a twenty-dollar bill. "Stop and get me a pack of Kool mild 100's, some B.C. powder, and a 7Up on yo way back."

"Ok," he said, and hurried out the door before she could think of somewhere else to send him.

"Damn, them niggas deep as fuck," Trigg said, almost drooling on himself.

"We done lucked up and hit the lotto cuz," Rarri said with a big ass smile on his face. You would have thought that nigga hit the Powerball how happy he was. He loved catching niggas slipping on their *Hood Day*, cause they were in big groups and crowds, making them easy targets. "The more, the better," he would say.

"Let's just hurry up and do this shit so we can get on," Spank said with an attitude. He might not have had aim, but one thing Spank hated most was sitting in a car. His luck was even worse than his aim. For some reason, every person Spank shot always lived. He shot a dude in the face at point-blank range, and he still lived. He put holes in a lot of muthafuckas, but ain't killed shit.

"Aye cuz, you mad or nah?" Trigg teased.

"On Yaahmpton, I ain't trippin', but thats on my momma, I won't drive no more," Spank said, not knowing how true his words were.

"Don't even trip cuz. Ima drive next time and let you shine, on yaahmpton," Rarri said, putting his hand on Spank's shoulder.

Spank was smiling now and nodding his head then said, “fa’sho.”

“Ight, but look; drive around the corner so we could park in the apartments behind them. We gon hop the wall and get craccin’….. just post up til we get back,” Rarri instructed.

“Yeah, just post up cuz,” Trigg joked, taking the smile off of Spank's face. Trigg always could get under Spank's skin, sometimes without even trying. Spank was older than Trigg, so he hated when he tried to school him, especially in front of Rarri.

When they pulled into the apartments, Spank backed into a parking spot, cut the headlights off, but kept the engine running. Rarri looked around the parking lot of the apartments to make sure nobody was watching them.

“Ight foo, we’ll be right back,” he said as him and Trigg got out of the car.

As soon as the doors closed, Spank lit a Newport. “Sit in the car… next time I’m craccin’ and y’all niggas sittin’ in the car,” Spank said, sounding like he was running shit and pointing in the rearview mirror.

When they jumped over the wall, all the attention was on them. It was red everywhere. Red hats, red shirts, red shoes… muthafuckas even had on red pants. Everything seemed to move in slow motion as they made eye contact, then Rarri broke the ice.

“What’s craccin’!”

"BOOM, BOOM, BOOM, BOOM, BOOM, BOOM, BOOM"... Trigg followed right behind him with his 30 round 9mm.

"PAT, PAT, PAT, PAT, PAT, PAT, PAT"...

All they could do was run and try to get out of the way as bullets ripped through the faces and body parts of their friends and loved ones. Muthafuckas was running over each other, hiding behind people, falling on the floor when they wasn't hit, all type of shit. One nigga even tried to use his aunty as a human shield. When bullets get to flying, all that homie shit is out the window, and it's everybody for themselves.

'CLICK! CLICK! CLICK!' "I'm out," Trigg yelled at Rarri.

"I'm still craccin'," Rarri yelled back, shouting at his moving targets. He ran up on one dude who was trying to crawl away from the scene and shot him in the face, then turned around to leave.

"Fuck that," he said and went back to put four more in what was left of the dude's head.

"Come on," he yelled at Trigg, and they started running back toward the wall. Once they jumped over the wall, they got back in the back seat and ducked down like they always did.

"Ight, go! Go! Go!" Trigg yelled to Spank, but the car didn't move.

"What the fuck you waitin' on, nigga, go!" Rarri yelled, but the car still ain't move.

Rarri got up to see what was going on and jumped back when he saw it. “What the fuck,” Rarri said.

“Why the fuck we ain’t movin’, and why the fuck Spank ain’t talkin’?” Trigg said as tears fell down his face. Fearing the worse, he still couldn’t look up.

“He can’t talk Trigg… he dead cuz,” Rarri said, feeling defeated.

“How is he dead?” Trigg cried.

“Somebody shot him,” Rarri said.

“Who shot ‘em?” Trigg asked.

“I don’t know,” Rarri said.

“How you don’t know?” Trigg screamed at Rarri.

“Nigga, I was with you!” Rarri screamed back.

“Fuck! We gotta get out of here. We goin’ to find out what happened. Let’s just get to the hood, first.”

“How we gon find out what happened and we don’t even know who did it?” Trigg asked with his head still down.

By this time, Rarri had to block Trigg’s crying out. It was bad enough that he had to push Spank’s body over to the passenger seat and drive all the way back. On top of that, every time Rarri looked over at Spank, Spank’s dead eyes was already looking at Rarri.

Somehow, they made it back to the hood with no problems. Rarri pulled up to a vacant house they kicked it at and sometimes fucked bitches in.

He hopped out, opened the garage, got back in the car and pulled in. When he closed the garage, he noticed Trigg still didn't get out the car and was in the same position. When he opened the back door, he grabbed his choppa.

"What we gon tell his moms, Rarri?" Trigg asked.

" 'We', ain't gon tell her nothin'," Rarri said with his head down.

"That's fucked up. We can't just not tell her nothin'. What if she—"

"I'ma tell her," Rarri cut him off.

"What you gon tell her?" Trigg cried.

"I'ma tell her I don't know what happened," Rarri said.

"But wh—"

"The last thing we need is for her to go to the police and try to have us be a witness to some bullshit…. You know how his momma is," Rarri's voice boomed.

He was clearly upset with Trigg and the way he was acting. Everybody in the hood knew Spank's momma was a snitch. Back in the day, she told on his father when the feds raided their house for drugs. Spank's father wasn't home, so when they kicked the door in and found sixteen kilos of powder, an arsenal of weapons, and a shook up wife who was 8 months pregnant, they used every trick in the book to get her to cooperate.

She told them everything and some. Shit they didn't even know nothing about, yet. The bitch even called

Spank's father pretending like her water broke, so he could come running home, only to be met by the punk-ass police and took to jail.

If it wasn't for the fact that she was about to birth his first child, she surely wouldn't have made it to the delivery room. He told niggas to stall her out and look after his son, so Spank always got stupid love in the hood from a lot of the older niggas. Especially the ones his father put on.

"I know. This shit just got me spooked how it all happened. I'm good. A nigga just need a blunt or somethin'," Trigg said as he got out of the car.

"Man, me too cuz. It's been us three rockin' and doin' our joints since the sandbox… now everything is just fucked up too fast for me to even process," Rarri said palm brushing his hair.

"So, what now?" asked Trigg.

"Now we just gon lay low until one of the homie's find Spank in here… we don't know shit, Trigg. You hear me? Nothing! Rarri said.

"Yea, I hear you,"

"I'm serious cuz," Rarri said more demanding.

"I heard you, my nigga. We don't know what happened," Trigg replied.

"Ight, let's get up out of here," Rarri said and hit the top of the roof twice on the car, then looked into the driver's side window and said, "I love you cuz."

It was like Spank was already waiting for Rarri with his eyes again. Rarri could hear Spank saying, "*Don't leave me here.*"

"I have to," Rarri whispered sadly.

"What?" Trigg asked, causing Rarri to turn around.

"Nothin'... we out of here," he said.

They went back out through the garage. Once he closed it, he looked around to make sure they weren't seen. He gave Trigg a dap.

"Ight, we gon link up in a couple days.... Remember, don't say shit to nobody cuz. Nobody!" Rarri instructed.

"I got you," Trigg assured, and the two went their separate ways.

A week had passed, and Rarri still hadn't seen or heard a word from Trigg. He wasn't answering his phone and when Rarri would go by his crib, his aunt would say she hadn't seen him. Rarri started to feel like she was lying.

To make shit worse, some little nigga was trying to get some pussy in the vacant and found Spank stanking the day after he was killed.

The funeral was pushed back another week because Spank's family wasn't even close to having enough money to bury him. They even set up a GoFundMe account but was only able to raise two hundred and twelve dollars.

Something was gon have to give, but if it didn't, Rarri was gon have to hit one hell of a lick so he could give

Spank a proper burial. It was the least he could do, but at 16 years old, wasn't much he could do.

All his life, he thought being gangster was everything. Now, as he faces a dilemma with the burden of burying one of his best friends, he feels different, he thinks different and see's different.

"I gotta get this money," Rarri said to himself.

"*But how?*" he thought. "I ain't gettin' no job, ain't robbin' no bank, and ain't enough money in purse snatchin'," he pondered.

"Fuck!" he said as he began to pace back and forth in his room. He did that for about an hour then laid on his bed and looked at the ceiling as if it was a T.V. Tired of thinking, he closed his eyes, trying to rest his brain a bit. He was just about to doze off when a thought caused him to open his eyes.

"Chu-Chu." Just as fast as he said the name, he was out the door.

***

"KNOCK, KNOCK, KNOCK."

"Who is it?" a female voice asked from the other side of the door.

"Rarri," he answered.

It sounded like ten different locks were turning right before the door opened.

"Hey nephew," the lady said and gave Rarri a big hug.

"Hey, aunty Heaven."

Heaven was Rarri's mother's sister. She also was a meth head, but somehow got one of the biggest dope dealers in Los Angeles; who was pussy whipped enough to marry her.

"Sorry to hear about your friend. Momma told me you was havin' a hard time since he died. Are you ok?" she asked.

"Yeah, I been cool," Rarri said with a half-smile that he forced on his face.

"Well, if you need anything, don't hesitate to ask," she told him.

"Well, that's kinda why I'm here… I was wonderin' if I could holla at Chu-Chu? I'm tryna help Spank's family out with some money for the funeral," Rarri told her.

"Nephew, now you know Chu-Chu don't do no business with no kids," Heaven said, pinching Rarri's cheeks.

"I know but I also know he'll do anything you tell him, so I was hopin' maybe you could talk to him for me… I ain't got nobody else to turn to," Rarri said, making sure she could see the water building up in his eyes.

"Look… I'ma talk to him, but I can't make no promises," she explained.

"Thanks, aunty. I knew you would understand," Rarri said and tried to kiss her on the cheek but she put her hand out to stop him.

"I'm only doin' this because I hate to see you cry, and you know that…. Yo momma probably cursin' me from her grave as we speak," Heaven said, shaking her head.

"She probably ain't trippin' under the circumstances," Rarri tried to assure her.

"Mmm-hmm, whatever. Well, you know what I gotta do to make him say yes, right?" she asked. "I mean, under these short circumstances."

"Um, cook him a fat ass meal?" Rarri asked.

Heaven laughed at his answer. She knew that he really believed it was actually that simple. At that moment, she decided that she was going to un-blind him so that reality would either make him or break him, but either way, he wasn't walking out of that house the same way he came in. She was about to turn Rarri into somewhat of a monster. To her, Chu-Chu was the devil. If Rarri was trying to go through Heaven to get to hell, he damn sure was going to fall hard.

"Ok look. Let me explain this to you as simple and straight forward as possible… once I walk into that room and close that door, I'm gon fuck, and suck, and throw this pussy back to bring out what you need. Do you understand?" Heaven asked.

"Bu—" Rarri started.

"Do you understand?" she cut off.

He paused for a minute to see if this was a joke, but she was straight-faced. Then he said, "Yea, I understand."

"Let me hear you say it," she responded.

"I understand," he said.

"No! Say, *I want you to fuck, suck, and throw that pussy back and bring out what I need*," Heaven ordered.

"Are you serious?" he asked.

"Bye Rarri," she said, walking to the front door to open it so he could leave.

"Ok! Ok! I want you to fuck, suck, and throw that pussy back and bring out what I need," Rarri said.

As soon as he said it, she took off all of her clothes until she was completely naked looking at him the whole time, then walked into the room Chu-Chu was in and closed the door.

Rarri couldn't believe what had just happened. After waiting for about an hour he fell asleep on the couch.

"I told you I didn't want to drive. Look at my head cuz. You just gon ditch me and leave me in a vacant. I thought we was boys?" Spank started grabbing him saying; "look at my face," over and over.

Rarri woke up to Heaven pulling on him trying to wake him up.

"Look at my face, I'm serious. These three is on me," she said and tossed three bags of powder on his lap. "That's 84 grams, Rarri. If you want to talk to Chu-Chu, come back with some money. I did my part. The rest is on you," Heaven said.

"How much do I need to bring back from this," Rarri asked as he was walking to the front door to leave.

“You figure it out,” she said as she opened up the door.

“Thanks, aunt—” Rarri started, but she cut him off again.

“No problem pimp. Just come back by when you ready,” Heaven said.

“Ight,” said Rarri, as he was about to walk off.

“Rarri!” she said so he could turn and face her.

“Yea?” he asked.

“How it feel to down yo first bitch?” Heaven asked, but slammed the door shut before he could answer. She put her back against the door, slid down in a sitting position and cried, thinking nineteen years back.

Chapter 2

It was the summer of 1997, and money was booming for Angel. She was 5'7'' with a coke bottle body, high yellow, light brown eyes, and if her hair grew an inch longer, it would have touched her ass.

Every trick wanted to fuck her, every bitch wanted to be her, and every pimp dreamed to have her on his team. Too bad for them, she had already chosen, and her nigga was far more aggressive than the pimps in Los Angeles.

He was a pimp from East Oakland who went by the name, God. God was known to go hard on a hoe, but with Angel, it was different. He would give Angel the world if he had it, and she knew it. Everything he knew about the game he shared with her, never holding nothing back so no slick bitch or con nigga could run it on her. She was game tight. His bottom.

Angel was counting her daily trap and smoking on a joint in the hotel suite her and God reserved for the week in Beverly Hills, California.

"Fifty-three hundred, babe," Angel yelled, and walked into the other room of the suite where God was laying on the bed watching T.V. Angel threw the money in the air, making it rain on God and jumped on top of him. She put the joint to his lips and he took a pull.

"Did you hear me?" she asked joyfully. "I made fifty-three—"

“I heard you,” he said cutting her off as he blew the smoke out.

“ugh,” she playfully pushed his face and climbed off of him. “You always tryna be all cool and shit…. Nigga, you know you happy.”

“I’m straight,” he said with a big ass smile on his face. “Just chillin.”

“Chillin’ my ass,” Angel said as she walked to the bathroom. “Don’t try to play me either… remember what you promised? Tonight, we livin’ it up.”

“Yea, yea, I remember,” he yelled after her.

As soon as he heard her turn the shower on, he got out of the bed and did his touch down dance.

He had been waiting on this day for a while now. It was Angel’s younger sister’s eighteenth birthday. She made him promise they would take that night off and take Cristy out. They were going to hit up a few clothing stores and go to the Santa Monica Pier.

By the time Angel stepped out of the bathroom, she was looking like a million and a half. She wore small booty shorts, a tight shirt that showed her perfectly formed stomach and her hair in two braids. To her surprise, God was dressed and ready to go. He dressed more like a gangster than a pimp. He had on some black 501 jeans with a matching leather jacket and some black and grey Nikes. The only thing to probably give him away was his chain. It was a fat gold rope, and the medallion was a gold, naked female in a laid-back sitting position, wearing high heels made out of red diamonds. He also had a matching gold grill. As they were leaving the room, he grabbed his Raider's hat and threw it over his neatly dreaded hair.

When they pulled up to Angel's mother's house in Compton, it was niggas up and down the street. It always looked like a block party was popping on Kemp Street.

"You ain't comin' in?" Angel asked with a smirk on her face.

"You know I can't stand yo momma," he joked but was dead serious. She disliked him just as much, if not more.

Angel and her mother used to be close before she met him, which didn't sit right with her. Angel had dropped out of school, stopped going to church and rarely came around since she had moved with him.

"Whatever," she said and got out of the car. "She can't stand you either," she finished and closed the door.

He waited until she was in the house and got out of the car. He lit a cigarette and fumbled through his pockets for his bankroll, but it wasn't there.

"Fuck," he said to himself, thinking he left it at the hotel room, but then he remembered putting it in the glove compartment. He walked around to the passenger side of the car, reached through the window to unlock the glove compartment, and grabbed two hundred-dollar bills. Before he could lean back out of the window, he heard a gun chamber in a bullet and felt it press the back of his cap. He froze in midstance.

"What that nutty like cuz?" a deep voice said from behind him.

“I…I…I ain’t even from round here, bruh.,” he responded, still stiff as fuck. Then he heard laughter behind him and felt the gun ease up off his cap. He recognized that laugh. It was only one person he knew that had a laugh like that.

“Muthafucka,” he mumbled and shook his head as the smile spread across his face.

“What’s up homie,” Crip Calvin said in his normal voice, as God was turning around.

Crip Calvin and God did a bid together in Delano State Prison. They earned mutual respect for each other during a racial riot between the blacks and Mexicans.

“The price of pussy, mane,” God said and gave Crip Calvin a dap.

“I see you cuz, I see you,” Crip Calvin said. “You still need that?”

“Do a fish need water?” God asked and handed him the two bills.

Crip Calvin pulled out a bag of coke. “This that raw, so you might want to step on it before you do ya thang,” he said.

“The only thing I’m mixin’ with this is some China, ya dig?” God said as he put it in his jacket pocket. He loved to mix his heroin with his coke.

“Still crazy than a muthafucka cuz,” Crip Calvin said, and laughed. “I’ma get with you later. Let me know when you slide back through this way.”

"Fa'sho bruh," God replied as he walked back around to the driver side of the car. As soon as he got into the car, he mixed his drugs and took a bump. He checked his nose in the mirror to make sure it wasn't dirty. Just as he was sitting back in his seat, Angel and Cristy was coming out of the house towards the car. They were almost identical in appearance. Cristy was just a shade darker, making her a caramel complexion and a little prettier in the face. He was in awe at the sight of them until he focused behind them and seen their mother looking at him coldly. Loving to get on her last nerves, he returned the same look so she could tell he was mimicking her. She flicked him off and slammed the door.

"Why you always tryna agitate my momma, babe?" Angel asked.

"Cause yo momma always tryna agitate me," he shot back. "Happy birthday Cristy."

"Thanks," she said shyly as they got in the car.

He went to the Compton swap meet before it closed and let Cristy go crazy getting any and everything she wanted. She had never spent that much money in her life. God stopped at a liquor store, got two bottles of Hennessy, and headed to Santa Monica. They smoked and drank all the way there.

By the time they got there, they were faded. They rode the rides, played games, and took a few pictures together. Cristy had never had that much fun before, and by now she was feeling herself. She even slid a few naughty looks at God on the under.

"Angel, come with me to the bathroom, I gotta pee," Cristy told her.

"Ok," Angel said. "Babe, we'll be right back, I'ma take her to the restroom," she told God.

"Ight," he said. Cristy gave him another one of those looks before they walked off. He knew this would be easy, but not this easy. He was in the middle of contemplating his master plan when three dudes approached him. He had been seeing them mean-mugging him a couple of times earlier but didn't trip because he wasn't there for that and as far as he was concerned, that comes with the territory of being a fly ass nigga. They were what he called, *bitchless niggas* because all night he didn't see them with not one bitch. It was one big gorilla looking dude with two little ones, standing next to him.

"Aye, where you from cuz?" the big one asked.

God looked at all three of them like they were clowns, then focused back on the crowd, scanning the bitches who walked by.

"I ain't even from around here, bruh," he replied. "Damn, how you doin' today, sexy?" God asked a female who was walking by.

"Fine," she said blushing and kept walking.

The big dude stepped in front of God, clearly upset cause he was being brushed off.

"I know you ain't from round here, that's why I asked where you was from cuz," he barked. "This Shoreline Crip."

“I’m from Babe Street,” God said, stepping to the side to get the view he once had.

The trio looked at each other confused and then burst into laughter. They almost had to hold the big one up, so he didn’t fall on the ground from laughing so hard. He was holding his stomach and wiping the tears from his eyes.

“Babe Street?” he asked, trying to catch his breath at the same time. “Where the fuck is that at, cuz?”

Angel and Cristy came out of the restroom walking towards God.

“Anywhere you see a bitch,” God said to the three dudes, and walked to meet Angel and Cristy halfway. The three dudes stopped laughing. When God reached them, he put an arm around them both as they walked.

“So, what, now?” he asked.

“Let’s take Cristy home and call it a night,” Angel said. “She’s had enough fun for one day. Plus, momma probably worried sick right now.”

“I don’t wanna go home. I want to go with y’all,” Cristy cried. “I wish we could do this all the time.”

“We could,” God added with a smirk.

Angel elbowed him in his side. “No, we can’t,” she said.

“Why not?” asked Cristy. “You act like I don’t know what you do, Angel, I’m not stupid.”

Angel laughed. “I’m not about to have this conversation with you, girl, especially not tonight.”

“Why not tonight?” Cristy asked.

“Yea, why not tonight?” God threw in, knowing he was getting on Angel's nerves.

“Babe shut up,” Angel said, trying to punch him in the arm, but he moved making her miss.

“Angel, I’m ready,” Cristy said, looking her straight in the eyes so she could see how serious she was.

By this time, they were at the car. Angel fumbled in her purse, pulled out a Newport and lit it. She looked at God and he put his hands up, shrugged his shoulders and took a step back.

“You think you slick,” she said pointing at God, then turned to Cristy. “And you think you ready.”

Angel took a couple more pulls from her Newport thinking of her master plan. She was going to take them both on a ride they would forever remember.

Angel pulled on the Newport, threw the butt and blew the smoke out.

“Fuck it! Let’s go back to the room.”

As soon as they got back in the hotel suite, Angel and Cristy went straight to the bathroom, turned on the shower and freshened up. When they came out, he went in. God came out of the shower in his boxers. Angel and Cristy was on the bed talking. He went and grabbed a joint he had in the ashtray and lit it.

“Babe, I ran the rules down to her, so she knows what’s up,” Angel said. “I just got one rule of my own.”

God went and laid on the bed so he could be between the two of them. “And what’s that?” he asked.

“She has to love and treat you the way I do, and you have to treat her the way you treat me,” Angel told him. “That’s the only way this is goin’ to work. So, what’s up?”

“I’m with it,” he said.

“Good,” she responded, and got up, grabbed an E-pill off of the counter, and put it in his mouth. “We already took ours.”

Angel started kissing God sloppily and playing with her pussy. She grabbed Cristy’s face and pulled it towards her’s and kissed her the same way, but Cristy pulled back and wiped her mouth with the back of her hand.

“What the fuck,” Cristy spat. “I’m not about to kiss you. You’re my sister.”

“What the fuck my ass bitch, you said you was ready right? Well, don’t freeze up now hoe,” Angel said and kissed Cristy again, but this time Cristy kissed back.

God was turned on by how Angel got down. She was one of a kind and he always loved that about her. He pulled down her panties and started eating her pussy while they kissed. She was riding his face in a slow, circular motion. Angel slid Cristy’s panties off and massaged her wet pussy, then she grabbed one of God’s hands so he could touch her wetness. Angel moved off of God’s face and put Cristy there. She put her hands on Cristy’s hips and moved them in the same motion she was moving. After she found her rhythm and God’s hands was gripping Cristy’s ass, she went down on him.

Angel spit on his dick so much that it was soaked under him. She sucked his dick like a pro, taking it all into her mouth. Every time she would come up, it would be even wetter. Cristy turned around so she could see Angel and ride God's face from the back in a sixty-nine position. Cristy grabbed his dick while Angel sucked it. When Angel came up, Cristy went down on it, making it even wetter. She moaned hard when she felt God smack her ass and spread her cheeks.

Angel jumped on his dick and began to ride him while he ate Cristy out. One bouncing on his face and the other bouncing on his dick. They switched positions over and over all night long. Cristy fell in love with God just like Angel, if not more.

They say that was the night God made Heaven, but if you ask me, I would say it was actually his Angel.

Chapter 3

"So, what you think?" Rarri said to Mook, who was pacing back and forth.

"Cuz, that shit fire as fuck," Mook replied excitedly. "Let me get a gram."

Mook was from the same hood as Rarri. Unlike Rarri, Mook was a party boy and a known coke head. Mook knew everybody who fucked with the powder, from the dealers to the sniffers.

"Ight look, I'ma shoot you three grams. Just slide me the bread for the other two tomorrow," Rarri said, and put a chunk of the powder on the scale.

"Fa'sho. Good lookin' out foolie," Mook said and shook Rarri's hand.

"Oh yea, what's that nigga Juice number?" Rarri asked.

After Mook gave him the number, he left. As soon as Rarri stepped outside the house, he called Juice.

"Yaah, what's the deal, who this?" Juice asked from the other end of the phone.

"This Rarri. Where you at? I'm tryna come holla at you on some money shit," Rarri replied.

“I’m where I’m always at,” Juice said and hung up.

Juice was what you would call a big homie. If you lived on the west side of Compton and smoked weed, crack, or sniffed coke, you went to Juice. He had the best of it all, and for the low. Juice had the pull, but Rarri was the one putting in work for the hood. Rarri had a big bone to pick with Juice but would save that for another day. Right now, he needed Juice’s money.

When Rarri made it to the Wilmington Arms Apartments, he went straight to the back where Juice would always be. Juice was sitting in his car with the door open, playing *West Side Connection.* He had one foot out and was drinking some Hennessy from a small cup.

“What’s craccin’,” Rarri said, and hopped into the passenger seat startling Juice a bit.

“Same ole bullshit,” Juice responded. “I heard you got some fire powder cuz… better than my shit,” he added.

“Damn nigga, how you know that?” Rarri asked.

Juice just gave him the *you-already-know* face.

“Mook,” Rarri said, shaking his head.

“Yea, cuz called right after you did, telling me he gave you my number and you had some shit that was killin’ mine,” Juice said.

“Yea, he said it was fire, but he didn’t compare it to yours,” Rarri told him. “I’m tryna dump this shit ASAP.”

Juice took a sip from his cup and turned the radio down. “How much you got?” he asked.

“Like, eighty-one grams,” Rarri responded.

"Damn, that's it?" You know I only fuck with big shit… I thought you at least had a nine-piece," Juice said and turned the radio back up, but Rarri turned it back down.

"I could get whatever you need, but I gotta get this off first," Rarri told him. "I'm tryna get this money up for Spank's funeral.

Juice smacked his lips. "Ight look; I'ma shoot you three stacks for the work and five hundred for the funeral, but I need a half-bird asap if you could swing that much, and if you could, I know a few more people who want some weight, too."

"Good lookin' cuz," Rarri said and pulled out the powder. "I'ma go grab that and come right back."

Juice pulled out a big roll of money, counted out thirty-five hundred and gave it to Rarri. "You already taxin' me cuz… don't take all day," Juice said. Juice paid extra for the coke because he knew he could cut it more than the coke he had been getting. He could tell Rarri didn't know what to do with it or what to charge, but Juice knew not to try and play him cause it would surely cost him his life.

"Fa'sho. I'ma be back in a minute," Rarri replied. "You gon be right here?"

"Naw, come up to the house," Juice instructed. "I do this lil shit outside."

Rarri pushed to another side of the apartments where all the younger people would be at. When they saw it was Rarri they came rushing over, giving him hugs and handshakes.

"What up my young nigga?" Tank asked. "We been on one for Spank, cuz, layin' shit out… everybody suspect right now."

"That's what's up," Rarri said. "Aye, where Bird at? I need her to drive me somewhere real quick."

"She upstairs in the house… Just go in. She been askin' bout you," Tank laughed. "I think you in trouble, lowkey though."

Rarri shook his head and walked up the stairs into the house. As soon as he opened her bedroom door and she saw it was him, she started going off.

"Nigga, where the fuck you been at?" You got me fucked up. Ain't answerin' yo phone now? So that's how we doin' it Rarri? Alright, bet. When I don't answer my shit, don't be talk—" she rambled but was cut off.

"Shut the fuck up cuz and put yo shit on. I need you to drive me somewhere, real quick," Rarri said and walked back out of the house.

Rarri and Bird had been together since he was fourteen and she was sixteen. Bird was the baddest bitch in the hood, but to Rarri she was the normal, typical girl who lived in the hood. She was nineteen and still lived with her momma. The only reason she had a car was because she somehow played this older guy for it, only to shake him for his shit. Bird loved her some Rarri. No matter what he did, she stuck by his side.

When Bird got to her car, Rarri was already in the passenger seat scrolling through his phone. She got in the car and turned it on with attitude.

"Where to, your majesty?" Bird asked being sarcastic.

Rarri turned so he could face her and then turned her chin towards him so she could look him in the eyes. "Bird, you know what happened to the homie Spank… I gotta get this money so I could make sure he get a proper burial," Rarri told her, then added, "Ain't nobody else doin' shit."

"I'm sorry babe, I didn't know you was tryna do all that… real shit… I wanna help. What you need me to do?" Bird asked while rubbing the back of his shoulder.

"Right now, I just need you to drive me to my aunty Heaven house," Rarri said.

"K," she replied, starting the car and pulling off.

When they pulled up infront of the house, Rarri got out of the car and told Bird to wait on him. Rarri knocked on the door expecting Heaven to answer, but it was Chu-Chu who opened it. He was standing there wearing only his boxers and a tank top. He also had on the three gold chains he never took off. His hair was salt and pepper, but his waves were still on smack for an older nigga.

"Didn't you just leave here earlier?" Chu-Chu asked, looking at Rarri suspiciously.

"Yea, I need some more… I'm out," Rarri said, as he walked past him, letting himself in.

Chu-Chu closed the door and walked over to his mini bar and made a drink, then went and sat by Rarri in the living room. He took a sip of his drink and set the cup on the table.

"What you workin' with?" he asked, getting straight to the point.

Rarri pulled out the money he had got from Juice and handed it to him. "It's thirty-five hunnit," Rarri told him. "I got somebody who wants a nine-piece right now."

Chu-Chu laughed. "This ain't enough for no nine-piece."

"Yea I know, but I was hopin' you could like, front me the rest," Rarri said. "I could bring the money back in a couple hours, fa'sho."

He studied Rarri's face for any signs of doubt but didn't see any.

"Look Rarri, I don't like to fuck with no kids cause I don't play no games, and this here ain't no playground... the only reason I'm fuckin' with you is because of yo aunty, but don't think you could get over on me and I won't trip."

"I'm already knowin'," was all Rarri said. "*This nigga got one more time to lowkey threaten me,*" is what he thought, though. What Chu-Chu didn't know was that Rarri didn't play no games either. Chu-Chu might lay a nigga out for some drugs or money, but Rarri killed for less.

Chu-Chu downed the rest of his drink and stood up. "Ight, come on," he said and started walking towards his room with Rarri behind him. As soon as they stepped into the room, he saw his aunt Heaven in the bed sleep. The room was plushed out with a 70-inch flat-screen T.V., nice bedroom set and different paintings on the wall. He led Rarri into his walk-in closet where he kept his safe. Rarri's eyes got big as hell when he saw it. It was a gun safe the size of a refrigerator. Chu-Chu blocked the nob out of

Rarri's view, put in the combination and opened it all the way.

"Check it out," he said, nodding his head for Rarri to come look. Chu-Chu loved to floss his shit so niggas knew he was on. When Rarri saw the inside of the safe, his mouth dropped open. It was about thirty bricks of powder, a few assault rifles and money stacked everywhere. He had never seen that much money or drugs in his life. He knew Chu-Chu had money, but not this much money. At that moment he looked up to Chu-Chu, in a way.

"Damn! So, you like, a real King-pin?" Rarri asked, looking at him amazed.

"Somethin' like that," he replied. "It took years of hard work and dedication to get this shit." Chu-Chu picked up a brick that was smaller than the other ones.

"Look, I'ma slide you a half key. Just bring me back ten stacks and you keep the rest," he told Rarri, and put it in a small bag, then handed it to him.

"Ight, I got you," Rarri said, as he was looking at the bag. Nobody ever looked out for Rarri like Chu-Chu just had. Rarri was going to show his loyalty to him 'til the end. If niggas got a problem with Chu-Chu, they got a problem with Rarri. A nigga bet not look at him the wrong way, cause if he did, Rarri fa'sho was going to fix his face with a bullet.

"Rarri," Chu-Chu said, interrupting him from his thoughts.

"What up?" Rarri asked, looking up from the bag.

Chu-Chu put both of his hands on Rarri's shoulders and looked him in the eyes. "If you ever play me, yo lil friends funeral won't be the only one you gotta pay for," he told Rarri and turned him around so he could see his aunt Heaven in the bed waking up. Chu-Chu put on his fake smile and walked out of the closet. "Hey baby, how'd you sleep?" he asked Heaven. Just like that, all the loyalty shit Rarri was thinking about went out the window. When Heaven saw Rarri coming behind Chu-Chu, she looked surprised and tried to cover her half-naked body with a cover.

"You back already?" Heaven asked Rarri.

"Yea, I gotta move fast right now," he replied walking out of the room, trying to avoid eye contact. When Rarri was out of the room, Heaven put on a shirt and went out after him.

"Rarri," she called after him as he headed for the door.

"What's up?" he asked, still trying to avoid eye contact with Heaven.

"I need to talk to you," she told him. "It's about your parents."

"What about 'em?" Rarri asked defensively.

Heaven sighed. "First off, your dad—" she started.

"Was a coward who left me for dead," Rarri finished, and just as he did, Heaven slapped the shit out of him before he could let another word out. Tears of anger grew in her eyes from what she had just heard.

"Your dad was a real nigga, and the only nigga I ever loved," Heaven blurted out on accident. Rarri could taste blood in his mouth from the hit.

"What the fuck is you talkin' about?" he asked like she was crazy. "You trippin' cuz."

"Look, just go and handle your shit.... When you come back, I'll explain it to you," Heaven told him. "You need to know the truth and what's expected of you, cause all this—"

She paused to wave her hand at him like he was filthy, with a look of disgust on her face,

"Ain't it," she finished, and stormed back into the room, leaving him alone to let himself out.

Rarri didn't understand why she was tripping. He sold all the powder she had given him earlier, and now he was about to sell more. Not to mention, this was all in the same day. Fa'sho, he could handle Spank's funeral now. Everything was going smooth.

When Rarri got back to Bird's car, she was in there sleep. He woke her up and told her to drive back to the hood so he could holla at Juice. The whole way back, they talked about how much they missed each other and what had been going on the last few days. Rarri explained to her how he was on some money shit, and how he wanted to be on. For as long as Bird knew Rarri, he had never talked like that. He was always on some gang banging shit. He never talked about getting out the hood, so she never thought about it. The only thing Bird cared about was what Rarri wanted, and no matter what it was, she was going to make sure he got it. If he wanted to shine, then he was going to shine.

"Well, I'm with you babe, whatever you need me to do, I'm with it no matter what it is," Bird told him as they pulled into the back of the complex.

"I love you Bird," Rarri said, and leaned over and gave her a kiss on the lips.

"I love you too, nigga," she said, giving him two more kisses. "Now, hurry up so we can head back before it gets too late."

Juice's apartment smelled like a marijuana clinic next to a crack house when Rarri walked in.

"What up cuz?" Rarri said greeting Juice with a handshake.

"Shit, been waitin' on you," Juice responded. "Tell me you got that."

"Yup, yup, everything good. I just need to weigh it up," Rarri told him.

"Fa'sho. It's a scale right here," Juice said and walked him to the table.

Rarri weighed out nine ounces and gave it to Juice, but he saw Rarri still had more.

"Hold on cuz," Juice said with a confused look on his face. "How much you got left?"

"Another nine," Rarri replied. "Why, what's up?"

"Damn, lil nigga, you on a half brick already? ...Where you gettin' this shit from?" Juice asked.

“From my people’s,” Rarri told him like it was nothing.

“You can’t plug me in?” Juice asked.

“Man, I’m still tryna get plugged in my damn self,” Rarri said honestly.

“Nigga, you plugged in already cuz, stop bullshittin’,” Juice laughed. “Ight look; let me give you sixteen for the whole thing?”

Rarri thought about it for a minute. He wasn’t making that much profit, but the flip was fast. After he paid Chu-Chu, he would still have six bands left. “Ight, run it,” Rarri said.

Juice walked in his room and came back out with sixteen thousand, then handed it to Rarri. Rarri just put it in the bag he had the powder in and gave Juice another handshake. “Hit me up when you need me to swing back through,” Rarri said and pushed back to Bird’s car. Rarri shook his head and laughed to himself when he saw she was sleep again. He opened the driver's side door and woke her up.

“Get in the passenger seat, babe, I’ma drive back,” he insisted.

“I got it,” she protested and tried to get herself together.

“Naw, I need you to do somethin’ else for me… scoot over,” Rarri told her again.

When Bird hopped in the passenger seat, he got in and started the car.

"What you need me to do from over here?" Bird asked while putting her hair in a ponytail and biting her lip with a half-smile. She thought he wanted some head on the way back while he drove. Rarri laughed because it was like he could read her mind.

"Naw, we gon do that later," he said making her pout, then tossed the bag in her lap. "Right now, I need you to count that."

Bird's face lit up when she opened the bag and saw how much money was inside.

"Damn babe," was all she could get out.

"Count out ten bands and put the rest in yo purse," he told her. "After that, you could suck on this dick," he added and pulled off heading towards Chu-Chu's.

After Bird counted the money, she sucked him up all the way there. Her mouth was making love to his dick slowly and passionately, but when they pulled up to the front, she started spitting, bobbing, gagging, and deepthroating his rod, making sounds he never heard before until he came.

"Shit!" was all he could say, as she stuffed it back in his pants.

She handed him the bag with the ten bands in it. "Hurry up this time babe, I'm tired," she told him.

"Ight, I'ma be in and out," he promised and then got out of the car. This time when he knocked on the door, it was Heaven who answered it and let him in.

"Well, it took you long enough," she said playfully and walked over to the bar. "Come sit and have a drink with me while we talk." He could tell she had already been drinking by the way she was talking and walking.

"I can't right now. I kinda promised Bird I would hurry up," Rarri said.

Heaven walked up to him with her drink in hand. "Well you kinda gotta break that promise," she said, then tried to put the cup to his lips to force him a drink, but he jerked back and it ended up spilling on his clothes. She started laughing so hard, it pissed him off.

"What the fuck is wrong with you? God damn," he yelled, trying to snap her out of her drunkenness, but she only laughed harder. "Where Chu-Chu at? I need to give him this money so I could leave," he asked, and she started laughing even harder. "Where he at?" Rarri asked again, this time angrier. Heaven was laughing so hard she couldn't even talk. She just pointed at the bedroom door. Rarri walked over and knocked on it and she started laughing even harder.

"He said… he said… he said come in when you ready," Heaven laughed. "He waitin' on you," she added and continued laughing like she told the funniest joke in the world.

Rarri opened the door and couldn't believe what he was seeing. Chu-Chu was tied to the bed, both his legs and arms were bound to a post and his mouth was duct-taped. He was trying to yank free as hard as he could, but he was tied too tight. When he saw Rarri open the door, he started yelling at him through the duct tape and yanking harder. Rarri closed the door back and walked back over to Heaven, who was now sitting on the couch with her legs crossed, sipping the drink casually with a smirk on her face, laughing to herself.

"What the fuck is goin' on?" he asked.

"Umm… nothin' much, just tiein' up some loose ends," she responded and chuckled.

"Why Chu-Chu tied up like that in there?" Rarri asked.

"Maybe you should ask yourself that question," Heaven said with a hint of attitude as she looked at him.

"I'm not even understandin' this shit cuz," Rarri admitted. He couldn't even think of a reason why he should ask his self that question. Heaven shook her head, took a sip of her drink then put the cup down.

"You don't think I heard y'all talkin' in the closet earlier?" Heaven asked. "Rarri, I gave you that work so you could flip it and make money, not so you could get fronted by a nigga and make his."

"But—" he started but was cut off.

"But what, Rarri?" Heaven asked, then finished the question. "Oh, wait! I was supposed to sit here and *hope* you made it back with his money? What if you would have gotten pulled over by the cops? What if the deal would have went bad and you got robbed or killed? You don't think I would be the one tied up or stuffed in a box somewhere because of it? He told you he would kill me, right?"

Heaven was hitting him with so many questions of what could have happened that he didn't even think about. All Rarri could do was stand there and look stupid while she drilled him. Heaven let a few moments of silence pass by so he could process what she was saying.

"Rarri, I think it's time you see what type of person yo dad was so you know who you are, what's expected of you and what way to carry yourself. But right now, I need you to do somethin' else," Heaven told him.

"Ight, what's up?" he asked.

"I need you to go in the room and get the combo to that safe," Heaven said. "After you get it, put him to sleep……. for good."

Rarri's smile was so wicked, it sent chills through her entire body. He grabbed her drink off the table, downed it and put the cup back down.

"Now you talkin' my language," Rarri said and walked to the bedroom. When he got to the door, he stopped and looked over his shoulder at Heaven. "Messy or clean?" he asked. This time, she was the one who was at a loss for words. "Messy," Rarri said after a moment, then walked in the room and closed the door behind him. Heaven didn't know Rarri's kill game was official, but she knew it was in his blood because of who his father was.

"Just like yo daddy," she mumbled .

The screams and cries that Chu-Chu made from inside the room was something she had never heard before. It was terrifying. Heaven was certain the sounds would haunt her for the rest of her life. Rarri came out about an hour later. He was so bloody; you would have thought he was injured.

“Bag the shit up. I’ma hop in the shower,” Rarri told her and went to the bathroom.

When Heaven walked into the room, she ran back out and threw up in the kitchen sink. It was the most horrific shit she had ever seen in her life. Chu-Chu’s face was split directly down the middle. It looked like somebody was trying to open it up and pull something out. It was blood everywhere, and the way the room smelled, she could tell Chu-Chu shit himself.

When she went back in, she covered her nose and walked straight to the closet with her head down avoiding the site on the bed. Heaven put all the bricks and money in two duffle bags, got some clothes for Rarri then went back to the living room.

“Fuck,” Heaven cursed herself. She didn’t want to go back into the room but needed to. Heaven ran back in and grabbed Chu-Chu’s cell phone off of the bedroom dresser and ran back out. Rarri was out of the shower wearing a towel around his waist.

“Here, throw these on and let’s go,” Heaven said, tossing him the spare clothes.

“Ight, go to Bird’s car out front and wait on me there,” Rarri told Heaven. “I’ll be right out.”

Rarri dressed quickly and went to make sure every window in the house was closed shut. He lit every candle he could find, putting them all in the furthest room and turned on the gas from the stove, then left out. When he got to the car, Heaven and Bird were already ready to go. Bird knew something was up when she saw Heaven putting bags in the car.

"Let's bounce," Rarri said and got in the car.

Bird pulled off. "What's goin' on Rarri?" she asked.

"Nothin'," he lied.

"BOOM!"

Right after he said it, the house went into flames behind them.

"Mmm…hmm, don't look like nothin'," Bird said and kept driving.

Chapter 4

"KNOCK, KNOCK, KNOCK."

"Who is it?" the voice from the other side of the door asked.

"Rarri," he responded. It was quiet for a few moments. "It's Rarri," he repeated.

"I heard you," the voice said. After about ten seconds, the locks turned and the door opened. Spank's mom stood in the doorway with tears in her eyes. "What do you want?"

"Can I come in?" Rarri asked.

"For what?" Spank's mom asked. "Ain't none of you muthafuckas thought to come by since my son got killed, so what the fuck you want now?"

"Look, my bad for not comin' sooner. I've been beatin' myself up over this whole situation," Rarri told her.

"Beatin' yo'self up?" Spank's mom asked in disbelief. "Rarri, what the fuck happened to my son?" she asked again, this time pounding at his chest and crying harder. She swung wildly at him. After a few hits nearly hit his face, he grabbed her and held her tight. "What happened to my son?... What happened to my son?" she kept asking while she cried.

"It's gon be ok," Rarri promised. "Everything gon be ok."

"No, it's not Rarri. We can't give him a proper burial.... Muthafuckas ain't lookin' out, and I ain't got the money for this shit right now.... Everything is fucked up," she cried to him.

"Don't nobody need to look out, I'ma take care of everything," Rarri promised. Spank's mom laughed sarcastically.

"How you gon do that Rarri? You ain't got no job."

Rarri let her go, dug into his pockets and pulled out a roll of money, then placed it in her palms. "This ten thousand right here. It's for you.... I'ma take care of all the funeral expenses, just let me know what it comes up to and I got it," Rarri told her.

Spank's mom's eyes were wide, and her face joyful as she looked at the money and listened to Rarri. "Where are you gettin' all this money from?" she asked happily, but Rarri changed the subject.

"Call when you need to meet up for the arrangements," he told her and put his number on a piece of paper before leaving.

The day before the funeral, everybody met at the wake in the Inglewood Cemetery. It was mostly family and close friends. Almost everyone came out of the building crying. Rarri was there before everybody, so he was the first to come out. He just wanted to make sure everything was on point before the actual funeral.

"What up Crip," a familiar voice said from behind Rarri as he walked out. When he turned around and saw who it was, his face lit up.

"Yaah what's the deal cuz," Rarri said, as he ran in to embrace lil Dink with a handshake and hug. "When you get out nigga?"

"Yesterday," lil Dink responded.

Lil Dink had went to Los Padrino's Juvenile Hall for taking a gun to school about a year ago. Lil Dink was a young hitter from the hood. He was close to Rarri, Spank, and Trigg. If he wasn't in jail, fa'sho Lil Dink would have been there the day Spank died.

"That's what's up foolie," Rarri said. "How you get up here?"

"My sis," Lil Dink replied and nodded to the car his sister was sitting in.

"Tell her she could sagg out… I'ma push you to the house later," Rarri told him.

"You whippin' now cuz?" Lil Dink asked surprised.

"Yea, a nigga got some wheels," Rarri said smoothly.

"Uugghh, you craccin' cuz," Lil Dink said, throwing playful punches at Rarri.

"Naw, *we* craccin'," Rarri assured him. "Hurry up. I'ma be over here at the whip."

"Ight…. I gotta holla at you about some shit, too," Lil Dink said and walked over to his sister's car.

Rarri walked over to his car and grabbed the blunt of weed he had in the ashtray, then went and sat on the trunk.

Lil Dink stopped and said what's up to some of their other homies who was chilling in and around some of the cars nearby. When he walked up to Rarri, Rarri handed him the blunt to spark.

"So, what's the deal?" Rarri asked.

Lil Dink sat on the trunk next to Rarri, hit the blunt hard and said, "I know who killed Spank," then blew the smoke out.

Rarri was so stunned by his words, he couldn't even speak, so Lil Dink just continued.

"I guess when y'all was tryna go slide on the east, these niggas from Lynwood was at Louis Burgers and seen y'all creepin'," Lil Dink explained and passed the blunt to Rarri.

Rarri took two big hits from the blunt then exhaled. "Why the fuck would some niggas from Lynwood give a fuck about us creepin' round that way?" Rarri asked him.

"Remember when I was fuckin' with that lil bitch out there and I flocked her house and came up, on them pistols, money and some jewelry?" Lil Dink asked Rarri.

"Yea," Rarri said, thinking back to that day.

"Well, I guess the guns were her brothers, and the money and jewelry was her momma's.... Ever since then, they been lookin' for me.... They thought Spank was me," Lil Dink told him.

Spank and Lil Dink did look alike. Most people assumed they were brothers. Some would call Dink— Spank or Spank— Dink on accident.

"How you find all this out?" Rarri asked as he passed the blunt.

"Nigga," Lil Dink said before pulling on the blunt." I got out the box and they moved me to unit Y1 'cause I was beatin' shit up in X2 upstairs.... But yea though, I'm chillin' in my cell and a nigga bang on the door. When I look up, I see it's one of that bitch's brother's.... cuz talkin' bout, "yea nigga, that's why I killed yo brother". Cuz ain't even get to finish his cigarette before I put one in his head,' how he seen y'all creepin' by Louis Burger, followed y'all to some apartments and did his shit thinkin' it was me and all that.... I'm tryna slide on these niggas tonight, cuz."

"You remember where they stay at?" Rarri asked.

"Come on now," he replied, hit the blunt again, passed it to Rarri then squinted his eyes to focus on the person in the distance walking towards them. "Oh shit, my nigga Trigg," Lil Dink said as he hopped off the car, ran up to him and embraced him with a hug. He was so excited that he didn't notice the change in Trigg's appearance until he stood next to Rarri. Trigg looked like he hadn't slept or bathed in weeks. His face was thinner, skin was ashy, clothes were dusty, and his smell was musty. The worst part was his eyes. They were big as hell and you could tell that he was on some type of drug fa'sho.

"What's up Rarri?" Trigg asked which turned out to piss Rarri the fuck off.

He hopped off of the car and got directly in his face. "What the fuck you mean what's up nigga? Where the fuck you been at?" Rarri was so angry, spit came from his lips. "You left me here to do all this shit by myself."

"So, it's alright for you to leave a nigga, but a nigga can't leave you?" Trigg asked.

Rarri knew he was speaking about him leaving Spank in the vacant house, so he tried to swing at Trigg, but Lil Dink grabbed him.

"What the fuck is wrong with you niggas?" Lil Dink yelled at them both. "We supposed to be slidin' for the homie, not tryna slide on each other."

"I'm ready," Trigg said.

"I ain't slidin' nowhere with cuz… look at him. He on somethin'," Rarri screamed. Everybody was looking by now, and Lil Dink didn't like making a scene.

"Ight, look… Trigg, you ride back to the hood with the homies and don't leave," Lil Dink instructed. "We gon meet up there."

"Ight," Trigg said and walked off mugging Rarri.

Lil Dink and Rarri got in the car and left. Rarri took Lil Dink to the Bloomingdale's store to pick out some clothes to wear and some shit to sport at the funeral tomorrow. Rarri explained to Lil Dink the situation that took place with Spank and the reason he was angry with Trigg. He even told him about the shit that went down with Chu-Chu. After hearing everything, he was just as upset with Trigg as Rarri was.

"That's still the homie though, cuz," Lil Dink said. "We gotta be here for each other, especially at times like these."

"Yea, I hear you," Rarri said sarcastically.

"Do you?" Lil Dink asked sarcastically. "You remember when my momma started gettin' high and lettin' her boyfriend beat me and touch on my sister?"

"Yea, I remember, cuz I hated seein' you go through that shit," Rarri said.

"Yea, well you ain't act like it," Lil Dink said coldly. "When we ran away and I stopped by your house, you ain't even offer to let us stay the night. Neither did Spank when we stopped by his, but Trigg did…. For a minute, I hated you and Spank. I felt like y'all ain't give a fuck about me, cuz."

Rarri didn't have to see the tears in Lil Dink's eyes to feel his pain.

"If it wasn't for Trigg, I wouldn't have never seen that the reason y'all ain't think to ask was because y'all ain't been in that type of situation before," Lil Dink explained. "We gotta be here for each other.

Lil Dink's words hit Rarri hard because he never realized how much his ignorance hurt one of his best friends.

"Let's go back and get cuz a fit real quick," Rarri said, as he wiped his eyes.

"My nigga," Lil Dink laughed and put his arm around Rarri's neck as they turned back around to go back into the Gucci store.

Big Tick was sitting in his car drinking lean and smoking weed as usual listening to his Mailbox Money CD by Nipsey Hussle, while almost dozing off every five minutes. His vision was so blurry, he couldn't tell the time as he held the phone to his face.

"Fuck," he said to himself taking the key out of the ignition. He opened the driver's side door to step out, but before he could get his foot on the ground, he was looking down the barrel of a .38 revolver.

"You lookin' for me?"

"BOOM, BOOM, BOOM, BOOM, BOOM, BOOM."

Lil Dink emptied all six rounds into his face before he could answer, grabbed his phone out of his lap and ran back to the getaway car.

When they made it off the block, he scrolled through the phone and found the number he was looking for, hit call, and then put it on speaker. After about four rings, a female voice picked up.

"Brandon, get yo ass in the house, they shootin' outside."

"This ain't Brandon bitch, call the coroner. Yo son dead outside," Lil Dink said, then threw the phone out the window and started laughing. "Two more to go."

"I got the next one," Rarri said, and turned up the radio playing E-40's *'Knockin' at the Light'* song.

Spank's funeral was craccin'. He wore an all-white Gucci suit with matching Gucci loafers. He rested peacefully in a Crip blue casket with white flowers around it and a picture of him painted on the front. People from all over came to pay their respects. It was muthafuckas from Compton, Watts, Long Beach, L.A., Pomona, even a few of

Spank's cousins from San Bernardino were there. Everybody from the same hood as Spank wore T-Shirts and sweaters that read *'R.I.P Spank'* with a picture of him on it. Some bitches had little booty shorts with *'R.I.P Spank'* on the ass of them.

Spank's mom was seated in the front, next to other family members wearing all black. Rarri was seated on the other side in the front next to his gang. Rarri, Lil Dink and Trigg wore the same fit as Spank. Every time Rarri looked over at Spank's mom, he couldn't help but notice the people around and next to her were mugging him.

"What the fuck wrong with them?" Lil Dink leaned over and asked Rarri.

"I don't know, but I ain't feelin' this, shit cuz," Rarri replied and walked up to the casket where Spank was resting. "I love you, cuz," Rarri told Spank as he planted a kiss on his forehead.

"Then why you leave me?" Rarri heard Spank's voice say loudly, causing him to jump back and trip over his own foot. Lil Dink and Trigg ran over and helped him up.

"You good?" Trigg asked.

"Yea, I'm straight," Rarri replied and looked back at the crowd of people who was watching him, and then he walked out as fast as he could before the ceremony started. Lil Dink followed behind him, but Trigg stayed. When they made it outside, it was people everywhere. It seemed like more muthafuckas was outside than inside, but either way, Spank was getting love.

"Aye, Rarri!... Rarri!"

He scanned the crowd looking for the person who was calling him until he saw who it was.

"What's the deal foolie," Rarri said as he walked up to Trouble and Lil Trouble was standing by a car smoking some weed.

"Shit, just came through to show some support," Lil Trouble said as they shook hands. "What's the deal Dink?

"Same shit different day," Lil Dink replied.

"Y'all niggas fly than a bitch cuz, I see you, bro, I see you," Trouble said, pointing to their matching fits. "Put a nigga on Rarri. I heard you craccin', on hood."

"Fa'sho, we gon talk. You already know," Rarri assured him. "How moms doin'?"

"She straight. Still trippin' as usual," Trouble said. "What about yo granny, how she doin'?"

"Still stuck in front of the T.V. like she gon miss somethin'," Rarri joked. "Y'all should come thr—"

"Look at this bitch ass nigga," Lil Trouble said, cutting Rarri off. All of them turned to see who he was talking about.

"Daaammn! Look at Darshawn though," Lil Dink said to Rarri as they slapped five twice." Cuz on his shit. He got like, four bad bitches."

Everybody stopped to stare at them as they walked by. The asses on all of them bounced at every step they took. All four could pass for sisters. It looked like they were imported from Brazil or something. These bitches were beautiful, almost to the point where they looked fake.

They followed behind him with their heads down walking towards the ceremony.

"Aye Darshawn!... Darshawn!" Rarri yelled until he got his attention. "Check it out."

He started walking towards them with the girls behind him. "What's up Rarri and Dink," he said as they shook hands. "Oh shit, the *Troubles*?" he greeted, with his hand extended to Lil Trouble, but Lil Trouble just left him hanging.

"Cough, cough, mark!" Trouble said fake coughing.

"Papi, I have to use the restroom," one of the girls said from behind him.

"Y'all go ahead. I'll meet y'all in there," he instructed, then yelled, "don't be on no reckless shit either."

"Ok Papi," one of them yelled back.

"Damn Darshawn. I ain't know you was craccin' like that cuz… you on, my nigga," Lil Dink said.

"Like a light switch, ya dig me, mane? But burn this; Darshawn flew once the sky turned blue…. I go by Pretty Me da P now," he told Lil Dink

Lil Trouble was giving Pretty Me da P the screw-face the whole time. He couldn't believe this nigga was back at it after hearing the shit that went down with Trina. He still had feelings for Trina, even if she was a hoe.

"I see somebody got his head from under the bed," Lil Trouble said sarcastically.

Pretty Me da P's face froze for a second as he flashed back to that night. He hoped Trina didn't tell people about what happened. So much, he convinced his self she wouldn't, but little did he know the streets was talking.

"I'ma go and catch this service. I'll get at y'all in a minute," Pretty Me da P said as he gave Rarri and Lil Dink a dap. He looked at Lil Trouble but covered his eyes when they made contact with his and walked towards the ceremony.

"What was all that about?" Rarri asked Lil Trouble.

"Man, that nigga a bitch, on Neighbor Hood Crip," Lil Trouble replied. "I wouldn't fuck wit cuz if I was you."

"Why, what cuz do?" Lil Dink asked.

Lil Trouble told them about the whole story Trina was putting out there, and how it happened after him and Trouble left from smoking with Pretty Me da P.

"Damn, that's crazy foo," Rarri said after hearing the story then asked, "do you think she tellin' the truth?"

"Nigga. When you ever known Trina to lie on a nigga?" Trouble countered.

"Never really, but shid, I never known her to be a hoe either," Rarri admitted, but then he thought about how Pretty Me da P's face looked once Lil Trouble made that remark about his head under the bed.

"We gotta make a play on this weak ass nigga," Rarri told them. "One of y'all got Bino number?"

Lil Trouble's face lit up. "I could get it," he said, already scrolling through his phone.

"Ight, do that and tell cuz to slide up here ASAP," Rarri instructed then texted Bird a paragraph of some shit to do. Honestly, Rarri didn't give a fuck about what Trina was going through or what Bino wanted. He just saw the opportunity to come up, so he took it.

The service was over, and everybody was coming out of the building to head to the burial site. Pretty Me da P was almost to the door when he spotted two familiar faces, he prayed to never see again, outside. It was Bino and Trina.

"Fuck," he said more loudly than intended as he turned back around to walk the other way, nearly almost knocking one of his hoes over.

"What's wrong Papi? You ok?" one of them asked.

"Yea, I'm good. I just need to use the bathroom," he lied. "Y'all go ahead. I'ma meet y'all at the car."

"We need the key, Papi," she yelled after him, but he was already on the move.

When he made it to the restroom, he went to the stall, locked the door, stood on the toilet and knelt down. About a minute later, the door to the restroom opened up.

"I know I just seen this nigga," Bino said to himself loudly. He walked over to one of the stalls and pushed the door open hard. Pretty Me da P flinched every time Bino pushed one of the stalls open. The closer Bino got the more Pretty Me da P trembled. Here he was again, hiding with his hands over his mouth, crying like a little bitch. Bino had just pushed the stall next to Pretty Me da P open when Bino's phone started ringing.

"Hello," Bino answered, then spoke into the phone as he sat down on the toilet, leaving the door open. "Hell naw, that nigga must have ducked off in the cut or somethin', but I ain't done lookin'… I'ma break his neck when I find him… I'ma finish searchin' this bathroom when I'm done takin' a shit… I ain't leavin' this funeral home until I find him."

Pretty Me da P could see Bino's shoes from under the stall. His mind was racing fast.

This is my chance", he thought. Pretty Me da P eased off the toilet as quiet as possible not making a sound and put his hand on the lock. With one quick motion, he twisted the lock, opened the door and bolted for the bathroom door to leave.

"Aye… aye… aye… I'ma catch yo ass, nigga," Bino yelled as he jumped off the toilet, still shitty booty, in pursuit of Pretty Me da P.

The inside of the building was empty, so Pretty Me da P made it out quickly. He could hear Bino tripping over things, so he knew he was on his tail. Pretty Me da P dashed and ducked by all the people outside until he made it to his car. He almost froze in mid-run when he saw Trina and Bird standing by the car next to his talking to his bitches. By the looks on their faces, he could tell Trina had told them what happened, but the only thing he cared about was getting the fuck away from Bino.

"I told y'all he was a bitch," he heard Trina say before he hopped in the car and made his escape speeding off. Everybody who saw it was in tears from laughing so hard.

“If y’all really tryna be poppin’, y’all should fuck with my bitch, Bird,” Trina said, nodding to Bird who was next to her. “Now, her nigga is the real deal.”

“Who is yo nigga?” one of them asked Bird.

“The one sittin’ on the Mercedes smokin’ the blunt,” Bird said pointing to Rarri, who was sitting on the Mercedes AMG CL450.

Chapter 5

Six months later

Rarri was sitting on the front porch of his grandmother's house smoking a blunt, lost in his thoughts. After the incident at Chu-Chu's, he had moved into his own place, but Heaven stayed so she could look after her mom more and get herself together. All she needed was a reason to kick her drug habit, and Rarri was it. Rarri made sure to stop by as much as possible to check on his grandma. He was proud of how Heaven cleaned herself up and was handling business for him. Heaven had also taken Bird and the four girls who used to work for Pretty Me da P under her wing. Rarri was just about to put the blunt out and go inside when Heaven came out.

"How do I look?" Heaven asked Rarri as she did a full 360-degree spin. Everything she had on was Gucci. Her dress, purse, and shoes. Even her accessories were Gucci. Her hair was long and curly, giving her a kinky look. A person would never think she was once a drug addict not too long ago. She looked flawless at that moment.

Rarri couldn't even respond. All he could do was look in amazement with his mouth open.

"I'll take that as a compliment," Heaven said smiling, then turned around and headed towards his car. She opened the passenger door and was about to hop in until she looked up and seen Rarri still in a daze. "Is you comin' or what?"

“Oh, yea,” Rarri said as he snapped out of his daze and jumped up walking towards the car. He hit the blunt one more time and put it out then hopped in the car. As he adjusted his seat and the mirrors, he couldn’t help but feel Heaven's eyes on him. When Rarri looked over, she was staring at him smiling, but she put her head down when they made eye contact and started fumbling through her purse still smiling.

“What?” Rarri asked.

“Nothin’,” Heaven replied, as she pulled out her lipstick and applied it in the mirror.

Rarri pulled down the driver's side mirror to examine himself. “I got somethin’ on my face or somethin?” he asked, still in the mirror.

“Yup,” she replied bluntly, still in the mirror, herself.

“Where?” he asked, looking at both sides of his face.

“You probably don’t see it yet,” Heaven replied as she sat back in her seat. “Let’s hurry up so we ain’t late.”

“I don’t get it though. How I don’t see it yet if it’s on my face?” Rarri asked.

“Boy, if you don’t drive this car,” Heaven started.

“Iight… ight… we out of here,” Rarri said, then started the car and pulled off. What Rarri didn’t see was that he was looking more and more like a boss each day. His waves were on smack, his chain was shining, and he was pushing a Maserati. It wasn’t many young niggas doing it like him in the hood.

Rarri and Heaven pulled into the luxury hotel in San Diego. He drove up to where the valet parking was and hopped out. Rarri handed the valet driver his car keys and tipped him a hundred dollars.

"Don't fuck my shit up cuz," Rarri said and walked over to the passenger side to open the door for Heaven. Heaven stepped out looking like she was ready for the red carpet. Everyone around looked at her in awe as she walked through the entrance of the hotel with Rarri. They made their way to the hotel restaurant with all eyes on them.

"How may I help you?" the waitress behind the counter asked as the two approached.

"We have a reservation with a Mr. Tony," Heaven replied.

The waitress studied them both for a brief moment before speaking. "Of course, right this way," she said, leading them to a table in the middle of the room. The restaurant was packed with people and almost every seat was filled. Rarri was looking around at the many faces in the room uncomfortably. He had never been in a place as nice or around as many white people before in his life. He felt out of place and honestly couldn't wait to leave… something didn't feel right.

"Don't worry. I'll do all the talking," Heaven told him as another waitress put drinks on the table. She could tell Rarri was tense about the whole situation. He waited for the waitress to leave before replying.

"Somethin' don't feel right," Rarri told Heaven. "I think we should sagg out."

“Do you know how hard it was to set up this meeting?” Heaven asked.

“Not as hard as it should have been.... I mean, if it was me, I would hav—” Rarri started.

“Good afternoon,” a man in a suit said, cutting Rarri off and seating himself next to Heaven. “I’m Tony.”

“Pleased to meet you, Tony, I’m Heaven,” Heaven introduced herself as she extended her hand.

Tony gently grabbed her hand and kissed the back of it without taking his eyes off of hers. “The pleasure is mine,” he responded in a heavy accent. Tony looked like one of those rich Cubans from the movies. He wore his jewelry under his clothes, but just by the parts you could see, you could tell every piece was expensive. He looked to be in his mid-forties without a gray hair on his entire head or face and still in shape.

Heaven blushed as she pulled her hand back slowly. “And this is my nephew, Rarri,” Heaven said continuing the introduction.

Rarri stood up and extended his hand to Tony, but Tony acted as if it was non-existent and kept his eyes on Heaven.

“So where are you from Heaven?” Tony asked.

Rarri sat back down feeling pissed and played.

Heaven hoped Rarri didn’t blow his cool over Tony’s arrogance. “I was born and raised here in California,” Heaven responded. “What about you?”

"I was born in Cuba, but I've been here in the states for about twenty years," Tony replied.

The two of them laughed, talked and flirted with each other for about twenty minutes as they drank wine. Rarri was beyond irritated as he sat in his seat while they bullshitted around, talking about almost everything in the world except what they came there for.

"God damn cuz, can we get to the fuckin' business already?!" Rarri said, cutting them off from their conversation of laughter. Heaven was slightly embarrassed and took a big sip of her wine.

Tony finally looked Rarri in his eyes and acknowledged him. "The business!... I almost forgot," Tony said sarcastically not breaking his stare from Rarri.

"CLAP! CLAP!'

Tony clapped his hands twice loudly and every person in the restaurant got up and started walking towards the exit, leaving them alone. The only people left besides Rarri, Heaven and Tony were six men in suits holding machine guns and blocking the exits.

"So, Mr. Businessman. What happened to Chu-Chu?" Tony asked calmly. "Why are you here and not him?"

Rarri and Heaven were quiet.

"BAM!"

Tony hit the table so hard that some of the drinks fell over. "I'm talking to you!" he yelled at Rarri.

"I-I-they killed him," Heaven cried.

"Who killed him?" Tony asked as he turned his attention to Heaven.

"I don't know who they were… everything happened so fast… one minute we were watching T.V., then all of a sudden we were being attacked by three masked men," Heaven sobbed. "They killed Chu-Chu after he gave them his safe combination and tried to take me with them… luckily Rarri here had heard the commotion and was able to set a trap, killin' two of them in the drive-way, but one of them escaped."

Tony eyed her cautiously to see if Heaven was lying, but her eyes only showed signs of pain and hurt. Her voice was so sincere and compassionate that he believed her every word. Little did he know that Heaven had mastered the art of seduction, manipulation, and deceit.

"I'm sorry for the loss you both have taken. Chu-Chu was a good friend of mine as well, and I surely send my condolences, but I can't help but wonder about the gain you must have taken in his death," Tony said.

"What do you mean?" Heaven asked.

"You said your nephew here killed two of them, but one fled, no?" Tony said but asked at the same time.

"Yes," she answered.

"Well, surely he did not flee with the money?" Tony questioned.

"No, he was not able to make off with the money… that's why I contacted you to see if we could continue business… I hav—"

Tony put his hand up to stop her from talking.

"That's going to be a problem," he said as a waiter put drinks on the table. Tony took a sip from the wine glass. "We are in a— how do you say?... um, um… a dilemma. You see, the only thing you have is *my* money."

"I don't understand," Heaven said with a confused expression on her face.

"He sayin' that Chu-Chu's money is really his money," Rarri spat out.

Tony pointed and smiled at Rarri. "Smart boy… I fronted Chu-Chu fifteen kilos, and I would charge him $20,000 a kilo for not paying up front. So, where's my $250,000?"

Heaven put her face in her hands and started sobbing.

"Hold on cuz, you movin' too fast homie," Rarri said as he tried to console Heaven.

"How do we know you gave him the kilos? Who's to say he didn't buy them from you?"

"I'm to say he did not buy them unless you are calling me a liar," Tony pressed.

"I ain't callin' you a liar; I'm just askin' how can we be sure?" Rarri asked.

"That's calling me a liar," Tony insisted. "There's no way for me to prove it to you. You're just going to have to trust me."

Rarri stood up with Heaven crying on his shoulder. "Ight well, look; we gon bring the money back," he told Tony. "I just got to go pick it up."

"Wonderful," Tony said and shook Rarri's free hand. "You go and pick it up… I'll show Heaven around in the meantime."

Just as Tony finished, two of the armed men walked up and grabbed Heaven from Rarri.

"No Rarri, don't leave me here, please, don't leave me with them," Heaven pleaded.

"How am I supposed to trust you if you don't trust me?" Rarri yelled at Tony.

"I trust you," Tony told him. "I just would like to get to know Heaven more…. Seeing as how you interrupted the good time, we were having to talk business."

Rarri looked over at Heaven who was now crying drastically.

"Fuck!" Rarri yelled.

"You have my word, I will not harm a hair on her head," Tony said with his hand over his heart then added "even if you do not come back."

"I'm comin' back," Rarri assured Tony then Heaven. "I'm comin' back." Rarri stormed out of the restaurant and out of the hotel. When the valet driver pulled up with his car, he hurried up and jumped in then pulled off.

Rarri walked into the hotel room and instantly smelled weed burning. He sat on the sofa and took off his shoes.

"Let me hit that shit," Rarri told Lil Dink.

Lil Dink passed him the blunt. "What's craccin'?"

Rarri hit the blunt hard two times. "It's lookin' good cuz," Rarri said and blew the smoke out.

***

"How do you like the view?" Tony asked Heaven who was looking out of the window.

"It's beautiful," Heaven admitted.

Tony had the best suite in the hotel and the biggest. Everything was plush from the extravagant rooms to the exquisite furniture. Even the carpet was luxury.

"Almost as beautiful as you."

"Tony, don't," Heaven replied sadly and put her head down.

"Don't what?" Tony asked in his heavy accent.

"You're acting like you're not goin' to kill me if you don't get your money," Heaven said, this time with anger in her voice. "Now you're complimenting me? I feel like a cow being lowered to its slaughter."

Tony kneeled down next to her so she could see his eyes, and then placed his hands on her knees. "I would never hurt you," Tony promised.

"Then why are you holdin' me here like a hostage?" Heaven asked.

"You are no hostage here… you can leave when you are ready," Tony assured her. "Your conversation is why I kept you here. You have a beautiful mind and I appreciate your company."

Heaven blushed shyly with a slight smile. She could tell Tony was being truthful.

"I enjoy your conversation too, Tony. You seem like a wonderful man… I bet plenty of ladies say that."

"You're actually the first one to ever say that," Tony laughed. "I want to be completely honest with you Heaven."

"I would hope so," Heaven joked. "I respect only the truth, no matter what it is."

"When I look into your eyes, I see a future. A future with someone I could love and give the world to. I see everything I need inside of you. Never, until today have I believed in love at first sight. You are not only beautiful, but you are very intelligent also," Tony said, the whole time looking directly in her eyes. "Be mines, Heaven."

"Tony, we just met. You're probably just feeling that way right now. Don't get me wrong, I would love to be with you, but how could I?" Heaven asked.

"Just by saying yes," Tony replied.

"Tony, you are royalty, while I'm just a regular girl from the hood," she said.

"Yet, here I am, the one on my knees," Tony responded quickly and placed a kiss on her thigh, sending chills through her entire body. He continued to kiss her thighs slowly and passionate. Each kiss was getting closer and closer to her pussy, making her wetter and wetter. She could feel herself dripping in her panties. "Just say yes," Tony said, as he continued to work his way to her pussy and lifted her dress slightly, exposing her bottom half, but Heaven didn't reply.

He could see the dampness in her panties and smell the sweetness. Tony moved her panties to the side and licked her clit softly, rotating his tongue in a circular motion as he wrapped his free hand around to her ass, holding her in place in the chair. He was making love to her pussy with his mouth. When he made his way to the hole of her box she moaned loudly and started to grind into his face, letting him taste all of her juices. Tony started fucking her pussy with his tongue and licking inside around her walls, making her cream. He had never tasted a pussy this good before in his life.

"Oh… f-fuck… Tony... right there… I'm about to cum," Heaven yelled as she fucked his face harder.

"Say yes," Tony said with a mouth full of pussy and started massaging her ass hole with her cream.

"Yes," she yelled.

"Say it again," Tony said.

"Yes," she repeated.

"Again," he demanded.

"Y-Yes… yes.... yessss," Heaven yelled and started squirting all over his face.

He kept licking her pussy as she squirted, then he licked her ass and she squirted again, this time, even harder. Tony licked all of her juices from her pussy and ass as she was shaking in the chair. After he finished cleaning her with his tongue, he stood and grabbed her hand. "Come, let's freshen up in the shower."

After they exited the shower, Heaven put it down on Tony giving him the best head and pussy ever, making him cum three times. Every time he would bust a nut, she would get him right back hard. After the third time, he couldn't handle anymore and fell asleep as she fucked him into a sex coma.

"Bing!" Rarri's phone messenger went off. When he saw it was a message from Heaven, he sat up straight on the sofa and swiped right.

HEAVEN: Got him.

Rarri's eyes grew big when he saw the message.

'Bing!"

His phone went off again, this time it was a picture message. When he pressed it to zoom in, he saw it was a picture of Tony in the bed sleeping like a big ass baby. He looked completely worn out and exhausted like he had never slept this good in his whole life. The message below read:

HEAVEN: Now that's' how you send a bitch.

RARRI: What time you want me to come back?

HEAVEN: Right now, silly.

RARRI: On my way.

"Wake yo ass up nigga," Rarri yelled excitedly and slapped Lil Dink on the leg knocking his foot off of the coffee table.

"What's the deal foo?" Lil Dink asked half-sleep.

“We on, cuz,” Rarri said as he lit a blunt. “Where you put the money at?

Lil Dink jumped up quickly and snatched off the cushion he was sitting on from the sofa. He reached in a hole he carved in and pulled out a mini duffle bag, then tossed it to Rarri.

“Damn cuz, you done cut the couch up and shit…. Fa’sho, we ain’t gettin’ the deposit back.”

Nigga fuck that deposit cuz, we on… they probably don’t even look under the shit anyway,” Lil Dink replied and snatched the blunt from Rarri.

Rarri acted like he was about to count the money as he slowly slid behind Lil Dink who was standing up hitting the blunt. Rarri tossed the duffle bag on the sofa behind him and grabbed Lil Dink in the chokehold. Lil Dink started squirming hard trying to break free from Rarri’s grip, but he was locked on too tight.

“Let me go!” Lil Dink warned.

“Naw nigga, I told you about that snatchin’ shit,” Rarri shot back. “I’m bout to fuck yo ass up now.”

Lil Dink used all of his might and lifted forward putting Rarri in the air, then brought him over his shoulder and slammed him on the couch. Lil Dink snatched him right up and put Rarri in the same chokehold he was just in and squeezed tightly.

“You still ain’t fuckin’ wit me cuz,” Lil Dink said half out of breath.

Rarri tapped Lil Dinks arm three times, but Lil Dink kept his grip. He tapped three more times. Lil Dink waited for a moment, and then let him go. Rarri collapsed and gasped for air. Lil Dink was standing over him, flexing.

"Eat yo Wheaties, lil nigga!" Lil Dink yelled down at Rarri.

"Fuck you cuz," Rarri replied.

Lil Dink put his hand out for Rarri to grab, then lifted him up and patted him on the back. "Maybe next time, cuz," Lil Dink laughed. "Maybe next time."

Lil Dink would always win the wrestling matches. He was the biggest out of Rarri, Trigg, and Spank. His time in juvie made him even stronger from working out so much. Lil Dink was the oldest out of the bunch and he was the first to get put on the Hood, so to him, they were the lil homies. Even though he was only a few months older, they looked up to him.

"Naw fa'sho, next time," Rarri laughed. "Come on, let's sagg out and handle this shit."

Afterward, Rarri went back with the money, Tony blessed him in the game, giving him Kilos for $8,000 apiece. He even let him keep the money he came with to put towards a purchase on top of however much he wanted.

Tony filled Rarri in on his feelings for Heaven and let him know to go through her for whatever he wanted. Tony still didn't like Rarri, but he did respect his hustle and the way he handled the situation he was in.

He planned on marrying Heaven in the near future if she allowed him to. She was irresistible to him, but little did she know how possessive he was. Or did she?

Chapter 6

Rarri and Lil Dink had the Hood craccin'. Every weekend was a party and the Arms was packed with homies and bitches from all over. Most of the bitches would come through in hopes of fucking a young nigga with money. Almost everybody had a foreign whip and money to blow. The only bitches who seemed not to be gold-digging were the ones who stayed in the Wilmington Arms.

Rarri made sure Bird put the bitches on, but not everybody was shining. Like every other Hood, you still had a circle of bummy muthafuckas who ain't got no hustle, and a crew of janky ass niggas waiting on you to get caught slipping. Rarri played the back and let Lil Dink be in the front. While Rarri supplied the drugs, Lil Dink setup the crews to dump it. So basically, if you wanted to get some work, you went through Lil Dink to get it.

Juice didn't like it, but he never complained, seeing as how he never had to pay upfront for anything no more, but he felt like he should at least be able to go to Rarri instead of Lil Dink because he was pushing a key and a half a week. He hated going through some little niggas to re-up, but he couldn't deny the fact that he was now making more money than he ever did before and was able to save his own money since being fronted. Juice's problem was that he wanted to be the man, but ever since Rarri got on, Juice wasn't him no more. He looked out for niggas, but Rarri was putting the Hood on, so he got way more love from his homies, especially the young niggas; they were deep as fuck. Fa'sho, the YTG's was craccin'.

"This nigga actin' like he forgot who first put cuz on," Juice said, then passed the blunt to Big Fatty as he mugged Rarri from a distance.

"Who you talkin' bout cuz?" Big fatty asked.

"This nigga Rarri," Juice replied.

"Man, let these young niggas eat cuz," Big fatty told him. "When the last time you seen the Hood cracc like this? Lil Fatty in a Benz? Baby Fatty jeweled up?

"I ain't hatin' on cuz . . . I'm just sayin' damn, can I get plugged? I'm the same nigga who gave cuz the money to get a half brick when he came to me, but now he on from that and I gotta go through Lil Dink to re-up? That's foul homie!" Juice said.

"I'm pretty sure cuz done slid that back and some," Big Fatty shot back.

"That ain't even the point homie. It's the principle ," Juice told him.

Big fatty and Juice grew up together, so he knew when Juice was tripping on some dumb shit. Unlike Juice, he was proud of how Rarri was conducting his business; especially since both of his little homies was getting money and craccin'. Rarri had done more for the Hood than a lot of muthafuckas put together ever did, and he was only sixteen. *A stunna and a gunna* with a good heart, he was a new breed of a nigga.

"Yea, I hear you." Big fatty hit the blunt and passed it back to Juice. "I'm bout to sagg out before the wife start trippin' . . . I'ma get wit you tomorrow."

Juice didn't say nothing. He just hit the blunt and kept mugging Rarri.

Rarri was smoking and drinking with all of his homies. Everybody was screaming the words to Terrance Cash *'No Sleep'* song as it played loudly through the speakers. Niggas was turnt all the way up. Some bitches was getting flipped in cars in the parking lot, while others out in the open.

It was about ten different dice games going on from ones to hundreds. Money was everywhere. A couple fights broke out, but for the most part, everybody was having a good time.

"I think it's time we stretch our wings, cuz," Lil Dink shouted to Rarri over the music.

"What you mean? he asked.

"I think we should start fuckin' wit some niggas from the other side, on some money shit," Lil Dink replied.

Rarri frowned. "The other side?"

"Yea nigga," he shot back.

"I don't know fool . . . I think we should just worry bout us right now. Shit been coo," Rarri said.

"But it could be better YAAH . . . we could lock the city up, Hood by Hood. Fuck all that beef shit, let's stack our bread. If niggas ain't wit it, fuck 'em. But whoever is, that's more money in our pockets," Lil Dink schooled.

Rarri thought about it for a minute, looking at the good and bad, but he had to admit Lil Dink was talking some real shit. It was simple: less beef, more moncy. At that moment, Rarri knew he had made a good choice by letting Lil Dink play the front.

"Who you got in mind?" Rarri asked.

"You remember my cousin, Travis?"

"Yea I remember cuz. I ain't know he banged though," Rarri said with a confused expression on his face.

"Yea, that nigga been on his shit Yaah," Lil Dink said matter-of-factly. "You heard if a nigga named Flock?"

"Yea from the west, but I never met cuz," Rarri explained.

"That's Travis," Lil Dink told him.

"That's crazy," Rarri laughed. "When you tryna link up wit cuz?"

"Tomorrow," Lil Dink said.

"Ight bet," Rarri told him as they dapped, then his phone went off. "Hello!"

"What you doin?" Heaven asked.

"Chillin' in the Hood. What's the deal?" he asked.

"Shit. I got a surprise for you . . . go to the front," Heaven told him before hanging up.

Rarri walked to the front with Lil Dink and a few other homies behind him. When they made it out the gate, Rarri saw Bird standing next to a stretched limo. When she saw him she ran up and gave him a hug. It had been almost two months since they had seen each other.

Bird, Mia, Tia, Dria, and Fia had been moving the coke out of town to some of Tony's clientele for Heaven.

"I missed you," Bird said before giving him a big kiss.

"I missed you, too," Rarri said between kisses.

"Aww, how cute," Lil Dink teased.

Bird flicked him off without breaking her kiss from Rarri.

"Ight, say bye to your friends. I'm stealin' you for the night," she told him.

"Ight . . . aye y'all, I'm bout to sagg out," Rarri told them.

"Cuz it's craccin' in the hood, fucc all that," Lil Dink replied.

"Naw!" Bird said and opened the back door of the limo. "It's craccin' in here."

Mia, Tia, Dria, and Fia was all sexing each other crazy. Tia and Dria were on their knees eating out Mia and Fia, while Mia and Fia were kissing each other.

"Daammnn!" All of Rarri's boys said at once.

"I'm goin' wit y'all," Lil Dink said and walked towards the door, but Bird closed it.

"No you ain't. This Rarri's birthday gift," she told him.

"It ain't even cuz birthday," Lil Dink said.

"Everyday is Rarri's birthday," she shot back.

Lil Dink looked at Rarri with a fake mad face and said, "you lucky cuz," then threw some play punches at him.

"Ight ight, Ima hit you tomorrow, fool," Rarri said and walked towards the door.

Bird stopped him and straightened out his shirt, then fixed the charm on his chain. "Babe, tonight is goin' to be one of the best nights of your life. I promise you . . . now open up."

Rarri frowned his face and moved his head back when he saw the pill in her hand. "What is that?"

"A molly, nigga!" Bird told him.

"I don't know cuz. I ain't never popped no molly before," Rarri admitted nervously.

"Trust me, you goin' to like it . . . look!" Bird said and put the pill in her mouth, then chased it with orange juice. "We all bout to be rollin'."

Bird pulled out another pill and put it in Rarri's mouth, then put the bottle of orange juice to his lips. Rarri drank some and swallowed the pill. Bird jumped up and down like a happy little kid and then opened the door for Rarri to hop in.

When Rarri got in the limo, Mia, Tia, Dria, and Fia were still going at it. They hadn't even noticed him in the limo until Bird closed the door behind her.

"Hey, Papi!" Mia and Fia said and went back to kissing each other.

"Hey, Papi!" Tia and Dria said and went back down on Mia and Fia.

The whole scene was breathtaking. Mia, Tia, Dria, and Fia all resembled Ayisha Diaz the model.

"What up y'all? Y'all on a molly, too?" he asked.

"Hell yea Papi, that shit feels good as fuck," Dria said. "Come here. Let me show you somethin'".

Rarri looked at Bird. "Don't look at me, we all yo bitches now. . . you gotta fuck them how you fuck me. They earned their spot," Bird said, and nodded to the stack of money next to her while she started rolling a blunt.

When he turned back to Dria, she was motioning him with one finger to come to her while she continued to eat out Mia's pussy. Rarri went over and sat down next to Dria on the floor of the limo. Dria grabbed Rarri's hand and guided it to her pussy that was dripping wet. She was so wet that it dripped down her thighs. Rarri's hand was instantly soaked and his dick grew hard as a rock.

Damn," was all he could say as he massaged her pussy, getting it even wetter.

"I haven't even got my pussy touched until now . . . it just keeps cummin' and cummin' on its own Papi!" Dria moaned. "Fuck me, Papi!"

"Me too, Papi! Fuck me!" Tia said.

"Us too, Papi! "Mia moaned.

"We want that dick, too," Fia finished.

“Me too, daddy! I want that dick, too,” Bird said from behind Rarri as she reached around his waist and unbuckled his pants.

She started stroking him with one hand while she drenched her other hand with Dria’s soaked pussy. After she was able to gather a small puddle of Dria’s juices, Bird poured it on Rarri’s dick then took him into her mouth, twirling her tongue slowly as she went up and down while moving her head from side to side all in one motion. Bird took his dick out of her mouth and slid under Dria so she could ride her face.

“Come fuck this bitch from the back while I eat her pussy.”

When Rarri stuck his dick inside of Dria, Bird tickled his balls with her tongue. Rarri started finger banging Tia as he slow-stroked Dria.

All of a sudden, he started feeling good. Too good! Rarri had never felt this good in his life. His entire body was tingling and everything was sensitive to the touch. When he took his shirt off, his dick slipped out of Dria’s pussy and into Bird’s mouth. Bird started twirling her tongue on the head of his dick and deep throating him wildly, then she stuck his dick back in Dria’s pussy.

“Oh my god,” Dria moaned. “F-fuck this pussy, Papi.”

Dria was popping her ass like a pro as Rarri fucked her and Bird licked her clit while she licked Mia’s pussy sloppily.

"I'm bout to cum," Dria said and started throwing her ass back harder. Bird put her hands around Dria's waist to help her throw it back faster and harder on Rarri's dick.

"Oh s-s-shhiittt," Dria screamed as she started squirting all on Bird's face and shaking like crazy.

Bird used four of her fingers and massaged her clit quickly from side to side, making her squirt again, this time harder and into Bird's mouth. She moved Dria from on top of her, slightly leaned up and spit all of Dria's cum on Rarri's dick.

"Next," Bird said and continued sucking on his dick until Mia slid down and got in the same position Dria was in while Dria went to eating out Bird.

Tia got on the left side of Rarri and Fia on the right. They took turns tongue-kissing him while he fucked Mia. Tia bent down and grabbed Rarri's dick and started sucking and spitting on it getting it wetter, then put it back inside of Mia. Fia stopped kissing Rarri to spit in Mia's ass so it could drip to her pussy and Rarri's dick.

The night had just begun and was surely going to get wilder. This was nothing but a warmup for them all. It was going to be more pill-popping, weed-smoking, drink sipping, dick sucking and pussy fucking than any of them intended on doing. Rarri leaned his head back and closed his eyes as he was about to cum to Mia bouncing on his dick and Bird sucking his balls.

"BING! BING! BING! BING! BING! BING! BING! BING! BING! BING!"

Rarri jumped up, startled by the alarm clock that was going off loudly in his room. He got out of the bed and unplugged it. His head was throbbing, and his vision was a little blurry. Rarri saw a figure on his patio but wasn't able to recognize it until he walked up closer. It was Heaven on her phone texting away and drinking coffee. He opened the sliding door, went outside then sat next to her as he lit one of Heaven's Newport's.

"Mornin'," Heaven said while never looking away from her phone.

"Good mornin'," he replied. "Man, I had the craziest dream last night."

Heaven laughed. "That wasn't no dream. They in the living room."

Rarri looked at Heaven dumbfounded and hurried back in the house towards the living room.

"Your welcome!" Heaven yelled after him, then mumbled to herself, "rude."

When Rarri made it to the living room, he saw all five of them sleeping in different sections, butt ass naked. He couldn't remember nothing that happened except for when he was in the limo, but the empty bottles of Ciroc and pills on the counter let him know it was craccin'. Rarri went to the bathroom to brush his teeth, then grabbed some weed and a blunt and went back to join Heaven outside.

"Thanks," he told her.

"No problem, pimp," Heaven replied. "You know I had to test all five of them bitches before I gave them my full approval, though."

While Rarri rolled his weed and smoked, Heaven filled him in on how she tested them for the last sixty days.

First, she had dudes pose as rich wealthy men; squares, pimp's and thugs, giving them expensive gifts and promising to take care of them if they would be theirs. This test Heaven did one by one secretly while each of them was alone, but every time they would tell Heaven about the gift and deny the men of sex. Heaven tested each of them over a half dozen times, but none of them failed no matter how expensive the gift. Heaven gave a guy a hundred thousand dollars who posed as a trick and told him to give it to them if they promised to be his. One by one, they all promised to be his for the money, but as soon as he went to sleep, they ran off with his money for Rarri. She kept all five of the girls away from each other so they couldn't tell each other what was going on. They all passed test one.

For the second test, she set up a fake police bust. The whole time they were out of town moving the drugs to Tony's clients daily. Heaven had some people posing as feds crack them and question the fuck out of them. I mean, these muthafuckas went hard as hell on each of them. One of the guys was actually a crooked cop on Tony's payroll who specialized in interrogating. Heaven promised him twenty-five bands for each one he had gotten to break, so you know he was pissed when he missed out on the hundred and twenty-five thousand, he thought he had comin. They passed test two, as well.

"Damn, that's crazy as fuck," Rarri laughed. "So, they solid?"

"Yup . . . I still got more to teach them, but they are all about you. Ain't no doubt about that . . . especially Bird. That bitch right there is the one. She reminds me so much of myself, it's crazy," Heaven said. "Don't forget who the real bottom is though, as you can see, I go harder than all, so ain't no competition. If a bitch don't push for you like me, you don't need her. Always remember that Rarri.

"What about Bird?" he asked.

"What about her?" Heaven shot back with a hint of attitude.

"You said she remind you of you, so how do I work that?" Rarri asked.

"No matter how much you love and trust a bitch Rarri, always watch her," Heaven schooled.

"What about you?" he asked.

"Even me," Heaven said with an even more stern face.

"BING!" Rarri's messenger went off. When he slid it open, it was a message from Lil Dink.

Lil Dink: Where you at fool?

Rarri: At the house, come scoop me up.

"BING!"

Lil Dink: on my way.

"I'm bout to hop in the shower real quick. Don't go nowhere," Rarri told Heaven and walked in the house to hop in the shower.

"Especially niggas," she mumbled to herself.

Lil Dink and Rarri drove down a back street in Compton. Everybody on that side wore burgundy or red in their clothing or shoes. Some niggas didn't wear either, but you could tell they were from around that way because they would throw up gang signs at the car and yell *whoop.*

They stopped in front of a house where two niggas were sitting on the porch. When Dink and Rarri hopped out, the two dudes jumped up and walked towards them.

"Aye, where you niggas from, blood?" one of them said as they approached.

"Parc Village, Compton," Rarri replied.

"Nigga this West Side, Bompton!" the other dude banged hard.

"And?" Rarri shot back and clutched his 357 revolver.

The other one drew his 30 round Glock 40.

"On Piru, I will lay yo ass out, boy!" You on the wrong side to be poppin' that hot shit."

"Man, fuck all this bullshit. Where that nigga Travis at?" Lil Dink asked, interrupting the standoff as he walked past them and up to the house.

Lil Dink walked right in like he owned the place leaving Rarri and the two dudes outside. He knew they wouldn't touch Rarri or bust no guns in front of that house.

"What up aunty?" Lil Dink asked his aunt Tammy and walked up and gave her a kiss on the cheek.

"Hey, nephew, where you been boy? Ain't seen you in a minute. You lookin' good," Tammy said.

"Tryna stay out the way. Where that nigga Travis at?" Lil Dink asked as he picked up a piece of chicken out of the bowl and took a bite.

"On that damn game," she replied, as she dropped some more chicken in hot grease.

"Ight," he replied and walked out of the kitchen into the hallway.

He stopped at a door that was cracked and stuck his head in. "What up Ashley?"

"Cousin," she yelled and hopped off of her bed to give him a hug.

"Aye, y'all, this my cousin, Lil Dink," Ashley told her two friends that were in her room.

"Hey!" they both said at once.

"What up?" he asked and turned back to Ashley. "Ima stop back before I leave."

Lil Dink winked at her two friends and walked off.

"Yo cousin fine as fuck. Is his chains real?" he heard one of them say as he went down the hallway.

Lil Dink made it to another room and walked in. As soon as he opened the door, the smell of weed hit his face and he saw Travis and two other niggas with Playstation 3 controllers yelling at the T.V. as they listened to YG's '*B.P.T'* song on the surround sound, loudly. When Travis saw Lil Dink, he paused the game and got up to shake his hand.

"What's brackin', nigga?"

"Same shit, tryna get rich," Lil Dink replied, then looked at the other nigga and said, "what's craccin'?"

"Bickin' it," one of them said and stood up with his hand extended. "Lil Flock, West Side, Bompton."

Lil Dink shook his hand. "Lil Dink, Parc Village, Compton."

The other one stood up with his hand extended too. "Baby flock, West Side, Bompton."

Lil Dink shook his hand. "Lil Dink, Parc Village, Compton."

"Yea, these my lil niggas I was tellin' you about," Travis said.

"Oh ok, fa'sho yaah . . . they wit the shitz?" Lil Dink asked.

"On Ru's," Travis said proudly.

"Let's holla outside. I got the homie with me," Lil Dink said and headed out.

When they made it outside, Rarri and the two niggas were smoking a blunt and talking like nothing ever happened. Turns out, they knew a lot of the same people and fuck some of the same bitches.

"That shit crazy, cuz," Rarri said smiling and shaking his head.

"Bitches ain't shit," Infant Flock replied as he hit the weed.

Flock, Lil Flock and Baby Flock introduced themselves to Rarri. Infant Flock and B-dog introduced themselves to Lil Dink. Flock sat down on one of the chairs outside as Infant, passed him the blunt. He hit it hard.

"What's brackin'?" he asked as he blew the smoke out.

Lil Dink and Rarri filled them in on the *Powder Plan* as they smoked blunt after blunt.

"So, what you think?" Lil Dink asked Flock.

Flock was thinking deeply on the situation with an undecided expression on his face. "I mean this shit sound cool and all that, but we ain't no dope dealin' type niggas, you feel me? We flock shit, blood, but fa'sho we could put the pieces together so we all could eat. I know some niggas from the Hood that will be wit it if we drop the work on em', especially this nigga B-dog. He the dope dealin' nigga.

"Yea, I'm wit that shit. A nigga been lowkey prayin' for a better plug, on Piru. If a nigga could be brackin' how y'all talkin' bout, we could fuck around and take over the city," B-dog explained. He always sold some type of drugs to keep some money in his pocket. B-dog always had the hustler's ambition. He just never had the right plugs to elevate his game until now.

His family was big, and almost all of them were from some Piru Hood in Compton, so he could touch a lot of sections with ease.

"Ight, bet . . . I'ma come back and get at you wit some work, today," Lil Dink said slapping five with B-dog.

"Aye! So, you say y'all flock shit, right?" Rarri asked Flock.

"All day," Flock replied.

"I got some shit for y'all. Just give me a minute to put it in motion," Rarri said as he hit the blunt.

Chapter 7

"Baby I'm hungry," Trina said as she walked into the living room with her sad face on. The only thing she wore was a T-shirt; no bra or panties, so you could see her nipples, and her hairless pussy was exposed.

Ima be blunt with you: Trina badd as fuck. She got that Megan Good type of look. Nice full lips, seductive eyes and a body that is out of this world.

"What you tryna eat?" Lil Trouble asked as he continued putting more coke on the scale without looking up.

Ever since Spank's funeral, Trina and Lil Trouble been inseparable. She felt protected when he was around because she knew how much he loved her. He promised that he would never let a nigga hurt her again, and he meant it.

Trina walked up and pushed him on the couch so that he was laying back. "First, I'm goin' to feed you, then we could worry about me," she said as she stood on the couch and squatted over him, putting her pussy to his lips.

Lil Trouble gripped her ass with both hands as he feasted. "Pop that ass for me," he said, and Trina started popping and twerking as he ate her out. He slid his middle finger in and out of her as she moved, making Trina's pussy wetter.

"Fuck my face," he said.

"I'm bout to cum! " Trina moaned and started riding his face wildly.

Lil Trouble's phone started ringing. When he tried to get up, Trina pushed down on him harder and started grinding wilder. "Wait, baby, let me cum on yo face first," she pleaded.

"Oh s-s-shiit," Trina screamed as she released on his face.

Lil Trouble licked her pussy a few more times before getting up. "I love the way you taste," he said as he got up and checked his phone.

"Put some clothes on babe, I got somebody comin' through."

"K," Trina said and went into the room to get dressed.

Usually, Lil Trouble wouldn't let niggas come by the house to buy no work, but this dude spent two bandz every other day, fa'sho.

"You still ain't told me what you wanted to eat," he yelled to her from the living room.

"Fuck it, let's just order a pizza and watch a movie," Trina said walking back into the living room putting her hair in a ponytail. She had on sweatpants, a tank-top, and some Nike blazers. Trina grabbed a blunt off the table, went in the kitchen and lit it from the stove, then walked backed in the living room and sat on Lil Trouble's lap.

"So?" Trina asked and took a pull of the blunt.

"I'm wit it, babe," Lil Trouble said as he grabbed the blunt from her and hit it. "You goin' to walk to the Redbox to get the movies?"

"Lazy ass," Trina replied playfully. "I got you . . . I guess you want me to order the pizza too."

"You already know," Lil Trouble laughed. "Here, take this with you," he added, handing her the blunt.

Trina turned around and gave him two kisses on the lips.

"Ight, I'll be back," she said and grabbed her cell phone and headphones. Trina put the headphones in her ears and headed out.

Lil Trouble finished bagging up the powder he was about to sell then cleaned off the table. After that, he rolled up a few blunts.

"KNOCK, KNOCK, KNOCK, KNOCK."

"Bout time," Lil Trouble said to himself as he walked to the door and opened it. "What's craccin' cuz?"

"Nothin' much, tryna power up and get this bread," the man said as he walked in and shook hands with Lil Trouble.

"Fa'sho bro, I got yo shit ready, right here," he said leading him to the living room.

He gave Lil Trouble the money and Lil Trouble gave him the coke.

"You tryna smoke cuh?" Lil Trouble asked and picked up a blunt.

"Hell yea," the man said. "What kind of weed you got?"

"I only smoke moonrock cuh," Lil Trouble responded, then sat down on the couch, lit the blunt and counted the money.

"You could sit down my nigga."

"Fa'sho," the man said and took a seat. "It's cool if I bump a line?"

"It's yo shit. Bump as many as you want to," Lil Trouble replied.

"Good lookin' . . . you chill peoples," the man said as he pulled out a chunk of coke and broke it down.

"Chill people's? Where you from out there, bro?" Lil Trouble asked.

"Newark," the man said and sniffed a line. "Newark, New Jersey."

"God damn nigga! What the fuck you doin' way out here?" Lil Trouble asked as he passed the blunt.

"My mom and pops brok—"

"BAM! BAM! BAM! BAM! BAM!"

"Shit, that's my girl," Lil Trouble said.

"We good?" he asked, slightly paranoid.

"Yea, she probably forgot her key again . . . hold up," Lil Trouble replied.

"BAM! BAM! BAM! BAM! BAM! BAM!"

"I'm comin'," Lil Trouble yelled.

When he opened the door, Trina was dancing and singing to *'Drunk in Love'* by Beyoncé. "We be all night . . ." Trina sang and gave Lil Trouble a kiss in the doorway.

Lil Trouble started off back to the living room while she locked the doors. When he sat down on the couch, he could still hear her singing to the music in her ears. When she walked into the living room, she was looking down, taking the movies out of the bag to show Lil Trouble.

"Babe this the homie Shawn," Lil Trouble said.

When Trina looked up, she dropped the movies. It felt like the world stopped and she couldn't breathe all at the same time.

"What's wrong?" Lil Trouble asked as he jumped up and rushed to her, but she couldn't talk. It was like she was choking on her own words. "Babe, what's wrong?"

When he looked into her eyes, he saw fear. By the time he noticed that what she was afraid of was right behind him, it was too late.

"BOOM!"

Lil Trouble didn't break his stare from Trina when he felt the burn in his back. He looked her directly in the eyes and said, "I love y—"

"BOOM! BOOM! BOOM!"

Shawn's bullets cut him off short, sending Lil Trouble falling to the floor.

Trina's scream was silenced by a gunshot to the chest. She fell next to Lil Trouble's body.

She could hear Shawn around savaging the house looking for drugs and money. Trina knew he found the stash when she opened her eyes and he was standing over her looking down at her with that evil grin.

"Please . . . I swear to God, I won't say anything," Trina cried.

Shawn chuckled. " I know. "

"BOOM!"

Everything went black for Trina.

***

Rarri was getting off the 710 freeway on Pacific Coast Hwy, heading East. He was feeling flexy as he swerved through traffic banging 'Trap Niggaz' by Future.

"RING! RING! RING!"

His phone started to ring from the Bluetooth in his car. He pressed the call button on his steering wheel to answer it. "Yaah what's the deal, Macky?"

"You out this way, yet?" Macky asked.

"I'm gettin' off on PCH right now," Rarri replied.

"Fa'sho ... Aye cuz, just meet me at the Wing Stop on 20th and Long Beach Blvd," Macky instructed.

"Ain't that a lil out of bounds for you?" Rarri joked.

"Them niggas from '20s goin' to press yo line."

"On Insane Crip, a nigga ain't gon press shit. I stay wit a '30, fool," Macky bragged.

The Insane Crips and the '20 Crips beef hard. Macky was telling Rarri to pull up in the '20 Crips, territory. A lot of them niggas couldn't wait to catch Macky slipping, yet here he was meeting other muthafuckas on they side like it was his. That's really the main reason they wanted to get Macky specifically. The nigga plain out disrespectful. He would disrespect them any way he could and every chance he got.

Macky was a short high yellow nigga with a big 20 crossed out on his neck. Damn near all his tattoos was disrespectful, too.

"Ight, I'ma pull up in about five minutes," Rarri said and hit the hang-up button.

When Rarri arrived, Macky was sitting in the passenger seat of his Audi, eating chicken with his baby momma. When he saw Rarri had pulled up next to him, he got out with the bag of chicken in one hand, and an *'MCM'* backpack over his shoulder.

"Wow! You a jockin' ass nigga, cuz," Rarri joked, referring to all the MCM apparel Macky had on. Everybody knew Rarri rocked MCM the most.

"Fuck you, cuz, I look better in it," Macky said and took a step back so Rarri could see the whole fit. Rarri put his head slightly out the window giving Macky a look-over, then sat back in his seat and said, "neva."

"Stop hatin' cuz, it don't fit you," Macky laughed then handed him the backpack. "It's all in there . . . get at me."

He hopped back in his car and Rarri opened the backpack to look at the money. “You don’t want yo bag back?” Rarri asked.

“Naw, keep it,” Macky said.

“So, you gon model on me like that cuz?” Rarri asked.

Macky didn’t say nothing, he just hung out the window, flicked him off with both hands and smiled as his baby momma sped off.

Macky and Rarri stayed flossing on each other. Who dressed the best, who fucked the most bitches, whose car was better? In all, Rarri would win because his money was longer, and he was younger. Macky was 19. Rarri was about to turn seventeen in two days.

Rarri lit a blunt he had already rolled and pulled off, heading back home to his condo in Hollywood. He had his radio blasting and was smashing on the freeway feeling himself, as usual.

Rarri saw a fly ass bitch pushing in a Lexus. When they made eye contact, she smiled, and he nodded his head saying, *what’s up?* The girl bit her lip in a sexy way as she admired Rarri, then floored it, speeding off and leaving Rarri behind.

“Ima crack this bitch,” Rarri thought happily as he sped up to catch her. Every time he switched lanes to get on the side of her, she cut him off, keeping him in the back.

They were driving around 100 mph and he was on her bumper the whole chase. Rarri hit his blunt deeply and started coughing so hard, that it fell in his lap almost burning a hole in his basketball shorts.

He was so focused on putting the cherry out, so he didn't get burned by the blunt that he didn't notice the girl switch lanes and was slowing down. By the time he saw what was going on he was passing her up, it was too late to react to what she was screaming, but he knew she was trying to get him to slow down. He looked up and saw the traffic in front of him, but there was nothing he could do.

"BAM!"

Rarri wrecked and passed out from the impact.

***

1998

"Tell that nigga if he want his fee to come get it his damn self. I don't need you bitches collectin' my shit," Candy said between the cracked door of her hotel room.

"So, you playin' with his money again?" Angel asked rubbing her hand in frustration.

"First off this my money, and if I don't feel lik—"

"BAM!"

Before Candy could finish what she was saying, Angel kicked the door as hard as she could and made her way in with Heaven behind her.

"What the fuck!" Candy said from on the floor holding her bleeding nose.

"What the fuck my ass . . . why I always gotta go through this wit you, Candy?" Angel asked as she searched the room. "This the second time."

"I'm not yo bitch," Candy screamed and tried to charge Angel but was tripped by Heaven.

Heaven flicked out a knife and stood over her. "Naw, you ain't, but you is my nigga bitch," she said, pointing the knife down at Candy.

"Ha!" Candy laughed sarcastically. "Yo nigga? I been around before both you bitches . . . y'all don't run me."

"Bitch, ain't nobody tryna run yo black, ran down, smoker body, ass," Angel said, as she looked under the mattress and seen the money rolled up.

"Really Candy?" Angel asked. "You keepin' this shit under the bed, now? . . . . You slippin' on yo shit.

"Whatever," she shot back.

Angel sighed, walked in the bathroom, wet a towel and brought it out for Candy's nose. She sat down, right next to her and tried to hand her the towel nicely, but Candy snatched it roughly anyway before putting it to her nose.

"Damn bitch," Angel said.

"Damn bitch, what? It's yo fault my shit bleedin'," Candy said.

"Now, you know not to fuck wit me," Heaven replied. They stared at each other for a moment then both of them burst out laughing. Heaven looked at them both like they were crazy, then sat down on the bed.

"What the fuck is so funny?"

"Time, baby girl . . . time is funny," Candy answered. "Now help me up bitch," she said with her hand extended out to Heaven.

Heaven looked at Candy then at Angel, who was still sitting down. Angel nodded in agreement, then Heaven helped Candy to her feet. Candy grabbed a Newport from off of the dresser and sparked it. Angel counted the money she had got from under the bed while she was still sitting down.

"Bitch don't try and play me. Candy ain't never been no short hoe," Candy schooled.

"Checkin' ain't cheatin'," Angel said and kept counting the money. Candy looked at her and smiled.

"You done came a long way from what you used to be . . . you know I don't mean to give you no hard time, you doin' everything you supposed to do. I just be missin' him on some square shit sometimes, all in my feelin's and shit."

"Sometimes? Bitch you always in yo feelin's," Angel teased as she got up. "Naw, but all bullshit to the side, you know I'm already knowin' what's up, so don't ever let it come between us. I'ma forever have love for Candy."

"Aaww," Candy said and gave Angel a big hug. "Now, get the fuck out my room before you make me cry, bitch."

"Ugh, you always kickin' a muthafucka out when I'm bout to get comfortable . . . come on Heaven," Angel said.

Heaven went to give Candy a hug before leaving, but she put her hand up stopping her.

"I don't do newbies . . . sorry," Candy said with her bottom lip poked out in her play sad face.

"Whatever," Heaven replied, feeling played as she walked out of the hotel room.

"I still don't get why y'all was laughin'," Heaven said when they made it back to the car.

"She used to be daddy's bottom when I first came around. When me or one of the other girls would mess up, she would come through and fuck us up. Sometime we would cry about it to her and she would be like, *"now you know not to fuck wit me."* I used to hate that shit, but it's a lot of shit I wouldn't know if it wasn't for her," Angel told Heaven.

"That was the big joke?" Heaven asked in disbelief. "Y'all muthafuckas is crazy."

"A lil bit," Angel responded.

"So, what happened? Why she ain't the bottom no more?" Heaven asked.

Angel took a minute before she replied.

"He always told me to take whatever I wanted in life, so I took her spot."

"What if somebody take yo spot, one day?" Heaven asked.

“First off, can’t a bitch breathin’ take *our* spot,” Angel replied, pointing at Heaven and herself. “Bitches like Candy get comfortable when they become a bottom. Bitches like us go harder . . . second! He really loves us, unlike the rest of these hoes he puttin’ on the blade. But in reality, we ain't no different from them. Some hoes just dumb and don’t know how to do shit but hoe, so they can’t prosper or think of more moves to make. Don’t ever be no *in the box hoe*, and don’t ever hoe for a nigga who ain't a son of God.”

“Preach bitch, preach,” Heaven said happily with her right hand to the sky and her left hand over her heart like she was really in the church listening to the pastor speak some deep shit.

“When you stay in pocket, you take off like a rocket, understand me!” Angel said, imitating an old school pimp.

“Oh shit! That’s what’s up,” Heaven laughed.

“Naw bitch, the only thing up is the price of pussyyy,” Heaven said, dragging out her last word like the pimps did in the movies back in the day. They both busted out laughing hard as hell for about a minute straight.

“You crazy as hell,” Heaven said. “So, where we goin’, now?”

“Let’s finish pickin’ up this money then go home . . . we gotta get ready for tomorrow,” Angel said and started the car and pulled off.

***

The next day

"I was wonderin' when you was goin' to stop playin' and start payin' some real pimpin'," Sir Master said after Heaven handed him a roll of money.

Sir Master was a pimp from Los Angeles, one of those fast-talking, limp walking, suit-wearing, gold chain swanging, every-finger-got a-ring, type niggas. Everybody in the game knew of Sir Master. He was a gorilla pimp. He once threw a bitch out of his moving car for being fifty-cent short of his daily fee. Can you believe that shit? Fifty-cent!! Two punk-ass quarters!! They say he got his name by making his black hoes call him Sir, his white hoes call him Master and ain't a bitch ever left his stable without him going across her face with a blade.

None of them would admit it, but most of the pimps feared him just as much as the hoes did, and he knew it. That's why he would harass any bitch on any blade at any time, no matter who her pimp was. Especially on *'Fig'*! As far as he was concerned, *'Fig'* was his blade.

He wasn't a gang member, but he had family from both Hoover and Denver Lane Bloods, which gave him access others didn't have.

"What my money smell like dad—" Heaven asked flirtatiously but was cut off by the mean look on his face. "I mean, what my money smell like Sir?"

Seeing how she corrected herself, put him back at ease, then he smiled and took a big smell of the money.

"It smells like a got a bad bitch," he said as he blew out, then he sat up on the couch, lit a cigarette from the coffee table and patted the seat next to him for Heaven to sit down. When Heaven sat down, he handed her the house phone.

"Now call that *would be* of a pimp you used to fuck wit so I could serve him his papers and let him know you sittin' wit some real pimpin'."

"Yes Sir," Heaven said happily, dialed God's number and handed it to Sir Master. The phone rang a few times.

"Hello."

"Say P. It's me, the nigga wit the tea, Sir Master . . . I got some good news and some bad news. Mane, I like yo style, so I'ma slide you the good news first. The good news is you could pimp strong and live long, ya dig. Bad news is, I'm sittin' next to a little hottie wit a nice body. She sa—"

"I don't mean to cut you off bruh, but do you got a cigarette on you?" God asked.

"Yea, I got one," Sir. Master replied.

"Do me a favor and hand her three of 'em for me," God instructed.

Sir. Master did what God told him to do.

"I did that," Sir. Master said.

"So, you say you knocked a bitch from me?" God asked.

"Yea, by the name of Heaven," he replied proudly.

"How much money you got stacked up at yo spot, bruh?" God asked.

“I’m sittin’ on eighty-seven thousand right now ‘cause I just cashed out on some more jewelry.”

“Do me a favor and go get that money and hand it to her for me, would you?” God asked.

“Hold on,” Sir. Master said and walked into his bathroom. By this time, his hoes were all standing in the living room wondering what was going on. A few moments later, Sir. Master walked out with a bag, tossed it to Heaven and picked the phone back up. “Done.”

“Damn bruh, you coo as fuck. You think you could do me one more favor tho?” God asked.

“Yea, just let me know,” Sir. Master replied.

“I need you to take off all yo jewelry, all yo hoes jewelry and any other jewelry in that house, and give it to the bitch you just cracked,” God said.

“Ok hold on,” Sir. Master replied, then went on to collect all of his other jewelry and the jewelry of his hoes. When he sat down on the couch, he relieved himself of all the jewelry on him and handed it to Heaven, who put it all in the bag. By now, all of his hoes were mad at what was going on, but none of them said a word that he could hear.

“Ok, that’s done, too.”

“Tell her she could leave now,” God instructed.

“You could leave now,” Sir. Master told Heaven.

Heaven got up and walked to the door and opened it, then looked back at the group of bitches.

“Step it up,” she said and walked out.

She saw Angel sitting in the car outside and ran to it excitedly and hopped in.

"It worked bitch," Angel yelled loudly.

"Hell yea it worked. I got everything from him," Heaven said.

"Come on, let's get out of here," Angel said and pulled off.

"Put me on speaker and call all of yo bitches so they could hear this," God said.

Sir Master did as told. "Everybody here, what's up."

"I know y'all wonderin' what's goin' on by now, so let me put it on y'all bluntly; Some real pimpin' goin' on right now. I go by the name of God and no, none of y'all can't be in my squad. The smart thing to do right now would be to leave because tomorrow he ain't goin' to remember nothin'. Only thing he is goin' to know is that his money and jewelry missin'. Let him know when he took a sniff off God's money, the only thing he smelt was the *Devil's Breath*," God said, then hung up.

Not many people knew what the Devil's Breath was back then. Some still don't know now. If you are one of those people, look it up.

Devil's Breath will make someone give you whatever you want, no matter what it is, they can't say no. The best part of the drug is that they don't even know they're on it. Everything seems normal until they wake up the next day to an empty house, or to find out they're bank account has been drained and they helped the muthafuckas do it.

***

"Aghh shit," Rarri said as he awoke to a terrible headache. For a second, his vision was blurry as he scanned the room noticing he was in a hospital. On the other side, he saw his aunt Heaven sleeping on the half-size sofa.

"Aunty! Aunty! Aun—" Rari called out in a whisper.

"I hear you Rarri," Heaven replied cutting him off. She turned and laid on her back looking at the ceiling while she talked, then sighed deeply before speaking again.

"You have to move more smarter. This—"

"I have to get out of here," he said as he tried to get up and off of the hospital bed, but one of his hands were cuffed.

"You ain't goin' nowhere right now," Heaven said, still looking at the ceiling.

"You fucked up Rarri, and I can't just get you out of this one . . . you totaled the car. You're lucky to even be alive, right now and to barely have a couple scratches. That's a miracle, itself . . . you flipped the car six times Rarri . . . six fuckin' times. I had to pay the muthafucka you ran into off just so they ain't press no charges."

"So, what I'm chained up for?" Rarri asked, which seemed to piss Heaven off even more.

She got up and walked to his bedside to look him in the eye.

"You chained up because they found twenty-thousand dollars on you and a pistol –they're tryin' to say you was smokin' weed and drivin', so they might throw a DUI on top of all that … then these muthafuckas all up in my ass tryin' to figure out where you gettin' all this money from, and why was you drivin' my car without a fuckin' license."

"You can't bail a nigga out?" Rarri asked.

"Don't you think I already would have done that if I could?" Heaven countered. "You're still a minor, they don't got bails for y'all… you gotta thug this one out. Thank God for Tony. He got you one of the best lawyer's money can buy. He says he can get you six months if you take the first deal, so yea."

"Six months? I ain't doin' no six fuckin' months," Rarri protested.

"Six months or six years? It's basic math Rarri." Heaven couldn't help but laugh.

"What's so funny?" Rarri asked.

"You cryin' over six months . . . that shit funny. . . I done did more than six months. Besides, you goin' to lil nigga jail, anyway," Heaven replied.

Now, this might sound stupid, but Rarri always wanted to go to jail before, but now it was different. Back then, he wasn't on how he was, now. Now, he had moves to make, but he knew he could still make moves from juvy.

"*Is the money makin' me soft?*" he thought to himself.

"Ight, fuck it. I ain't trippin'. Just make sure business keep movin' in my section, so I get out still on point," he said, and Heaven gave him a *'come on now* look. One thing was certain about Heaven; she handled business!

"KNOCK, KNOCK, KNOCK."

"That's yo boys. . . I'ma let y'all talk for a little bit," Heaven said, then walked to the door and opened it for Lil Dink and Trigg.

"Yaah! What's the deal foo? You out here Nascar racin' and shit ?" Lil Dink asked as soon as he walked in.

"Hell naw, a nigga was tryna crack this lil bitch and wrecked my shit cuz." Rarri thought back to the moment he saw her face. "I ain't seen a bitch that bad, ever, my nigga."

"I bet. You almost died over that pussy," Trigg teased, and they busted out laughing.

Lil Dink and Trigg filled Rarri in on what happened to Lil Trouble and Trina getting shot and robbed. None of them could believe it, still. Trina died and Lil Trouble was on life support, so nobody knew exactly what happened. If it wasn't for the nosy ass pizza man, who pushed the cracked door open, Lil Trouble would have died, too.

"Damn, that shit crazy as fucc foo. I hope that nigga make it," Rarri said sadly. "What's up wit Big Trouble?"

"He sick! That shit got him trippin', right now. Everybody suspect— especially how it happened in the Vill."

The Vill is some apartments on 8th Ave and Slauson called Dorset Village. It's in the 60's territory. That's what shocked everyone around. Some thought it had to be someone from the same area to pull that off because nobody was bold enough to try to hit a lick in the '60s but the '60s. It was unheard of.

"See if he need some help and look out for him," Rarri told them. "Look, I'm bout to be down for a lil minute. I'ma need you to be on point. The work goin' to keep comin' as usual . . . Heaven goin' to lace you up on the program."

"Ight, bet," Lil Dink replied.

"What's up wit you, Trigg, you ready to get craccin' now?" Rarri asked.

Trigg opened his mouth, but no words came out.

"You ain't heard?" Lil Dink said and put his arm around Trigg's shoulder. "This nigga done squared the fucc up."

"Squared up? What the fucc this nigga talkin' bout Trigg?" Rarri asked.

"Yea man, I been tryin' to get my stuff together . . . I go to church now, got a job and a baby on the way," Trigg said proudly.

"What the fucc?" Rarri said in disbelief. Never had he thought Trigg would be the square type, but he had to admit it was better him going the church route than the smoker route. "You got my support, my nigga. I respect it, bro."

Trigg leaned in and gave Rarri a hug. "I appreciate that bro. I love you, man."

"Aww, ol' mushy ass niggas," Bird said from in the doorway with Mia, Tia, Dria, and Fia behind and beside her. They were so caught up in the moment, none of them noticed that the door had opened.

"Here bro," Lil Dink said and handed Rarri some weed, and a lighter wrapped in plastic. "You goin' to have to cheek it. They don't strip search in L.P. Happy Birthday bro, I love you," he finished as he and Trigg headed out.

'Happy Birthday?' Rarri thought to himself. "How long I been sleep?" Rarri yelled to Lil Dink, but he was already out the door.

"Almost two days," Bird answered. "Now let's hurry up, we ain't got too much time."

Bird stood at the foot of the bed, Mia and Tia on the left, and Dria and Fia on the right of the bed. Bird lifted his hospital gown up, laid between his legs and went to work sucking him up.

"We goin' to miss you, Papi," Dria said as Fia rubbed his head.

"I'ma miss y'all too," he moaned.

"Damn, bitch, share the dick," Tia said and went down on him as well, then Mia and Dria.

All five of them were going crazy on his dick. He could hear them slurping and spitting on him wildly. When he felt Bird put his balls in her mouth, his toes curled, and his entire body trembled and tensed up.

"Oh shit, I'm bout to nut," he moaned, and they all at once licked the head of his dick as he exploded, sharing his seeds. It was pure bliss. Mia grabbed some towels from the restroom, and they all wiped up.

"Ok Papi, we goin' to come visit you when we can, and know we holdin' it down until you get out, stackin' this paper up," Mia promised.

"Ight, make sure y'all send me a gang of pic's too . . . I'ma miss y'all," Rarri instructed.

"You got that, Papi," Dria said, then they all kissed the back of his hand and walked out.

About thirty minutes later, two detectives walked in. One was a short fat white guy with a bald head; the other was a tall black man with curly hair.

"Mr. Ransom, I'm detective Moore and this is my partner, detective Benson. We know right now you're in some deep shit. It seems as if your—"

"I ain't got shit to say," Rarri cut off before the detective could finish.

"Have it your way," the tall black one said, and they both walked out, leaving Rarri to his thoughts for a second, then two uniformed police came in and read him his rights and took him away.

Chapter 8

"The Chinx leavin' right now on Piru," Lil Flock said to the other Flocks.

They had been scoping out a house lick that Rarri put them on, about a month ago. Really, Heaven told Rarri and he told them so they all could profit from it.

"Who gon knock?" Lil Flock asked them.

"I got it, Blood," Flock told him, then hopped out the mini-van, walked to the front door of the house and rang the doorbell. When nobody answered, he banged on it loudly four times. Still, nobody answered, which was the green light to go.

He waved to the van for them to come on, then he jumped the gate to get out of sight of the neighbors. When all of them were in the backyard, it was go time.

"Who got the CP?" Lil Flock asked, referring to the center puncher.

"I got it," Baby Flock replied. "Let's go through the side door."

"Naw blood, hit the kitchen window. We goin' through there and we out in 60," Flock instructed.

"Ight," Baby Flock responded.

"I'm goin' in first," Infant Flock insisted.

Infant Flock was the youngest and somewhat wildest. He was always the first to want to do some shit.

Baby Flock pushed the window with the CP then it shattered, and Infant was through the window followed by the rest of the Flocks.

Once in the house, they all split up, each going into different rooms to cut time. No more than fifteen seconds later, Baby Flock found the room they were looking for.

"Aye I found it, blood," he yelled through the house.

The first to come in with Baby Flock was Infant, then Lil Flock followed by Flock.

"Damn blood," Flock said in excitement.

"I'm bout to go get the van . . . put everything by the door," Lil Flock said and ran out.

"Help me grab this bitch," Flock said, referring to the four-foot safe.

"Infant put them jewelry boxes in this pillowcase."

They carried the safe to the front door and Infant grabbed the jewelry from in the room.

"KNOCK, KNOCK!"

Flock opened the door then they carried the safe to the van and hopped in.

"Easy money," Lil Flock said and sped off.

When they pulled up to Flock's house, Heaven was sitting on the hood of her car in the driveway smoking a cigarette and texting on her phone.

"What the fuck she doin' here?" Infant asked out loud.

"I don't know . . .. I ain't tell the bitch we was hittin' the house, today," Flock told them. Lil flock put the car in park, then they all hopped out and walked up to her.

"So, I see everything went well," Heaven said while she continued to text on her phone, not once looking up.

The four of them looked at each other with a dumbfounded expression.

"How did you know we hit it already? I ain't call you," Flock asked.

Heaven chuckled, put her phone in her back pocket, finally making eye contact with Flock and took a pull from her cigarette before speaking.

"I had y'all followed ever since Rarri told y'all about it," she replied and nodded at the two all-black SUVs a few houses down, then signaled for them to move in. "We'll take it from here."

The two SUVs pulled up and eight armed men jumped out. Two of them hopped in the mini-van while the others guarded it. They moved like professionals; swift and strategically. Everything about them was on point.

"Hell naw, that's our lick," Infant said and tried to storm off to the van, but Lil Flock grabbed him before he did something stupid.

"Chill bro," Lil Flock told him. They all knew how cold Heaven could get. Lil Dink made sure to let them know not to get on her bad side.

"Aww, he's cute," Heaven teased like she was talking about a little baby. "Let's get one thing straight: this is *MY* lick . . the only reason y'all are involved is because Rarri wanted to put some money in y'all pockets. I could have easily had this done a long time ago, without y'all . . . talkin' bout y'all lick! Who y'all know in Pelican Hill? Y'all didn't even know y'all was bein' followed all this time."

"Ight, whatever. Fuck all the bullshit. How we goin' to split this shit up? What we goin' to get half the jewelry or what?" Flock asked.

Heaven chuckled again, hit her cigarette one last time then threw the butt. "Naw, y'all ain't gettin' none of the jewelry . . . the man y'all took it from will track each one of y'all down once you pawn it and slit your throats then send you back to y'all momma's in a box, so this what we goin' to do," Heaven said, then reached in the car and pulled out a Gucci backpack and handed it to Flock. "It's four hundred bandz in here, a hundred for each of y'all."

All they heard was a hundred bandz each and wasn't no arguing after that.

"Is that coo?" Heaven asked.

"Hell yea," they all said at the same time.

None of them ever seen that much money in their life, and never thought they would have. It was a surreal moment.

Heaven hopped in her car and started it up. "I'ma let you know about the next one in a few days," she told Flock.

"The next one?" Flock asked, shocked.

"Yea! This was the test run. The big fishes are next, so y'all get ready to step it up," Heaven told him then pulled off and the SUVs followed.

"I think I'm in love, Blood," Baby Flock said as he lustfully watched Heaven disappear down the street.

***

"KNOCK! KNOCK! KNOCK! KNOCK!"

"Ransom," Dickson called into the single-man cell in unit R-S which was the box/sho program.

"Yea," Rarri answered from under his blanket, still half-sleep.

"Get up and get ready. You goin' to unit-Y," Dickson told him.

This was music to Rarri's ears. He had been temporarily housed in the box due to too many fights.

Rarri was set trippin' on any and all of his enemies and planned to trip on the ones where he was going, too.

What started off as a six-month term doubled his first thirty days when he beat the shit out of some little nigga from Santana blocc with a jail made brass knuckle.

Rarri got his things together quickly and was on his way.

As soon as he stepped in unit-Y, all the other kids started banging on their door and yelling out what gangs they were from. Rarri just stayed quiet. He wasn't with making scenes and shit. He just laughed and nodded his head.

He was almost to the office when he had a flashback of when he crashed, and time seemed to move in slow motion at the sight in front of him.

Sitting in a chair behind the desk was the same girl he tried chasing on the freeway, looking just as beautiful as she did that very day. He couldn't believe it.

Dickson handed her Rarri's profile folder, said a few words and left. "*I wonder if she remember me*?" Rarri thought to himself.

"Cell-5," she said when she looked up from his folder at him, but he couldn't move.

"You—" Rarri started.

"Cell-5," she said louder, cutting him off and pointing towards his cell.

"*Nope*," he thought to himself as he walked to his cell with his bedroll. "*She don't remember a nigga.*"

"You have a visit today. Family members will arrive shortly, so be on your best behavior or I'll cancel it," she yelled rudely.

"Yes ma'am," he replied sarcastically and walked into his cell.

"Where you from?" Rarri asked the kid already in the cell, not wasting no time to press his line.

“I’m Fly-Nitty from west side Hoover street” he replied aggressively.

“I’m Rarri from west side Parc Village Compton Crip,” Rarri said just as aggressive.

“Fa’sho groove. I heard bout you,” Fly-Nitty said with his hand extended, and they shook hands.

Rarri made his bed as Fly-Nitty filled him in on how the unit was run.

“Yea groove, this a chill unit. Niggas ain’t really trippin’ in here,” Fly-Nitty said.

“Well I’m trippin’,” Rarri promised bluntly, then laid down and rested for a minute.

About an hour later, they called him for his visit. When he came out, he saw Heaven sitting at the table looking mad as fuck.

“Hey aunty,” he said as he gave her a hug while she was still seated.

“Don’t *hey aunty,* me,” she barked. “What the fuck is wrong wit you? You gettin’ in fights, catchin’ extra time and shit? The girls been waitin’ to come see you, but you fucked that up. I had to pull some strings just to get here today.”

“Rarri sighed deeply. “Yea, yea, yea, I miss you too . . . how granny doin’?”

“Same ol stuff, stuck in front of that T.V. She said she ain’t comin’ to visit you in no jails, but to tell you she loves you and stay out of trouble . . . I ain’t told her you caught no more time, yet. I don't know how or when I'ma do that." Heaven replied.

"Tell her I love her, too . . . what's new, though?" Rarri asked.

"Nothin' really, everything movin' smoothly out there. The girls holdin' it down. They really on they shit, now. Lil Dink on point as usual... um, what else? Oh yea, the Flocks did good on the lick, so I'ma plug them wit some people I know to teach them how to be better at what they do . . . only thing missin' a beat is you," Heaven said.

"Damn, that's what's up. Everybody on they shit," Rarri said proudly.

"Everybody but you," Heaven shot back. "You gotta lead by example Rarri . . . move like a boss, not like a boy."

That shit hit Rarri hard. Everybody was waiting on him, here he was bullshitting and catching more time.

"I'ma try to—" Rarri started.

"Failures try, Rarri. We out here depending on you to *do* better, so do it . . . here, I brought somethin' for you," Heaven said, and handed Rarri a thick journal looking book. The title read, *'The Book of God.'*

"What kind of Bible is this?" he asked.

"Visits are over," the staff worker said.

"It's your dad's Bible. Don't let nobody else read it and you study it, Rarri. Study it more than anything else, and you will see how you need to conduct yo'self. Live those words in there for me, that's all I ask of you," Heaven said in a hurry.

"I'ma see what's up," Rarri said nonchalantly.

Heaven smacked the table loudly causing everyone else to stop and look. "No, promise me."

Rarri looked around slightly embarrassed. "Ok, I promise."

Heaven smiled brightly and gave him a kiss on the cheek. "K . . . I'll bring the girls up here next week. Love you," she said and walked off.

Rarri went into his cell, sat on the bed and opened his book.

"I had everything I wanted growin' up. My pops was a pimp from L.A. and my momma was a hoe from Oakland, so I was destined to be great, understand me? Both of them groomed me up since diapers. From middle school to high school, I stayed with a ring on every finger and a fat chain around my neck.

I got kicked out of school in the 7th grade when the principal found out I had lil bitches suckin' dick for lunch money. Most kid's mommas would have went upside them wit a switch or grounded them but when I walked into the house that day, my momma was happy. All she said was, "you gon be some big ol' pimpin," then took me shoppin'. I only had three friends, Reese-Money, Pay Day and Fantastic. They mamas and daddies was pimps and hoes, too.

My pops taught me to put B.A.B.E before everything. "Break a bitch easy'; it's not a phase, it's a lifestyle," he would say. "Don't be no Crip or no Blood, be a boss. Hoods die off; B.A.B.E street forever. Never forget that."

I wanted to be like my pops soo bad, but he schooled me on how to be better.

I ain't look up to gang bangers or square niggas. I admired pimps and go-gettas.

My life was so unordinary that I wasn't easily influenced. My pops kept me round hoes, daily; who spoiled me like I was they pimp too.

I knocked my first real hoe from my pops at fourteen and served him his papers like a real 'P'. Boy, was he proud?

It didn't last long though. He knocked her back two weeks later, but I popped at the bitch every chance I got.

"I'ma teach my son everyt—"

"Lunchtime!" a voice said through the intercom and the cell door slid open.

Rarri ate his food as fast as he could and went back into his room to read more of his father's words.

The next week when Heaven and the girls came to see him, they could feel the change in him.

"So how you likin' the book?" Heaven asked.

When Rarri smiled she knew the answer.

All the other kids were in awe of Rarri's bitches. Every time he had a visit, all of them would be looking through their door windows. They especially liked how they would kiss the back of his hand when they were leaving. It didn't take long before he was the one all the others wanted to be like. They would ask him hundreds of questions, only to be brushed off. The only person Rarri talked to was Fly-Nitty and niggas from Compton . Other than that, he was reading his book or working out.

"Ransom, you got mail," Ms. Brown said and slid five envelopes under his door. "I see you are well-loved out there," she added flirtatiously, looking at him with her light blue eyes and smiling like a girl in love. Her skin looked so perfect and her kinky curly hair was the only thing to make her look mixed with black. She looked exactly like Star on the T.V. series. Rarri knew she looked at his pics and seen how he be flexing out there.

"Yup," is all he replied, then picked up his letters and sat back on his bed like she was nothing, leaving her feeling played before she walked off.

"That bitch be on your groove. You playin'," Fly-Nitty said as he got up and looked out his window at Ms. Brown as she walked back to the office.

***

Five months went by without Rarri saying no more than two words at a time to Ms. Brown. While everybody else starred and gave her attention, Rarri didn't even look her way, something she wasn't used to.

One night his door slid open around midnight.

"Ransom, come to the office," Ms. Brown said through the intercom.

"What the fuck!" Rarri said angrily as he got up and walked to the office.

"What's up?" he asked her.

"That's what I'm tryna figure out. You walk around here like you don't see me, wit your little attitudes and chip on your shoulder, like you better than everybody," Ms. Brown fussed.

"I am," Rarri said bluntly.

"What?" she asked in disbelief.

"I am better than everybody and yea, I do got a chip on my shoulder. Bout time you realized it," Rarri answered coldly.

"You know what, go back to your cell," Ms. Brown told him,

"No!" he replied.

"Excuse me?" she asked.

"I said no. What, you can't hear either? Cause you damn sure can't remember shit," Rarri barked.

"What the fuck are you talkin' bout Ransom?" Ms. Brown asked.

"You don't remember me?" Rarri countered her question.

"Remember you from where?" she asked.

"That's crazy," Rarri half laughed. "I'm the nigga that crashed tryna get at you on the freeway. I'm here for tryin' to get yo damn number."

Ms. Brown put her hands around her mouth in shock as she thought back to that day. "*This is him*", she thought to herself.

"Oh my God, I'm so sorry," Ms. Brown said as she got up and hugged him tightly.

"It's coo," Rarri replied.

They talked all night, and the rest was history after that. Rarri had it poppin'. Ms. Brown was bringing him phones and weed to smoke. She even met with Heaven and the girls outside of work. She contemplated quitting when Rarri got out, but Heaven talked her out of it. As far as she was concerned, that was Rarri's call, not hers. While all the other kids called her Ms. Brown, Rarri called her Stacey. He promised himself he wouldn't have sex with her until she hit his mitt with a big ball of money.

Rarri found himself in his father's book. It was so much in there that he really had to study it and take his own notes. Besides his father's life story, it was a game manual he called, *'The Cheat Code.'*

'The Cheat Code' was basically a blueprint of every blade in America. It had the times to hit them and times not to. It also had a list of the best cities and hotels to hit. Rarri had two main plans to do when he got out. The first one was to pick up where his pops left off and continue the tradition. Second, he was going to start his own record label and sign Fly-Nitty as his main artist. Rarri heard niggas rap before, but Fly-Nitty was the hardest he ever heard and he had his own style. All he needed was a shot to get in the game.

Rarri wanted to be independent and get all his money. As far as he was concerned, wasn't nothing a major label could do that he couldn't do.

He incorporated '*B.A.B.E Street'*. Before his release, *'B.A.B.E Street'* wasn't just a label, it was a lifestyle. Something with a real meaning behind it.

***

"Run me, my money, bitch," Pretty Me da P said and snatched the crumpled-up bills from Porsha.

After being chased by Bino at the cemetery, he moved to Orange County with his cousin, *another wanna-be pimp*. Nobody knew of Pretty Me da P out there, so it was easy for him to get back at it. Girls always gave into him with ease. His long curly hair, light brown eyes, and fair complexion was all he needed. He could easily pass for the thuggish type when he wore out his hair in two braids but really drove them crazy with the four plats hanging out a snapback.

"What the fuck is this?" he asked as he thumbed through the bills inside his car while she stood outside the window.

"It's slow out here, right now," Porsha complained.

"Come here," Pretty Me da P told her, and she put her head through the window.

"SLAP!"

Pretty Me da P slapped fire from her ass.

"It ain't never slow for a hoe, bitch. Now go get my doe," he yelled, and Porsha ran off and did what she was told.

"Damn cuzzo, you got her trained," Amazin laughed.

"Fuck that hoe. The bitch stay short," Pretty Me da P replied.

"I could dig it. A nigga need some bitches like this," Amazin said and pressed on a video on his Instagram showing some bitches popping ass and throwing hundreds everywhere. Pretty Me da P snatched the phone and scrolled down, looking from picture to picture and watching some of the videos in shock.

"This shit crazy,"

"Them bitches poppin' right!" Amazin said. "They get like, three thousand likes every time they post shit."

"Man, I used to fuck wit these bitches," Pretty Me da P said, still scrolling down the profile.

"Hell naw. You bullshittin'," Amazin replied.

"Nigga they name Mia, Tia, Dria, and Fia. That other bitch named Bird. I ain't never fuck wit her, but I had the other four on my pimpin'," Pretty Me da P said as he pointed them out individually.

"Wow, they fuckin' wit this nigga?" he asked himself when he saw a picture of Rarri with a screen text that Read: **Free Papi**.

"Yea, them bitches be postin' a lot of pics of him . . . I think they ho'n for P, but he locked up or some shit," Amazin explained. "You know him, too?"

"Yea, somethin' like that," he replied.

Pretty Me da P was salty over the whole situation. He couldn't believe Rarri knocked him for his bitches. He really didn't like how much they were popping. Ain't no way in hell Pretty Me da P could compete with Rarri, but he had to get some type of get back.

"Text me them bitches profile names," he said as he handed Amazin back his phone.

"Ight, I got you," Amazin said and sent the text.

"BING!"

Pretty Me da P looked at his phone and opened up the message box asap.

Text: Pretty bitch 1, Ratchett bitch, Nasty bitch, Gutta bitch, Rarri Bitch.

"This they profile names?" he asked surprised.

"Hell yea. Them bitches crazy," Amazin replied.

"Ight . . . I got somethin' for these muthafuckas," Pretty Me da P said as he put his phone down and drove off.

***

Trigg was lying in bed kissing on his baby momma, Jessica's stomach. Her dad was the preacher of the church Trigg went to. He helped him get a job and took Trigg under his wing teaching him how to work on cars and how to be a man of God. Now that Jessica was seven months pregnant, Trigg spent most of his time at home. He even stopped going by "Trigg" and stayed away from the hood. He was growing up and was now far from the boy he once was. Now he was a young man with a family on the way.

"You know how much I love you, right?" he asked.

"No, how much?" Jessica asked.

"I was talkin' to the baby, but I love you too, tho," Trigg replied playfully and laughed.

Jessica swung at him but missed.

"You better not stop lovin' me, Maurice, I'm not playin' wit you," Jessica warned.

"Never," he replied as he kissed her on the lips.

"KNOCK! KNOCK! KNOCK! KNOCK!"

Trigg gave her two more kisses then got up. "I'll be back babe," he told her.

"Who is that?" she asked.

"Dink! We goin' to look at some baby cribs for the baby," he told her and headed for the door.

"I thought you was done hangin' out wit hoodlums," she asked sarcastically and sat up on the couch with her arms crossed.

"I told you before babe, Lil Dink and Rarri are like my brothers," he assured her. "They support what I'm doin' for you and my child."

“Yea, I hear you,” Jessica replied and grabbed the remote to the T.V.

“Ight, I love you. Be back in a minute,” Trigg said and walked out the door.

“What up nigga?” Lil Dink asked as they shook hands. “When I’ma get to meet the wifey, cuh?”

Even though the door was closed, Trigg looked back like Jessica could hear their convo.

“She trippin’ right now bro . . . she’ll probably be calmed down bout time we get back.”

“You said that last time foo,” Lil Dink said as he shook his head. “I bet you still ain’t told her sister bout me, huh?”

“I ain’t even goin’ to lie dawg, I forgot,” Trigg half lied as he got in Lil Dink’s car.

The truth was Trigg wasn’t going to try and hook them up because Jessica’s father would be upset with him for doing so. As much as he did for him, he owed him some sort of respect and loyalty.

“How you know I ain’t tryin’ to settle down too? I need a lil sexy chocolate church girl like yours to keep me out the way like you,” Lil Dink joked. “Be a house nigga.”

“Oh, you a funny guy . . . know darn well you ain’t tryin’ to slow down no time soon,” Trigg said while he put his seat belt on. “What’s this, a BMW i8? You loud bro. How long you think—”

“Ight. Ight. Ight. I was just fuckin’ wit you, cuh, don’t lecture me down,” Lil Dink replied then turned his radio up full blast playing 'M and M's by Migos and pulled off.

Thirty minutes later, they pulled up in front of an apartment complex.

"Oh snaps," Trigg said when he noticed where they were at. "I ain't seen Ms. Benitt in a while."

He hopped out the car before Lil Dink and walked ahead of him on the way to the apartment excitedly.

It's been months since he saw Spank's mom, and he couldn't wait to let her know about the baby and how good he's been doing.

When Trigg knocked on the door nobody answered. When he started to knock again, Lil Dink stepped in front of him and twisted the door, then moved to the side for Trigg to go in first. Trigg looked at Lil Dink suspiciously.

"She probably sleep," Lil Dink shrugged.

Trigg walked in with Lil Dink behind him, so he never saw the .45 with the silencer on it that Lil Dink held in one hand behind his back.

Lil Dink locked the door while Trigg walked into the living room. Trigg's eyes grew wide in shock when he saw that most of the room was covered in a plastic tarp and Spank's mom was tied to a chair with her mouth duct taped. She looked so relieved when she saw him, and tears of joy and anxiety ran down her face. Trigg immediately ran up to her and untaped her mouth.

"You have to help me, please," she begged.

"It's ok. Everything goin' to be ok," Trigg replied and started to untie her.

"I wouldn't do that if I were you," Lil Dink warned from behind him.

"What the fuck man?" Trigg screamed. "What's wrong wit you?"

"A lot," Lil Dink replied bluntly.

"Please, Trigg! Help me!" Spank's mom cried.

"What the fuck is you doin' man?" Trigg asked. "This shit is foul dawg."

Lil Dink put his gun on the counter and sparked a blunt, then sat on a nearby stool. "Tell him what you told me," Lil Dink told Spank's mom as he blew smoke out into little circles.

She shook her head slowly as more tears flowed out, not wanting to say a word.

"Tell me what?" Trigg asked her calmly, but she didn't reply.

"Tell me what?" he asked again.

"Please! I'm sorry," was all she replied.

Lil Dink got up then walked up to Spank's mom and flicked ashes in her face, causing her to jump a little.

"What the fuck man?" Trigg said as he fanned the ashes off of her face.

"That's the same shit I was wonderin' at Spank's funeral— why is they lookin' at us all crazy . . . I ain't understand that shit, I couldn't put my finger on it, then one day I get a call—" Lil Dink explained.

"Please!" Spank's mom cried.

"Shut up bitch!" Lil Dink barked, then began talking to Trigg.

"I get a call from this bitch talkin' bout she want a hundred thousand, or she goin' to the police and tellin' them how her son died and how you and Rarri was responsible—"

Trigg put his head down in disbelief.

"Yup," he assured as he hit his blunt again. "She told me that you told her everything . . . everything! What the fuck is wrong with you, cuh? You know she been a snitch, and you goin' to tell her some shit like this? You buggin' cuh. How you goin' to raise your son from prison doin' life Trigg? They goin' to charge you for Spank's murder cause y'all was comittin' a crime when he got killed, not to mention the nigga's y'all shot up, too. You think yo lil church bitch goin' to hold you down through all that?"

Trigg just kept his head down as he let it all sink in. He knew he was wrong for telling Spank's mom, but he had to clear his conscience at the time.

Spank's mom was better off asking for the money. Blackmailing them was the wrong thing to do. Rarri made sure she got five bandz a month already, so now she was just being plain out greedy.

"You could have just asked for the money," Trigg said with his head still down, feeling defeated.

"I'm sorry," she cried.

Lil Dink knelt down. "But dig this; I got shit to do… people to see, bitches to fuck you know, shit like that right. So this one on you. I did my part. It's time you did yours," he whispered in Trigg's ears, then got up and headed to the door.

"The thang on the counter. I'ma be in the car."

"Please Maurice, don't," Spank's mom begged when she heard the door close.

Trigg lifted his head so that he could look her in her eyes.

"Please!" she begged once more.

"you should have kept your fuckin mouth shut!" he barked angrily and taped her mouth back up.

Chapter 9

"Let me get a hood bro," Bullet asked Crazo as they were walking through the apartment complex together.

Crazo took a cigarette from his pack and handed it to Bullet. "What happen to that bitch from brims you was fuckin' on? Tell her to come through so we could flip that bitch in the Vaco."

"That bitch on some Hollywood shit," Bullet replied then lit his cigarette. "To keep it real, I think she ho'n now or somethin', cause she been flexin' on the gram."

"Yea?" Crazo asked with a look of surprise.

"Hell yea," Bullet said as the two walked into a hallway and up the stairs to one of the complexes.

Bullet knocked on a door that was to the right while Crazo stood on the stairs. A moment later, an old man who looked to be in his late fifties had opened the door and just looked at Bullet without saying anything.

"Is Jamal here?" Bullet asked.

"No," the old man replied and slammed the door shut.

"Bitch," Bullet said under his breath and turned to walk back down the stairs, passing Crazo. "Come on cuz."

"Damn, bro still ain't comin' outside? Why cuz actin' like we bout to t-treat him?" Crazo asked following Bullet back out the hallway.

"Some niggas get put on and get spooked when they see how hood we be," Bullet schooled.

Jamal had got put on 60's about a month ago. Everything was fun for about a week, then shit just started getting crazy, too fast for him. He joined the gang for protection so people from the '60s wouldn't target him, but lately, it seemed like a war inside the 60's. Homies were targeting homies. He didn't think the *"you ain't a real 60 til you kill a 60"* quote was real before he got put on, but now he saw firsthand that these niggas was really crazy. Their gang banging was too much for him to handle, so he moved with his aunty in Texas.

"Where you think cuz go?" Crazo asked as he stepped out of the hallway with Bullet.

"I don't even kn—"

"BOOM!"

Bullet took off running as soon as he heard the gunshot, not looking back to see if Crazo was ok or not. He bent the corner of the complex before Crazo's body hit the floor. He didn't know what happened and he damn sure wasn't about to stand around and find out. The bullet from the .357 left a golf ball size hole in Crazo's face. Blood fell from his nose like a turned-on faucet as his body twitched from shock.

Trouble stepped from out of the hallway, tucked the burner in his hoodie, threw on his hood and pushed off. He had been waiting in a vacant apartment downstairs, scoping niggas that walked by. When he saw Bullet and Crazo, he knew it was time to make his move. The two of them stayed in the Vill all day every day, so he wasn't buying that *nobody knows what happened to his brother* shit.

To him, it had to be an inside job, so everybody was suspect, and Trouble was willing to kill anybody he ran into from his hood until he found out what happened to his little brother. If it wasn't for the nosey ass pizza man who pushed the cracked door open the day Lil Trouble and Trina was shot, fa'sho Lil Trouble would have died. Since the shooting, he's been in a coma. Unfortunately, Trina didn't make it. Trouble been on one and was going to stay on one until he found the nigga who did this. If his little brother died, he would forever blame the set.

***

"Breaking news. Two teen bodies were found this morning in the Inglewood Cemetery. The 18 and 19-year-old boys are reported to be brothers both from Lynwood, California. The cause of death at this time is unknown, but both were apparently beaten with some sort of object. The bodies were discovered nude in what the witness say's appeared to be a sexual position. Detectives are looking into this also as a hate crime. Here's footage of an earlier statement from the witness who found the bodies," the reporter said, and then a video popped up enlarged on the screen, minimizing the live feed.

"Can you tell us what you saw this morning here at the cemetery?" the reporter asked before pointing the microphone at the elderly white woman.

For a brief moment, she hesitated, thinking of how to word the scene properly. She looked like a typical old white woman who probably still went to work at the same place for the last 30 years, not ready to retire her government job. Her grey hair a bit frizzy from the blowing wind and her makeup poorly done, she was a bit on the heavy side but not fat and her clothes looked like they came from a garage sale.

"Well, I was just leaving from where my husband is buried like I do every Monday, and I saw what looked like two naked people in the distance . . . I walked over to confront them, thinking they were doing something they shouldn't have been doing here, but as I got closer, I noticed the two weren't moving. When I approached them all the way, I noticed they were both actually dead," the woman explained. "Then I called 911 for help.

"Can you explain how the two bodies were positioned?" The reporter asked.

Again, the woman hesitated.

"Well . . . um . . . one of them was sitting up against the gravestone and the other one was laying between his legs with his head in his lap . . . like . . . he was . . . you know…"

"Suckin' his dick!" Trigg cracked and started busting up laughing menacingly at the T.V.

He had caught them niggas slipping the night before and placed the bodies at Spank's gravesite. Lil Tick and Baby Tick was no longer. Trigg's baby momma stepped back quietly from the living room where she was watching him and into her room, slowly closing the door then locking it. She couldn't believe what she had just seen and heard.

"He killed them," she thought to herself. "I have to get out of here."

Chapter 10

"Ding Dong! Ding Dong! Ding Dong! Ding Dong! Ding Dong! Ding Dong! Ding Dong!"

"I'm comin' God damn," Heaven yelled as she walked to the door, but the doorbell kept going off. When she opened the door it was Bird, Mia, Tia, Fia and Dria. All of them rushed her with hugs and kisses, knocking her down to the floor.

Tia was on top of Heaven humping her like they were having sex. "Oh yea! Give it to me baby! Right there! Right there! Take this dick, bitch! Who's your daddy? Who's your daddy?"

"Take this pussy! It's your's daddy!" Heaven yelled as she thrusted up, matching Tia's pumps. Mia and Fia were holding her arms down while Bird and Dria kept kissing her face.

"Aww!" Tia moaned loudly like she was cumming hard. All of them started laughing as they were getting off the floor.

Heaven's house was immaculate. As soon as you walked in, you couldn't help but feel small because of how spacious it was. The twin set of stairs and chandelier made of Gold and glass was out of this world. The painting on the ceiling of Angels, half-naked men and women looked like it cost a million, itself. The carpet was so soft it felt like you were almost floating through the house. Everything between the front and back door was extravagant. As they walked past one door down the hallway, they always looked into it at the beautiful indoor pool. The light that came from the water hit the entire room, giving it an exotic take. It was something that should have been at a Spa Resort. There were laying chairs, couches, electric fireplaces, a two-sided Jacuzzi, a bar area, all types of shit. Although Heaven stayed with Tony most of the time, she still wanted her own personal space, so she convinced him to purchase this 9-bedroom house for her.

"Bout time y'all bitches made it back," Heaven said as they reached the kitchen. "What took y'all so long?"

"We had to make a lil detour and book this nigga for these," Bird replied and pulled out a pouch, then poured out the contents on the counter for Heaven to see. "How much you think this worth?"

Heaven picked up one of the diamonds and examined it. "It's worth some money fa'sho... what, y'all bitches hittin' jewelry stores now?" Heaven joked.

"Somethin' like that," Dria said as she sat down on one of the stools.

Heaven put the diamond down, walked to the refrigerator, grabbed a carton of orange juice and went back to the counter where the diamonds were. "Ima have my guy come look at 'em . . . how many is it?"

"Twenty-three," Fia said quickly like she had counted them a thousand times.

Heaven took a drink straight from the carton of juice, then passed it to Mia who took a sip then passed it along. That was one of the reasons why they liked Heaven so much. She wasn't too good to drink or eat with them. Sometimes, they even slept in the same bed, took showers with each other and all types of shit. Heaven was like the big sister none of them ever had. It wasn't nothing they couldn't come to her about, and no matter what, she always had their backs.

"Ight, I got y'all," Heaven said then added, "Ain't you, bitches forgettin' somethin'?"

"Oh yea," Mia said taking off her Gucci backpack and handing it to Heaven.

She opened it and skimmed through the stacks of money then closed it back. Heaven grabbed the carton of Juice from Bird, took another sip, and then set it back on the counter. "Come on, I gotta show y'all somethin'," she said and walked off with them on her trail. She stopped at an all-white door, pushed it open and backed to the side for them to walk in first. They all just stared in, none of them moving. It was so dark in there, you couldn't see the bottom, but the stairs going down let you know it had to be a basement or some sort of underground room.

"Um . . . why is it so dark down there?" Fia asked pointing into the room.

Heaven pulled out her .38 snub she slipped in her pocket while she was in the kitchen. She only drew it out, never pointing it at them. "If y'all bitches don't hurry up, I'ma pop one of y'all right here," she said pushing Bird, who was in the back of the line which caused her to push the others forward. They walked down as slow as they possibly could.

"Sis you sure thi—" Tia started.

"Shut the fuck up bitch and keep walkin'," Heaven cut her off, pushing Bird again. "Hurry up!"

When they made it to the bottom the lights cut on.

"Surprise bitches!" Heaven yelled happily.

All five of them started screaming and jumping up and down when they saw the five Bentleys in the garage. Each one was jet black and had each of their names on the headrest, just like Heaven's. They ran to the cars and jumped in the one that had their name on it, taking in all the features and admiring the peanut butter interior.

Dria hopped out and gave Heaven a big ass hug with tears in her eyes. "I love you, Heaven."

"I love you too, bitch," Heaven replied pushing Dria away from her and wiping the tears from Dria's face. "Fuck all this mushy shit, let's push out and go shoppin' . . . I got us VIP reservations at the Seven in Hollywood tonight, Drake and Lil Wayne performin'."

"Fuck Drake and Lil Wayne let's go see Papi," Tia said eagerly.

"Ain't no visits today," Bird replied then started twerking. "But we could send him a freaky ass video of us pop'n ass and fuckin' each other tonight . . . you know he love that shit."

"Y'all think he be fuckin' ol girl in there?" Fia asked.

"Hell yea," Tia replied as she grabbed Dria by the waist, bent her over and started hitting her doggy style. "Papi be fuckin' that bitch like Bam! Bam! Bam! Bam!"

"Fuck this pussy Rarri," Dria said as she threw that ass back at Tia. "Fuck! This! Pussyyy!"

Fia pushed them apart. "Stop it," she said angrily and charged them. Tia and Dria started laughing as Fia softly punched.

"Aww somebody jealous," Mia said, and everybody started laughing. Everybody but Fia.

"Fuck y'all," Fia said then hopped in her car and started it. "Let's go . . . you ugly bitches is gettin' on my nerves."

Heaven pushed a button on the wall, opening the garage and walked out to her car while everybody else jumped in theirs and pulled out. They hit the streets six Bentleys deep, racing through traffic all the way to the nearest Bloomingdale's.

Chapter 11

Halloween

Lil Dink was now moving bricks all over Compton. The Nutty Blocc's, Palmer Blocc's, Front Hood's, Spook Town's, South Side's, Atlantic Drive's, Farm Dog's, Mona Park's, ward lanes and Carver Park's was all fucking with Lil Dink from the start. Now he was fucking with all the west side Piru's, Tree Top's, Elm Street's, Lime Hood's, Mob's, Fruit Town's, Cross Atlantic's and Lueders Park Piru's.

Even though most of the hoods beefed with one another, he still supplied them the same regardless of the bullshit. It was always one hood telling him to stop fucking with the other, but he wasn't trying to get involved with the drama. He just wanted to make money and fuck on bitches. It was still a few hoods he didn't fuck with because of past beef, but he maneuvered through others and got their money that way, never directly doing business with them. It wasn't personal, he just didn't trust them.

Lil Dink rose up from his bed in frustration as Monica continued to softly jerk his dick.

Monica was a bad bitch who lived in the Wilmington Arms. She was twenty six, 5'4", dark brown complexion with hazel eyes and had the body of a goddess.

Lil Dink swore to himself when he was younger, he would bag her one day when he got older. Now nineteen and super popping in the hood, it was all but hard to get her on his team.

Monica had always been his fantasy girl, and she falls under a different category of bitches to him.

He hoped this one thing would go away, but it only seemed to get worse, and today he reached his boiling point. He had to talk to her despite the awkwardness of the conversation.

"What's wrong babe?" Monica asked jerking his limp dick softly. "You want me to suck it?"

"Naw, I gotta talk to you bout somethin'," Lil Dink said removing her hand as he slid out of the bed and lit the cigarette on the dresser.

"Ok let's talk," Monica said, sitting up Indian style in the bed and smiling happily as she finger-combed her long curly hair back. "What's up, babe?"

Lil Dink took a long pull from his Newport. "*How do I say this shit,*" he thought to himself. "*Fuck it, just be real with her. She'll understand. Just don't sugarcoat it.*"

"Babe!" Monica said, snapping him out of his thoughts.

She looked so flawless at that moment. Lil Dink thought about saying never mind, but he had to say something. The last 3 months with her was the best times in his life and truly, he didn't want to fuck that up.

"Ight! You gotta promise me not to start trippin'," Lil Dink replied.

Monica's face turned angry. "What, you got another bitch pregnant? I'm not about to be no nigga side bitch, Dink. If that's wha—"

"Naw, it ain't nothin' like that," Lil Dink said, cutting her off before she went on one. "See you already trippin' and I ain't even say shit' yet . . . never mind cuz."

"Ok! Ok! I ain't goin' to start trippin'," Monica replied, forcing herself to calm down, putting her smile back on.

"Promise!" Lil Dink said. "Naw, matter fact, promise, promise!"

Promise, promise was their way of double promising. Meaning they really, really meant it. Monica hated when he made her promise, promise, but she would do it to him to get the truth out.

Monica sighed deeply and folded her arms. "I promise! promise!" she said reluctantly.

Lil Dink took another pull from his Newport then blew the smoke out before speaking and looked her straight in the face.

"Yo pussy be stankin' cuz, I *know* if I could smell that shit, you could too . . . you ain't scrubbin' yo shit right or what? Like what's the issue?"

Monica's jaw almost hit the bed. She couldn't believe this nigga. She picked up the remote and threw it at him as hard as she could, barely missing his head. "Fuck you!"

"Come on babe," Lil Dink protested, but she wasn't hearing it.

Monica was out of the bed putting her clothes back on. “Fuck you Dink . . . you a lil ass boy. I ain’t got time for this shit. I don’t need no nigga tellin’ me how to wash myself, I’m a grown-ass woman.”

“Babe, you promise, promised,” he reminded as he tried to grab her arm to stop her from leaving.

Monica looked him in the eyes one last time. “Fuck you, Dink,” she said as she yanked her arm free from his grip and left out the room.

Monica knew her pussy stank—sometime, but that didn’t give him the right to comment on it.

“Fuck you too, bitch!” Lil Dink yelled after her, standing there, butt ass naked, still smoking his cigarette. “I was tryna help yo stank ass,” he said to himself.

He walked over to his ringing phone, picked it up, and pressed the answer button. “Yeah what’s the deal?”

“I need two of them thangs,” Juice said from the other end of the line.

“Ight bet! Give me like an hour,” Lil Dink replied.

Juice smacked his lips and hung up.

“Weird ass nigga stay smackin’ his lips like a bitch,” Lil Dink said to himself.

Now that Monica was gone, he was thinking about what bitch to fuck with tonight for Halloween. He didn’t feel like going to no parties, he just wanted to get a couple dollars and chill around the house. Lil Dink didn’t party as much since Rarri got locked up. A function wasn’t the same without his boy to turn up with him, and Trigg was busy plotting on niggas and shooting shit up.

***

"Why I gotta do it?" Infant Flock asked with an attitude.

"Cause you the littlest nigga, Blood," Lil Flock said.

"Hurry up and put this shit on man . . . stop bullshittin'," Flock said handing Infant Flock the costume trying to keep a serious face.

Infant Flock snatched the costume from him, went to the back of the van and put it on. When he jumped back in the second seat next to Baby Flock, everybody was looking at him.

"Huh Blood, you forgot yo mask," Baby Flock said, handing him the mask.

"Ight, so just make sure nobody home. Y'all don't want me to go in?" Infant Flock asked after he put the mask on.

They couldn't hold it in any longer. All of them started busting up laughing hard as hell. Infant Flock looked like a real Ninja Turtle. The kid costume fit him too good like it was meant for him to have that muthafucka. The small, compact, buff body of the costume made it even funnier.

Flock, Lil Flock, and Baby Flock were laughing so hard they couldn't even breathe. Infant Flock was pissed the fuck off. He snatched the mask off his head.

"Fuck that, I ain't doin' this shit no more."

"Ight! Ight! We just fuckin' with you," Flock said trying his hardest not to laugh and put back on his serious face. Lil Flock and Baby Flock did the same. "Just let us know if it's clear, then we goin' to come so we could push in at the same time . . . act like you trick or treatin' . . . if nobody answer the doorbell, check the back and we good to go."

"Ight." He looked at Lil Flock and Baby Flock to make sure they wasn't even thinking about laughing. "I'm bout to get brackin'," he said after putting the Ninja Turtle mask back on and extended his fists to give them daps. They all avoided eye contact with him as they dapped his fist. As soon as he exited the car and closed the door, he could hear them burst out laughing. He shook his head and walked towards the house, holding his pumpkin container half-filled with candy.

Infant Flock was the youngest out of the four of them. At fifteen, he still had the body of a twelve-year-old, so he was able to squeeze into smaller spaces than the rest of them. He was 5'2 with the heart of a giant and known to be with the bullshit. Infant Flock was that little nigga in the hood that's always starting shit and trippin on muthafuckas twice his size. One thing he hated most was niggas bigger than him doing bitch shit. Especially turning down fades. He would always say what he would have did if he was the next nigga size. "*If I was that big, I woulda knocked blood out,*" was his favorite line.

After ringing the doorbell about twenty times, he went to the side of the house and opened the gate leading to the backyard. The backyard was one of the largest and best-looking ones he had ever seen. The swimming pool had a little waterfall built to it. The barbeque pit was fancy and built into the rocks around it. There was a tennis and basketball court. It even had a little mini house back there, probably for the kids.

He looked through the back sliding door to make sure the house was empty. All the lights were off, and he was sure it was empty, but he decided to knock on the glass just to make sure one last time. Better safe than sorry. If someone did answer he would just act like a nosy little kid.

"Knock! Knock! Knock! Knock! Knock! Knock! . . . . Knock! Knock! Knock! Knock! Knock! Knock!"

He pulled the walkie-talkie from under the candy in his pumpkin basket and was about to tell them it was clear when he heard heavy breathing and what sounded like keys moving towards him.

He scanned quickly to the right in the darkness where he thought it was coming from but didn't see anything. A soon as he turned left, he was tackled to the ground by two big ass German shepherds.

At that moment, he saw his life flash before his eyes. He could hear the growls and smell the breath of the two dogs, but he didn't feel any bites. That's when he realized they weren't trying to kill him, they were humping the shit out of him, trying to get some turtle pussy. *"Not this turtle,"* Infant Flock thought as he pushed the one on top of him away and turned to attempt to get on his feet, but the dog was back on him in his favorite position. He tried to shake him off his back, but it had its paws wrapped around him good, while the other one humped at his face.

When the two dogs would get in each other's way, he could hear the growls and barks of them scuffling, but they stayed positioned. After the fighting, they continued humping on him harder, this time. He tried to crawl away, but the dogs just moved with him, still humping. He couldn't turn at all because the one on his back had him pinned down.

Infant Flock couldn't shake these muthafuckas. He tried his hardest to get them off, but they were too heavy. When he did almost get free, the one on his back gave him a warning bite on his shoulder.

"Ok! Ok!" Infant yelled and stopped struggling. "Fuck! Blood."

The only choice Infant Flock had was to let them finish doing they shit. Never in a million years did he think he would be getting raped by two dogs trying to flock a house. Even though he didn't get penetrated he still felt violated. This was something he was fa'sho going to take to his grave.

"What's takin' Blood so long," Lil Flock said, looking out the window nervously.

"I don't know," Flock replied with the same expression of concern. He had been trying to get through to Infant Flock for the past five minutes but wasn't getting a reply. He was just about to try again when Infant Flock finally hit back.

"It's clear."

Bout time, Blood," Flock said over the walkie-talkie, then all of them got out of the van and headed towards the house with stockings over their faces.

“Oh shit,” Baby Flock said when he stepped into the backyard and seen Infant Flock petting two big ass dogs.

“They don’t bite . . . we good,” he assured them.

The three hesitated, but then pursued when the dogs didn’t move.

“Them muthafuckas big for nothin’,” Flock said.

Lil Flock went to one of the bedroom windows and slid it open. It was unlocked just like she said it would be. Heaven made sure to always have an inside person in on the licks they hit. She was out dining with the owners of the house, feeding them while at the same time secretly robbing them blind.

Lil Flock hopped in, followed by the rest of them. Once inside, Flock and Infant Flock went one way while Lil Flock and Baby Flock went the other.

Lil Flock and Baby Flock quickly made it to the room where Heaven said the safe was. Both of them took a side and carried it to the front door, then went back to searching for more shit finding nothing worth taking, so they just went to join Flock and Infant Flock.

When they found them stuffing jewelry in their bags in the dark, Baby Flock turned on the bedroom light, grabbed a pillow from the bed, took it out its case and started helping them.

Lil Flock walked over to Infant Flock and squinted down at the backside of his costume. “What’s all that slimy shit on the back of yo ass, Blood?”

Infant Flock stopped what he was doing and turned around to see what it was. "Oh yea, that's probably from when I fell in the backyard," he lied when he saw it.

Everybody had stopped doing what they was doing and was now looking at him.

"Blood, that shit on yo mask too," Baby Flock said.

Infant Flock wiped the side of his face that Baby Flock was looking at and immediately felt the slimy stuff they was talking about. When he looked at his hand, he almost threw up in his mask. He ran out of the room and found the kitchen.

Flock shrugged his shoulders as Baby Flock and Lil Flock looked at him. "Come on, let's get up out of here," he said walking out of the room with them behind him.

When they made it to the front door, Lil Flock and Baby Flock both took a side of the safe, then picked it up again.

"Infant! Come on, Blood," Flock yelled then opened the front door to leave but was stopped by an old man holding a shotgun.

"Don't fuckin' move," the old man barked. "The cops are on the way—you're goin' to jail, buddy . . . all of ya's," he added, waving the shotgun at the three of them.

Lil Flock and Baby Flock was so shocked and frozen, they still stood there with the safe in their hands scared to move or put it down.

"Sir, we—" Flock started.

“Shut your face,” the old man ordered. “I don’t want to hear it.”

This old man was pissed the fuck off. He was so angry, his face was flared red and his hands were shaking. He kept his eyes on them in the awkward silence, and hardly spit out a glob of chew tobacco.

After a brief moment, Flock built up the courage to speak again. “Sir I was just tryi—”

“I said shut it,” he barked again, this time pointing the gun at his face and cocking it simultaneously. “I been watchin’ this neighborhood for the last thirty years ... I see and hear everything around here.”

Just as he said it, the police sirens could be heard in the distance and he lowered his gun a bit easing up.

“Fuck!” Lil Flock cried out.

“Yup . . . the three of ya’s is fucked,” the old man said with a smirk on his wrinkly face.

“Excuse me, Mister.”

The old man jumped almost out of his skin, startled by the voice that came from behind him. He couldn’t help but turn around, and as soon as he did a brick smashed right into his face, knocking him out instantly. His body hit the floor hard. Standing behind him was Infant Flock in his costume. He had slipped out the back door when he heard what was going on.

The sirens were getting closer.

“Come on, the boys comin’,” Flock said, and all of them ran to the van.

Lil Flock and Baby Flock double-timed with the safe. Police coming or not, they weren't leaving without it. Real Flock shit.

Chapter 12

"Fuck Snoop and that Long Beach movement bullshit," Macky said as he snatched the Aux cord from the car stereo, cutting off the new *'Beach City'* song that everybody was starting to bang. "I don't fuck wit 20's on babies," he added.

Macky knew the song was hot but he couldn't stand Snoop 'cause he was from 20 Crip. He hated 20's just as much as Longos, probably even more.

When Macky was 8 years old, he had witnessed his pop's murder. He would forever remember that day. Macky was walking down the street with his father heading towards his grandmother's house when a car pulled up and a short black ass, nigga hopped out with a gun in his hand. Macky's father stood in front of him, shielding him from the man.

"Come on Tah, I'm wit my so—"

"Fuck insane." the man said coldly and blew his brains out with no remorse at all. He pointed the gun at

Macky's face and pulled the trigger, but the gun had jammed.

"Fuck insane." he said again and hit Macky in the head with the butt of the gun, knocking him out cold.

Macky never told police what the man looked like or what type of car he was in. The only person he told the details to was his uncle Toon, who was his pop's brother. That's when he found out the nigga that shot his pops name was Tah Tah.

Macky could still see the shook up look on his uncle's face. The nigga didn't want no funk with Tah Tah. He was spooked. That was the day he found out his uncle Toon was a bitch. Never again did he speak another word to his uncle after that.

"You trippin' cuz. Snoop puttin' the whole city on right now," Trey Smooth said and hit the blunt. "He bringin' us together and shit—"

Macky snatched the blunt out of his hand with so much force he snapped it in half. "Get out my car, cuz."

"You fa'real my nigga?" Trey Smooth asked surprisingly.

"On babies," Macky replied straight-faced.

Trey Smooth didn't ask him again. He knew better. He stepped out of the car then looked back in at Macky. "You still goin' to let me hold that powder?"

Macky drew out his .45 and pointed it at him quickly. "Close my door," he said through clenched teeth.

Trey Smooth closed the door and walked off down the street.

Macky was disgusted with these new niggas from the hood. Most of em' wasn't bout shit no more. All they wanted to do was party; none of em' wanted to put in work. Niggas was in it for show, but not Macky. He was a real one. He looked like a pretty boy type nigga that could have been a model if it wasn't for the streets. Money didn't calm Macky down, it intensified his gangsta. It gave him more resources to kill. He had more guns now since Rarri started having bricks dropped on him. Macky was known to hop out the car fly as a muthafucka only to kill a nigga. If you ever saw somebody jeweled up in designer clothes shooting a block up on the east side of Long Beach, it was more than likely Macky. He had a circle of niggas in his hood that was just like him. They were really insane. It was nothing to shoot a nigga then go to sleep and dream about some other shit.

Macky pulled out a small bag of powder and put some on the middle console. The passenger door opened just as he was dividing the lines. Macky didn't bother to break his concentration from what he was doing to see who it was because he already knew it was his boy.

"What up third?" Kill Kill said as he sat in the car and closed the door.

"Same shit, different bitch," Macky replied as he took in a fat ass line through his nostril. "You know how it go cuz," he added and passed Kill Kill the rolled-up hundred-dollar bill used to funnel the powder.

"Hell yea," Kill Kill said before bumping his line. He put his head back and sniffed in three times deeply to feel the drip of the powder hit his throat. He bit down a couple times noticing his front teeth were numb. "This shit fire, cuz."

Kill Kill was a dark, skinny young nigga fresh out of high school. He got his name from his first mission putting in work, followed by the second one in the same day, killing two people from two different hoods. Kill Kill loved to put in work. Killing a person made him feel better about himself. In control of people's lives, he felt like God. It was his choice if a person would live or not. He could never go too long without shooting somebody. Kill Kill had a killing problem. He really didn't care who it was, he just had to kill something. It never mattered where a person was from to him. Kill Kill was just in it for the kill. The only tattoo he had was a 23 under his left eye.

"You ready?" Macky asked, getting straight to the point.

Kill Kill didn't say anything, he just gave him a look that asked, "*are you serious*?"

Macky smiled hard. "I'm just askin', my nigga."

"When you known me not to be ready cuz?" Kill Kill asked as he pulled up his shirt showing off his .40 Glock which was his signature gun.

"Remember that one time when we was bout to bust on the Chongos and you froze up?" Macky clowned.

"Cuz . . . you, always, bringin', that, shit, up . . . I keep tellin' you the burner fell down my pants leg . . . Bout time I grabbed it, you was already craccin' and everybody was gone . . . what was I supposed to do, shoot in the air or somethin'?" Kill Kill responded while Macky kept laughing.

"On insane, you bet not *ever* fuck up in front of me, cause I ain't gon never let that shit go."

Macky started laughing harder. He knew Kill Kill didn't freeze up that day; it was just funny because Macky knew how to get under his skin. Every time he would bring it up, Kill Kill would get hot. Kill Kill hated when Macky played with his kill game. Macky and Kill Kill were best friends, so they knew almost everything about each other. Almost everything!

"I'm just fuckin' wit you third," Macky admitted after catching his breath. "Where the whip at?"

"Around the corner," Kill Kill replied.

Macky reached in the back seat of his BMW i8 and grabbed two identical Jason hockey masks. He gave one to Kill Kill and they both got out of the car. They walked around the corner to Raymond Street, hopped in the G-ride and pushed off.

Macky and Kill Kill jay-walked across the street on Atlantic and headed inside the Poly Apartments, also known as the PAs. One of Macky's bitches had let him know about a Halloween party, a nigga named Corn was throwing in the apartments. She gave him the apartment number and time the party was going to jump off. It was kids in costumes trick or treating throughout the complex.

Macky and Kill Kill spotted niggas hanging outside and around the apartment, they were looking for. Immediately, he recognized a few faces he couldn't stand and his blood started to boil as he got closer and closer, finally standing in front of the group outside. Macky and Kill Kill just stood there looking through their masks at the niggas in front of them.

"Look at these weird-ass niggas cuz," one of the dudes in a black and gold Pirate's hat said, and they all started laughing.

Macky and Kill Kill just kept looking. Kill Kill turned his head to the side, studying the group in front of him.

"Oh shit, that one crazy right there," another dude said talking about Kill Kill, and they all started laughing again.

The dude in the Pirate's hat walked up and stood face to face with one of the masked men. "Y'all niggas ain't scarin' nobody cuz," he said and pulled off Macky's mask. His face dropped when he saw it was Macky, and the crowd behind him stopped laughing. Time seemed to slow down.

"oh shit!" one of the dudes yelled loudly as he turned to run in the house, as did everybody else. The one who took off Macky's mask turned to run, too but was dropped.

"BOOM!"

Kill Kill put him down quick and started shooting at niggas who were cowering over each other, trying to get in the house first.

"BOOM! BOOM! BOOM! BOOM! BOOM!"

Macky casually picked up his mask and put it back on after dusting it off, then drew his .45 as they advanced into the apartment.

The music was still playing but everybody was screaming and running towards the bedrooms down the hallway.

"BOOM!"

Macky put one into a nigga who was crawling on the floor hurt from the bullet Kill Kill hit him with.

"BOOM! BOOM!"

Kill Kill shot two bitches who were trying to hide in the kitchen. The face shots killed them instantly.

Macky headed into the hallway and seen a dude trying his hardest to push open a door that seemed locked. He was trying to turn the knob and push in with his shoulder. Macky could tell the door wasn't locked because every time the dude pushed it, it would slightly open but immediately close back like people were barricading it with their bodies.

"Come on y'all, let me in man— please!" he begged and tried harder when he saw Macky gaining on him with Kill Kill behind him. "Don't kill me, man, please."

Macky looked at Kill Kill. "Ain't this the same nigga that was dissin the other day?" Kill Kill shook his head up and down. Macky aimed his burner at the boy's head then pulled the trigger. Brains and skull fragments flew on the wall behind him. Macky was so close, he could hear the bullet crack into his head and the squishy sound of brain mixing when leaving one's head. He loved the way blood sung when it hit the floor.

"BOOM! BOOM! BOOM! BOOM! BOOM! BOOM!"

Macky could hear screams as he shot at the door, then he pushed it open forcefully.

Everybody was at the other end of the room curled into balls trying to shelter themselves with their own bodies. All of them crying and begging for their lives. It all fell on four deaf ears.

"Trick or treat muthafuckas."

"BOOM! BOOM! BOOM! BOOM! BOOM! BOOM! BOOM! BOOM! BOOM! BOOM!"

Macky and Kill Kill ruthlessly lit it up, then ran out and back to the G-ride.

"Where we at now?" Kill Kill asked as he started the car and pulled off.

"Let's slide through the Chongos," Macky said as he put in a new clip.

Chapter 13

4 Months Later

Rarri stepped out of the door like a brand-new man. His once slim frame was now built from all the working out that he did while locked up. The sun gave his curly afro a shine and graced the bronze color of his skin, which matched his eyes. Rarri sprouted to the height of 6"1" quickly within the time of his small bid. His father's book opened his eyes to a whole new world. A world Rarri desperately wanted to master, and he was willing to give his all to accomplish this new goal of his. He knew now, it was in his blood to break on a bitch. Heaven gave him his father's book so Rarri could be like his father. Rarri learned to respect his father and he admired the man more than anyone on earth, despite never meeting him in person, but he did not want to be like him or on his level. Rarri wanted to surpass him. He wanted to be better than his father. He wanted to be better than everybody. The best Mack, hustler, player, and pimp. A true finesser.

Heaven couldn't hold her cool any longer as Rarri and his grandmother walked towards the car. She ran up and gave him the biggest hug she could with teary eyes.

"I missed you so much," she said holding onto him tightly.

"I seen you almost every week since I been down, ain't nothin' to miss," Rarri joked.

Heaven let go and punched him in the arm. "Rude ass . . . that's why I was just playin', I ain't miss you either," she added with a playful attitude and started walking back to her car. "Come on momma."

"She lyin'," Rarri's grandmother whispered to him.

"I know," he replied with a smile.

All Heaven could talk about was what it was going to be like when Rarri got out. She even had a room at her house arranged *just* for him, which was the master bedroom. Heaven tried her hardest to get her mom to move in with her, but she refused to leave her home in Compton. Even though it was in a rough neighborhood, she loved it. The memories from that house were priceless to her, along with moments she cherished deeply.

The gang members never gave her problems at all. They would sometimes help her take groceries into the house when noticing her struggle to carry them from her car. One time a smoker had snatched her purse and took off running. A guy named Moss chased him down, beat his ass and brought it back. A lot of people hated the Nuttys, but she had found to love them. She would live her last moments in that neighborhood no matter how much money Rarri and Heaven made. She was staying. If it wasn't for Lil Dink, Rarri fa'sho would have been from Nutty Blocc. He loved them niggas too, especially Crip Calvin. He always looked out for him when he was young for some reason. Moody, nutt , and Mike Dog would too. Rarri got his first gun from moody, first weed sack from nutt and caught *his* first body with Mike Dog, so they were surprised to hear he got put on Park Village, but it was all love. N.F.V, Nutty Front Village 4life, despite the bullshit that's going on, right now. Rarri would forever love the Nuttys and the Front Hoods.

When they got in the car, Heaven handed him a brand-new cellphone. It was a Galaxy S7 Edge. "It's already activated, you just gotta sync yo contacts."

"Fa'sho," Rarri replied immediately, finger fucking the shit out of his new phone.

Heaven laced him up on everything that's been going on recently as they drove to his grandmother's house. She would shake her head from side to side when Heaven said something she didn't like.

When they made it to the house, he went directly to the shower to wash off that jail smell. When he got out, he put on some basketball shorts and a tank top, then slid into his Jordan slip-ons and went into the kitchen where his grandmother was dressing the table with food she had been cooking since last night. This time as they ate, his grandma was the one who couldn't stop talking. She reminisced and told stories about Rarri's childhood. The same stories she would always tell over dinner for the Lord knows how many times. No matter how many times she told the stories, they still never got old.

Rarri's favorite story was when the police threatened to take her to jail because he stopped going to school. She swore up and down she didn't know he wasn't going to school no more and swore that she hasn't seen him in weeks. The police weren't buying it and told her she was under arrest.

"Rarri get yo ass out here," she yelled as soon as they cuffed her up.

His second favorite was when Heaven went to jail for a warrant, she didn't know she had trying to get his grandma's car out of the impound cause Rarri went for a joy ride while she was in the hospital and got pulled over. They let him go but took the car. Heaven called from jail swearing to God she was going to kill Rarri once she got out. He was so spooked; he packed some clothes and ran away after he hung up the phone in her face. Rarri didn't dare come back no time soon. At least not until Heaven calmed down, which ended up being a month later.

After stuffing his face and laughing so hard to the point of almost throwing his food up, Rarri pushed his plate away and leaned back in his chair. When everybody was done, his grandma started to clear the table.

"How come you never tell stories about my pops?" Rarri finally asked as she made her way closer to him.

She froze for a minute, as did Heaven. Both of them looked at him, but he kept looking down at the table. He knew her next words.

His grandmother put a hand on his shoulder and a loving smile on her face. The smile he hated. Loving, serious, and firm all in one. "I told you . . . I'm yo daddy," she said and turned to walk away. Rarri grabbed her hand on his shoulder so fast, it startled her and Heaven. His eyes were closed, and he sighed deeply with sadness. This would be the last tear he would ever drop. Rarri eased his grip on his grandma's hand and rubbed the top of it softly, letting her know that he was sorry, then got up and stormed to his room, slamming the door behind him. As he laid on his bed staring at the ceiling, he could hear his grandmother and Heaven arguing but couldn't make out what they were saying.

Forty minutes later, Heaven busted into his room with tears in her eyes and a wet face.

"Pack yo shit, we leavin'," Heaven cried.

"All my clothes at my apartment still," Rarri replied as he sat up. "I don't wear none of this no more."

"Well come on," she said and walked off with Rarri on her trail.

"Where we goin'?" he asked when they were outside on the porch.

"To pick yo shit up, then I'm droppin' you off," Heaven replied as she walked down the steps and to her car.

Rarri stopped at the second step, slightly confused, then turned around when he heard the door behind him open. It was his grandma with an angry look on her face and a beer in her hand. She took a big sip of the tall can of Old English. Rarri hadn't seen her drink in years. She was a recovering alcoholic. She must have had it stashed somewhere because he didn't see it in the refrigerator, earlier. She was an angry drunk, and Rarri didn't want to be around when she started tripping.

"Drop me off where?" he asked looking back at Heaven.

Heaven turned around as she opened her car door and looked directly into her mother's angry, drunken eyes, then said, "at yo granddaddy house . . . yo *real* daddy's father is still alive… now come on."

Rarri didn't waste any time. He almost ran to the passenger side and hopped in.

"Cristy, don't bring yo ass back to this house you, bitch," Rarri's grandmother yelled and threw her beer at Heaven's car splashing beer all over it, barely missing Heaven.

"You ain't gotta worry bout that. I won't be comin' back nowhere near this muthafucka," Heaven said and jumped in the car and backed out.

Rarri's grandmother picked up a rock and tried to hit Heaven's car again but missed. "I hate you!" she yelled as she almost fell off the curb. "I hate you!"

After they stopped by Rarri's apartment so he could pack up some clothes, they drove to San Bernardino and got a hotel room. The next day, Heaven took Rarri to get his hair dreaded by her homegirl Ashley who worked at a shop called *'Allstarz'*. Ashley did dreads better than anybody she knew. Ashely hooked Rarri up with some of the neatest dreads that money could buy, then he went and got an edge-up on the other side of the salon by the barber while Heaven got her hair done. He smoked a blunt with Ashley, then they headed to the Bay.

Bird, Mia, Tia, Fia and Dria was hot he didn't come see them yet, but they calmed down when Heaven let them know they had to handle something important. Rarri facetimed with them almost all the way up north. They even gave him a little freak show. He missed his bitches and couldn't wait to get it popping like they always did. He told them he would call them back after he got some sleep, and then passed out for a minute. He woke up when he felt the car come to a complete stop.

Heaven reached in the back seat, grabbed his MCM duffle bag and handed it to him. “Come on,” she said as she opened up the car door and got out. Rarri got out and followed her to the house with his bag in hand. The house looked like it had seen some times. It wasn’t run down, but it could surely use a good painting. Other than that, it was a nice-looking house.

“KNOCK! KNOCK! KNOCK! KNOCK! KNOCK! KNOCK!”

She waited for about ten seconds.

“BAM! BAM! BAM! BAM! BAM! BAM! BAM! BAM! BAM! BAM! BAM! BAM!”

The door swung open hard.

“What is your prob—” the old woman in the doorway started to yell but froze when she saw Heaven. She hadn’t seen her since her son’s funeral.

Heaven looked the old woman up and down. She had to admit, the years had been good to her and secretly, Heaven prayed her body looked that good when she got older. The stand-off was cut short when Heaven saw God’s father stand next to his wife in the doorway. He almost looked the same as he did the last time, she saw him, except his hair was grayer and his face a bit wrinkled. For a second, she felt like she was looking at an older version of God and was slightly short of breath. Heaven quickly gained her composure and pulled Rarri next to her, giving him a kiss on his cheek.

“Call me when you ready,” Heaven told him then walked off back to her car.

Rarri's grandparents stood there shocked with an unbelieving look on their faces as the two studied his face. They undoubtedly knew this *was* their grandchild.

Rarri couldn't help but notice he had the same features as the old man in front of him. Especially his eyes; they had the same eyes. His grandmother was now holding on tightly to his grandfather. They were hurt and happy at the same time. The moment was unreal.

"Y'all goin' to let me come in?" Rarri asked with his most charming smile, unknowingly, the same one his father used on them all the time. His grandmother's knees grew weak and she would have fallen to the floor if she wasn't holding onto his grandfather so tightly. He felt her almost go down but caught her in time. The two of them were holding onto each other for dear life, cause Lord knows Rarri's grandfather was near having a heart attack.

After a moment, his grandmother reached out for his hand. When Rarri put his hand in hers, she pulled him in closer and hugged him, followed by his grandfather. They were hugging him so tight, he could barely breathe. His grandmother broke down into sobs while his grandfather cried silently.

His grandfather reached out with one hand open towards Heaven who was watching from her car and shook his head up and down, letting her know all was good. Heaven dried her eyes, started her car and drove off feeling relieved.

When they walked into the house, Rarri was taken back. It was more up to date than he expected. It looked more like somewhere some younger people would have lived instead of some old folk. It had a 90-inch sharp television in the living room. He could tell it was a smart T.V. because of the built-in camera at the top. The leather sofas were up to date, not them old kinds you see at most older people's houses with the plastic still over them. In the center was a statue of a tiger laying on top of a large Persian rug. There wasn't a speck of dust on none of the tables or the entertainment center.

There were tall frames made of glass that had pictures on the shelves. He could see some of them were of his father when he was a kid and some of his grandparents. It wasn't hard to see that his grandfather was big pimpin' back in his day. The gold chains, watches, bracelets, and rings on every finger told it all. Not to mention the prostitutes standing behind him with their heads down. He noticed one of them didn't have her head down and looked pissed. He chuckled to himself and moved to another picture next to that one. It was a picture of his father when he was about twelve. He was jeweled down in an all-white Gucci sweat suit, throwing up the P sign to the camera. In another picture he looked a couple years older, sitting on top of a Benz rocking a red and black Bill Blast sweater with the matching loafers, always throwing up the pimpin', but this time with both hands.

There were also pictures of his grandmother with his dad and some of her by herself. She wore big gold earrings and also had chains, bracelets, and rings on. Everything she wore looked expensive in every picture. Her hair was short and curly and almost the same color as her rich brown skin. She looked like she ran shit. Her poses were real boss like and her eyes were flirtatiously firm, yet those of a fearless person.

Rarri turned and saw his grandparents sitting on the couch then went and joined them. He set his bag down beside him as he sat down. When he looked at them, they were staring at him with happy smiles on their faces watching his every move in awe. It was an awkward silence. Nobody knew what to say.

"Um . . . . . . y'all got somethin' to drink?" Rarri asked breaking the silence.

"Yea!" his grandmother replied as she quickly jumped up and started for the kitchen. "What you want, water, soda or juice?" she yelled from the kitchen.

"Soda is coo," he said over his shoulder looking into the kitchen. When he turned back around, his grandfather was still stuck on him with that smile which made Rarri laugh a little. His grandmother returned handing him a canned soda and a cup holder, then sat back down next to his grandfather on the sofa across from Rarri.

"Thank you," he said after taking a drink and sitting the can on the table over the cupholder.

They held each other's hand as they watched him, still stuck with smiles. They looked at him like he was God. Literally!

"Well, my name is—" he started

"Rarri," his grandfather finished. He said it with so much pride.

"If y'all knew my name, how come y'all never came to see me or pick me up?" Rarri asked after a few seconds passed.

Both of their faces became serious and concerned as they let go of each other's hands.

"We tried plenty of times but," his grandmother stopped to choose her words correctly, "It was just too much goin' on."

"The last time I popped up demanding to see you, I got shot right here," his grandfather said lifting up his shirt so Rarri could see the bullet wound on his chest. "And right here, too," he added, pointing to a spot on his ribs. He left out the bullet wound on his ass.

"Why would somebody shoot you for tryin' to see me?" Rarri asked. "I don't get it, my granny ain't never say nothin' about none of this. I just found out about you yesterday."

His grandparents looked at each other and shook their heads looking upset but didn't say anything.

Rarri knew something was up. He didn't know what it was that they weren't trying to tell him, but he wanted to. He unzipped his bag and pulled out his father's book, holding it for them to see.

"I already know what type of shit y'all used to be on. It's all in here. He wrote about the both of y'all . . . this my Bible and I'm pickin' up where he left off, regardless . . . so if y'all don't want to keep it real, it's coo. I'm used to everybody lyin' to me anyway, but from what I've been readin', I would think I could come to y'all for the truth."

"We would never lie to you Rarri, but are you sure this is the lifestyle you want to live?" his grandfather asked, and then added, "the same lifestyle that took your father?"

Rarri looked at him in the eyes. “I’m sure.”

His grandmother smiled and rose from the couch. She walked to the glass frame, opened it, grabbed a picture then went and handed it to Rarri. “What do you see in there?” she asked as she sat back down.

Rarri studied the picture. It was the same one he was looking at when he first walked into the house. “I see my grandpa standin’ wit his hoes behind him,” he replied, putting the picture back down.

“Look closer,” she said and then asked, “ain't nothin’ in that picture familiar to you?”

Rarri picked it back up and studied it again.

“That’s enough,” his grandfather said for the first time, raising his voice at his wife.

“Naw, he wanna know the truth so I’ma tell him the truth,” she yelled back at him.

“I said that’s enough,” he barked.

“You see the bitch without her head down lookin’ like she got an attitude?” she asked.

“Yea,” Rarri replied still looking at the picture. “What this gotta do with him gettin’ shot tho?”

“That out of pocket hoe is yo granny,” she told him then added, “that bitch had him shot when he came to see you.”

Rarri looked closer at the picture. It sure was his grandmother, standing there with the rest of the prostitutes wearing hoe attire. He couldn’t believe it was really her.

Rarri wasn't mad at all, but he did want to know what the fuck was going on, 'cause this shit was crazy.

"Ok, so you was pimpin' on her back in the day. That still don't explain why she had you shot," he said as he sat the picture back on the table and looked at his grandfather for an answer.

He was shocked at how well Rarri took in everything. He didn't seem to be moved, even the slightest bit. That's the moment he knew for a fact that his grandson was really built for this shit.

"I'ma give it to you straight, cause I see you don't want it no other way," he replied then added, "I had to kick the bitch . . . she was lazy as fuck, stayed short and always out of pocket. Ain't no way in hell I was bout to hold a hoe wit no doe, ya undastand me?"

Rarri didn't say anything, he just nodded in approval.

"She wanted everything, but ain't wanna do shit to get it. Always complainin' bout the next bitch instead of worryin' about her damn self. You see, she was the type of hoe no pimp wanted. A possessive hoe. A ask you *where you goin'* and *who you wit,* type of bitch. A hoe who wanna be yo only hoe so you got no choice but to let her go, cause *ain't* no hoe runnin' yo show... a hoe that love you so much she don't wanna see you wit nothin' cause she jealous of everything. A *why you need money when you got me, I had a dream pussy should be free,* type of bitch . . . it wasn't long before she found out she didn't have what it took to be my bottom, and that's when the out of pocket shit started happenin' . . . first, it was the fights wit yo granny right here over dumb shit."

"Which I won," his grandmother threw in with attitude.

His grandfather gave her a look that said *shut the fuck up*, then continued.

"Second was when she would get drunk and make scenes, talkin' reckless to a 'P' in front of other pimps . . . third was when she got pregnant by a trick, ran off wit him, had the baby, came back alone wit a fee hoe'n up for a couple months, then the bitch turned around and got pregnant by the same trick again, runnin' off for a second time . . . that was it for me. Yea she was fine. Real fine! But I couldn't let *no* hoe keep embarrassin' my pimpin'. I never found pleasure in beatin' on a bitch. That's not my job. So when she came back wit my fee like she always would, I had a different plan in mind this time . . . I still remember it like it was yesterday. I was choppin' game wit my 'P' partners in East Oakland on International Blvd when she walked up tryin' to speak to a 'P'. She was lookin' better than ever and ready to go. I was damn near bout to send her and forget everything that happened when she handed me the six rolls of bills. That was the biggest fee a bitch ever handed me at the time, but I still had somethin' to prove cause ain't no price on my pimpin' . . . . . . I stripped her for everything she had and h*ad on*, sendin' her away butt-ass naked for every hoe and pimp on the blade to see. That was when I started B.A.B.E St, 'cause I broke a bitch easy in the streets. I kept it a secret from most pimps 'cause I wanted it to have more meanin' to it than just pimpin'. Almost anybody could be a pimp, but everybody can't be from B.A.B.E. Anyway, after that day my game elevated to a whole new level. The hoes flocked like never before. The only way for me to go was up with all the toes I had down.

I was never lookin' back. Well, at least I thought I wasn't. I was so in my own world, silly me forgot what I did to Katey a year back on International, but she didn't. One night, I was walkin' to my car and a white man pushed up on me wit a knife, stabbin' me eight times. *"That's from Katey,"* he said as I fell to the ground, holdin' my stomach and turned to walk away. That's when I drew my pistol and shot that cracker in the back of the head. I ended up doin' four years in prison for manslaughter, cause ain't no self-defense law in California. Later, I found out *that cracker* I shot was the same trick that got Katey pregnant. *That cracker* was yo other granddaddy."

"Damn!" was all Rarri could say. This shit was deeper than he thought.

"When I found out my son was messin' round wit Katey's daughter's, I tried all I could to talk him out of it but his mind was made up. That's when I knew he loved yo momma." Rarri's grandfather chuckled then added, "and yo aunty."

The three of them laughed at the last part.

"After yo momma and daddy died, I popped up at Katey's house demandin' to see you every day for about a week straight, but she would never bring you out or let me in. I wasn't goin' to give up on seein' my grandchild that easy. . . no sir... I was back on her porch and arguin' wit her through the door again the next day. After about an hour, some niggas came and told me to leave, but I wasn't hearin' them either, so I brushed 'em off . . . that's when they jumped me and dragged me off the porch. I tried to fight back but it was just too many of them... they beat my ass and shot me in the street like a dog. Before I blacked out, I looked at the house and seen Katey standin' on the porch with you in her arms smilin' down at me. I never knew she could be that cold, but after almost dyin' *twice*, I found out the hard way."

His grandfather paused then sighed in relief. "That's the whole truth."

Rarri sat there for a minute digesting it all. He wondered why Heaven never told him none of this. "Thanks . . . I appreciate that."

"You welcome," he replied.

That awkward silence was filling the room again as all of them were deep in thought.

"You wanna see yo dad's room?" his grandmother asked.

"Hell ye— I mean yea," Rarri replied excitedly, then followed his grandma down the hall.

When they got to the door his grandmother said, "gon 'head and open it up."

Rarri paused as he placed his hand on the doorknob, then looked at his grandmother again. He didn't know why he was nervous, but he was. His heart was beating fast and he felt his palms began to moisten, making the knob a bit wet.

"This *yo* daddy's room," she said looking him in his eyes and pointing at him. "Go on in there."

Rarri turned the knob and stepped inside. He stood there for a moment taking in the detail of the room. He immediately knew why his name was Rarri; almost everything in the room had a Ferrari symbol on it. The covers on the bed, the pillows, the curtain and a neat pile of folded towels. There was a big Ferrari symbol painted on the wall and toy model Ferrari cars nicely placed on a few shelves.

“He always said if he had a son, he would name him Rari with an extra ‘R’ for rich,” his grandmother told him.

Rarri didn’t say anything. He was still in awe of his father’s room. He walked over to a long dresser that was attached to a big mirror and noticed all the gold chains neatly spread across the top. Each had its own different medallion. One was a Ferrari symbol, another said B.A.B.E., another was a hand throwing up the pimpin’, but the one that really caught his eye was the one of a naked bitch in a laid back, sitting position wearing high heels made out of red diamonds. Rarri touched it gently, admiring the diamonds and thickness of the rope.

“Put it on. They yours now,” his grandma assured him.

Rarri picked it up, then sat it back down.

“Not yet . . . I wanna earn ‘em.”

His grandma smiled as she stood next to him and they looked at each other through the mirror. Then she opened up the top drawer and grabbed one of the books. Rarri’s mouth dropped open in surprise. It was filled with books. The same type of book like the one Heaven had given him.

“My dad wrote all of those?” Rarri asked, pointing at all the other books.

"Yup, he sure did," she replied as she closed the drawer back and handed him the book she took out. "This your other bible . . . me and yo granddaddy goin' to give you the game, but studyin' these books will give you way more. When you done wit that one pick up another, but, don't skip them. They're placed in order. Take yo time, but don't be no snail. Oh, and don't tell him I said it, but yo daddy could out pimp yo granddaddy, blindfolded."

When his grandma left out of the room, Rarri sat down on the bed and read the title of the book out loud to himself. *"THE CHEAT CODE."* Then he opened it up to the first page.

"The first rule in pimpin' is simple: it ain't no rules."

That was all it said on the heading part of the first page, so Rarri turned to the next, but there were no words on the paper. Neither the next page or the page after that. Rarri placed his thumb on the side of the book touching the last page slightly lifting it up, then removed his thumb towards his index finger, letting the pages fall as he scanned them for words to no avail. The pages were blank. The only thing visible was bumps and ripples. It looked like someone poked over and over on the other side of the page. Rarri scanned through the book again and noticed all the pages had the same bumps, then closed it. He walked out of the room and found his grandparents in the kitchen. He couldn't believe what he was seeing and hearing, really what he was hearing.

"You lil stupid ass, I don't give a fuck, I don't give a fuck, I don't, I don't, I don't give a fuck, bitch I don't,

give a, fuck about you or anything that you do, don't give a fuck about you or anything that you do."

These two old muthafuckas were singing along to Big Sean's '*IDFWU*' song as they danced. Not only did they know the hook, they knew all the verses too... especially E-40's! Rarri watched in amazement as he recorded them on his phone. He had to post this shit on Snapchat. The caption on the video said, **"I got the flyest grandparents."**

This was Rarri's first post since his release. Immediately comments started to pour in:

"Wya?"

"What's the deal?"

"Hit me!"

"Lmao"

"You out?"

"Roll up."

"Yaah!"

"Lol"

"Cute!"

He didn't respond to none of them.

His grandpa gave his grandma a kiss, then headed out the kitchen. "Come on Rarri, let's go for a ride. I want you to meet some people. He followed him out of the house.

Rarri stopped at the sidewalk when he saw his grandpa walk around to the driver's side of a smoke grey AMG CL450.

"What's wrong?" he asked when he saw the confused look on Rarri's face.

"This the same car I got," Rarri admitted.

His grandpa put on his strongest country accent and said, "ole jockin' ass nigga," then hopped in his car.

Rarri laughed as he got in. He didn't expect him to be this cool. He didn't even dress like an old nigga. He had on a red Polo sweater; some blue True's exposing his brown Gucci belt, everything fitting him slim. His Gucci loafers matched his sweater. Still, buss down with the jewels as he was in the pictures Rarri saw, and his gray waves at a 360.

His grandpa saw the admiration in his eyes. "I ain't never been no Cadillac pimp," he said as if he could read Rarri's mind then added, "understand, this is regular," as he pressed play on his phone that was connected to the Bluetooth system in his car and blasted Drakeo's song *'Regular'*. They pulled off into traffic bobbing their heads. His grandpa pulled open the center console and grabbed one of the already rolled blunts.

"Fire him up," he said passing it to Rarri, then handed him a lighter.

Rarri hit the blunt and inhaled deeply, blew out the smoke then started coughing his life away, uncontrollably. His grandpa started laughing his ass off, then grabbed the blunt from Rarri and hit it hard like it was nothing, blew the smoke out without a single cough and hit it again as he swerved through traffic. Rarri was still coughing and sweating like a muthafucka.

"What kind of weed is that?" Rarri asked after catching his breath, barely able to even talk.

"Moonrock!" he replied hitting it again. "I get mine's extra dipped at my homeboy clinic," he added after blowing the smoke out.

Rarri took little baby hits when the blunt was back on him and passed it quickly back to his grandpa who flicked it out the window when it was about half an inch long.

Ten minutes later, they pulled up on a street that was crowded with prostitutes. His grandpa parked but kept the engine running as they watched what was going on around them.

"Grandma gave me another one of my pop's books," Rarri said breaking the silence. "She told me to study it, but the muthafucka ain't got no words in it."

His grandpa looked at him and smiled, then back to the streets. He liked Rarri's lingo.

"You gotta crack the code," he replied then repeated, "*you* gotta crack the code."

Rarri was trying to figure out what code to crack. "*It's a fuckin' book, not a smartphone*," he thought to himself.

"Just take it slow, you got time."

His grandfather rolled his window down and pressed the horn five times. About eight different hoes walked by dropping rolls of money through the window and into his lap. Rarri was shocked at how good they looked. These wasn't no old hoes, these bitches had to only be in their twenties, and they was fine.

"Love you, daddy," they would say but kept walking.

"I know," he replied to some and, "I love me, too," he replied to others.

"They don't love me, Rarri, they love my pimpin'," his grandpa said, popping his collar, excitedly.

"You still in the game?" Rarri asked in disbelief.

"This ain't a phase, it's a lifestyle," he schooled. "I don't know no eighty-year-old hoes, but I do know some eighty-year-old pimps . . . A bitch hoe'n ain't got shit on yo pimpin' . . . Rarri, you gotta pimp strong to live long, you understand me?"

"Yea, I could dig that," Rarri replied coolly while nodding his head.

"Ight . . . count this for me," he said and handed Rarri the money that he had just got from his bitches, then he pulled off.

After a couple blocks and bending a few corners, he pulled over parking in front of a house that had luxury cars filling up the driveway.

"Here," Rarri said handing him the money. "It's four bandz."

"Ok, good lookin'," he replied, then put the money in the middle console, then added, "Don't ever count no pimp's money for him Rarri . . . that's what hoes do," he chuckled then got out the car.

"Awww . . . you muthafucka," Rarri said to himself as he stepped out the car too and followed his grandpa.

They walked along the side of the house towards the back. Rarri could hear music and loud chatting. His grandpa opened the latch to the back gate and walked in with Rarri behind him. Rarri immediately noticed the group of young niggas congregating. Nobody in sight looked to be near thirty, and the bitches sitting with their feet in the pool all looked bad, but none of them turned to make eye contact, so he wasn't too sure.

"What's up 'P'?" a short light-skinned nigga with tattoos all over his face yelled over the music to his grandpa as he and Rarri were approaching.

"My bitches when they standing next to yours," he joked, then gave the little nigga a P-shake. All the other niggas laughed and gave him a P-shake as well. Rarri had noticed all of them were jeweled up and everything they had on was designer. That's when he wished he would have brought his shit with him before Heaven brought him out to the Bay.

"Who this?" the short light-skinned nigga asked, looking at Rarri.

"This my grandson, Rarri," he told him.

"Oh ok, fa'sho 'P', he replied then extended his hand to Rarri. "I'm Money-Mike, but everybody call me Twin."

"Ight fa'sho . . . fa'sho," Rarri said as he shook his hand.

Money-Mike looked at him with a skeptical expression when he didn't P-shake.

"You some pimpin'?" he asked.

Rarri didn't know what to say. He couldn't say yea, but he didn't want to say no, either. So, he just said, "somethin' like that."

All of them niggas started laughing.

"'P' part-timin'," a tall dark-skinned nigga rocking Armani shades and a Franko chain joked, then they continued laughing at the new joke.

A stocky brown skinned nigga with a Mohawk bent down and pointed at Rarri's Nike's then yelled loudly, "what are those, tho?"

They were all cracking up.

"Look at bruh jeans," another one said. Everybody looked and laughed some more.

Rarri was pissed the fuck off. He was so mad he didn't even hear the rest of the jokes, but he knew they were still bagging on him. *"I got more money than all you weird-ass niggas,"* he thought to himself.

After they kept going on and on, Rarri had snapped.

"Cuz, you niggas is weird as fuck," he barked, then stormed off back to his grandpa's car.

Rarri wasn't used to being *the joke*. He didn't like that shit at all, not one bit of it. He really didn't like how his grandpa just stood there and let him get clowned on by some niggas he didn't even know. "*What type of shit is that?"* he thought to himself.

A moment later, his grandpa was walking back to the car with all the young niggas behind him. Rarri stood up from the hood of the car and met them halfway.

"What, y'all niggas tryna get down or somethin'?" Rarri asked, stretching his arms ready for a fight.

Money-Mike walked up smiling at him. "Say 'P', don't ever let niggas manipulate yo demeanor... you gotta stay boo, balm and bollective, Blood."

"Rarri . . . these yo cousins," his grandpa said with a laugh.

"Aww," Rarri replied with a smile, slightly embarrassed. "My bad, man."

Everybody laughed as they gave him a real handshake and a hug as they introduced themselves. The one that said he was part-timing was his cousin Josh, the one that clowned his shoes was his cousin Tae Tae, and the one that clowned his jeans was David, also known to the world as J-Money, Pay Day, and Dolla.

"Let's slide up in the house," Money-Mike told everybody, and they all walked back to the backyard, then into the house.

As soon as they hit the living room, Rarri knew why Money-Mike said everybody calls him Twin when he saw a nigga that looked just like him, only with different tattoos, choppin' on four bitches sitting on the couch with their heads down.

"Y'all bitches think this a game, an X-box or a PlayStation 4. I ain't out here play pimpin' hoe, I'm bout my doe. I need moe if you can't hit my mitt, go! I don't give a fuck if you far from swine, pretty or fine without a dime, you can't dine and damn sho not on mine, ya understand? Look at me hoe."

The hoes looked up at him.

"Now look back down bitch! I ain't done choppin' on you hoes. If y'all can't sell pussy, collect cans! I don't give a fuck what y'all do, just hand me, my bandz. Daddy need to be designer from his hat to his pants, is what a dumb bitch thought. What about my shoes, hoe? You see my waves on swim, I need to be bust down from the grooves to the shoes, that's the new news bitch. Let me kick my feet up while you get yo shit beat up, bring my bread don't ketchup, keep up, I ain't no Kermet the frog nigga sippin' out a tea-cup, a big ass elephant runnin' around for a peanut, a old nigga poppin' pills cause he can't get his meat up, bitch I'm Money-Mitch, filthy rich, without me you ain't shit but a filthy bitch. I wouldn't fuck a broke hoe wit a filthy dick. I'm milky, silky and builtly fit. Ain't a flaw in my future, I'm really it. I got two words for a hoe without me; Silly! Bitch! My chili thick, I'm really slick bet not ever hear you hoes say give me shit! I rock Gucci, Louie and Fendi mixed, chain so long it say gimmie dick. I don't human traffic, I really pimp. This Rolli real, it don't tick. I blow kill bill sick. Addicted to the life, real whipped. This ain't no field trip bitch, break bread or fake dead. Hoe up or blow up and get slapped if you ain't got it when I show up, understand me? Put some wheels on them heels and pay my bills. I need a hoe, not a bitch wit skills. A real hoe follow the rules, see a *nigga* on T.V. and turn to cartoons."

"Breathe on them hoes 'P'... breathe on them muthafuckin' hoes 'P'," Rarri's grandpa yelled loudly and proudly at his nephew, Money-Mitch like his favorite team just won the championship game after that last shot before the buzzer, with nothing but net. Money-Mitch always chopped on a bitch the best. He was the reason that house was called the *Chopp shop*. Money-Mitch never needed a reason to chop on a bitch; he would chop on a hoe just cause he felt like choppin' *and* was known to chop a pimp when he broke him for a bitch.

Money-Mitch turned to his uncle even more excited than he was and said, "Oh yea, I'ma breathe on her but if she ain't got my doe I'ma bob and weeb on her. If she ugly throw a weave on her. Ashy, Grease on her, understand me?"

"That's what the fuck I'm talkin' bout mane," Rarri's grandpa said as the two gave each other an aggressive hug.

"Y'all bitches go play in the pool," Money-Mitch instructed his hoes.

They got up and walked out with their heads down. Rarri was surprised at the big smiles he could see on the visible part of their faces. "These bitches like this shit," he thought to himself.

"That's Rarri?" Money-Mitch asked his uncle, pointing at Rarri.

"The one and only," he replied.

"What up cuzzo?" Money-Mitch asked as he gave Rarri a handshake and a hug in the same motion. "I'm Mitch, but everybody call me Twin or Money-Muthafuckin-Mitch cause I—"

"Go hard on a bitch," Rarri cut off with a laugh. "I see you mashin' cuzzo. I see you."

Money-Mitch was buss down like a muthafucka. The grill in his mouth looked to cost about sixty bandz, probably more. He had on about nine different chains, his bracelet was diamond crusted and about an inch and a half wide, the boogers on his ears were diamond crusted letter M's. He was shirtless, showing off his tatted-up body. His pants, briefs, belt, and shoes were all coke white and made from Gucci. He had Money-Mike designed on the side of his head and dyed red.

Everybody took seats throughout the living room. Money-Mitch passed the blunt box around and everybody grabbed their own already rolled blunt.

"So how long you goin' to be out here for?"

"I don't even really know yet, but fa'sho for a few months," Rarri replied as he lit his blunt.

"Shid, we got a extra room if you tryna post up here," Pay Day told him then added after hitting his blunt, "this where all the bitches be, anyway."

"You got some toes yet?" J-Money asked

"Naw! Not yet . . . I need to go find some, like ASAP," Rarri replied.

"Check this 'P'. I got this lil fine bitch I could pass you, but we gotta split the doe, tho," J-Money said.

Rarri chuckled. "Good lookin' out, but I'm not never takin' no *hand me down* hoe. . . I need a bitch who ain't never hoe'd before, know what I'm sayin'? A turn out I could burn out."

Everybody in the room went crazy.

"Oh shit!" Money-Mike yelled. "Cuzzo ain't green."

Little did they know, Rarri had more game than he put into view. His father's book taught him to never expose his hand and how to game others by *acting* gameless. This whole time he was running game and these niggas ain't even know it, not even his grandpa. What, y'all thought he was studying his father's book this whole time and didn't learn nothing? Rarri knew every word in that book like the back of his hand. "Friendly competition," he thought to himself.

Nobody knew how fast his mind was actually racing. Every move was just another calculated step towards mastering his game and yea, this was *his* game. He already had everybody in the room categorized; all it took was a few words and a brief look into one's eyes for Rarri to read a person. They thought like pimps, he thought like a B.A.B.E St nigga. The two were the same and completely different at the same time. Like Pepsi and Sprite, one dark and one light. Both sodas, but fa'sho nothing alike. One thing he knew fa'sho was that the five of them were the real deal. Their advantage over him was an experience and being raised in the game. Rarri was raised by gangs and nothing else, but for some reason, he took to pimping like a pro. It was so complex and deeply rooted in him that he didn't even understand how he understood the game so good.

Heaven brought Rarri to the Bay so he could learn more about his father and be around his grandparents. She knew he would pick up game along the way because it was in his blood. Rarri had every intention to take his time, stay humble and just enjoy being around his grandparents. That was until his grandpa brought him around these niggas. Now, he had a new agenda and task to achieve at all costs, fuck everything else. Just that fast, Rarri's intentions shifted to something else, something more exciting. For him! He didn't give a fuck about these niggas being his cousins, he wanted to knock them for every bitch they had. All of them. Every last one! Especially the twins. "Friendly competition," he thought again.

"Wassup with that extra room?" Rarri asked.

Chapter 14

The next morning

Rarri and his grandma went to cemetery where his father was buried. His grandma brought flowers and Remy to pour as she always did. She was emotional and couldn't hold her tears as she talked to her son about Rarri's arrival and how happy she was to spend time with him. Then she prayed.

"I wish you could be here in person to meet your boy and be in his life how we were in yours, but I know you are here without a doubt, in spirit. Son, shine your light on Rarri and give him the knowledge he needs to survive in this world, 'cause Lord knows he has the heart. I'm askin' you to bathe him in your game son. Give him the game he desires, and more. Give him life, son, wake his game up. Let him breathe, let him breathe so he can achieve. This marathon ain't over yet, it's just beginnin'. You planted the seed that's gonna grow into a forest and a jungle 'cause he can't be just a tree. Make him big, not small. Bigger than yo daddy. Bigger than you. Bigger than any muthafucka thinkin' bout steppin' foot in this here game, son. Take BABE through new trails and new heights, luxury hotels, and overseas flights. Let him be what you couldn't and see what you wouldn't. This is *yo son*, make him the symbol of this lifestyle. Internationally known by every and all. He ain't come here to struggle, he came to ball, pimp hoes and stand tall. Jump off and don't fall. He need that blessin', that blessin' only you could give him. The blessin' you been givin' him his whole life. He don't know it's been you, but I do. Right now, I'm askin' you to bless *harder* and to keep blessin'. He grateful for the blessins you've been givin' him, but it ain't enough. It ain't never enough! He need more and you goin' to give it to him cause if you don't, when I die and come up there or wherever we at, I'ma go on and kick yo ass."

Rarri's grandma finished her prayer with her son's favorite slogan, slightly mocking him playfully.

"Now, *do you understand me*?"

Rarri chuckled at that last part. She went hard on that prayer to her son. He could tell his grandma really believed his dad was the God of game, and the one and only Game God. Deep down, Rarri believed it too. She believed he was put on this planet for one purpose, and one purpose only; to leave a message.

When they left the cemetery, Rarri immediately felt a lot more confident about himself and his game. All of a sudden, he just *knew* he was *that* nigga. His grandma was taking him to the twin's house. Rarri enjoyed sleeping in his dad's room last night, but he wanted to be where the action was and around some people his age. Well, that's what he told his grandparents.

They were at a stoplight waiting on it to turn green when Rarri saw her. She was a short, thick, long-haired, green eyes, light-skinned, bitch with nice full lips, a pretty face, and rocking some booty shorts that made her ass look too good to be true. They locked eyes, and as the car drove off slowly and she walked by going the other direction, she never broke his stare. She actually was breaking her neck, so much that she had to turn her body with her cause her head couldn't turn no more. "*Her*," a voice said in his head.

Rarri turned to his grandma. "Grandma pull over, I got one," he said excitedly with his hand already on the door handle. As soon as she pulled over, he was out of the car.

"Aye!" he yelled at the girl who was now walking away. When she turned around, he signaled with his hand for her to come to him and said, "Check it out!" which she happily did.

Rarri stayed standing where he was. He didn't want to seem thirsty, like her.

"Hey," she said when she approached him then added, "wassup?"

He immediately noticed the extra pop she was doing with her hips and how she was standing in front of him still swinging her hips. She was *already* throwing that pussy at him.

"That's what I'm tryin' to find out …I see you walkin' down the street swangin' that thang for a nigga and all that. What's the deal?" Rarri gamed.

She blushed with a big smile and said, "that's how I always walk."

Rarri smiled with his playful, *yea-the-fuck-right* look. "So, you ain't put that extra pep in yo step when you seen a nigga?" he asked.

"Nooo!" she lied, still smiling. "I really walk like that."

Rarri's smile faded and his face became serious. "Oh ok, my bad, I must have been trippin' then," he said then turned to get back in the car.

"Oh, it's like that? You ain't tryna fuck wit me now?" she asked ghetto than a muthafucka.

"Not if you goin' to lie to a nigga," Rarri replied then added. "I don't fuck wit bitches who be lyin."

Her expression became mad and sad at the same time as she quickly got flooded with emotions and thoughts. *"I'm not a liar. Did this nigga really just call me a bitch?"*

Rarri opened the car door and was about to hop in.

"Wait!" she said, then smacked her lips and sighed deeply with frustration. "I did."

Rarri turned around with a confused look on his face. "Did what?"

She tightened her lips in order to break her smile and squinted her eyes giving him that, *'I know what you're up to stare.'*

"I put a lil extra on it," she mumbled as she rolled her eyes.

Rarri closed the door quickly like he was surprised, put his hand to his ear as he ran up and bent down to her height.

"Hold up! I ain't catch that, what you say?" Rarri asked playfully.

"I said!" she replied raising her voice a little, then lowering it to her normal level and added, "I put a little extra on it… when I seen you." She was smiling from ear to ear.

Rarri eased up and stood straight looking her in the eyes. "Was that so hard?"

"Naw, it wasn't…I just didn't want you to think I was thirsty for the dick," she honestly replied.

"First off, I *know* you thirsty for this dick," Rarri told her.

"How you know that?" she asked with attitude.

"You just said I didn't want you to *think* I was thirsty for the dick… which means… you thirsty for this dick, you just ain't want me to know," Rarri joked then added, "It's coo, I like thirsty bitches."

"First of all, you rude…second, I ain't no bitch," she replied with her neck on a swivel.

"Who told you that?" Rarri asked with a smile.

"I told me that," she shot back.

"You know the worst lies you could tell is the ones to yo'self, right?" Rarri asked and told her at the same time.

"I'm not lyin' to myself. I just don't consider myself a bitch," she said.

"Is that right?" he asked.

"It sho'll the fuck is," she replied crossing her arms and looking at him through bruised eyes. She didn't like what he was saying, but for some strange reason, she couldn't turn and walk away.

"Come here, let me show you somethin'," Rarri told her and walked to the car, then knocked on the passenger window. When the window rolled down, both of thcm leaned down to get a view of the driver.

"Grandma, what do you see standing next to me?"

His grandma looked from him to her, then back to him and said bluntly with a sour expression, "A bitch!"

"And what is you?" the girl shot back with attitude.

His grandma looked her dead in the eyes and said, "an *old* bitch," with just as much attitude.

The girl's mouth dropped open.

"Thanks, grandma," Rarri replied and stood up straight, as did she.

"That's crazy," was all she could say.

"Is we goin' to fuck or what? Cause right now you bullshittin'," Rarri asked with a smile.

"Damn nigga, you just straight to the point, huh?" she replied.

Rarri smacked the side of her thigh and said, "you know you like that shit."

She smiled. "Yea . . . I do," she admitted swinging her hips from side to side. She had been dripping in her panties the whole time, talking to Rarri.

Rarri opened the back door for her. "Get in, bitch," he joked.

She shot him a dangerous look, tightening her lips again to stop herself from smiling. Then she happily got into the back of the car.

Rarri had his grandma drop them off at a Hotel. As soon as they were situated in the room, she undid Rarri's pants and went to work, sucking his dick like a pro. She took her time sucking him soft and slow, making love to his dick with her mouth. She would go all the way down until she choked, making her mouth more wet each time. She twirled her tongue around the head of his dick and popped her lips, seductively moaning in every motion. She was making a mess, a sexy mess. She was gagging and gurgling on his hardness with the mouth of a porn star. She sucked his balls gently as she stroked him with her hand, then took him back into her mouth, this time bobbing her head faster, still stroking him at the same time. She was so wild with it, spit was splashing her face, which seemed to turn her on more than Rarri cause she only went harder. She would come up, pulling his dick out of her mouth gasping for air like she was just underwater and go right back down. Her moans were turning into soft cries like she was punishing herself with his dick. Her face was almost completely wet. She slid her shorts and panties off and was playing with her pussy and fingering herself while she continued sucking his dick.

"I'm bout to cum," she moaned loudly, still with his dick in her mouth. "Aaaarggh! Awww! I'm cummin'! I'm! Cummin'! I'm! I'm. . . I'm cummin'!" she started shaking uncontrollably and moaning in exhaustion, still with her mouth around his dick. Rarri grabbed her by the hair and started moving her head up and down quickly. She sniffed her nose from running and sucked as she felt the tears fall from her eyes. These were the tears she loved. The tears that came from sucking dick and gagging so much that you can't stop them from falling. Rarri stood up, still with a grip on her hair and dick in her mouth. Then he started fucking her face roughly as she moaned in pleasure, fingering herself again. When he let go of the hair, her head kept moving back and forth. She grabbed his dick with her free hand and twisted while pulling on it at the same time.

"Cum on my face...Cum on my face."

Even though her mouth was stuffed, Rarri knew exactly what she was saying. He was hearing her clearly. Just the thought of cumming of her face had him ready to go. After a few more bobs of her head, Rarri felt the build-up coming and pulled out of her mouth. She jerked his dick over her face with her mouth open and tongue out until he came, then she smeared his nut all over her face using his dick. She put his dick in her mouth one more time and sucked to make sure not a drop was left to drip, then she popped it out loudly. Rarri fell back on the bed and blew out hard in exhaustion.

"Damn, that shit was bomb," he panted as she was walking away to the bathroom.

"Uh-uh! Don't pass out. That was just the warm-up. I'm bout to hop in the shower and get ready for that second nut," she said and walked into the bathroom then yelled, "I'ma show you a bitch!"

"Aye! Ight, stop playin', my bad . . . what's yo real name?" Rarri yelled as he sat up.

She poked her head out of the bathroom. "Remember… it's bitch!" she replied, stuck her tongue out at him and closed the door.

Chapter 15

After three days of fucking and getting sucked on, Rarri knew all he needed to know about the girl he was lying next to. Her name was Laelani, but everybody called her Lae Lae. She was twenty-three, had a five-year-old son that lived with her sister, born and raised in the bay area, didn't have her own place or a job, wanted to go back to school to be a nurse and get her NA. After she got her NA, she was going to open her own nursing home for disabled children and have another side for homeless elderlies who couldn't afford to stay in other homes and blah blah blah blah, all that same bullshit the rest of these hoes be saying but never end up doing.

"You ain't ever thought about gettin' yo own place?" Rarri asked as she rubbed his chest.

"Hell yea, all the time," she replied.

"What's been stoppin' you?" he asked.

"Nothin' really, I just been bullshittin'," she admitted. "Ever since my momma died, shit just been goin' downhill for me… I don't got no help out here no more."

"Sorry to hear that about your moms. I lost mines too . . . and my pops," Rarri told her with glossy eyes as if he was holding back tears and sat up straight in the bed.

"Aww, baby I'm sorry," Lae Lae said as she sat up too and rubbed his back. "I didn't know."

"*Duh bitch, I'm just now tellin' you,*" he thought to himself.

"It's coo . . . I know you understand how it is," Rarri replied. "I really don't got nobody either, so I gotta make shit happen on my own cause ain't nobody goin' to give me nothin'. I mean I got my grandma, but I don't like askin' people for nothin', you feel me?"

"Yea I feel you. I'm like that too cause muthafuckas always wanna throw what they done did for you in yo face. I hate that shit," Lae Lae said.

"So, what you be doin' out here to get money?" Rarri asked.

"I been puttin' in applications, but ain't nothin' been comin' through," she replied. "Somethin' is goin' to give though."

"Check this out," Rarri said as he got out of the bed and went over to his bag. He put the bag on the bed, unzipped it and pulled out a fat roll of money. Then he tossed it to her and said, "count that!" before walking to the bathroom. She was shocked at the fat stack he had. She had never felt this much money in her life. All crispy blue-faced hundreds. She counted it out in thousands, placing ten bills in each separate stack on the bed.

"It's thirty-eight hundred dollars. Where did you get this from?" she asked as he came from the bathroom.

That's when he knew he had found the right bitch.

"I had to grind for it," he replied bluntly.

"I need to grind where you be grindin' at …wassup, you goin' to put me on or what?" she asked him.

"I don't know if you ready for all that yet . . . I be really on my shit, so I don't got time to be playin'," he told her.

"Please!" she begged. "I'm not goin' to be playin'... I promise."

Rarri waited for a minute. "Ight, get dressed."

The only thing she had to put on was the same outfit she had on when they met a few days ago. He picked a hotel that was across the street from the mall just for this reason. After she put her clothes on, Rarri counted out fifteen hundred from the roll of money and put the rest in the dresser as she watched him.

"Can you grab my hat out the bathroom?"

"Yea, I got you," she said and hurried to the bathroom. "I don't see it."

"My bad, it's right here," he yelled as he pulled it out of his bag and threw it on. "That's the mall across the street, right?"

"Yea, that's it... what we goin' there for?" Lae Lae asked.

"I can't have you walkin' round wit me in the same fit... we goin' Shopin'," Rarri told her.

Lae Lae couldn't control herself. She ran up and gave him a big hug and kiss on his cheek.

She was like a happy little kid in a candy store at the mall. They bounced from one store to the next. Rarri picked out most of the dresses and heels but he let her pick a couple out herself too. He even stopped at Sally's Beauty

Supply so she could get things she needed to hook her hair up with. They stopped at a nail shop and got her hands and feet done. Rarri picked the design, color and the type of nails to put on her. He got her makeup did professionally at the MAC booth by some white bitch who looked good as fuck at doing makeup, judging by the woman she hooked up who was in front of Lae Lae.

Lae Lae stepped out of the mall looking and feeling better than she ever did. Rarri ordered a pizza about forty minutes before they left the mall so it could arrive at the room shortly after they got there.

Rarri noticed that room service had been to the room because the bed was freshly made, and the trash was empty. Immediately he went and got in the shower while Lae Lae awed over her new clothes and her new look. About five minutes later, the pizza had arrived and Lae Lae was in the bathroom asking him for the money to pay for it.

"Look in my pants."

She went in his pocket and pulled out the seven crumpled up one-dollar bills, then searched the other pockets, finding nothing but a few coins.

"It's only seven dollars in yo pocket. He said the pizza is nineteen eighty-five baby," she told Rarri.

He peeked his head out the shower curtain and said, "Use the money that's in the dresser."

"Oh yea." She had forgotten he put the rest of his money in the dresser before they left.

When she opened the dresser, she saw him put the money in, her heart sank. She quickly opened the other drawers, but all of them were empty.

"It's nothin' in here babe," she yelled to him.

"What?" he yelled back over the running water, barely able to understand her.

"It ain't in here," she replied louder, still looking in the empty drawers like it would just pop up.

Rarri cut the water off and hopped out the shower, quickly grabbing a towel and covered his lower half, not bothering to dry off completely. He stormed to the dresser looking through each one in frustration.

Lae Lae saw the pizza man looking just as frustrated as Rarri.

"Can you give us a minute please?" she asked and closed the door, not waiting for his response.

"I put that shit in here," Rarri barked, pointing at the dresser.

"I know you did babe, I seen you put it in there," she replied.

He looked at her suspiciously.

"I didn't steal yo money," she said with an attitude like she knew what he was thinking.

"I know you didn't," he replied. "It had to be them room service muthafuckas."

Not even two minutes later, Rarri and Lae Lae were in the main office demanding that the person who cleaned their room be searched. Lae Lae was making a bigger scene than Rarri. She was swearing up and down she was going to beat a bitch ass if that money didn't show up. The manager told them if they didn't calm down, they would have to leave the hotel. He promised to get down to the bottom of it and would contact them in their room once he did.

Rarri paced the room back and forth as they waited for the manager. When the phone rang, Rarri rushed to it and picked it up quickly. "Hello…"

He listened in silence for about twenty seconds. "Naw that's alright, thank you," he replied then slammed the phone down.

"What they say?" Lae Lae asked with her eyes glued to Rarri.

"He said he didn't find anything on the person that cleaned the room, but I'm more than welcome to file a police report. I don't fuck wit no police," Rarri said as he sat back on the bed.

"I didn't take the tags off none of the clothes. We could return them and get yo money back," she told him.

"Hell naw: that's out … I got that shit for *you* . . . we ain't takin' nothin' back," he replied.

She felt so many emotions for him at that moment. Here he was, broke with only seven dollars to his name and over a thousand dollars' worth of clothes he bought for her that he could take back easily, but wasn't going to because he wanted her to look good and keep her things.

"So, what we goin' to do?" she asked.

"I don't even know… I ain't got shit to start with now," he replied.

"Yo people's won't front you nothin'?" Lae Lae asked him.

"*She think I sell dope,*" he thought to himself.

"My cuzzin' would, but I'ma have to pay him back like ASAP cause he got a lot of shit goin', plus I still gotta pay my half of the rent," Rarri replied in a defeated tone.

Lae Lae rubbed his back and asked," What *we* gotta do to get back on track? Whatever it is, I'm wit it."

Rarri looked at her. "You sure? Cause I do got *one plan.*"

"I'm wit you babe, whatever it is, I'm down," Lae Lae told him.

An hour later, Rarri had her down on the blade with his grandpa's hoes while the two of them sat in the car and chopped game.

"Good lookin' out on lettin' me hold that four bandz," Rarri told his grandpa.

"Come on now, you know grandpa goin' to always lookout, but I ain't let you hold nothing; I let you have it, that's the least I could do for my 'P' child," his grandpa replied, palming the top of Rarri's head and playfully shook it softly.

Rarri patted the money he had in his pocket. The money he pretended was stolen. What Lae Lae didn't know was that Rarri had the money the whole time. He grabbed it out the drawer when he told her to get his hat out of the bathroom. Rarri bagged a new bitch with an old trick.

Lae Lae turned her first date and was hooked.

"It's easy babe, them niggas be nuttin' fast and they got some little ass dicks," she said, laughing as she undressed for her shower then asked, "Are we goin' back tonight?"

"If you want to," Rarri replied but thought, *"hell yea we goin' back tonight. Nine hundred ain't enough."*

"We might as well get all the money we can, right?" she asked standing there naked.

Rarri looked up from the money he was counting with a smile. "We might as well."

"You know I was thinkin'," she said and paused for a minute. "All the other girls be in they own little groups and shit, watchin' each other's back . . . I know two bitches who would be with this shit fa'sho . . . especially Meeka. She already be fuckin' niggas for free, anyway. I mean, it's up to you though. I was just thinkin'."

Rarri rubbed his chin like he was in deep thought. "Fuck it . . . hit them, bitches, up when you get out the shower."

Lae Lae smiled and hurried to the shower. She texted both of them before she got in and sent them a few pics of her new look. By the time she got out, she had over a dozen text messages and at least half a dozen missed calls from both of them. Lae Lae called Meeka and they three-wayed Fonda. After she told them what he told her to say, them hoes was on they way.

To make sure they were serious, Rarri had them catch the bus to the hotel room he was staying at with Lae Lae. Once they got there, he didn't waste any time giving them the run-down of how shit was going to go.

Meeka was tall and petite, pretty in the face with some ugly ass feet. Her complexion was almost the same as Rarri's, just a shade lighter. Her hair was cut short to neck level with a good-looking curl to it. She was decent; Fonda, on the other hand, needed a good fixing. Light skin don't fit everybody and damn sure not her. The bitch looked like she should have been born black; face whooped, hair torn back. What she did have was body. Fonda was short and thick; real thick. Rarri was going to put a wig on this pig if it was the last thing he did.

He took them shopping, just like he did with Lae Lae, not spending as much, but had them looking and feeling the same as she did. Meeka didn't need that much work to look good like Fonda did. After a good makeover and a blond China bang wig, she was brought to life. Yup, Rarri Frankensteined that hoe and she was ready to go.

After shopping, they got some sleep. He had to switch to a room with two beds. Him and Lae Lae slept in one bed, Meeka and Fonda in the other.

Later that night, his grandpa took him to down the bitches in the right spots as they sat in the car and chopped game again.

"I see you climbin' fast 'P', that's what I'm talkin' bout. Breathe on these hoes," Rarri's grandpa said, then passed him the blunt. Rarri hit the blunt lightly, still scared from the first time he smoked with his grandpa.

"Hell yea… I ain't bout to play wit this shit," he replied after blowing the smoke out.

"That's what I like to hear mane… if you play wit it, you ain't gon stay wit it... gotta mash daily cause tomorrow just a maybe, ya undastand me?" his grandpa schooled then added as he pointed. "speakin' of maybe, look at baby."

When Rarri looked to where his grandpa was pointing at, his blood boiled as he steamed. Meeka was talking to a pimp who was hanging out the sunroof of a red Benz in the middle of the street. Lae Lae was pulling at her arm, but Meeka stood her ground and kept talking to the nigga choppin' at her. She was definitely feeling his game.

Rarri bounced out of the car and stormed towards them.

"Aye, bitch!" he yelled at Meeka.

When Lae Lae seen Rarri, she let Meeka's arm go and walked back to the sidewalk.

"Babe, she ain't listenin'," she yelled to him.

Meeka saw Rarri and power walked up to the pimp's car. Before Rarri could get to her, the pimp was out of the car and putting Meeka in the backseat.

"Get yo ass out the car bitch," Rarri barked as he walked up to the car before the door closed. To his surprise, the 'P' didn't close the door; in fact, he opened it more, but he did put his hand out to stop Rarri from entering or grabbing her out.

"Hold on 'P', what's the deal? Talk to me, mane," the pimp said to Rarri, still with his hand guarding the entrance.

"That's my bitch," Rarri yelled pointing past him.

"Calm down 'P', you movin' too fast," he replied smoothly then added, "What they call you?"

"They call me, Rarri," Rarri told him as he looked him in the face seriously.

"Ok ok that's what's up 'P', nice to meet you," he said cooly playing with his chin hair with a smirk on his face then added looking at Lae Lae," Well look, they call me Success cause I'm the best, ya understand me? And around here, I'ma put ya hoes to the test, just like I do the rest. Ain't a pimp, exempt, no sir. I ain't slackin' on my mackin' just cause *you* ain't crackin'. Slippin' on my pimpin' just 'cause *you* simpin'. I'm out here from the bay to L.A. Money demandin', everybody wanna touch Success, look how close *you* standin'. Askin' for yo bitch back, better get back. I'm bout to break on this bitch like a Kit-Kat, ya understand me? Step ya game up an-

"Success, what up 'P'?" Rarri's grandpa said as he walked up on them. He had to cut Success off cause he was choppin' the fuck out of Rarri, and he knew Success was nowhere near done. He was going to chop until Rarri got hot. Success never gave a fuck about another nigga's feelings. He was a real smooth and cutthroat at the same time type of nigga. Success would probably break his daddy for his momma if she was out of pocket; he was that serious about his pimping. Oh and don't think it's going to be a secret or a discreet encounter when he serve yo papers. The main reason niggas hated to get knocked for a hoe by him was that Success was going to make the biggest scene he possibly could. His favorite thing to do was record a bitch, asking her who she *used* to hoe for and who she got knocked by, then post it on his Snapchat, Instagram and his Facebook. He was a real asshole by nature.

Success was a black-ass, stocky nigga, about 5'8", kept his hair wavy and stayed bussdown with diamonds. He was about 25 or 26. Nobody really knew his age or real name. Success didn't have no close friends 'cause he always tried to get a nigga for his bitch. He one of them type of niggas you just don't bring to yo house for no reason at all. Other pimps might not have liked him, but they respected his pimping without a doubt.

"Oh shit, what up 'P'?" Success said and gave Rarri's grandpa a 'P'-shake, then added, "I'm just servin' and swervin'... check my new toe's out mane."

Success moved out the way so Rarri's grandpa could see Meeka sitting in the back with her head down.

"Oh ok, I see you," his grandpa replied as he looked in the car.

"She bad ain't she 'P'?" Success yelled dramatically. "Say she ain't bad 'P'... say she ain't bad 'P'."

"She bad 'P'... she bad," he replied.

By this time Rarri was hot as fish grease. Success was clowning hard. He wanted to knock this nigga out so bad, his hands were shaking. What really pissed Rarri off was that Success was acting like Rarri wasn't standing there no more, and he was talking loud as fuck. He wanted to knock that smile off his face, but one thing Rarri knew was that this was a no-contact sport. Yea, he probably could beat Success up in a physical fight, but how would that help his game? Success would still be the better 'P' after the fight, no matter how it turned out, and that's what Rarri wanted to be; the better 'P'. He calmed down. A little bit.

Rarri could see Meeka with her head down, grinning like this shit was funny.

"I just got her from bruh, right here," Success said pointing at Rarri and then looked at him.

"Good lookin' out 'P', I really appreciate it, mane. I been on one all day. Matter fact, here."

Success handed Rarri's grandpa his phone, stood next to Rarri, crossed his arms and posed, then dramatically yelled, "flick us up 'P'... flick us the fuck up 'P'."

Rarri's grandpa had to chuckle at that one. Success was a muthafuckin' fool. He couldn't help but act an ass. Rarri moved out of the way.

"I ain't bout to take no picture of y'all 'P'," Rarri's grandpa said through a smile handing him his phone back. "That's my grandson, mane."

Success looked at both of them a couple times and seen the resemblance. "Oh shit 'P', my bad, mane. I ain't even know O.G. was yo folk," he said giving Rarri a 'P'-shake and a hug, taking away the tension.

"It's coo man, I ain't trippin'," Rarri said with a smile for the first time.

"Naw 'P', walk wit me, mane. You could get the bitch back," Success said, putting his arm around Rarri's neck and walking him up to the car. The back door was still open. Rarri's grandpa put his head down almost in embarrassment, but he still was smiling.

"Go on and chop at the bitch 'P'," Success said with his left arm still around Rarri's neck. He had his face to the sky with his eyes closed.

Rarri bent down and looked at Meeka with the biggest smile on his face. "Come out we bout t—"

"Sike!" Success said as he slammed the door shut and started busting up laughing into tears. "I got em good 'P'… I had to mane."

Lae Lae put her hand over her mouth, his grandpa shook his head and Rarri stood bent down for a good five seconds not believing he really just fell for that shit.

Success laughed all the way to the driver's side of his Benz. "You will never forget me 'P' . . . you will never forget the story of Success."

He hopped in and gassed it, leaving Rarri looking at his taillights. Fonda had bent the corner when Rarri, his grandpa and Lae Lae were walking back to the car. She had just came from a date.

"Come on, we out of here," Rarri barked.

The drive was quiet on the way back to the room, and even quieter once they got there. Lae Lae just stared at Rarri sympathetically as she bit on her lip in frustration.

Fonda was looking at both of them, trying to figure out what was going on. After about thirty minutes she finally built up enough courage to ask the million-dollar question.

"Where Meeka at?"

Rarri gave her a cold stare.

This the part of the game that hasn't been taught. What do you tell yo bitch, when she ask about yo other bitch when you know she just got knocked by a nigga flyer than you?

"Shut the fuck up!"

That night, Rarri drilled on Lae Lae and Fonda til the next morning, letting them know how serious he was about his pimping, and how he wasn't mad cause Meeka was obviously a weak ass bitch. It was better she left now than later. He was just hot 'cause he got her all dolled up for the next nigga. Rarri said he was about to put their hoe'n to the test. As soon as he said that, him and Lae Lae secretly thought about Success. He could still hear his squeaky voice in his head. "You will never forget me, P…you will never forget the story of Success."

Rarri shook it off. "Is y'all bitches ready to go hard, or go home?"

"I'm ready to go hard," Lae Lae spoke up, then Fonda," I'm ready to go hard too . . . *we* ain't no weak bitches, fuck Meeka."

How they saw it, Meeka left them too so it was—fuck her.

Rarri called his grandpa and told him he wanted to get a room in the Pit. His grandpa tried to talk him out of it, but Rarri wasn't hearing it; that's where he needed to be. The Pit was one of the roughest areas for pimps *and* hoes. It was a place where a pimp had to worry 24/7 about a bitch choosing another nigga, and it was a place where hoes had to worry about gorilla pimps either kidnapping them, robbing them, rapping them, all types of shit. It was the Pit of Pimps.

The hotel his grandpa took them to was a far cry from the one they had just left from. Rarri had Lae Lae put the rooms in her name. He told her to get two separate rooms right next to each other. He did this so one room could be used for a place to take the tricks, and the other could be used for them to sleep in. He stressed the fact that having two rooms meant going twice as hard, and they agreed.

There were pimps hanging out in cars and standing around the parking lot, smoking weed and chopping game. Some pimps had buckets, some had foreigns. Some were fly, others was dusty. Some tall, some short, some fat, some skinny. It was probably one of every type of pimp there. That's when Rarri thought of what kind he was going to be, and that was the best.

"Fuck!" he said in his head as he once again thought about Success, hearing that squeaky voice of his. *"You will never forget me 'P'... you will never forget the story of Success."*

Lae Lae and Fonda returned to the car with the room keys. Lae Lae gave Rarri two keys, one for each room.

"Grab y'all shit and go on to the room . . . I'ma be up there in a minute," Rarri instructed.

Lae Lae and Fonda got their bags from the back seat and headed to the room with their heads down. As soon as they were about fifteen feet away from the car, about six or seven pimps ran up on them, followed by three more, and started chopping at the bitches hard, trying to make them smile or look up, but they stayed in pocket. A couple of them even stood blocking in front of them, but Lae Lae and Fonda just moved around, keeping their heads down. One pimp even bent down low, as he back stepped in front of them while chopping his game trying to get them to make eye contact with him or laugh. He was doing all type of silly shit while he chopped at them. Waving his hands, making goofy faces, barking at them like a dog, making monkey noises and shit. The nigga even got on his knees and started chasing them. All the other pimps started busting up laughing, even Rarri, and his grandpa as they watched from the car.

Ain't no rules on how to chop on a bitch; you could chop however you please. Some niggas chop to make a bitch cry, and some chop to make her laugh. Some chop to build her up and some chop to put her down. Shid, some niggas don't even chop at all 'cause they don't need to; bitches just hoe up off of swag, personality or gangsta for them. It could be the smallest or the biggest thing to do that would knock a bitch, but it does have to be something. It could be something you ain't even know you did or the fact that you don't pay her no attention like other niggas, so she mad cause you ain't do nothing at all, but you still did something by not doing nothing, because sometimes doing nothing does something to her. Yea, it's that crazy. But if you got a girl who ain't a hoe/prostitute, you don't just come out and say, " Hey, will you be my prostitute and sell that pussy for me?" and she'll say, "I surely will sell this pussy for you." In a perfect world, it probably would work like that, but in reality, it's nowhere near that simple.

If a bitch told you she only prostituted because a pimp *asked* her to, more than likely *the bitch* is a liar. A pimp wouldn't need game if it was that easy. Choosing is a choice and it's *her* choice to choose, but that mean she'll get chose. Don't get me wrong, it's gorillas out here who be forcing bitches into prostitution, but a gorilla ain't a pimp, he a trafficker. Giving bitches rides and blacking they eyes. Ain't nothing pimp, player or cool about him. He can't let her leave cause he don't know how to breathe. Only a chump gotta throw a bitch in the trunk and force her to do some shit. A real 'P' will pop that muthafucka open and say, "bitch get in," letting her jump in her damn self on some fly shit. Then have her get back out cause he was only testing his game and seeing how far her hoe'n was really goin.

"I see you tryna put yo pimpin' on another level… the Pit goin' to either make you or break you, Rarri; ain't no in-between in this here game, ya understand me?" his grandpa schooled as he looked over at him.

Rarri looked at his grandpa for a second then back out the front window. "Only hoes break grandpa… only hoes break," he replied and got out of the car. He walked right up to the group of pimps and introduced himself like a real nigga would.

"He goin' to be some real pimpin'," Rarri's grandpa said to himself with a proud smile and pulled off.

Rarri chopped game for about thirty minutes, getting the run-down of the area from the other pimps. They swapped numbers after blowing some weed his grandpa slid him. All of them was cool as fuck, especially the nigga who got on his knees and started chasing Lae Lae and Fonda. His name was King Doe.

King Doe was a short, brown skinned ugly little nigga with a lot of tattoos and some long nappy dreads. He had about four chains on. All of them looked to be 10k. King Doe was fly though. Rarri could see that most of his money probably went towards his clothes. King Doe was funny than a muthafucka too, it was hard not to see that his personality made him a good 'P'. He could make hoes laugh, and sometimes they've been crying for so long, all they wanna do is fuck with someone who could make them smile.

Rarri noticed a girl approaching them who didn't have her head down. She was about 5'4", caramel complexion, skinny thick and had on a black weave that was styled covering her right eye. Her and Rarri made eye contact as she walked by them. Her eyes were a beautiful light brown, well the eye he saw. She smiled and kept walking. Rarri looked at the other pimps like they were crazy. They had harassed the fuck out of Lae Lae and Fonda a moment ago, but let this bitch just walk by not paying her no mind.

"Aye!" Rarri yelled after her and she quickly turned around with a smile.

"Hold on 'P'," King Doe said, putting his arm out to stop Rarri from leaving. "I ain't even goin' to let you go out like that."

Her smile faded as she dropped her head and walked off sadly.

"What you mean 'P', y'all ain't just see that bitch out of pocket? She was *eyein'* a nigga," Rarri said excitedly.

All of them started busting up laughing. Rarri didn't understand what was so funny.

"You a foo 'P'," King Doe said between laughs then added, "you's a muthafuckin' foo 'P'…that shit comedy," and started laughing harder.

"What y'all talkin' bout? I don't get it," Rarri asked then admitted.

"You said . . . you said... hold on wait up… let me catch my breath 'P'… let, me, catch, my, breath, 'P'... got damn… aw shit . . . my stomach hurt mane… I think I'ma throw up . . . I think I'ma throw up . . . aw I'm good . . . aw shit… ok I'm good, I'm good 'P', I'm good." King Doe wiped the sweat from his forehead and the tears from his eyes, trying his hardest to stop laughing. "You said… *you* said the bitch was *eyein'* you."

"What's so funny about that?" Rarri asked with a sour expression.

"The bitch only got one eye 'P', that was Betty Wap," King Doe joked then added, "Fetty Wap lil sister."

They all started laughing again.

"Don't nobody fuck wit her… she ain't got no folks . . . nobody ain't tryna have they pimpin' be the laugh of the Pit, fuck no," another pimp named Kali told Rarri.

Rarri kind of felt bad for her, but he ain't want to make no joke of his pimping either. Especially not right now; he was trying to bounce back from yesterday. He wasn't going to fuck with Betty Wap, but he wasn't going to be mean to her either.

"Oh ok, good lookin' out 'P'," Rarri told them chuckling to himself and giving them 'P'-shakes. "I'ma get wit y'all later," he said then pushed to his room.

When he got to the room, Lae Lae and Fonda was already dolling each other up ahead of time. Rarri smiled and threw his bag on the bed.

"That's what I'm talkin' bout. If y'all stay ready, we ain't gotta get ready . . . we ain't doin' no playin' out here, y'all was lookin' good out there. Ain't nothin' better than a hoe in pocket, if a bitch lookin' she goin' to get tooken'. We got one week to make what we need, then we out this bitch. I need a band or better from both of y'all. Don't even think about goin' to sleep short, cause for damn sho y'all goin' to be short of sleep fuckin' wit me. This is where it count at, if y'all could make it here, y'all could make it anywhere. We need to stack up and move on, get out our own whip and all the shit."

"We goin' to get our own car, babe?" Lae Lae asked excitedly.

"You damn right we is, ain't no need for us to keep gettin' rides from muthafuckas . . . it's two of y'all we gotta elevate. After we get up, we goin' to my spot, fuck these motels," Rarri gamed.

They was ready to get going, the only thing stopping them was time. They still had a few hours until it was time to step-out. That's when Rarri thought he might as well break Fonda in and see what that pussy felt like. She was ugly, but that body wasn't. Rarri fucked both them bitches together, then sent them out happy as fuck a couple of hours later. Fonda couldn't believe Rarri could fuck the way he did. Lae Lae had to pin her down to stop running so much from the dick. Fonda creamed so much, Rarri's dick was almost completely white. He didn't even know it was possible for a bitch to cream that much in one session. Fa'sho, Rarri was hitting that again. Lae Lae freaky ass sucked him clean after the session was over.

Rarri hoped in the shower, got dressed and pushed out. He didn't have the designer shit everybody else wore. All he brought out there was his different pairs of 501 jeans, two black hoodies, two pair of black and white forces and some regular white tees. Oh, and a black and gray Raiders hat. He didn't bring no jewelry or money with him.

Rarri didn't see none of the niggas he met earlier so he bailed off, walking down the street smoking a blunt. He didn't want to get lost, so he didn't bend no corners. Rarri was just trying to meet as many 'P's as possible and get his name out there while he was going to be around, and maybe, just maybe, come up on another bitch.

It was a lot of police out, harassing bitches and shit, trying to catch them slipping.

He walked by a group of pimps who was congregating and Poli-Pimpin'. They were standing next to a row of foreign cars, all wearing designer clothes and buss down.

"What up 'P'," Rarri said as he was walking by, but none of them responded; they just stopped talking.

Soon as he passed them, he could hear them laughing. They was the pimps too good to talk to pimps that wasn't on their level. Real conceited ass niggas. Pretty boys wearing colored contacts and cotton candy cologne, acting cool ass niggas. Basically, a circle of Pretty Me da P's. Rarri wouldn't have hung out with them no how. He just kept pushing; confrontations wasn't going to benefit anyone.

When hoes seen him coming, they crossed the street to the other side. When he was far enough, they would go back to their corner. It was more hoes out than Rarri had seen on the other blades his grandpa took him to, and the pimps were jumping out, pulling over, running up and basically throwing shit at bitches.

After walking for about maybe a mile, he turned around and headed back to the room. He passed all the same people. The hoes crossed the street again, and the funny acting pimps laughed once he passed again. Rarri was almost to the room when Lae Lae came running from around the corner crying with two niggas chasing her. She immediately ran behind Rarri.

"Babe, they tryin' to get me," she cried.

The two dudes stepped in front of Rarri and he noticed they had guns in their hands and was breathing hard. One had dreads and the other had short hair. Both of them had on black hoodies with black cotton gloves. Their eyes were bloodshot red and real glossy.

"What's goin' on 'P'?" Rarri asked matching their stare.

The two didn't say nothing. They just looked at him angrily. The one with the short hair bit down on his lip hard as he looked at Rarri. Rarri knew that look they was giving him. It was that '*nigga I could kill you* look, and they knew that look Rarri was giving them was that *I don't give a fuck* look. That moment was tense and terrifying at the same time.

"We out," the one with the dreads said and they pushed off. Real always recognized real.

Rarri turned to Lae Lae. "What the fuck was they chasin' you for?"

"I don't know, they just hopped out the car and started runnin' towards me, so I ran," she replied honestly.

"Call Fonda and see where that bitch at," Rarri instructed and then continued walking to the room with Lae Lae in front of him.

"She standin' in front of the hotel. I could see her, right there," Lae Lae pointed ahead.

As soon as they walked up, Fonda handed Rarri the money she had made.

"How much is this?" he asked as he counted it.

"$990," she replied happily smiling. "I told you I was goin' to get it, daddy."

"You still short. I told you don't think about gettin' no sleep until you bring a band back," Rarri told her. "Go get the rest."

"You goin' to really send me to go get ten more dollaz?" Fonda asked in disbelief.

Rarri gave her a look that said it all, then he looked at Lae Lae. "What you got?"

Lae Lae pulled out a ball of money and handed it to him with her head down.

"What the fuck is this?" Rarri asked flickering through the crumpled-up bills.

"A hundred," she mumbled lowly.

"A hundred, huh? Well look, teamwork is dream work, so y'all go get that nine hundred and ten dollars, *together* and don't come back without it," Rarri replied and walked off on them heading to the room. He didn't shout or scream at them; actually, he talked to them with a smile on.

"Come on bitch. Let's go get this money," Fonda told Lae Lae then added jokingly, "broke ass."

"Fuck you, hoe," Lae Lae laughed as they walked off. "How did you come up on that shit so fast?"

"Girrrl, you know how I do," Fonda replied with a smile. Everybody knew Fonda was good at stealing.

Lae Lae's mouth dropped in disbelief. "You stole it?" she asked, eyes crack head wide.

"Hell yea, I stole it, these niggas be slippin' . . . I mean, I went on a few dates, but fuck that, I'ma get this shit anyway I can. He didn't tell us we couldn't jugg," Fonda told her.

Lae Lae bit down on her lip as she thought. "Show me how to do it too. I ain't tryna be out here all night if I ain't got to."

"It's easy. Just go in they pocket when y'all fuckin' or when you suckin' they dick . . . it *'would'* be better if we both was in the car though, cause sometime that shit don't be workin'," Fonda schooled Lae Lae.

"Ok, ok I get it. Yea, I think I could do that," she replied.

"How much?" A paisa yelled as he followed them slowly in his work truck.

"Which one?" Fonda asked in her Mexican accent she always put on when talking to Mexicans.

"Both! How much for both?" he asked back.

"A hundred fifty ," Fonda told him as she and Lae Lae slowed their pace.

"Ok! Come! Come!" he replied excitedly.

They looked at each other and smiled, then hurried to the car and got in.

When Rarri bent one of the corners in the motel, he saw Betty Wap standing in front of his door knocking.

"What's the deal?" he asked as he approached, which startled her a bit.

"Oh nothin', I was just wonderin' if um... if-if-if, if you was tryna smoke?" Betty Wap asked nervously showing him the rolled blunt in her hand.

Rarri looked at her with a sour expression for a moment then said coldly as he put the key in the door, "Hell naw."

Betty Wap's head sank and she turned to walk away sadly.

Rarri let her take a few steps.

"Aye!" he called after her then added with a smile on his face. "I'm just fuckin' wit you… come on."

"Oh my God," she said with her hand over her heart and inhaled to catch her breath, then exhaled dramatically. "I thought you was serious."

"Naw, you good," Rarri told her, then walked in the room with Betty Wap behind him.

"Here, you could spark it," Betty Wap said handing him the blunt.

"What's yo name?" Rarri asked as he fished in his pocket for a lighter.

"Marquesha. . . but everybody calls me Betty Wap," she replied happily. She didn't seem bothered at all by the name Betty Wap, it actually sounded as if she liked it.

"Ok, ok. They call me Rarri," he told her as he lit the blunt and inhaled the smoke. His face became sour and he tried to blow the smoke out as quickly as possible while handing her the blunt back.

"What's wrong? Are you ok?" Betty Wap asked with a worried expression.

"Hell naw, that weed bullshit," Rarri replied while trying to spit out the shake that flew in his mouth and added, "put that shit out."

She rushed and put it out in the ashtray on the little dresser next to them. "Oh, I'm sorry… the dude I got it from said it was top shelf."

Betty Wap looked sad now cause she knew she just blew her moment of ever getting Rarri. She nervously finger-combed the bang over her eye, which was something she always did unintentionally when nervous, scared, happy or sad.

"Well, that nigga don't know good weed," he told her as he went to his bag, unzipped it, grabbed a nugget from a plastic baggie and a blunt then handed it to her. "Roll that up."

Betty Wap couldn't believe it. She thought fa'sho he was going to make her leave. She rolled the blunt like a happy little kid. Rarri was surprised at how perfect Betty Wap could roll.

As he talked with her, he couldn't help but notice how sweet she was. Rarri could tell Betty Wap had a really good heart. She was a cool person, just a little dingy and a little gullible. She had the dorkiest yet cutest laugh he had ever heard. Betty Wap could talk, talk, talk and keep talking, then turn around and talk some more. She told story after story after story. Rarri could see she was having the time of her life talking, so he didn't stop her; he actually liked her talking. He thought a lot of the stories she told were funny, some of them made him laugh almost into tears. She knew everything about everybody. If Rarri hadn't known better already, he would have thought everybody around was her friend cause Betty Wap didn't say a bad thing about nobody. She even spoke highly of King Doe, like he was her friend or something. "King Doe! Yea that's big bro right there," she said a couple times. Even though they treated Betty Wap bad, she didn't care cause they were all she really had. She talked to Rarri for hours between rolling more blunts.

"I ain't tryin' to be rude but . . . "Rarri paused for a moment, then asked the question he had been wondering about all night. "What happened to yo eye?"

"Oh, my daddy shot me," she replied like it was nothing then asked, "you wanna see it?"

Rarri waited a moment, confused by her response and how nonchalant she was about it.

"Yea, fuck it, let me see that muthafucka," Rarri told her as he leaned towards her with both hands on his knees.

Betty Wap leaned in, meeting him halfway and lifted her bang as she cleared her throat.

Her eye looked like it belonged on a monster or one of them crazy looking pit bulls. It was pink and meaty looking. Kinda tight like a China-man's eye, but without the white part and slightly wet with a little sleep in the corner.

After examining it for a minute, Rarri leaned back and Betty Wap let her bang fall down, finger combing it back over her eye how she liked it.

"Damn, so yo pimp did that to you?" Rarri asked in disbelief, wondering why somebody would do someone so sweet like this.

"Uh-uh, my daddy, like my father, he shot me when I was six," Betty Wap told him again like it was nothing.

Rarri's heart sank to his stomach.

"What he do that for?" he asked through hurt eyes and a hint of anger on his face.

"Well… he was my momma pimp. I had got sick for about a week straight and my momma had to keep runnin' me back and forth to the doctor 'cause I kept getting sicker. One night, he came in my room and said I was comin' between his money and shot me in the face," she said.

"Where they at now?" was all he could think to ask.

"My daddy in jail, still. They gave him twenty years for shootin' me in my eye . . . and my momma... well... I don't know where she at," Betty Wap replied then added, "she probably still mad at me."

"What she mad at you for?" Rarri asked in disbelief.

"Duhh, for takin' my daddy away from her," she said like Rarri should have known that already.

"Betty Wap, he shot you in *yo* face. How is that yo fault?" Rarri asked, trying to make sense of the situation.

"Cause if I wouldn't have *stayed* sick, my momma wouldn't have had to keep missin' money, and my daddy wouldn't have had to shoot me," Betty Wap told him like it was one plus two equals three simple.

"Betty Wap . . . he didn't have to shoot you 'cause you got sick. Kids get sick all the time. . . ain't no way in hell I would shoot my own daughter. Especially over no shit like that," Rarri replied.

Betty Wap didn't seem at all moved by what Rarri was saying. The whole time he was talking, Betty Wap was smelling her top lip wondering what it smelled like as she looked and listened to Rarri.

"And that's why they say the game ain't what it used to be . . . my daddy don't let no bitch come between his money, not even his own daughter," Betty Wap schooled then added, "he some real pimpin' . . . my momma only mad cause he in jail, but when he come home, we goin' to all be a family again . . . just watch, you'll see."

Rarri couldn't believe what Betty Wap was saying. You would think she would be mad at her father for doing what he did to her, but she actually praised him and couldn't wait for him to get out of prison, cause when he did, they were surely going to live happily ever after, just like people did in the movies.

Rarri knew at that moment why Betty Wap talked about everybody like they were her friends, even though they treated her bad. She had been done worse. Waaaay worse. In Betty Wap's world, they all loved her and only treated her bad cause they had to. One day, somebody was going to see she was worthwhile and let her be on the team. Betty Wap wouldn't be picky either. She didn't care who team she was on; she just wanted to belong to some *real pimpin*.

Chapter 16

Betty Wap was willing to do almost anything. Whatever she had to do, she would do no questions asked. Pimps would always make her do silly things with promises of choosing her *if* she could do the silly shit they told her to do.

Once, a pimp told her he would pick her up if she could do a thousand push-ups. Betty Wap immediately got on the ground and started doing as many as she could, no questions asked. A crowd formed and people laughed, but she didn't care cause she was finally getting chose. By the time Betty Wap finished, the crowd was gone, and it was just her and the pimp. She got off the ground exhausted, dirty and sweaty. She was so out of breath she couldn't stand up straight.

"So, what . . . corner . . . you want me to… work?" Betty Wap asked between breaths, with her hands on her knees looking up at the pimp.

"That one right there," he replied pointing.

When Betty Wap looked up and seen he was pointing at the moon, her heart sank as did her head. The pimp just walked off laughing.

Betty Wap told herself that the reason she never got chose was because she wasn't doing what they told her to do correctly. Even the time she ended up in the hospital for drinking dishwashing liquid, she swear to this day it's only because she drunk it too fast, being in a rush to get chose.

"Next time, I'ma take my time," Betty Wap told people when she got out the hospital.

"No pimp want a hoe who always fuckin' up," she reminded herself, constantly.

Rarri felt sorry for Betty Wap, but she didn't feel sorry for herself; that's what he liked about her. He promised to look out for Betty Wap while he was around. He wasn't going to choose her, but that didn't mean they couldn't be friends.

In some strange way, Rarri liked Betty Wap. He didn't know why; he just did. She seemed innocent, even though he knew she was a prostitute, her mind seemed pure and uncorrupted by all the bullshit life had put her through. She seemed unphased by it all and was determined no matter what to keep trying.

Rarri grabbed another nugget of weed and a blunt. "Let's smoke one more," he said handing the weed and blunt to Betty Wap, then pushed to the bathroom to take a piss.

After using the restroom, Rarri washed his face in the sink and tried to forget about Betty Wap's life story that killed his high. He still couldn't believe what her dad had done to her.

"That's a bitch ass nigga," Rarri said to himself as he dried his face with a towel. Then he inhaled and exhaled, pushing the bullshit to the back of his head as he looked himself over in the mirror and walked out of the bathroom.

"So, I was thinkin', maybe you could slide back through on—"

Rarri stopped dead in his tracks when he saw Betty Wap laid across the bed completely naked in what looked like her sexy position. "What you"

Before Rarri could finish his question, the door flew open and in came Lae Lae and Fonda. Their conversation of laughs and giggles was cut short when they saw Betty Wap on the bed laid back with the unlit blunt in her mouth and Rarri standing there like he was just about to hop in the bed and beat that thang up.

Betty Wap hurried and covered herself with the blanket, startled by their interruption.

Lae Lae and Fonda's mouths both dropped open with a disbelieving smile as they stood in the doorway.

"You want us to come back?" Lae Lae asked and tightened her lips to break her smile like she always did.

Rarri gave her his *bitch please* face. "Come in and close the door," he said to Lae Lae and Fonda, then turned to Betty Wap. "Betty Wap put yo clothes on."

Lae Lae and Fonda came in and closed the door, and Betty Wap put her clothes on not even the slightest bit embarrassed.

Lae Lae and Fonda sat on the other bed with their heads down trying not to laugh.

"What y'all got?" Rarri asked.

Lae Lae reached in her bra and pulled out a roll of money, then handed it to him with her head still down trying not to make eye contact.

"It's all here?" Rarri asked as he looked down and flicked through the bills counting.

Lae Lae shook her head up and down, but Rarri didn't see.

"You don't hear me talkin'?" he asked looking at them.

"Yea, it's all there," Lae Lae replied.

By the sound of her voice, Rarri could tell she was holding her laugh. "Oh, this shit funny to y'all, huh."

Lae Lae and Fonda busted up laughing. Betty Wap's crazy-ass started laughing too not knowing what they was laughing at, she was just laughing 'cause they was laughing. Rarri looked at Betty Wap and started busting up laughing too.

He knew Lae Lae and Fonda was laughing 'cause they thought he was about to fuck Betty Wap, and Betty Wap was just laughing 'cause well, that's just Betty Wap. She didn't even know why she was laughing. That was just her way of trying to fit in.

Rarri ended up explaining the situation right there in front of Betty Wap so it wasn't no misunderstandings. He explained to Betty Wap that he did think she was beautiful and that he would love to pick her up, but the timing was wrong ... he had a lot going on at the moment. Rarri told her to give him some time to get himself right because he wouldn't want to misguide her by not having his things in order when bringing new toes to the table. Then he kindly excused her but told her to come back later to smoke and talk. Betty Wap walked out of the room happier than she was coming in with the thoughts of Rarri one day picking her up once he got back on his feet.

"Aw babe, you so sweet," Lae Lae told him after Betty Wap left.

"Yea, that was nice daddy," Fonda added.

They knew he would never fuck with Betty Wap; he was just being nice.

"Do me a favor and treat her nice would y'all? Everybody around here be doin' her foul she think they her friends but they not," Rarri informed.

"We got you, daddy," Fonda assured. "Ight," he replied with a smile then added, "Now go hop y'all fonky asses in the shower so we could go to sleep."

Lae Lae and Fonda threw pillows at him playfully then went and got in the shower.

Rarri recounted his money and threw on something more comfortable.

Chapter 17

Money was so good that week, Rarri decided they were going to stay a little longer. He had found a car on Craigslist, and after brokering the deal with the owner, Rarri called his grandpa and asked him if he could take him to pick it up.

"Y'all bitches wake the fuck up," Rarri said as he snatched the covers off of Lae Lae and Fonda, then went and opened the curtains letting the sun into the room.

"Noooo! We just laid down," Lae Lae cried and put a pillow over her head. Fonda didn't say anything. She just covered herself with the bedsheets.

"Ain't nobody tryna hear that shit, get the fuck up," he said taking her pillow and snatching the sheets off of Fonda. Both moaned and whined in frustration. "I'ma be outside. Just throw something on and come on," Rarri added, then pushed out of the room.

Lae Lae and Fonda dolled up a little bit, cause wasn't no way in hell they was stepping out looking the way they were looking just waking up. Lae Lae was talking shit all the way to the parking lot.

"This nigga fuckin' trippin'. I don't know about this shit no more, I'm bou—"

Lae Lae's mouth dropped when she saw Rarri sitting halfway out of a Dodge Challenger with the music blasting as he rolled a blunt. It was candy red sitting on 22's.

"Yea bitch, you bout to what? Huh? I can't hear you," Fonda teased Lae Lae then ran up to Rarri. "Daddy tell me this your car! Tell me this your's daddy."

"I told y'all we ain't out here playin' no games, ya understand me? This ain't shit, we bout to go the fuck on one," Rarri told them excitedly then stepped on the brake and pushed the ignition button starting the car up. "Y'all bitches get in."

Fonda hurried and ran to the passenger side, beating Lae Lae by a split second, then hopped in the front seat.

"Uh-uh bitch get in the back," Lae Lae told Fonda.

"Naw, I got here first . . . don't be mad 'cause I beat you," Fonda laughed and pulled the lever lifting the seat up for Lae Lae to get in the back.

"First of all, I got here first. I'm the one that called you and told you to come fuck wit *us*, remember? Or did you forget?" Lae Lae replied with attitude as she busted Fonda's bubble, taking the smile right off of her face.

"Wow, are you serious?" Fonda asked with a disbelieving expression. She hoped her longtime friend was just playing around.

"Hell yea! What the fuck?" Lae Lae said with a disgusted look on her face.

"Whatever," Fonda replied, rolling her eyes, then got into the back seat.

Lae Lae tightened her lips to break her smile as Fonda got into the back, then she got in cheesing from ear to ear.

"Damn babe, this shit fly," Lae Lae told Rarri as she rubbed her hands across the dashboard, then over the leather of his seat. She peeped her head in the back and nodded in approval, admiring the interior. When she turned to Fonda, Fonda was looking at her with her sourest expression. Lae Lae dramatically rolled her eyes with the same look on her face but turned back around with a smile. "So… where we goin' babe?"

Sometimes, that's all it takes for a friendship between two hoes to be easily broken—the front seat."

Rarri took them to Denny's and talked about the next moves to be made. He told them they were going to stay in the Pit for two more weeks and be gone after that to his house. He couldn't help but notice how distant Fonda was acting. She barely even spoke two words the whole time there.

"What's wrong wit you?" he asked.

"Nothin' I'm good," Fonda replied as she picked at her food.

"You sure?" Rarri asked, not believing her.

"Yup," she lied, trying to avoid eye contact with him so he couldn't read her.

"I gotta use the bathroom," Fonda added then dropped her fork with attitude and walked off to the restroom.

Rarri watched her walk away with a concerned look on his face. “What’s wrong with that bitch?”

Lae Lae looked back to make sure Fonda was out of ear’s reach then turned back to Rarri. “I don’t know, but I would watch that bitch, babe. She sneaky as fuck . . . she stay stealin’ from muthafuckas. That’s why she don’t got nowhere to go now... and this mornin’ before we came out the room, she was talkin’ bout how she tired of this shit and all that, but changed up as soon as she seen you sittin’ in the car . . . I mean, I fuck wit her, but I don’t trust her like that . . . especially after that shit wit Meeka.”

“Ight . . . keep an eye on that bitch,” Rarri told her and continued eating his food.

When Fonda came back the vibe was awkward, so Rarri asked for the check and bounced back to the room. Soon as they got there, Fonda took a shower and dolled up. Lae Lae was in the bed laying down watching T.V., and Rarri was sitting at the table pre-rolling blunts when she came out of the bathroom, dressed and ready to go. Rarri watched suspiciously as Fonda grabbed her purse and cell phone, then double looked at herself in the mirror, straightening her wig and clothes. Lae Lae sat up in the bed looking at Fonda, hoping she wasn’t doing what she thought she was about to do.

“Where you goin’?” Rarri asked.

“You said go hard or go home, right? Well I’m tired of sittin’ in this muthafucka,” Fonda replied, and Lae Lae sighed in relief, but that was short-lived once Fonda continued.

“We sittin’ in here like some lazy ass bitches when we could be out bringing more money to the table... I’m not bout to be playin’ wit my hoe'n no more... yea that car coo or whatever but it’s other bitches who puttin’ they daddies in foreigns, fly ass chains, and designer clothes. They hoe'n ain’t no better than mine, I could put you in all that shit too . . .” Fonda looked over at Lae Lae and added, “by myself,” then walked to the door. She looked at Lae Lae again, this time with a smirk. It was a *bitch please* smirk. Fonda rolled her eyes and happily opened the door and left.

Lae Lae looked over and seen the look on Rarri’s face. It was a look of surprise, happiness, and approval all in one. The fact that he didn’t even say a word let Lae Lae know he felt what Fonda was saying. Lae Lae smacked her lips, got out of the bed and went to the shower. When she got out, Rarri watched her dress with a slight attitude, taking her sweet time, huffing, puffing and blowing and shit.

“I know you ain’t trippin’ on no competition,” Rarri teased as he walked up and grabbed on Lae Lae’s waist pulling her towards him.

“Move,” she cried in irritation as she tried to free herself from his grip.

“What you mean move?” he asked playfully and started tickling her as he wrestled her to the bed. Rarri knew her spots enough by now. Lae Lae was laughing uncontrollably and trying to break free.

“Aww! Ok, ight. I’m done,” Rarri screamed in pain as Lae Lae bit him on his chest.

"Uh-uh... no you ain't," Lae Lae replied, still with her bite locked on his chest and started undoing his pants. "Now you gotta beat this pussy up," she added as she pulled his dick out slid him inside of her wet pussy.

"Fuck," Rarri moaned as he thrust slowly getting her more and more wet each time. Lae Lae was still biting on his chest which turned out to turn him on. After about 5 minutes of missionary, he turned her around and started beating it up from the back. Rarri was pounding her shit, making her pussy talk.

"KNOCK! KNOCK! KNOCK! KNOCK! KNOCK!"

"Hold up I'm comin'!" he yelled.

"Me too," Lae Lae moaned. "Oh shit, I'm comin'."

"KNOCK! KNOCK! KNOCK! KNOCK! KNOCK!"

"I said hold up, I'm comin'," Rarri yelled again, then started fuckin' Lae Lae faster and harder as he controlled her by the waist. When he felt the build-up, he pulled out and nutted on her ass. He quickly grabbed the towel Lae Lae had used to dry off with from the shower and wiped himself with it before passing it to her. She wiped her pussy and the back of her ass off, then pulled her dress back down.

"KNOCK! KNOCK! KNOCK! KNOCK!"

Rarri snatched the door open.

"Hey," Betty Wap said, letting herself in. "Hey, Lae Lae."

"Hey wassup Wap?" Lae Lae replied as she grabbed her purse and headed out of the room like a happy little kid.

Betty Wap had been stopping by on the regular now. Rarri kinda looked forward to their daily conversations, well really Betty Wap's talking. After a week, she still didn't run out of shit to talk about, and she kept Rarri updated on what was going on around the area. Betty Wap might have been in denial about a lot of shit and desperate than a muthafucka, but she was no dummy. What Betty Wap lacked was commonsense; other than that, she could count, read and hold a decent conversation. Her life was so corrupted by pimping and hoeing, she believed it more than most people. Bitches got different reasons for being in the game; some hoe to pay the rent, others hoe to pay a pimp, but Betty Wap hoe'd because she was raised to believe that's what she was put here to do. She believed in hoe'n just as much as any pimp believed in pimpin, and with or without a pimp, Betty Wap was going to keep hoe'n.

The fact that her and Rarri's parents were in the game is probably why they got along so well. Rarri couldn't understand why he understood Betty Wap out of all people, but he did. He felt connected to her, but not in a sexual way. It was more of a homeboy type of connection. Rarri felt bad too, because eventually at some point in time, he was going to have to let her know he wasn't going to fuck with her how she wanted to fuck with him.

After Rarri told her he would pick her up once he got on his feet, Betty Wap couldn't wait. All she mainly talked about was how her life would be better when she started fucking with Rarri. She had it all planned out, from the corners she was going to work, the times she would work, to what she would wear and some more shit. Betty Wap even showed Rarri a list of all the pimps who was going to be mad after seeing how hard she was going for him and what they missed out on. She made the list after leaving his room the morning he told her he would pick her up once he was on his feet. Betty Wap didn't show him the list of the future kids they were going to have when they decided to settle down and get out the game. Naw, not yet. She would wait until the time was right to show him that list 'cause it was special. She kept that one on her at all times, just in case she thought of something new to add. The only time Betty Wap lied to Rarri was about having to use the restroom so much. Secretly, she was only making adjustments to the list.

"So, I see you got some new wheels," Betty Wap said as she sat down on the bed.

"Yea, I grabbed a little bucket," Rarri replied, then lit one of his blunts and sat back down at the table.

"That ain't no bucket . . . it's a 2012, but it's still fly," she said excitedly.

"How you know what year it is?" Rarri asked.

"I love cars . . . I got all types of car magazines that I collect. But anyway, now that you got some wheels are you pickin' me up?" Betty Wap asked with a smile.

"I just gotta handle a few more things," Rarri lied as he passed her the blunt.

Betty Wap studied his face with a now unsure expression and a half-smile. She wouldn't say nothing to Rarri, but Betty Wap didn't believe him. She knew the look on his face better than anybody. It was the same look she had been getting her entire life. Betty Wap pushed that feeling to the same place in her mind where all the other things she refused to believe were at and told herself what she wanted to hear. Just like that, Betty Wap was back smiling.

"Ok, well don't keep me waitin' forever." She hit the blunt then added, "It's money to be made we missin' out on."

"I'm already knowin' Wap... I just thought about somethin'," Rarri said with a confused look.

"What's that?" Betty Wap asked.

"You stay comin' over here, but ain't never invited me to yo room," he told her.

"Oh," she replied and hit the blunt.

"Oh? What you mean oh, Wap?" Rarri asked as he grabbed the blunt from her, took a pull then added, "What, a nigga ain't good enough to slide through? I ain't trippin'. That muthafucka probably dirty, anyway," Rarri chuckled as he thought about how dirty Betty Wap's room probably was. He imagined old pizza boxes and McDonald's bags scattered all over the place. Dirty clothes, filled ashtrays of cigarette butts smoked to the filters along with boo-boo weed roaches. He didn't even wanna think about the bathroom, fuck no.

"Um no. My room ain't never dirty. I clean my shit daily, even after it's serviced, so yea," Betty Wap replied with a hint of attitude behind her smile.

"Yea?" he asked with his *yea the fuck right* expression.

"Boy, ain't nobody gotta lie to you," she laughed but was looking at Rarri thinking how fine he was. Betty Wap done undressed Rarri about 20 times since she walked through the door.

"Well come on, let's push to yo shit," Rarri said and headed towards the door.

"Can I use the bathroom real quick?" Betty Wap asked. "Dang," she added like he was being rude.

"Aw shit she stallin' 'P'," he joked running in small circles and laughing hard as hell.

"Ain't nobody stallin', I gotta use the bathroom for real," she replied as she walked to the bathroom and closed the door behind her.

***

Betty Wap put the key in the door to her room then looked at Rarri.

"Come on, let's just go back to my shit," Rarri said, turning around to walk away.

Betty Wap rolled her eye and opened the door, then walked in with Rarri behind her. Soon as he walked in, he was stunned.

Betty Wap wasn't bullshitting. Her room was spotless, but what really shocked him was how different her room was from all the others. Unlike other rooms, Betty Wap's had a stove area, a small living room with two sofas, a coffee table and an entertainment center with a 50-inch flat-screen T.V. She walked back and opened another door that led into the bedroom. In there, was two twin beds, a computer desk, and another 50-inch T.V. sitting on top of a dresser. She opened her closet and showed him her clothes. Everything was neatly organized. Betty Wap noticed the dumbfounded look on his face.

"Yup, busted yo bubble," she teased as she closed the closet door, then went and sat on one of the beds.

"Like a muthafucka, I ain't even gon lie," Rarri replied and sat down on the other bed. "How much these rooms hittin' for?"

"This the only one like this… except the owners, his is better," Betty Wap said.

"How you get this one?" he asked as he lit a blunt.

"I'm just coo wit the owners," she said like it was nothing as she sat up and grabbed an ashtray out of an empty drawer, then handed it to him.

"What, he like a trick or somethin'?" Rarri asked and passed the blunt.

"Dang, you all in my business," Betty Wap laughed before hitting the blunt. "Naw, he ain't no trick, tho . . . I been down here runnin' the streets since I was 13. One day, I caught a date and he brung me to this Motel to handle our business or whatever. Everything was goin' coo then the nigga just snapped out of nowhere, talkin' bout how I was goin' to go to hell for being a prostitute, and how I should be ashamed of myself. He started shoutin' verses from the bible at me as he undressed his self . . . I was so scared, I ran to the corner of the room and balled up, cryin' . . . he didn't look that evil when he picked me up. I don't even think he saw me as a person at that moment, 'cause he was lookin' through me like I wasn't even there no more . . . I tried to let him know I was only 13 and was only out here cause I was hungry and homeless... when I said I was sorry and tried to pray to God for forgiveness lettin' him know I wouldn't do this no more, the guy got even madder and started beatin' on me, callin' me a liar. He threw me on the bed and said he was goin' to fuck the shit out of me then kill me."

Betty Wap started busting up laughing as she passed the blunt to Rarri.

"How the fuck is that funny Wap?" he asked in disbelief.

"The situation wasn't funny, but him talkin' bout he was goin' to fuck the shit out of me was… as soon as he said it, I looked down at his little ass dick, and knew he wasn't fuckin' the shit out of nothin'... even at thirteen, he couldn't do no damage to me, his shit was really that little . . . like the size of my pinky and it was rock hard. I wasn't tryin' to laugh, but I couldn't hold it in for nothin', even after the ass beatin' he just gave me. What made it, even more, funnier was when he looked down at his little shit noticin' that's what I was laughing at... he looked sad and embarrassed, which made me laugh even harder," Betty Wap told him.

"Hold on . . . so, you laughed at the nigga who was tryin' to rape you?" Rarri asked. "What happened after that?"

"He got mad as fuck and tried to jump on the bed but ended up fallin' on the other side. I used that split second and ran to the door. Luckily, soon as I opened it the owner was right there talkin' to somebody, 'cause he was on my ass. I ran behind the owner and some other dude. They saw I was butt-ass naked, beat-up and tryin' to get away from ole boy and went in there and beat his ass way worse than he beat mine . . after that, the owner was bout to call the police, but I begged him not to... I told him about my situation and how I just left a foster home because of the men who would touch on me there and how I didn't want to go back. He ended up lettin' me stay in a room next to his and gave me a job, I just had to promise not to run the streets 'til I was old enough to make my own decisions. He knew I wasn't bout to go to school or none of that bullshit cause I really *wanted* to hoe. Soon as I turned 18, I quit and hit the streets. He let me keep my room, I just gotta pay rent," Betty Wap said.

"Betty Wap … you got some crazy ass stories, my nigga," Rarri finally admitted as he passed her the blunt.

"They might be crazy to you, but it's just life to me," she replied before hitting the blunt. "Shit happens."

"BAM! BAM! BAM! BAM! BAM! BAM! BAM! BAM! BAM! BAM! BAM! BAM!"

"Who the fuck is that bangin' on yo door like that, yo nigga?" Rarri asked, not noticing how jealous he sounded.

"No! Don't no niggas come here... you the only nigga I *ever* let in my room," she replied as she walked to the door. Whoever it was, they were still banging on it like the police.

As soon as Betty Wap opened the door, Kandice ran in and shut the door fast.

"Betty Wap, please let me stay here for a minute, Supreme trippin' agai—"

"BAM! BAM! BAM! BAM! BAM! BAM! BAM!"

"Bitch bring yo punk ass out here for I shoot this muthafucka up," Supreme yelled and started kicking the door hard as fuck.

"I can't keep you here . . . what if he start trippin' on me too?" Betty Wap told her.

"Betty Wap please, he goin' to kill me this time," Kandice cried.

"What did you do?" was all Betty Wap could ask.

"BAM! BAM! BAM! BAM! BAM! BAM!"

"I didn't do nothin'," she cried.

"Bitch I ain't playin' wit yo dumb ass, run my money," Supreme yelled and continued kicking the door.

Rarri walked into the living room and seen Kandice next to Betty Wap crying. "Who the fuck is that at the door, Wap?"

"It's her pimp, Supreme," she replied.

Soon as Kandice saw Rarri, she ran over to him and fell to her knees, begging him to not make her go back outside. Rarri noticed Kandice was a pretty little chocolate bitch. She almost looked dead on Kelly Rowland, Kandice was just a little thinner and her lips a bit bigger. She was some real work, but Rarri didn't want to get in no drama. Then a thought, better yet a voice memory, popped up in his head:

"*You will never forget me '... you will never forget the story of Success.*"

"What's yo name?" he asked her.

"Kandice," she replied through tears.

"Well look Kandice, I'm some real pimpin'... come at me correct or hop yo fonky ass back outside wit *Supreme Scream*," Rarri told her smoothly.

"Kandice started pulling money out of everywhere and setting it on the table. "That's welve hundred."

"Count that shit for me, Wap," Rarri said to Betty Wap, then looked back down at Kandice. "I'ma tell you this one time . . . I don't fuck wit no lyin' ass bitches at all, no matter how much money on the table, so tell me what happened as simple as you can."

"I don't want to pay him no more cause we ain't gettin' nowhere. . . so, I ran off yesterday, now he trippin'… I don't got no problem payin' some real pimpin', I know how it go," Kandice cried to him.

Rarri looked at her for a minute, then went to the door and opened it just as Supreme was about to kick it again, which caused him to fall in slightly. Supreme adjusted himself looking silly than a muthafucka, over here sweating and shit from kicking the door and yelling so damn much. Supreme looked like a got damn fool. *"No wonder why Kandice ain't tryna pay this nigga,"* Rarri thought.

"Where that bitch Kandice at 'P'?" Supreme asked trying to look around Rarri.

"Ain't no Kandice up in here," Rarri replied deciding to play with Supreme.

Supreme looked him in the face with a sour expression. "I just seen the bitch run in here, bruh … what, you out here savin' hoes 'P'?"

"Savin' hoes? Naw, I ain't never save no hoe before . . . matter fact, hold on, I'm lyin'. It was this lil chocolate Kelly Rowland lookin' ass bitch I met about a minute ago who did say her name was Kandice, but I changed it to Kandi when I saved her," Rarri said like he was in deep thought.

"When you saved her?" Supreme asked in disgust.

"Yea… I saved her from some weak ass pimpin'... she came up in here talkin' bout some nigga name Supreme Scream who be screamin' and shit . . . Rarri started busting up laughing. "Can you believe that shit 'P'?... A nigga named Supreme Scream who be screamin' 'P'. Wat the fuck was that nigga thinkin' namin' his self, Supreme Scream? I'm tellin' you 'P', that's why we gotta stick together, it's niggas out here named Supreme Scream runnin' round screamin' and shit. What the fuck he screamin' about? The niggas pimpin' so bad, he always mad? His scream must be Supreme, that's why Supreme named his self, Supreme Scream, cause when Supreme do scream, it be some real supreme shit he be screamin'... I don't know, what you think Supreme Scream be screamin' for?

Supreme just looked up at Rarri with his lips in a knot. He was so mad, he couldn't even talk, so Rarri continued as Betty Wap and Kandice giggled behind him.

"Honestly, I think Supreme Scream be screamin' Supreme Sc—"

"It's Supreme!" Supreme yelled. "Just Supreme, that's it."

Rarri looked at him, confused. "Oh... oh, that's yo boy or somethin'?"

"I'm Supreme," he replied through clenched teeth.

Rarri acted surprised. "You bullshittin' 'P' . . ." he told him, then looked over his shoulder at Kandice. "Aye Kandi! It's a ugly lil nigga out here wit a big ass head actin' like he Supreme Scream."

Kandice got up and walked to the door, then looked over Rarri's shoulder at Supreme. "Yea, that's him," she said and went back to sit down next to Betty Wap.

"My bad my nigga. You know these hoes be tryna prank a 'P' sometimes. I'm out here lookin' for the hidden cameras and some more shit. Ain't no way in hell I thought yo lil funny lookin' ass would have been Supreme Scream…wait up… I gotta ask . . . why the fuck you always screamin, Supreme? Is that why they call you Supreme Scream, 'cause you always screamin?" Rarri asked.

"It's just Supreme! Don't nobody call me Supreme Scream, 'cause I don't be screamin'," Supreme screamed.

"You screamin' right now 'P'," Rarri told him.

"That's 'cause you makin' me scream 'P', callin' me Supreme Scream and shit... stop callin' me Supreme Scream and I'ma stop screamin', got damn... it's just Supreme... no scream," Supreme screamed again.

"So, so, so, so, so now it's my fault you be screamin'?" Rarri asked with a chuckle.

Supreme exhaled deeply, trying to calm himself as best as he could, and for the first time talked normal. "Look, I'm tryin' to let you know I don't be screamin' and my name is Supreme. Just Supreme... no scream 'P'."

"So, so Supreme really don't be screamin'?" Rarri asked.

"I just told you that," Supreme screamed.

"Yea, but you screamin' again 'P'," Rarri replied.

"That's cause you keep talkin' bout this screamin' shit when I specifically told you I don't be doin' no fuckin' screamin' 'P'," Supreme screamed, then screamed some more. "What part of Supreme don't do no screamin' don't you get nigga?"

"Now I see why they call you Supreme Scream, 'P'… it's 'cause Supreme Scream, scream so much he don't even think he scream no more . . . I just met you, now you screamin' at me talkin' bout I'm the reason why you be screamin' when you know damn well niggas been callin' you Supreme Scream way before you even met me Supreme. So, don't be screamin' at me, my nigga. I'm tryna figure this shit out just as much as you is 'P'," Rarri told him, then hit his blunt.

"Ain't shit to figure out bruh, I keep tellin' you don't nobody call me Supreme Scream 'cause I don't be screamin', like that . . . the only reason I'm probably screamin' right now is 'cause you keep tellin' me muthafuckas call me Supreme Scream when I know for a fuckin' fact, don't nobody call me Supreme Scream. It's Supreme. Only Supreme, no scream 'P', damn," Supreme screamed.

"Ight I think I got it," Rarri said with a serious face. "Yo name Supreme, not Supreme Scream 'cause you don't be screamin', like that. The only reason you screamin' right now is 'cause people been tellin' me, yo name is Supreme Scream when it's really just Supreme wit no scream. Everybody just been lyin' on Supreme spreadin' rumors, talkin' bout Supreme be doin' some extreme screamin', when Supreme don't even scream extreme. The only time Supreme scream is when muthafuckas tell Supreme he be screamin', 'cause he know damn well he barely even scream, like that?"

"Exactly 'P', that's what I been tryin' to tell you," Supreme said with a smile. "Don't nobody be callin' me Supreme Scream, 'P'…just Supreme, that's it... no scream."

"Ok ok . . . I get it, I get it," Rarri replied as him and Supreme gave each other a 'P' shake. "Well look, I gotta handle some shit, I'ma get at you in traffic 'P'."

"Ight fa'sho 'P'. You stay up bruh," Supreme said and walked off.

Rarri closed the door and stood there.

"KNOCK! KNOCK! KNOCK! KNOCK! KNOCK! KNOCK!"

"Who is it?" Rarri asked.

"Supreme," Supreme said.

"Who?" he asked again.

"Supreme," Supreme replied a little bit louder.

"Who?" Rarri asked once more.

"Supreme!" Supreme screamed.

Rarri snatched the door open fast. "Damn Supreme, you screamin' again 'P'."

"That's cause you actin' like you ain't hear me, 'P', so I had to scream, *Supreme*. The only reason I screamed, *Supreme* was so you could open the door, 'P', other than that I wouldn't have even had screamed," Supreme explained calmly.

"So … now it's my fault you screamin' again?" Rarri asked. "You can't keep blamin' this shit on me Supreme, I'm not the reason you be screamin' . . . now I see why they call you Supreme Scream. It's not 'cause you like to scream; Supreme *love* to scream. That's why Supreme Scream extreme. I mean, why else would they call you Supreme Scream if yo scream wasn't Supreme. You know what I mean?"

Supreme snapped.

"Maybe I am screamin'! It ain't my fault I'ma fuckin' screamer. I grew up in a house full of niggas who be screamin'. That's the only reason people tellin' you Supreme be screamin'. How the fuck they goin' to speak on my screamin' when I'm Supreme and I don't even know why I'm screamin'?" Supreme screamed in exhaustion. By now he was sweating in frustration thinking deeply about his screaming disorder.

Rarri put a brotherly arm on his shoulder. "You gotta embrace the scream, Supreme. Stop runnin' from it. You just said you grew up in a house full of niggas who be screamin', so the only reason Supreme be screamin' is cause he was raised to scream. Supreme was born to scream, that's why they call you Supreme Scream, 'P'."

"It do kinda got a ring to it, huh?" Supreme asked with a smile looking up at Rarri.

"That's what I been tryna tell you 'P'. Ain't nothin' wrong wit Supreme Scream cause Supreme do scream," Rarri told him, sincerely.

"Yea, you right 'P' . . . I do like to scream, now that I think about it. I be feelin' good when I scream at a muthafucka. Screamin' make me feel Supreme. Everybody just assume I be mad when I'm screamin', but that's just some Supreme shit they don't get," Supreme said with passion.

"That's what I'm talkin' bout 'P', embrace the scream Supreme . . . matter fact, you gotta own that shit, 'P'. Let me hear you scream, *Supreme Scream*," Rarri said, pumping him up.

"For real?" he asked like a happy little kid whose parents told him he could open a present early before Christmas.

"Own that shit Supreme... scream Supreme Scream, 'P'... scream, Supreme Scream," Rarri told him seriously.

"Supreme Scream!" Supreme screamed

"Scream it louder 'P'," Rarri cheered.

"Supreme Scream!" Supreme screamed as loud as Supreme could possibly scream.

Rarri and Supreme laughed for a minute. Supreme felt better than ever.

"Yea, you did that, 'P' . . . you lookin' like a whole new nigga, now," Rarri told him.

"Good lookin' out 'P'. I appreciate that shit. I owe you one fa'sho," Supreme replied as he gave Rarri a P-shake. "What up wit the bitch, Kandice, tho?"

"I told you 'P', her name Kandi now... I don't think she goin' to fuck wit you after seein' you get played like that in front of her," Rarri said.

"Ain't nobody ever played Supreme Scream, especially not in front of no bitch," Supreme replied with confidence.

"'P'… I just convinced you to change yo name to Supreme Scream, actin' like niggas been callin' you Supreme Scream, Supreme. Really, I ain't never even heard of Supreme. I just started callin' you Supreme Scream cause Kandi said a nigga named Supreme was bangin' on the door and I heard you out there screamin'. Then I get you to say you grew up in a house full of niggas who be screamin' and that's why you a screamer. On top of that, I get you to scream Supreme Scream as loud as you could possibly scream, Supreme. Makin' a fuckin' fool of yo'self . . . . . . she already done hit my mitt, but I'ma real nigga so I'ma let you chop at the bitch…let me keep it real wit you tho 'P'... it ain't lookin' good.

Rarri moved out of the way so he could see Kandice sitting next to Betty Wap crying laughing. Kandice couldn't even breathe she was laughing so hard.

Supreme's ego was shot out of the sky. Nobody had ever manipulated him like that in his life. It hurt so much to see these hoes laughing at him and his pimpin, that deep down he really wanted to cry. He felt it coming too. "Keep the bitch!" Supreme screamed and stormed off angry.

Rarri started crying laughing... After he recuperated, Rarri laced Kandi up on his program, with all the dos and don't's. He asked Betty Wap to let her stay there, and of course, she said ok. Then he went back to his room and recounted the money he just broke Kandi for. After that, he called Fia on Skype and talked to his favorite bitches. Rarri was missing them like crazy and they damn sure was missing him too. Bird laced him up on everything that was going on in the hood. Mia, Tia, Dria, and Fia kept asking him when he was coming back so they could get some dick. Rarri just told them soon cause he really didn't know exactly when that would be. They started putting on a show for him, getting it popping. Rarri loved the way Fia stayed lit. She was always the one tryna hog the camera, showing him how freaky she could get. Fia never let him down and would always find something new to do. Rarri was stroking his dick quickly, feeling the buildup coming, just as the room door opened. He fumbled with the phone trying to turn it off, forgetting his dick was out.

"Oh shit, don't let me stop you," Fonda laughed as she shut the door behind her.

"It ain't even what you think," he replied.

Fonda looked down at his dick that was now standing at attention... "Yea, I bet," she laughed. "You want me to handle that?"

"I don't know you be runnin" Rarri joked sarcastically. "I'ma let you taste it tho 'cause you been on yo shit."

"Aye!" Fonda cheered, then threw a roll of money on his lap and went to the bathroom to brush her teeth.

Rarri counted out five hundred dollars. "What the fuck this bitch out here doin?" he asked himself. It had only been a couple of hours and the blade wasn't even booming around these times. Whatever she was doing was fine by him. Fonda turned out to be a natural. Oh, and her head game... *oh Lord,* the bitch head game was out of this world. Never would he had thought Fonda could out-suck Lae Lae. Yea, Lae Lae was cold with her mouthpiece, but she wasn't close to fucking with Fonda. What Rarri really liked most about Fonda wasn't how she sucked dick; it was what she did after sucking his dick. Fonda didn't waste no time trying to sit around and talk to a nigga or none of that bullshit other hoes be doing. She went to the bathroom, freshened up and went right back out the door to go get some more money. A real stomp down bitch.

About an hour later, Lae Lae came into the room as Rarri was getting out of the shower. She was talking about how slow it was and how the police was hot. All she handed him was a hundred and twenty dollars and sat down on the bed complaining bout how much her feet hurt. Rarri didn't say nothing, he just got dressed and pushed out the room, then went to the cemetery where his dad was buried. He spent a few moments at the gravesite, then went and sat down on a nearby bench next to some old man. Rarri had so much on his mind, and for some reason, being at that cemetery calmed him more than any other place he had ever been. Here is where he found answers to his questions… for the past week, he had been calling an Uber driver to bring him up there at all hours of the day, sometimes before the sun even came up. Rarri would bring

Remy to pour and blunts to smoke as he asked his father questions. It's crazy how he never heard a voice respond, but when he left the cemetery, he always knew what to do. "If only I could figure out how to cr—"

"I see you got some new wheels," the old man said cutting Rarri off from his thoughts.

"I thought you was blind, man," Rarri replied to the old man.

"I am... see?" The old man said and took off his shades so Rarri could see his eyes. They looked like eyes you would see on a dead man. "Just 'cause I'm blind don't mean I'm not aware of my surroundings young buck. Now is you goin' to let me hit the weed, or are we goin' to sit here and talk about my eyes all day?"

Rarri laughed as he lit the blunt and passed it to Blind Bill. Rarri and Blind Bill would smoke weed and trade stories. Blind Bill loved to tell stories about his late wife and about how life was back in his day.

After he left the cemetery, he drove to his grandparent's house and chilled with them for a minute, then went back to the Pit. Rarri was quickly making a name for himself in the Pit. He made sure to introduce himself properly to the pimps and players around town by chopping at they hoes every chance he got. Rarri didn't give a fuck if he was walking; a bitch was going to hear what he had to say. Now that he was driving, Rarri couldn't wait to hop out on a bitch, cause one thing they would know when seeing him now is that he ain't out here bullshitting with his pimping. He got dropped off in the Pit with nothing a week ago and turned it into something fast. No bitch want to hoe for a nigga who don't know what to do with his dough... Rarri was up and down the blade, pulling up on hoes trying to knock a bitch to no avail, so he went to the motel. The parking lot was packed with muthafuckas. Rarri got out and mingled with the other 'P's. They congratulated him on the new car and recognized his pimping. Some niggas been down there for years and was still walking or driving a beat-up ass car; only the strong progressed in the pit.

"I ain't even bout to lie 'P'. I pushed up on both yo hoes tryna knock one of them bitches from you, but they wasn't even fuckin' wit a nigga," Peso told Rarri and everything, but the music stopped. All heads were turned to Peso.

"Man, fuck y'all . . . I keep tellin' y'all muthafuckas I'm Puerto Rican, Black, and Creole."

Everybody started busting up laughing. They knew damn well he wasn't Puerto Rican, Black or Creole .. Peso was a full-blooded Mexican, but a real nigga at heart. Shid, he talked more black than most niggas did. Peso was known to pick a bitch up acting like he barely knew English until he got her in a room, then he would chop on her sounding like a straight nigga. Some of the other 'P's didn't like that shit, but everybody knew one thing about Peso; he wasn't no bitch. Peso would shoot it out or fight, he really didn't give a fuck. However you wanted to handle it, he was with it, that's what Rarri liked about him. A lot of pimps be quick to hit a female but quicker to run from a nigga.

"I'ma get wit y'all in a minute 'P'," Rarri laughed and pushed to Betty Wap's room.

Kandi was already ready to push out and so was Betty Wap. Betty Wap gave him a spare key to her room just in case he needed to go in while she was gone. As they left, he went back to his room and found lazy ass Lae Lae still laying in the bed. He chopped on that bitch and sent her out. 30 minutes later, Fonda came in and hit his mitt with another $650, freshened up, then pushed back out. Rarri rolled a few blunts then went back out too.

Soon as Rarri hit the parking lot, King Doe didn't waste no time asking, "you fuckin' wit Betty Wap, 'P'?"

"Hell naw! Who told you that?" Rarri asked.

"Betty Wap 'P' . . . I tried to get her to hit some laps around the parking lot and she said naw cause she fuckin' wit Rarri," King Doe explained. "Say it ain't so 'P'... say, it, ain't, so, 'P'... please say it ain't so."

"Naw, she trippin' 'P'. I ain't pick her up, but I do got this lil bitch I knocked from some nigga named Supreme, stayin' at her room," Rarri told him.

"Oh ok . . . yea, I heard about you knockin' Kandice. You's a fuckin' foo, 'P'," King Doe said, then screamed, "Supreme Scream!"

"How you hear about that?" Rarri asked as they laughed.

"The lil renegade bitch, Tasha that stay right next to Betty Wap. She was standin' in her doorway lookin' the whole time. . . 'P' that's on my pimpin', Tasha put that on her hoe'n, she ain't never seen a nigga get served like that in her life... she been talkin' bout that shit all day. It's only a matter of time before everybody find out cause Tasha fuck wit everybody . . . the bitch some real live hoe'n. If I was you, I would chopp at the bitch 'P', she feelin' yo pimpin'," King Doe told him.

"If her ho'n so good, why she ain't got no folks?" Rarri asked.

"Her nigga went to jail a few months ago . . . 'P' was some real pimpin'. Ever since he got locked up, she been out here still gettin' it. Niggas been tryna get her but she ain't fuckin' wit it . . . I be sellin' the bitch weed and playin' the lil brother role, tryna get in where I fit in . . . I already told her don't be talkin' bout that Rarri shit in front of my bitches . . . 'P', if you ever knock me for a hoe, don't serve me or chop on a nigga," King Doe said, then screamed in his Supreme voice, " just Keep the bitch!"

They both started laughing as they walked to the circle that was popping. Soon as they saw Rarri everybody yelled, "Supreme Scream!" and started laughing.

" P, we just heard how you did Supreme... that's crazy bruh," Peso said. "You already makin' niggas the laugh of the Pit."

"Nigga's get served every day," Rarri replied smoothly.

"Yea, but not on camera 'P' . . . niggas don't get served like this, ever... I've never seen no shit like this," Peso told him, then scrolled down on his phone to a video and pressed play.

There it was; Rarri serving Supreme from beginning to end. When Supreme walked off, Tasha turned the camera to herself and said, "Daaaamn!" He could see she posted it on her page. The video already had two hundred and twelve hundred likes and over four hundred comments. Fa'sho, it would go viral.

"I ain't even know the bitch was recordin' me," Rarri told them.

"Man, that bitch Tasha record everything... she said she thought he was bout to whoop Kandice ass again, but then you came out," T-Mack said.

T-Mack was a fat, black ass nigga, but he had bitches and stayed fly for a big nigga.

"Man, fuck all the bullshit. Y'all niggas tryna carpool or what?" King Doe asked.

"You ain't sayin' nothin' 'P', let's bounce . . . we in my shit," Peso said and walked to his car followed by Rarri, King Doe and T-Mack. T-Mack got in the front, Rarri and King Doe got in the back.

"Is y'all rollin' wit me?" Peso asked once everyone was in the car and pulled out a bag full of Molly's.

"Hell yea!" T-Mack and King Doe said at the same time.

"How much you sellin' these for?" Rarri asked as he pulled out a roll of money.

Peso, King Doe and T-Mack all looked at him and laughed.

"I ain't no drug dealer 'P'. . . I'ma muthafuckin' pimp . . . grab some of them muthafuckas bruh," Peso said, then popped two Molly's and passed a bottle of water around.

Rarri grabbed eight Molly's out of the bag, then popped two and put the rest in his pocket. Don't ever tell a Compton nigga to just grab something without being specific, 'cause more than likely he going to take more than you was expecting. That's just how Compton niggas is.

They went and posted in front of a liquor store, drinking orange juice and smoking weed as the pills kicked in. Peso had the Sauce Twins banging through the stereo of his Lexus . . . something about their music had all of them ready to chop at bitches, so every bitch that walked by got chopped on. Some of the bitches talked back, some didn't. That's how it is sometimes. Shid, some of the bitches cursed them the fuck out, but that didn't stop the fun. After that, they drove up and down the blade jumping out on bitches, hitting 'P' circles and all types of shit. They even parking lot pimped in front of a few clubs, chopping at bitches as they came out 'cause the only ones old enough to get in was T-Mack and Peso.

Rarri had never had this much fun in his life. Rolling around with niggas who was like him was a feeling he would never forget. The Molly mixed with the rush of knocking a bitch was pure bliss itself. Rarri was taking pictures every chance he got. He had bitches take pictures of him, Peso, King Doe and T-Mack, and he took pictures with bitches he was meeting. They ended up going to some after-party, and all started acting a fucking ass . . . some of the bitches flocked Rarri 'cause he wasn't too pimped out to have fun like a normal nigga. Rarri ended up being the life of the party and he didn't even know nobody or who party it was. The night was lit, so Rarri decided to hit Peso up for some more pills. They was all ready to pop again, so they went to Peso's car and all popped two more Molly's.

Rarri secretly popped three; he still had the other Molly's in his pocket that he was saving for a rainy day.

When they went back into the party, bitches swarmed them tryna get a dance. Everybody was faded. Rarri was dancing with this little Mexican looking bitch who he had his eye on. After a few songs, she grabbed his wrist and led him to the bathroom. "Aye!" Everybody cheered when they seen where they were headed. As soon as they closed the door, the little Kim Kardashian looking Mexican bitch dropped to her knees and started undoing his pants in a rush. As soon as she put his dick in her mouth, he felt the Molly's hit him hard as fuck. He felt good. *Toooo* good. He repeatedly inhaled and exhaled deeply as he held the back of her head with one hand and his balance on the sink with the other, then after about 2 minutes he blacked out.

Rarri jumped out of his sleep and noticed he was in his motel room, then exhaled in relief. He looked over at the next bed and it was empty. '*Fonda on her shit,*' he thought to himself, then looked over at Lae Lae who was laying under the covers next to him. *'No wonder why they call this bitch Lae Lae. Her lazy ass stay layin' down,*' he thought as he snatched the covers off of her bout to chop on the bitch, but it wasn't Lae Lae under the covers; it was Tasha fine ass. Rarri admired her sexy tattooed covered body for a minute. She was inked up for real. Even her titties was tatted up. Tasha looked like one of those video vixen, bitches. She kind of favored Nu-Nu off of ATL, kind of! She wasn't that bad, but her body was killing Nu-Nu's.

"Nooo! Daddy, I'm tired," Tasha cried and pulled the covers back over her.

Rarri was shocked. He eased out of the bed and started putting his clothes on, then checked his pockets to make sure his money was still there.

"You bout to leave?" Tasha asked as she came back from under the cover.

"Yea uh, I gotta go take care of some shit . . ." he replied still in shock then asked, "how I end up over here?"

Tasha's look said, *no this nigga didn't.* "You knocked on my door yesterday mornin' around 4 in the morning askin' if I wanted to pop."

"So, I been over here for a whole day? In this room?" Rarri asked. "What was we doin' for a whole day?"

"Aw hell naw," she replied with attitude. "Are you serious?"

"I don't usually pop pills, I probably blacked out or somethin'," Rarri explained.

"We talked and fucked all day . . . literally all day… you got my shit hurtin'. My pussy ain't never been this sore, *ever*," Tasha told him putting emphasis on every word, especially *ever*.

"Oh ok. So, I beat that thang up?" he asked with a smile.

"No, you didn't beat it up, you murdered this muthafucka," Tasha laughed and held her pussy in her hand for comfort.

"That's what I'm talkin' bout . . . let me go handle some shit, and I'ma slide back through later," Rarri told her then turned to leave.

"Ight . . . don't forget about me," she said in her sexy voice.

"I won't," he replied and opened the door.

"You ain't goin' to take the money?" Tasha asked stopping Rarri in his tracks.

"What money?" he asked back.

"The money in the dresser . . . " she said pointing to the drawer. "Remember you said you was pickin' me up?"

"Oh yea," Rarri fake remembered as he opened the drawer and looked inside with a confused expression. "How much is that?"

"Three hundred," Tasha replied. "I had to put money on Blue books, remember?"

Rarri closed the drawer back and chuckled. "Don't ever come at me short, talkin' bout some other nigga . . . Rarri don't split nothin', I ain't no piggy-back pimp bitch... I'm really out here," he told her and pushed out the room.

Tasha felt her pussy get moist. Everything about Rarri made her wet. Even the way he called her bitch. Rarri didn't raise his voice or sound rude. He called her a bitch with a smile on his face and said it so nice and calm that it could almost be manipulated into a compliment.

"This nigga got game," she told herself with a smile and laid back down for a minute.

Rarri went right next door to Betty Wap's room to check on Kandi. When he walked in, he immediately seen Kandi sleep on the couch. Betty Wap heard the door open and opened her room door, then went back to lay down. Rarri went in Betty Wap's room and sat down at the computer desk where he seen the money laying at. He immediately started counting the bills. It was twenty five hundred.

"Damn, Kandi made all this?" Rarri asked Betty Wap in excitement.

"Naw, that's what I made," she replied happily.

"Oh," he replied looking down at the money in his hands as he thought deeply.

"What's wrong, daddy?" Betty Wap asked.

Rarri set the money back down and walked over to the bed next to Betty Wap, then sat down. He sparked the blunt she had in the ashtray and pulled on it hard.

"Wap, I can't take yo money . . . I know I said I was goin' to pick you up, but I can't."

"Why not? You picked Kandice up," Betty Wap said.

"Cause I don't give a fuck about Kandi or none of these other bitches... Wap, you like the sister I never had... on everything, I will feel bad if I take yo dough. I ain't goin' to be able to do it Wap. I just can't do it," Rarri tried to explain.

"You can't or you won't?" Betty Wap asked with a tear in her eye, but refused to let it fall, so she blinked it away. "Nevermind, it don't even matter... I knew you wasn't goin' to pick me up anyway, I'm not dumb."

Rarri felt bad. Real bad, but he just couldn't fuck with Betty Wap like that. He really cared for Betty Wap, and if she was anybody else, he would have broke on her, no questions asked. Unlike these other niggas, Rarri really didn't 'need' these bitches money; he 'wanted' their money, but he didn't want Betty Wap's money. She was the only person Rarri ever felt sorry for and genuinely cared for with no hidden agendas behind their relationship. He didn't give a fuck what people thought; he looked at Betty Wap like a real friend and trusted her more than most people, for some reason.

"Wap, don't even say it like that, cause it's not like that," Rarri said truthfully.

"It don't even matter what it's like Rarri. All that matters is that you're not fuckin' wit me . . . so whatever, I'll live," Betty Wap replied.

Her words hurt him just as much as his hurt her.

"I'ma always fuck wit you Wap, just not like this. Not right now," he explained.

"Can I hit the blunt, damn you doin' all this talkin'," Betty Wap said.

Rarri passed her the blunt. "So, you ain't mad at me?" Rarri asked.

"Hell naw," she replied and hit the weed then added. "You just saved me."

"From what?" he asked seriously.

Betty Wap hit the blunt again then said, "from some weak ass pimpin'," and started laughing.

"Fuck you Wap," Rarri laughed. She really hit him with his own shit.

"What? I'm just sayin'," she joked.

"Oh, so my pimpin' ain't up to par now?" he asked.

'I'ma hoe so I don't know but uhh... yea, you lost some major points . . . I ain't goin' to tell nobody tho . . . unless you make me mad," Betty Wap said.

"Unless I make you mad? You ain't bout to be blackmailin' me Wap, that's out," Rarri laughed.

"Alright, well just drive me to the mall and we'll call it even," Betty Wap told him.

"That's a deal . . . let me go wake these bitches up so they could go too," he replied and headed out.

Rarri got $1,700 from Kandi and told her to get dressed then went to his room. When he got there both Fonda and Lae Lae was sleep. He woke them up and told them to get dressed. Fonda hit him with twenty two hundred; Lae Lae hit him with twelve hundred. Rarri knew who was the real stomp down, now. Lae Lae was falling off. He hopped in the shower and freshened up, washing Tasha off of him.

After he got dressed, he rounded all the bitches up. Rarri introduced Fonda and Lae Lae to Kandi, letting them know she was some new toes. Then he dropped them off at the mall. He slid Kandi and Lae Lae $1,000 and gave Fonda $1,500, then pushed to the cemetery. He talked to his father for a minute, then went and smoked with Blind

Bill, hearing some more of his stories. After that, he went to his grandparent's house and ate as he filled them in on what's been going on in the Pit. Lae Lae called and said they were all done shopping, so he went and picked them up. All four of them came out smiling from ear to ear and talking nonstop. Especially Betty Wap. Rarri felt bad, cause for the first time, Betty Wap looked like she was actually fitting in with other people. She just wanted to belong somewhere. Everybody put their bags in the trunk and got in the car.

The whole way back to the room, they each talked Rarri to death. Telling him what they bought and all the weird shit that was going on at the mall. It was so damn loud in his car, he couldn't wait to drop them off at the room. Fa'sho, he was splitting these bitches up 'cause they're too damn loud together. '*These hoes havin' too much damn fun in my shit,'* he thought in frustration. It was equivalent to having too many kids in the same house after leaving a candy store.

Rarri pulled into the Motel and noticed it was packed kind of early. He rolled down his window and hollered at King Doe. "What up 'P'—"

Psssh!

His back window shattered, and all the girls screamed. Instinctively, Rarri immediately put the car in park and jumped out quickly just in time to see Supreme little big-headed ass running off at top speed.

"I'ma beat that lil nigga ass," Rarri barked. He was hot. Rarri hadn't been this mad in a long time. Everybody was quiet. None of them ever seen him look the way he did at that moment. He looked like a killer. He didn't have to say another word, but they all knew after that look that Rarri had probably caught a couple bodies before. Rarri started busting up laughing when he saw the brick Supreme threw. For a minute he thought Supreme shot at him.

"That nigga did that, 'P'," he said with a smile as he examined the hole in his window.

"Y'all bitches grab y'all shit and go to the room."

After he calmed down, everybody joked about it. The shit did look funny, especially how Supreme little ass was running. He bent the corner like a roadrunner. Rarri didn't dare chase him. Supreme had to really have been hurt to do some shit like that. Breaking a nigga window was some real bitch shit. Supreme might as well have tried to break in his room and bleach his clothes next, cause he was on some hoe shit.

"All he doin' is makin' yo pimpin' look that much stronger . . . he could never sit in the Pit again 'P' after breakin' a nigga window cause he got broke for a bitch . . . It's a spot right up the street that fix windows. You wanna push up there?" King Doe asked.

"Yea come on, fuck it," Rarri replied and got back in his car.

About an hour and a half later, he pulled back into the Motel like nothing ever happened. Rarri told King Doe about how he ended up at Tasha's room and knocked the bitch but can't remember nothing that happened.

'I told you 'P'. I knew that bitch was on you," King Doe said excitedly. "So, you don't remember if the pussy was fire or not?"

"I don't remember shit, 'P'," Rarri admitted.

"You *was* fucked up, but you ain't pass out or none of that type of shit . . . check yo phone 'P'. You was takin' pictures and recordin' shit all night . . . I know you probably got that bitch on camera doin' somethin'," King Doe told him.

Rarri pulled out his phone and scrolled down his pictures and videos. Sure enough, there was a video of him fucking Tasha and one of her sucking his dick.

"Damn 'P'! I wish that was me fuckin' that bitch instead of you, I ain't even goin' to lie," King Doe joked seriously, then said in frustration, "you dumb 'P'. How you not goin' to remember this shit?"

"Them Molly's . . . that's the second time some shit like this happened... "Rarri laughed. "Her pussy ain't got gold in it, fuck that bitch . . . matter of fact, that's what I'm not goin' to do."

"I hope you ain't sayin' what I'm thinkin' you sayin' 'P' . . . please don't be sayin' what I'm thinkin' you sayin'," King Doe pleaded.

"I'm sayin' I ain't fuckin' wit the bitch . . . fuck Tasha. That bitch ain't nothin' new. She just like the rest of these hoes and her hoe'n damn sure ain't got shit on my pimpin'," Rarri explained.

"Noooo!" King Doe cried as he put his face in his hands. "Don't do this."

"What I am goin' to do is have her send me that video of me servin' Supreme," Rarri said and immediately texted her, telling Tasha to send it to his phone or Gmail.

King Doe started busting up laughing. "You gotta get the fuck out the Pit . . . we don't want you here no more... yo welcome is worn out... you come around here thinkin' you all this and all that, stirrin' up trouble wit Tasha when niggas done ran through the lion's den wit porkchop drawers on tryna get to the bitch and you just pass her up like she ain't shit. . . Rarri, you know what? You ain't shit and you ain't never gon be shit. You ain't never goin' to be nothin' but a pimp... a pimp all the hoes hate but love at the same time. Got damn, I wish I was you right now. The Pit bout to be lit as it can get and you ain't goin' to hear the end of this shit. If niggas ain't know yo name, they goin' to know it now. You's a bad muthafucka. Badder than a Michael Jackson knife fight at the train station 'P', and that's bad. You kickin' more bitches than a Kevin Gates concert wit this one bruh... I'm talkin' about gettin' away wit murder like O.J., 187 to zero like Gucci, spazzin' on Sway like Kanye 'cause the bitch don't got all the answers like you do 'P'…I love this shit!"

"You crazy K.D. It ain't even all that serious," Rarri chuckled.

"See… you lookin' at me like that 'cause you don't know Baby D . . . you don't know Baby D like I know Baby D, that's why you lookin' at me like that," King Doe said imitating Mike Epps on '*Next Friday*'.

"You actin' like the bitch gon shoot me or somethin'," Rarri said.

"Naw, she ain't goin' to shoot you, but she might try to stab you," King Doe replied seriously.

What Rarri didn't know was that Tasha was known to stab a muthafucka like it was nothing. Pimps or hoes, she didn't give a fuck. Even her previous pimp slept with one eye open. Rumor has it, Blue called a couple of his homies from jail talking about how he sleeping better in there than he was next to Tasha. She done stabbed Blue so many times over the years that everybody knew she would be the death of him. One time she caught him with a bitch she didn't like and Blue shined her off like she wasn't shit and walked right past her. Tasha was so mad, she threw a knife at him and it stuck right in the middle of his back nearly paralyzing him. The bitch he was with ran and Tasha ran to his side crying, telling him how sorry she was. Blue was probably just as 'crazy cause he always took her back and everybody else was just as crazy cause they still wanted to fuck with Tasha crazy ass. Hey, they say crazy bitches got the best pussy, that's probably why everybody wanted the bitch.

"I ain't never hit a bitch, but if she run up tryna stab me, I'ma punch her up like a nigga, 'P'. . . I swear to God," Rarri said just as serious.

"Just watch yo back bruh, don't sleep on that hoe," he laughed.

Rarri thought deeply for a minute. He didn't have time to be playing *catch me if you can* with no bitch. This was not what he signed up for.

"You know what? . . . I'ma fuck wit her for a lil bit and ease my way out," Rarri told him after sitting in silence for almost a full minute.

King Doe started laughing.

Later that night, Fonda went to jail for prostitution. When Rarri called to see how much her bail was he found out she had a probation hold, so it wasn't nothing he could do to get her out but wait. She called the next day acting like she was his sister as they talked on the phone just in case the police were listening. Fonda told him what had happened and when she would be going to court. Rarri used Betty Wap's debit card to put $100 on his phone for jail calls and he put $300 on her books. Fonda was a real bitch and he recognized it, so he stayed real with her, too. Now that Fonda was gone, he decided to move Kandi in his room with Lae Lae so she could have some company. Rarri broke his rules down on Tasha and kept an eye on that bitch. A close eye. Turns out she did have some good pussy. If it wasn't for the fact that Rarri done had better, he probably would have been stuck, too.

Chapter 18

He was enjoying the Pit, but money wasn't the same since Fonda went down. It had been a month and Rarri was still there. The hotel rooms was starting to hurt his pockets and Kandi and Lae Lae wasn't going as hard as Fonda was. Them bitches was lazy and starting to complain too damn much over every little thing . . . he didn't even chop on them bitches no more, he just let them talk and complain whenever they felt like it . . . he even took them shopping, spending nothing on himself and they still complained. Then there was Tasha— all she wanted to do was fuck on Rarri and lay up all damn day and talk about how much she didn't like Lae Lae and Kandi... Tasha wasn't compatible with other bitches and always had something to say... shit was going downhill. Luckily, King Doe was a real nigga and told Rarri how Kandi and Lae Lae was complaining about his program to other hoes. That was all he needed to hear.

"Y'all pack y'all shit and meet me at the car," Rarri instructed Kandi and Lae Lae then walked out with his bag. They did so reluctantly.

"Ight 'P', I'ma get at y'all later," he told King Doe and Peso as he was pulling out of the Motel.

"Stay up bruh, and slide back through when you get a chance," King Doe said.

"I better see you in traffic, 'P'. Don't be sleepin'," Peso added.

“You already know ‘P’, I’ma see y’all in a minute,” he responded and pulled off.

“Where are we goin?” Lae Lae asked after about fifteen minutes of driving.

“To my people’s spot . . . that room shit was getting too expensive,” Rarri told her.

After about another fifteen minutes, he pulled up to his cousin’s house and got out. “What y’all waitin’ on, come on.”

“Oh my God, you live at the Chopp Shop?” Kandi asked.

“You been here before?” Rarri asked skeptically.

“No, but everybody knows about this house... ain’t this where some dudes named Money-Mike and Money-Mitch stay at?” Kandi asked.

“You not talkin’ bout the twins, are you?” Lae Lae looked back and asked Kandi before Rarri could even reply.

“Yea that’s them... that’s who I’m talkin’ bout,” Kandi said.

“Oh shit, I didn’t know we was com—”

“If y’all bitches don’t shut the fuck up talkin’ bout some other niggas, I’ma give y’all somethin’ to really talk about,” Rarri barked, cutting Lae Lae off. “Now get the fuck out the car and don’t be on no out of pocket shit when we get up in here.”

“Kandi smacked her lips but did as she was told and so did Lae Lae.

Rarri had already called Money-Mitch and told him he was coming ahead of time. When Money-Mitch opened the door, he was fly than a muthafucka as usual.

"What up cuzzo?" he said as he embraced Rarri with a 'P' shake and a hug, then turned his attention elsewhere. "And who is these lil sexy bitches? Ok, I see you cuzzo."

"They ain't nothin' but some toes . . . where that room at so I can put these bitches up wit the clothes?" he asked.

Money-Mitch laughed. "You a fool 'P'… come on, it's this way," he said then walked off with them behind him. "I heard you been kickin' up dust in the Pit and I seen that Supreme scream video. You ain't waste no time, I like that... but yea here go yo room right here."

Money-Mitch opened the door to a room that was fully furnished. The carpet was rose-red but everything else from the bed to the curtains was coke white, even the T.V. on the wall was white. It looked like nobody had ever slept in there before by how neat and organized everything was.

"Damn, this muthafucka fly cuzzo," Rarri admitted as he turned to Money-Mitch just in time to catch him eyeballing Lae Lae.

Money-Mitch acted like he was looking at something else, then looked at Rarri. "Yea it's boo, this the guest room . . . my room is where it really goes down at."

"*This nigga think he slick*,' Rarri thought but said, "Oh ok, I'ma have to check you out, later . . . where everybody at?"

"They in the back. Come on, let's go and chill for a minute... I'ma send my bitch up here to give yours a tour and a rundown of the house rules," he replied.

"Ight bet." Rarri gave them a look that said a million words before he walked out of the room.

When they got to the back yard, Pay Day, Dolla, J-Money and Money-Mike was sitting on the couch outside on the patio.

"Supreme Scream!" they all screamed when they saw Rarri.

"Keep the bitch!" Dolla screamed like Supreme and they all started laughing as they embraced him with P-shakes and hugs.

"Bout time you came to fuck wit yo rellys. I was startin' to feel like you ain't like me or somethin', mane," J-Money said.

"Naw 'P', I just had to get some toes and a couple dollas before I came through," Rarri told him as he sat down.

"Yea, I heard you been in the Pit... that was a good choice to start off there before comin' to the shop," Money-Mike said.

"Yea, why you say that?" Rarri asked.

Everybody chuckled.

"That's a good place to start off cause it's some real pimpin' goin' on around there, but around here we go more harder on these hoes and run through bitches easily ... it ain't one nigga in the Pit who could make it in the Chopp

Shop, 'P'. Them niggas don't come around here," Money-Mitch replied as he lit a blunt. "Especially not wit no hoes."

"It's more cutthroat here at the Shop. That's why they call it the Chopp Shop, bitches dream to be on the team, 'P'. The blade is coo for some bitches but you wanna spread yo hoes out. Ain't no way in hell I could go back to babysittin' a bitch . . . we really sendin' hoes out of state '*and*' keepin' them local. You wanna elevate yo game so you don't gotta stand over these bitches 24/7 cause when you in her mental, she goin' to bring it back every time. Western Union and Money Gram is a muthafucka, not to mention Pay-Pal . . . this shit is set-up for a 'P' to win," Pay Day schooled.

"So how y'all be knockin' hoes if y'all too good for the blade?" Rarri asked.

"I ain't never said we too good for the blade . . . in my personal opinion, a nigga can't say he some pimpin' if he ain't never played the blade. That's like a lion being born and raised in a zoo talkin' bout he king of the jungle... I ain't sayin' he can't be king of the zoo, but he can't be a king in the jungle 'P'. He ain't nothin' but a big ass cat actin' like a lion. He don't know nothin' bout sendin' a bitch off to bring that food back. That's why we sayin' you made the right choice by playin' the blade first, but don't limit yo pimpin' to just playin' the blade... some bitches you will put on the blade won't make shit, but when you put her on the net, she'll be boomin'. Vice versa. You gotta see what type of bitch you dealin' wit, like can she hold a respectable conversation or is she just a dumb hoe. What type of game she got about herself. Is she a outgoin' type of bitch or do she got a diffident personality? It's all types of questions you wanna figure out before you send a bitch so you could know exactly where to send her that will be most profitable for you . . . every bitch got a common denominator that could be dominated," Pay Day replied.

Rarri nodded in approval. Pay Day was kicking some real game.

'*This shit might not be as easy as I thought it would be,*' Rarri thought to himself.

"That lion shit was a coo analogy, but King Kong the one who really fucked the game up 'P'," Dolla said and hit his blunt.

"What the fuck is you talkin' bout Dolla? King Kong was the shit," Money-Mike asked as he sipped his lean. His eyes were so low you couldn't even see them no more. Dolla was fucked up too.

Dolla stood so he could get his point across and he was a bit upset at Money-Mike's comment. "Maaan, King Kong wasn't shit but a gorilla pimp runnin' around snatchin' white bitches up, climbin' on top of buildin's and knockin' planes out the sky and shit, rippin' and runnin', tearin' the city up all over that fonky, punk rock ass, bitch. The nigga ain't have no game about his self 'P'. Not even a drop of finesse wit his clumsy ass. That's why they throwin' human traffickin' at muthafuckas now cause of niggas like that . . . fuck King Kong!"

Money Mike jumped up and started going off. "Fuck you Dolla! It ain't his fault he caught jungle fever when he seen that bitch. Wasn't nobody else around for him to fuck wit. That was probably the best pussy he smelt in his life. Not once did he try to penetrate or violate her in no type of way at all. At least he ain't no rapist or some weird-ass nigga wit a fetish of getting' shitted on... Yea he probably took her against her will, but that's only cause the bitch was on him first, reckless eye ballin' and tryna touch on him and shit. You wouldn't be sayin' none of this if he was standin' right here, right now. Wit yo scary ass. I didn't wanna say this, but you sound like a fuckin' hater right now 'P'. You the nigga wit no game about his self. What type of pimp hate on a monkey?"

Dolla was hot at the two last statements. He didn't want to say what he was thinking, and he tried not to, but pride is a bitch he couldn't control. "I will knock yo bitch . . . any one of em."

Everybody went crazy in excitement and laughter. J-Money and Money-Mitch jumped up and started running around screaming, "Oh shit, oh shit... goddamn," over and over. Rarri and Pay Day was slapping fives aggressively as they laughed.

Money-Mike and Dolla just stood there looking at each other, grinning. They would have been toe to toe if it wasn't for the coffee table between them.

Money-Mitch and J-Money came back with their imaginary chainsaw's in hand imitating the sound of its motor and the sound it makes when cutting things, then Pay Day joined in with his. Rarri didn't know what was going on, but whatever it was he liked it. He did know Money-Mitch, J-Money and Pay Day was pumping shit up.

"So, you really wanna do this?" Money-Mike asked looking up at Dolla. "You challengin' *me*?"

"Like I said, any one of 'em," Dolla replied looking down at Money-Mike who was now palm brushing his hair thinking deeply with a smile on his face.

The chainsaws stopped as Pay Day instigating ass ran up with his imaginary microphone pointed at Dolla. "So . . . what bitch did you have in mind 'P'?"

"I mean it's like I said, 'any one of em' 'P'... put me in the garage wit the bitch and she goin' to get chopped, re-built and brung back brand new, ya understand me?" Dolla said feeling his self and every word he spoke.

"You know the rules 'P'. Drop a name," Pay Day said into the mic, then pointed it back at Dolla.

Dolla smiled and adjusted his Rolex, even though it was already on perfectly he just wanted to make them wait a minute 'cause right now they was on his time. Dolla loved the attention and the spotlight he was getting. He looked at Money-Mike, then everybody else, then back at his Rolex. "I was thinkin' bout, Kayla."

"Oh shit!" Money-Mitch screamed and him and J-Money was running around laughing again.

Pay Day looked at Money-Mike and chuckled. "What bitch you pickin' 'P'?"

Money-Mike sat down and took a sip of his lean. A big sip. You know Pay Day messy ass followed him down with the mic to the side of his face.

"You know I wasn't goin' to go for the gusto, but fuck it, the bitch be on me, anyway. Tell that nigga I want Nicole, 'P'. I mean, I might as well start wit his bottom then work my way to the top."

Everybody went crazy. Pay Day even started running around screaming with Money-Mitch and J-Money for a minute, then he ran back up to Money-Mike with the mic again. “Is you sayin’ what we thinkin’ you sayin’?” Pay Day asked almost out of breath. “Break it down to us ‘P’. Break, it, down.”

“Why chase a horse when I could walk into the stable?” he asked smoothly, then jumped up with ambition. “I’m Money- Muthafuckin –Mike. What’s a Dolla to a Blue face? You wanna see a trick? Tell this dog to turn around and show his true face. Before you breathe on my hoe, use some toothpaste… when Dolla holla, they run screw faced. I’m the shit, you ain’t even a turd…. ‘P’! This stanky breath nigga got nerve. When I’m done, he goin’ to be mad, sad and cryin’ on the curb… I’ma show y’all how to turn ‘fly’ into a featherless bird. When I’m done, they ain’t even gon put you third. It’s only two choices: Mike the pimp or Dolla the nothin’ ass nerd. I’ma do you so dirty, muthafuckas gon mistake you for a overgrown germ, pimpin’ out a fanny pack and a perm. You understand me? You gon learn my pimp hand stern. I’m the one, ‘P’... wait yo turn. The crown ain’t given, it’s earned. Boy, this nigga gon burn. ‘P’ step yo game up, I fuck wit metaphoric hoes so it’s like I’m wasting money throwin’ Dolla’s in this urn, ya und—”

“Ight, ight, ight, don’t chop ‘em to death ‘P’. We family ‘P’... we family,” Pay Day yelled as he tackled Money-Mike playfully on the couch to stop him from choppin’ Dolla to the point of no return.

Money-Mitch, J-Money, and Rarri was going crazy.

Dolla had one of those nasty looking smiles on his face as he nodded up and down in approval. He had to admit Money-Mike was choppin' like a muthafucka. Thank God for Pay Day.

"Naw, he wanna challenge Money- Mike- the-Great. I want action at every bitch in the stable. Every last one of 'em," Money-Mike yelled from under Pay Day. Pay Day was trying to cover his mouth, but Money-Mike kept moving his head out of the way.

Money-Mitch, J-Money, and Rarri went even crazier. Pay Day the pump-up artist ran off screaming. "Money-Mike too hot! He too hot! I'm burnin' 'P'! I'm burnin," then jumped in the pool fully dressed.

Now Dolla was wishing he would have kept his fucking mouth shut. Money-Mike always taking some shit to the next level. He always got to up the ante.

"I bet you wished you would've shut the fuck up now," Money-Mike chuckled to Dolla.

"Nigga, you ain't got me worried about it. I'm ready," Dolla lied.

"Well let's stop wastin' time then," Money-Mike replied then rushed in the house with Dolla behind him.

Rarri got up to follow them in the house.

"Naw 'P', they bout to be back out," Money-Mitch said stopping Rarri.

Rarri went and sat back on the couch. "What they about to do?"

“Well at first they was goin’ to grab the bitch that each of them picked to chop at, but Twin duce crazy-ass challenged Dolla at every ho he had in the house, so now it’s a whole different story,” J-Money told him.

“I caught that part, but what’s a challenge and why they goin’ to the garage?” Rarri asked.

Pay Day was walking back from the pool when he heard Rarri’s question. “It’s like this: when a nigga challenge you, y’all both get to pick a bitch to chop at from the other ‘P’s team in the garage for thirty minutes. The garage is the backhouse. See this is why I’m glad we think ahead, cause I had my bitch make some big ass flashcards just in case somebody got challenged to multiple hoes. All the cards look the same on the back but got different answers on the front. One say ‘choose’, the other say ‘stay’. After it’s all done the bitches flip the card to show what they chose.”

“So basically, the goal of the game is to knock a nigga bitch in 30 minutes or less,” Money-Mitch put it shortly.

“Y’all niggas is burnt the fuck out ‘P’,” Rarri laughed.

Money-Mike and Dolla came out with 4 hoes each.

“What the fuck, daddy. I’m tired... Don’t nobody feel like playin’ y’all little dumb ass game,” Kayla cried to Money-Mike as she rubbed her sleepy eyes in frustration.

“Bitch! Shut the fuck up. You playin’ the game,” he replied smoothly with a smile.

Kayla was his bottom bitch, so she done played this game plenty of times, and to her, it was stupid cause wasn't no way in hell she was going to leave Money-Mike. They had been through too much.

"Oh my God," she whined and folded her arms with an attitude. Kayla was the only bitch bold enough to talk back to him sometimes, but she knew her limits well. Other bitches wouldn't even dare cause fa'sho he would fire or smack fire out of the bitch.

Kayla was a badd, blond hair, blue-eyed white girl. The fake titties and ass on her would make any nigga bite his knuckles in excitement like Rarri was doing. The three bitches with her was cool, but they didn't have shit on Kayla. She walked and talked like she knew she was that bitch in charge. Two of the girls on the side of her were Hispanic and the other one was black, also known to the world as Bionca, Gabby, and Raven. None of them looked happy to be playing this game. Even though they never played it before, Kayla had told them all about it.

Dolla, on the other hand, had all black bitches. Two caramel complexion and two dark. Not one of them was ugly. All of them were dimes with the most petite bodies that had just the right amount of ass. Everything on them was real and looked real good too. Nicole was the baddest of the group. Her skin was chocolate and smooth. Her hair was long and curly with kinks. Her eyes were a light hazel brown and her lips were full and sexy.

I bet she could suck a mean ass dick, Rarri thought. *Damn, them eyes sexy as fuck.*

"Dolla's bitches didn't ask no questions or talk back. They were just waiting to do as told them. Rarri studied Nicole's face for a split second along with her body language and laughed to himself. Behind her was Tyonna, Kelly, and Terri.

Pay Day stood and cleared his throat dramatically before speaking loudly.

"Money-Mike, Dolla. Do y'all give me permission and authority to referee this challenge?"

"Yup," they both said at the same time as they sized each other up.

"Lil ass nigga," Dolla joked.

"I'ma teach you that you ain't got to be tall to ball 'P'," Money-Mike replied, then winked at Nicole as he licked his lips.

"Do y'all give y'all's hoes permission to listen to me throughout this challenge as I inform them on the rules and guidelines of this here game and swear on yo pimpin' that you will not harm, hit, threaten or fire any one of your hoes for followin' the rules of this game?" Pay Day asked.

Both Money-Mike and Dolla put their 'P' signs in the air. "I swear."

"Well then, let's carry on," Pay Day said in his white man's voice, then turned to the girls.

"Hoes and bitches, bitches and hoes. How this is goin' to end nobody knows, but as of right now at this moment y'all are nobody's toes. So, for the first rule, I need all y'all to take off y'all's clothes."

"That ain't how you play the game!" Kayla yelled.

"Damn, I was just playin' Kayla. You need to loosen up, you too stiff. Too damn stiff. Money-Mike, you need to un-stiffen this bitch or when she get older, she goin' to be walkin' round like this."

Pay Day lowered his head, brought up his shoulders and started walking around with a hunch-back and a funny look on his face.

Everybody but Kayla laughed.

"Man, get on to the game 'P'," J-Money said.

"Hey! You cut me off again and we're goin' to be next buddy," Pay Day told J-Money still talking in his white man's voice, then turned back to the girls.

"The people these days... now back to the business... the rules are simple and easy .. . just like all you bitches standin' here, right now."

"Fuck you, *Play Day*," Kayla shot back. She was heated.

'Oh, so you goin' to go there?" he asked in a surprised tone. Pay Day hated getting called Play Day. Some bitches called him that 'cause he was always playing.

"Daddy, I'm not playin' this game no more. He ain't even doin' it right," she whined to Money-Mike.

"Pay Day, stop playin' and do this shit or we goin' to have to substitute you," Money-Mike said.

"Maaan, both of y'all stiff than a muthafucka. Stiff and stiffer makin' the game borin' and shit. It's supposed to be fun 'P'. The game is supposed to be funny and fun," he replied.

"Pay Day!" Money-Mike and J-Money said at the same time, both ready to get on with the game.

Pay Day did play too fucking much sometimes. He sagged his face and made the most expressionless, lifeless expression, which looked funny as well.

"Well they don't wanna have fun, so let's just not smile or any of that bullshit people do when they happy, 'cause this is not a game anymore . . . It's serious . . . like I was sayin' before, the rules are simple and easy. Usually, we start wit thirty minutes, but since it's so many of you bitches... oops! I meant ladies. Since it's so many of you ladies, we agreed it shall only be for ten minutes. You have to give the 'P' ten minutes of your time so he can let you see why he is the better 'P'. After your fifteen minutes are up, grab the card of your choice and step back outside so the next girl can go in. Do not show your card to anyone until the game is over. When everyone is done, the cards will be turned at the same time. . . pimpin' is a sport and there are no poor sports here at the Chop Shop. None of us will stop fuckin' wit each other over the choices y'all make. This business is not personal, to us. To be a boss you have to know how to take a loss. If you do choose a new 'P', the previous 'P' has the burden of carryin' your bags to your new room. The best part of this is that he, the previous 'P' cannot keep anything he has bought you. Anything of value or sentimental value that was given or bought for you is yours to keep . . . now let's let the games begin … 'P' to your rooms."

Money-Mike and Dolla walked to the back house and both of them went in separate doors.

The backhouse, AKA the garage had two divided sides which allowed them both personal space to chop.

"First up is stiffy . . . I mean Kayla and Nicole. Nicole, you on the right door... Kayla, yo stiff ass on the left," Pay Day told them.

"Whatever Play Day," Kayla shot back as she and Nicole walked up towards the backhouse, then she looked at Nicole. "You know you wanna come home. Stop playin' and fuck wit some real pimpin'. Money-Mike will get you right bitch."

Nicole rolled her eyes and smiled, then opened the door and walked in as Kayla walked in her door.

Pay Day knocked on the doors ten minutes later and both girls came out with cards, then went and sat down. Next was Tyonna and Bionca, then it was Kelly and Raven. After that was Terri and Gabby. Pay Day knocked on the doors once more for Terri and Gabby to come out ending the game. Dolla and Gabby came out, but Terri and Money-Mike was still in the room.

"Knock! Knock! Knock! Knock! Knock!"

He knocked again.

" 'P', y'all time is up!" Pay Day yelled. "Y'all goin' to make me open the door mane, my hand is on the knob."

"Oh shit," Kayla laughed and ran over to where Money-Mike's room was, as did everybody else.

Pay Day looked at Dolla. "I don't know what to think Dolla. They probably came out when I wasn't lookin' and went to the store or somethin'. Now that I think about it, Twin did say we was out of Kool-Aid 'P'."

Dolla was lowkey sweating now, and everybody was crowding around making it even better.

"I'ma give y'all til the count of three and I'm comin' in 'P'! My hand is on the knob …One … two . . . three," Pay Day pushed the door open and everybody went crazy.

Terri was sucking the shit out of Money-Mike's dick while he counted some money in his hand, dramatically re-counting it over and over.

"She broke bread, so I let her give me some head 'P' . . . you ain't never got no head like this Dolla," Money-Mike was yellin holding the money in the air that he just got from her.

"Her daddy name Chris Tucker, that's why yo money been short. The bitch a natural-born Tucker and she been Tuckin' dollaz on Dolla just to bring to lil ole me, ain't that somethin'?"

Everybody was going wild, running around screaming. Kayla pulled out her phone and started to record Terri as she sucked on Money-Mike. "Suck that dick, bitch."

Kayla even grabbed some of Terri's hair and moved her head up and down for her, occasionally pushing it down further to make her gag. This was the type of shit Kayla loved, and fa'sho she was going to fuck the shit out of him tonight. She controlled Terri's head until he came in her mouth. Then he pulled his pants up and went outside for the card turn.

Terri was the only bitch who ended up choosing to leave; everybody else stayed where they was at.

"Go get my bitch bags 'P'. She ready to move," Money-Mike told Dolla.

Dolla gave him a 'P'-shake and a hug. "You did that 'P'."

"Of course, I did. I'm Money-Mike the great. I don't know why you was tryin' to fuck wit me Dolla. You know I'm that nigga out here… now go get my bitch bags and stop stallin' P'," he arrogantly replied and fanned him away as his bitches crowded him in victory.

Two Weeks Later

Money was becoming scarce and Rarri's pockets were starting to touch. Lae Lae and Kandi wasn't popping at all some nights, making close to nothing. On top of that, the bitches had the nerve to blame it all on him, always complaining about the times he put them down or where he put them down at. Lae Lae was making a habit out of talking reckless to him in front of others. He talked to her about it, but the bitch just wasn't hearing him.

Kandi seemed to always show out in front of his cousin's hoes, either smacking her lips or just having something to say every time he told her something. She especially acted funny in front of NeNe. NeNe was hands down the baddest bitch in the Shop. She was Puerto Rican, Cuban and Black and thick as fuck. NeNe could have easily been a model, but Money-Mitch had her mental. Her long jet-black hair went down to the middle of her back and her skin complexion was the perfect shade of brown. Her face was beyond pretty and more than beautiful. She was surely smacked by God before she came out of her mother's womb. Rarri fantasized about her more than he meant to and caught himself thinking of her whenever he fucked on Lae Lae or Kandi. He wondered what she felt like on the inside and if she could suck dick as good as he imagined she could. Everything about NeNe screamed sex appeal. Everything about her was sexy and she knew it. This was a bitch Rarri had to have. She was the one he was looking for. NeNe would establish his name in the game if he knocked her from Money-Mitch 'cause she was his bottom bitch.

Despite almost being broke, he was grateful to have Lae Lae and Kandi; proud even. They were important to him and he appreciated everything about them. This might sound crazy but the only reason he let them talk back and get out of pocket was cause of love. Love for the game, love for pimpin', but most importantly love for BABE ST.

Rarri finished talking with his dad and made his way over to where Blind Bill was seated. He sat down next to him and lit a blunt. Rarri hit it a few times then tapped Blind Bill on the arm so he could hit the blunt. "It's on you O.G."

"Hold on youngsta, this the good part," Blind Bill replied. Blind Bill was moving his hands on a page in a book. He was so focused; his mouth was wide open as he used his mind to visualize things.

"What the fuck is you doin'?" Rarri asked as he hit the blunt and looked at Blind Bill like he was crazy.

"What it look like I'm doin' fool? Just cause I'm blind don't mean I can't read," he shot back, and everything came together in Rarri's mind all at once. The news seemed to hit him harder than the weed 'cause as soon as he heard it, Rarri started coughing uncontrollably, almost as if the weed became stronger.

He dropped the blunt and ran full speed to his car then popped the trunk. Rarri immediately began rummaging through all of the junk and clothes in search of his bag that he kept his father's book in until he found it. Then he closed his trunk and ran back to where Blind Bill was. He had finally cracked the code. These weren't bumps and ripples in his father's book. It was Braille. Braille is a system of printing for the blind in which letters and numerals are represented by raised dots.

"Hey, what you doin' man? Give that back," Blind Bill yelled as Rarri snatched his book from him.

"Hold on Bill, I need you to read somethin' for me," Rarri replied and handed him his father's book. "I need you to read this one."

"So, I'm supposed to just stop my readin' to read what you want me to read? You got issues Rarri, anybody ever tell you that? Some real twisted issues. I ain't been able to put my finger on it, but somethin' is wrong wit you, boy. I can't see it, but I could feel it," said Blind Bill.

"It's important Bill. My bad for snatchin' yo book, I was just too excited. My pops wrote this book. I been tryin' to figure out what's on these pages since I been out here," Rarri explained.

"I didn't know your dad was blind," Blind Bill replied as he opened the book.

"He wasn't, he just wrote it like that," he told him.

"That don't make sense, but hey a lot of shit don't these days . . . ok, let's see what we got here," Blind Bill said and began feeling the first page. "The Cheat Code."

Blind Bill turned to the next page and started reading.

"The first rule in pimpin' is simple: it ain't no rules . . . what type of book you got me readin' youngsta? Is this some type of trick you playin'?"

"Naw this ain't no trick or no type of game, just read the book for me, Bill," Rarri said and grabbed the blunt off the ground then re-lit it.

Blind Bill sighed and shook his head then continued reading. "The first rule in pimpin' is simple: it ain't no rules . . . not for a BABE Street, nigga. A rule is a regulation. A regulation is a principle, rule or law for controlling behavior. To be regulated means to be controlled in agreement with rules or laws or to be directed. No man should follow anything that hasn't been written by God . . . most of the rules written by pimps are self-serving guidelines of laws others should obey. A list of their instructions, so I ask you: what is he who is instructed by a pimp's rules? Exactly! Hoes follow instructions and rules. A man with morals need not follow these rules because he knows right from wrong and values conducting himself in the right way at all times. A man without morals could easily be a pimp, but a man without morals could never be from BABE. The meanings of BABE are more than just pimpin', but pimpin' is a big part of BABE because BABE is a part of everything. Therefore, someone who is not a pimp can be from BABE. A man can Break-A-Bitch-Easy just as a woman can Break-A-Boy-Easy. Therefore, a woman can be from BABE just as equally as a man. BABE street is a belief, a lifestyle, a religion, a family and so much more. Be-A-Boss-Everyday. We do what the fuck we want to do. Anyone seeking to limit what we stand for should rightfully be expired. We are for each other as we are for ourselves. Selfless. Inspired by love, peace, unity, and greatness. Motivated by wealth, loyalty and respect. We are those who accomplish, win and succeed. We are the most ambitious. To my people I don't teach instructions or rules; I'm here to give game you could use. I am the best but all of you will be better. Not here in person, but in spirit I will see it through. I was born to die for this cause. My very existence was only based on leaving a message, but don't get it fucked up: I am the game, God! Now close your eyes and visualize as I introduce the real *Cheat Code* of BABE Street. Not the dud I put in the Book of God about pimpin'; this is flawless, the lawless game."

Rarri closed his eyes as Blind Bill read his father's words. It was so much game being said, he wondered how his father wrote it all. He was speaking of future game to use. He talked of things that wasn't created yet. God was ahead of his time. He was even ahead of Rarri's time. After about three hours, it became too much to process. Too much game to contain and comprehend in one day, so Rarri ended the session.

For the next seven days, he spent as much time as he could handle at the cemetery listening to Blind Bill read. The book was so good, Blind Bill was looking forward to their sessions. It took exactly seven days to finish, and on the last day, Rarri departed from Blind Bill. He left the cemetery feeling good and decided to stop by the Pit to show his face. Besides that, he wanted to see who all was going to "The Show" tomorrow that was being held at the park. "The Show" was a function that pimps threw every year. Pimps from all over would show up and show out. Dressed to impress, the whole scene was flamboyant. It was a friendly competition of who could bring the most hoes, who could dress the best, whose car was better and whose jewelry cost the most. And don't show up at The Show trying to show out in some fake shit, 'cause you will get exposed and labeled as a fraud. Muthafuckas be walking around with diamond testers trying to catch niggas slipping and play pimping. This was Rarri's first show to attend and he couldn't wait. Making connections is real important and getting your name out there is priceless. It was going to be some real congregating and Poli-pimping going on around that muthafucka fa'sho.

When Rarri pulled into the parking lot of the Motel, he noticed a crowd standing around the back of a grey Charger, so he pulled into the parking spot next to it and got out.

"K.D, what's the big ole deal 'P'?" he asked as he gave him a 'P'-Shake, then greeted the others around.

"Nothin' much what's up wit you?" King Doe asked not looking Rarri in the eyes.

King Doe was always animated, so Rarri instantly caught wind to his dry response.

"Oh ok, ok," Rarri said suspiciously. "Shit, I was just stoppin' through to see if y'all was goin' to the show tomorrow."

"Yea, I'ma see you up there," he replied dryly.

King Doe was definitely hiding something from him. For a minute, Rarri thought it was because he cut Tasha off and maybe she was in his ear, but he knew King Doe wouldn't act funny over no bitch. But then again you never know; niggas switch up all the time.

Everybody seemed to stop talking since he entered the circle. Everybody except the big muscle head ass nigga they were crowded around before he came.

"What up 'P', I'm Rarri," he introduced himself.

"Fa'sho 'P', I'm Big Tommy," Big Tommy said as he gave Rarri a 'P'-shake. "You wanna see my new toes?"

Rarri chuckled, then turned to King Doe who was trying to shush Big Tommy with his pointer finger to his lips signing him to be quiet. When Rarri turned his way, King Doe tried to play it off like he was scratching his lip and looking somewhere else, hoping he wasn't caught. Rarri turned back to Big Tommy who obviously wasn't paying attention to King Doe.

"Yea let me check that bitch out 'P'," he said straight-faced.

Big Tommy dug in his pocket, pulled out his car key, pressed the trunk unlock button then opened the trunk. When Rarri stepped forward, his blood boiled. Betty Wap was curled up inside looking dumb as fuck. It was actually sad to see her in there like that. Betty Wap looked up and seen Rarri, then laid her head back down. Even though she didn't speak to him, her eye said a million words. She was trying to get chose and Big Tommy had her camped out in the trunk thinking she was going to get picked up. Betty Wap dropped a tear, not because she was in the trunk; she cried because Rarri seen her in the trunk. This was the first time Betty Wap felt embarrassed in front of someone. She didn't care if a million people saw her in the trunk as long as Rarri wasn't one of them. He was the only person she knew who cared about her how a brother cares for his sister. She never seen someone look so hurt and upset by her actions. Betty Wap didn't know what was going on inside of her head. So many emotions was flooding her all at once.

Everything she bottled up her entire life was hitting her hard. Being shot by her dad, being raped by different men, being played by pimps and snaked by hoes. She relived all these times at once in the back of that trunk. Betty Wap balled up and let out a loud painful cry. She cried so hard, everyone around felt it in their chest; it was heartbreaking. Some of them knew Betty Wap for years and never once had anyone witnessed her cry. None of them ever heard a person cry like this. Not as bad as Betty Wap. Her cry was so long overdue, it came out as an uncontrollable scream.

"Shut up bitch!" Big Tommy yelled as he slammed his trunk shut, and she immediately began pounding and kicking, still screaming at the top of her lungs. "This bitch cra—"

Rarri hit Big Tommy in the chin as hard as he could, dropping him instantly and was on him sending blow after blow to his head. Everybody else jumped in and started stomping Big Tommy the fuck out. He was getting attacked in too many places to cover. King Doe kicked him in the side of the head and Big Tommy was out cold. Rarri went into his pockets and took his keys then popped the trunk. When he opened it, Betty Wap jumped into his arms and sobbed.

"I'm sorry Rarri . . . I'm sorry," Betty Wap cried to him.

"It's alright Wap . . . everything goin' to be alright. You gotta stop doin' this shit," he said as he held her tightly. "Promise me you goin' to stop doin' this."

"I promise," she replied. Betty Wap felt a tear fall on her face and knew it was his. '*This is what love feels like,'* she thought to herself as he held her.

"Go to yo room . . . I'ma be there in a minute," Rarri instructed as he released her. Betty Wap seen the rage in his eyes and knew what type of nigga he was behind the pimping. She noticed the same look on his face when Supreme busted his window. It was the same look on her dad's face when he walked into her room when she was six and the same look her mother had when she accidentally baptized her for too long when she was seven.

Betty Wap grabbed his arm as he tried to walk off. Something about the way she held his arm calmed him. It was an understanding grip she had on him.

"Don't… it's too many people out here," she said calmly.

Rarri looked around and noticed all the people standing around watching as Big Tommy continued to get beat by King Doe and all the other pimps. Nobody was going to call the police after hearing Betty Wap cry like that. Big Tommy needed a good beating to set him straight. Some people even cheered them on.

"Whoop his muthafuckin' ass!" one woman holding a baby yelled.

"Bout time y'all stuck up for that girl! She ain't never wronged nobody!" another one shouted.

At some point in time, Betty Wap done almost looked out for everybody around there, only to be taken advantage of. She loaned money out and never asked for it back, convinced the owner of the Motel to give certain people extensions so they didn't get kicked out. King Doe knew firsthand how good of a person Betty Wap was. If it wasn't for her, he would have been on the streets a long time ago. She looked out for her people and this was the first time any of them had looked out for her.

"I ain't goin' to do nothin' stupid. I'ma meet you in the room in a minute," Rarri assured her with a smile.

Betty Wap studied his face for a second. "K," she replied and walked off.

Rarri pulled a crowbar from Big Tommy's trunk then beat his legs and feet until he knew Big Tommy would forever be a cripple. Nobody didn't have time to be getting chased by that big ass nigga. Rarri heard about Big Tommy; he was a gorilla pimp.

After everybody was satisfied, they walked off laughing, slapping fives about the whole thing and bragging about what they had done. They was pumped up and feeling good.

"My bad 'P' . . . a nigga should have been put a stop to this shit. Lowkey, we been making ourselves look weak letting niggas come around and treat Betty Wap like that when all she do is look out for us... I ain't never heard nobody cry like that 'P' . . . I seen my daughter screamin' in that trunk," King Doe admitted

"I seen my daughter too, bruh," Kali said.

"I seen my sister, " Ricky-Rick added.

"I seen my niece," T-Mack admitted.

"I seen my momma bruh," Greedy said sadly.

"When he slammed the trunk on her, it was like… I felt like... like he wasn't goin' to let her out or somethin' . . . it seem like he was tryin' to keep her in there… I thought he was goin' to do her like he did Naomi," King Doe added sadly.

Everybody knew Big Tommy killed Naomi. He locked her in his trunk for four days straight in the summer. She died within the first 24 hours and he spent the other three days riding around showing people the body like it was cool.

"That's why I got off on him, my nigga . . . he wasn't bout to do Wap like that in front of me. That nigga ain't no pimp, he a gorilla," Rarri replied.

Everybody sat in silence for a minute.

"We good?" King Doe asked with his hand extended to Rarri.

Rarri looked at him straight-faced, then down at his hand. After glancing a few more times from his face to his hand, Rarri smiled and shook his hand embraced with a hug. "Yea, we good 'P' . . . I ain't even goin' to lie, I was lowkey spooked. I ain't know if y'all was goin' to help me or jump me, so I had to give that nigga everything I had 'P'."

They all broke out laughing.

"What you would have did if Big Tommy would have ate yo punches?" T-Mack asked.

"Shiiid, I would have done what any other pimp would do," he replied.

"What's that?" Greedy asked.

"Rarri gave him the *are you serious* face and said, "run fool!"

They all started dying laughing.

After that, King Doe lit a blunt and they all laced Rarri up on what's been going on since he been gone. Supreme been on a stakeout for his car. Numerous people spotted him creeping with a big ass rock. He ain't had no toes since Kandi left him, so he was tripping off of that. Oh, and Tasha. Boy oh boy, Tasha been talking dumb shit about Rarri, calling him everything but a pimp, swearing he's everything but a pimp, which was kind of true 'cause Rarri wasn't just a pimp so he wasn't at all offended.

He wrapped up his conversation with them and went to holla at Betty Wap. He talked with her for almost an hour, making sure she was okay, then headed back home so he could get some sleep and be ready for '*The Show'* tomorrow.

When he pulled up, Rarri seen his grandpa's car outside and smiled. "Just the man I need to see," he said to himself as he got out of his car and walked towards the house.

He could see the inside through the screen door and heard Money-Mitch talking as he got closer.

"I'm just sayin' unc . . . niggas ain't breathin' how we breathin'. We ain't sittin' around playin' wit this shit. The Shop ain't no playground. We really out here pimpin'. Our names be ringin' from mashin' so hard. Muthafuckas can't make it in the Cho—"

"Chop Shop, yea we know," Rarri joked as he walked in cutting Money-Mitch off. He sat the two bags of clothes down he bought from the mall earlier for Lae Lae and Kandi to wear tomorrow.

Rarri gave his grandpa a 'P'-shake. "Who you choppin' on now 'P'," he asked Money-Mitch.

Everybody got quiet.

This was the second circle to go mute when he came around, today. Rarri looked around at everybody in the living room. J-Money was scrolling through his phone, Pay Day was looking for change in the sofa, Dolla was tying his shoes that didn't have laces and the twins wasn't smiling, which was kind of odd cause them two muthafuckas stay smiling. Now they was all straight-faced and shit, but he knew something was up because Pay Day was damn sure hiding his smile. Rarri's grandpa was in deep thought and looked a little bit upset.

"Niggas ain't getting' ready for the show tomorrow? I got Lae Lae and Kandi some fly matchin' outfits that match my shoes 'P' . . . .I can't wait for tomorrow to come, man, we goin' to have niggas hidin' bitches 'cause they damn sure goin' to be out of pocket when they see me mane, ya understand me?" Rarri said excitedly.

Pay Day couldn't hold it in any longer and started busting up laughing.

"What you laughin' at cuzzo?" Rarri asked Pay Day with a smile, but Pay Day was too busy laughing to hear him.

"What's up wit this nigga?" Rarri asked Dolla with his same smile.

"Maaan, you gotta ask them, niggas," Dolla laughed as he pointed to the twins which caused J-Money to start laughing too.

"What these niggas laughin' at 'P'," Rarri chuckled.

"Fuck it, Ima keep it real wit you 'P'," Money-Mitch said. "You gotta start breathin' on these hoes cuzzo . . . You lettin' these bitches run around doin' whatever they want to do ... got them layin' up all day while you gone. They walkin' around this muthafucka like they run this bitch. Don't no bitches run the Chopp Shop, 'P'. We built a reputation in here and you got bitches thinkin' this a vacation resort or somethin'. They ain't bout to be kickin' they feet up in the shop without puttin' in work. You gotta start puttin' yo game down cuzzzo or you goin' to drown in this water. If you don't get back on yo shit quick, you ain't goin' to make it out here 'P', I'm tellin' you."

"Fa'sho cuzzo, Ima step it up on these hoes. You right. A nigga lowkey been bullshittin', but I'ma bounce back 'P'," Rarri replied and gave Money-Mitch a 'P'-shake.

"That's what I'm talkin' bout 'P', get back on yo shit. I don't like seein' you like this. We need you to breathe in these streets cuzzo," he said sympathetically, then pulled out a roll of money and handed it to Rarri. "Here, this should keep you afloat until you get back right... me and Twin put this together for you . . . I mean… it's the least we could do."

"Damn. Good lookin' out y'all. Ima make this shit work, watch," Rarri said happily with a smile as he put the money in his pocket. Then he picked up his bags.

"I'm bout to go breathe on these hoes and get them ready for 'The Show', ya understand me, mane? Niggas bout to be mad 'P', on my pimpin', they bout to be mad," he added excitedly and attempted to walk off.

"Boom! He just blew his pimpin' up," Dolla whispered to J-Money, and they both chuckled on the low.

"Rarri!" his grandpa called loudly.

"What up G-Man?" Rarri asked.

G-Man was a nickname he came up with for his grandpa, so he didn't make him feel old by calling him, grandpa.

"You goin' to have to catch the next show," he replied.

"Why? They canceled it?" Rarri asked in disbelief.

His grandpa shook his head in frustration. *Where is this boy's common sense?* he thought to himself but said, "you can't go to no shows without no toes 'P'."

"I got toes 'P'. I ain't buy these dresses for me," Rarri replied and held up the bags for his grandpa to see.

"You *had* toes," he shot back.

"What you talkin' bout G-Man?" Rarri asked, confused.

"He talkin' bout the toes you had, 'P' . . . Lae Lae fuckin' wit me now and Kandi chose up on Twin," Money-Mitch told him. "You don't got no more toes 'P'."

Rarri looked down at the bags in his hand and shook his head. "How y'all just goin' to snake me for my bitches like that?"

"Ain't nobody snaked you for shit... they ain't feelin' yo program, you know how this shit go," Money-Mike spoke up.

"You's a damn lie, they ain't say no shit like that . . . y'all niggas is scandalous bro," he said with a look of disgust. "Y'all niggas is scandalous."

"You trippin' cuzzo," Money-Mike told him.

"Trippin! Y'all muthafuckas is janky, 'P'! I'm not hearin' none of this shit y'all talkin' bout! Niggas ain't loyal at all! And stop callin' me cuzzo! I don't even fuck wit y'all like that! I should have never came to this muthafucka in the first place! Y'all niggas set me up! I know y'all did, 'cause y'all ain't got nothin' else better to do but be scandalous to a muthafucka! Greedy ass niggas wit no morals!" Rarri barked.

His grandpa looked at him questionably after hearing his last statement. Rarri noticed all the girls standing around now, so he stormed to the room he had been staying in, packed his shit and left without saying another word to anyone.

Chapter 19

The Show was lit. Everybody was up there, from the little leagues to the big leagues. Even a few celebrity 'P's like Sunny-D, Chucky, Franko, Banker, The real King Doe, Charlie Mack, Prestige, Boy Wonder, Magnificent, Lavish, Supernatural, Ching-Ching, Veezy, Future, 8-Chains, Mookie, Spectacular… the list goes on and on.

Money-Mike, Money-Mitch, J-Money, Dolla and Pay Day was all amongst the upper class 'P's. Niggas was showing the fuck out and bitches was walking around half naked in big ass groups. The park was going up. About ten different niggas got exposed for wearing fake jewelry within the first thirty minutes. Another seven got knocked within the hour, leaving hoeless. It was wild. Real wild. Money-Mike and Money-Mitch was chopping on everything moving, having a ball.

Rarri pulled up a couple hours after the show began. The scenery was unlike anything he had ever seen before. He lit a blunt, pulled on it for a bit, then hopped out still smoking.

Betty Wap walked up. "Are you ok? I seen Lae Lae and Kandi. Everybody talkin' bout how you got knocked by the twins."

"Yea, I'm good. I ain't worried bout that shit . . . who you up here wit?" Rarri asked as he passed her the blunt.

"Tasha . . . she brung me up here with her and now she actin' funny in front of her friends so I just been chillin' by myself until we leave," she replied then hit the blunt.

"Oh ok... well I'ma get wit you later. Let me go mingle for a minute," Rarri said as he walked off. "Keep the blunt."

"Ok… if you need some money, let me know and I got you," Betty Wap yelled to him. Rarri looked at her, smiled then kept walking towards the circle of pimps.

Everybody was dressed up in designer clothes and wearing jewelry over jewelry. Everybody except Rarri. He wore some black basketball shorts, a gray hoodie, and his Nike slip-ons. When he pushed up, all the P's got quiet and mumbled once he passed. Some even laughed. They all knew he was the one who got knocked by his cousin's, last night. The twins had been telling all the pimps. Lae Lae and Kandi had been telling all the hoes.

Rarri had quickly become the laugh of the show and he felt it. When he walked up on his cousins, they seemed to be acting funny, too. All five of them. The only P's who seemed to have his back was those he knew from the Pit. Peso told him don't sweat it, and if he needed something to let him know. So did T-Mack, King Doe, Greedy, Ricky-Rick, and Kali. They did want to know why he never told them he was the twins relatives. He just said they weren't important and pushed off. When he walked back by his cousins and the other P's, he could hear them talking about him and laughing. He even saw Lae Lae and Kandi pointing him out to Meeka bitch ass. The three of them laughed as he looked over at them. He even tried to say what's up to Tasha, only to get the cold shoulder and laughed at by all the bitches she was with. Rarri wasn't getting no love. He seen his grandpa talking to Success and brushed right past them. His grandpa tried to call after him and Success funny ass had the nerve to yell, "Run Forest, Run!" Rarri just kept on walking.

He walked to his car, sat on the hood and watched everybody for about twenty minutes, then went and popped his trunk. Rarri pulled out all of the clothes he had in there and threw them in a pile. Then he pulled out a golf club, walked to the front of his car and started smashing the headlight and the grill over and over. Then it was the hood and the front windshield. After that was the side windows, rearview mirror, and the doors. Everybody ran over there to get their laugh on.

"That's what niggas do when they get knocked for they bitches," Tasha said as she recorded Rarri from her phone. "This how they act when ain't no pimpin' left in them."

Rarri jumped on top of the roof of his car and started smashing the back window and side windows. Everybody had their phones out recording him. He was looking like a wild man doing all that swinging. Rarri looked past the crowd and seen his grandpa smiling at him and chunked up his 'P'-sign then hopped down.

"I could record y'all muthafuckas too," he said and pulled out his camera then started recording them back, which made most of them laugh. Success was the main nigga getting' everybody fired up while he recorded Rarri.

His cousins made their way through the crowd and approached him. " 'P', you embarrassin' yo'self out here . . . we think it's time for you to leave... you at the show wit no toes and you doin' some weird shit, right now," Money-Mitch said. "You kn—"

"Give him the bitch back 'P'," Success joked.

"You know you makin' a fool of yo pimpin'," Money-Mitch finished.

Rarri had the camera on Money-Mike, then he turned it back on himself and talked to the camera. "See this the shit I been havin' to deal wit. Moral-less men, speakin' on my pimpin' cause he's just a pimp. Well, I ain't just a pimp... I'm from B.A.B.E Street; these niggas are beneath me."

Rarri walked to his trunk and grabbed the lighter fluid, then started squirting it over the clothes and the ground.

"Beneath you?" Money-Mike laughed. "Nigga you doin' all this over a bitch. What part of the game is this?"

"It's the part of the game you ain't learn yet: dexterity and being proficient," Rarri replied. "Oh yea, I forgot this."

He pulled out the money the twins gave him last night, threw it over the clothes then poured the rest of the lighter fluid over the clothes and bills. Rarri pulled the Zippo lighter he bought from the store, lit it then threw it over the clothes causing it to flame and instantly burn the money.

"I don't need nothin' from none of you hoes. I'm the son of God, who the fuck is y'all? This is everything I bought since I been out here and the twenty five hundred, I got from these two funny actin' ass niggas who played me cause another two dead beat beach bum ass bitches bounced like a beach ball," Rarri laughed into the camera then pointed it back at them.

"What part of the game is that? You niggas payed me for some bitches that was already yours 'P'. That's some weak ass shit. Only reason bitches fuck wit y'all is cause y'all on already. Them bitches ain't loyal. Matter of fact, I challenge all you niggas. Let's play my game." Everybody looked to the right as five Bentleys pulled in, back to back and parked in back of Rarri's car, blocking it in.

Bird, Mia, Tia, Fia and Dria got out of the car with their hands full. Everybody was star-struck, even the pimps.

"Oh shit, that's the Bentley Bitches!" some bitch yelled to everybody else in excitement.

"It sho'll the fuck is," another bitch said.

Bird, Mia, Tia, Fia and Dria walked up to Rarri and began undressing him, then redressed him in an all-white Gucci jumpsuit with the matching red bottoms. Fia opened his Gucci Tech backpack and started pulling out chain after chain after chain, then placed them all on him. Mia put in his earrings, Tia locked on about nine of his bracelets, Dria slid his rings on his fingers and Bird put on his Rolex watch. Rarri just looked at every pimp that was standing around like they were stupid, then he turned his attention to their hoes. They was so busy laughing at him they forgot they hoes was out of pocket looking at him.

"Now look at my bitches, then look at yoself . . . ain't no comparison. My bitches really shinnin' out here.

They shine like I shine, they eat like I eat and spend like I spend 'cause loyalty is priceless. Raise yo hand if you pulled up in a Bentley today."

None of the bitches raised their hands.

"Exactly my point. Y'all rockin' these cheap-ass outfits thinkin' y'all doin' somethin' in costume jewelry, but y'all hoes ain't worth shit... but it ain't too late to be great. I'm pretty sure most of y'all followin' my bitches on Instagram or Snapchat, that's how y'all knew they was the Bentley bitches, so Ima make this easy 'cause right now, y'all niggas lookin' sleazy. Hit my bitches inbox when y'all tryna choose-up. Don't get at me directly unless y'all tryna choose up right now. Who tryna be on the winnin' team?" Rarri asked.

Bitches didn't waste no time running to his side. Rarri was damn near knocked over from the hoes who rushed to him, smiling, ready to be on the same team as the Bentley Bitches.

"Bitch get yo ass back over here. You got me fucked up!" Success yelled at Diamond, his bottom bitch as he tried to grab her from the crowd, but Rarri intervened, stopping him just in time.

"Hold on 'P', you movin' too fast . . . talk to me, mane," Rarri told him.

"Ain't nothin' to talk about 'P', tell that bitch to come back over here," Success said seriously.

Rarri looked over his shoulder then back at Success. "It's a lot of bitches over there, 'P'. You gotta be more specific."

“He talkin’ bout the Rox Brown lookin’ bitch with the blue dress on,” Rarri’s grandpa chuckled.

“Oh, the Rox Brown lookin’ bitch,” Rarri said sarcastically, looking at his grandpa. “She bad, ain’t she ‘P’? Ain’t she bad! Say she ain’t bad ‘P’.”

“She bad ‘P’. She bad,” his grandpa laughed.

Rarri looked at Success who was pissed the fuck off. “I got her from bruh right here. Man, I appreciate that ‘P’. I been on one all day. Matter of fact, here.”

Rarri handed his grandpa his cell phone and turned the camera function on, then stood next to Success with his arms folded. “Flick us up ‘P’. Flick us the fuck up ‘P’.”

Rarri’s grandpa took about four pictures of them.

“Hold on, get one like this,” Rarri said as he put his arm around Success’s neck.

“Don’t fuckin’ touch me!” Success yelled loudly as he yanked away from Rarri.

“Damn ‘P’, my bad, I ain’t know you was trippin’ like that,” Rarri replied sincerely. “You want the bitch back?”

“I just gotta handle some business with her tonight cause we had some big money lined up. After that, you could come pick her up or I will drop her off to you ‘P’,” he explained.

“Yea, I feel you ‘P’ . . . go hurry up and grab that hoe, you could get the bitch back,” Rarri told him.

Success didn't waste no time to start power walking towards Diamond. Rarri crept up behind him and yelled, "sike!" as he tripped him.

Success hit the ground hard. Rarri started running around laughing. Diamond covered her mouth and Meeka's dropped open wide.

"I got you good 'P' . . . I got you good. How you fall for your own trick ,'P'. What— you forgot?"

All the other hoes started laughing.

Bird, Mia, Tia, Fia and Dria was loving the way Rarri was clowning. They never seen him like this before. It was turning them on; he was acting a straight ass.

Success got up and tried to tackle Rarri, but Rarri moved out of the way just in time and Success fell again, this time, scraping his face on the concrete. He got up looking crazy as fuck. Never had he been in no situation like this, now he was the laugh of 'The Show'. Success stormed away to his car with Meeka behind him.

"Ima get wit the rest of y'all later," Rarri told the other pimps who was standing around looking stupid, then he walked away.

Bird tossed him her car keys. "Y'all pick the bitches for tryouts and get a room."

"Ok daddy," she replied, and they began picking bitches to take with them. Those who didn't get picked was going to be assed out of luck, cause fa'sho, the pimps they tried to leave was going to be all over them. Rarri opened the door to Bird's Bentley then thought about something.

"I need a loyal ass bitch I could trust to be on my team. Somebody I could really rely on."

All the bitches ran up yellin'," me, right here, I'm loyal, you could trust me, me, me, me, me, me."

Rarri scanned the crowd looking for the perfect companion to chill with, and after a few looks there she was. The one he had needed on his team. The person he could build into something new. The person he could grow with. The one he envisioned on his team more than any of the rest. NeNe. She was standing right next to NeNe away from the crowd but listening to everything.

"Betty Wap! Come on, we out of here," Rarri shouted to her.

"W-w-what?" she asked, confused.

"I told you I was goin' to pick you up when I was ready," he said with that million-dollar smile.

"W-w-w-what I gotta do?" she asked.

"All you gotta do is get in Wap. That's it," he told her seriously.

Betty Wap put both her hands over her mouth to stop herself from crying out loud as a tear poured down her face. This was the happiest moment in her life, cause she believed Rarri was picking her up. She knew he wouldn't lie to her and she felt bad for not believing him before. All the other bitches was shocked and puzzled, not believing he would pick Betty Wap over them.

"I'm bout to leave yo ass Wap, you playin'," Rarri said and got in the car.

“Noo, I'm comin’!” Betty Wap yelled and rushed to the passenger side. “Move! Watch out! Bitch, get out the way!”

Betty Wap didn’t want to be rude, but this was no time to be bullshitting and these bitches was standing in the way like they didn’t hear her just get chose by the flyest ‘P’ around. She pushed and shoved anyone in her way until she was in the car. Once she was in there, Betty Wap hugged him tightly and rocked back and forth, happily.

“Wap, chill out,” Rarri laughed.

Betty Wap let him go and sat back in her seat. “Ok my bad, I’m calm…I’m calm.”

The whole way back to the Pit, Betty Wap was finger combing the fuck out of her bang and smelling her lip wondering what it smelled like. Rarri passed his ringing phone to Betty Wap and told her to put it on speaker for him.

“Hello.”

“So, is you goin’ to let me come back?” Lae Lae didn’t waste no time asking.

“Naw, I ain’t goin’ to be able to do it,” he replied.

“Why not? I swear I won’t talk back no more or be out of pocket in no way at all, babe. Just give me one more chance,” she whined.

“It’s about trust Lae Lae,” Rarri told her.

“You could trust me, babe, I won’t fuck up again,” Lae Lae promised.

Rarri sighed deeply. “It wasn’t thirty eight hundred.”

“What are you talkin’ bout?” she asked.

“That day I had you count that money at the motel a couple days after we met. I gave you four thousand , not thirty eight hundred . . . See, the only reason I fucked wit you in the first place was cause I knew I couldn’t trust you after you tucked two hundred of my money. I needed a bitch I couldn’t trust so I could accomplish my goal. What, you think I took you to the Chopp Shop on accident? You think I just let you run over me for no reason? Bitch please, I got more game than a lil bit. Sit close and you might just learn somethin cause I ain’t even got started yet. Thanks for contributing to my legacy Lae Lae, I appreciate you more than you think, but you will never be on my team,” Rarri explained.

“Rarri that’s fuc—” Betty Wap hung up before she could finish. Lae Lae kept calling back to back to no avail.

Rarri was going to show everybody what he was about.

Betty Wap couldn’t stop laughing as she reenacted every bullshit line Lae Lae tried easing her way back in with. The two of them cracked on her the entire drive to the room.

“She sounded so hurt Rarri, I bet she cryin’ still,” Betty Wap joked as she turned the doorknob to her room, pushed it open and walked in with Rarri behind her laughing too.

“Yea, that bitch did . . . she still blowin’ up my phone like I’m bout to change my... hold on, what you doin'?" Rarri asked looking at Betty Wap like she was crazy.

"My feet hurt," she whined, kicking off her shoes and rubbing the back of her foot, as she sat on her sofa.

"Naw Wap, muthafuckas not bout to be on no lazy shit my nigga," he said as he lit a blunt, inhaling some of the best from the West. "Go pack yo shit."

"Pack my shit?" Where we goin'?" she asked with concern. "Is you goin' to follow directions or ask a million questions?" Rarri counter questioned.

Betty Wap let out a playful breath of air as she got up and headed to her bedroom.

Rarri smiled as he pulled on his blunt again, sat down, put his feet on the table, crossed one foot over the other, leaned back and exhaled heavily, blowing the smoke to the ceiling.

"That's what the fuck I thought!" he yelled playfully after closing his eyes.

"You know what yo problem is Wap?" she couldn't help but laugh as she packed her clothes neatly in her no-name duffle bags. Betty Wap loved his sense of humor and his down to earth personality. "Naw, what's my prob—"

"Yo problem is you don't respect me!" Rarri yelled, cutting her off and continued clowning.

"A nigga gotta scream like Supreme and all that . . . muthafuckas actin' like I ain't the best catch of the year, all in my ear. I'm on that, *how I'm this fly, I ain't dress in the mirror* type shit, you understand me Wap?"

"Yea, I understand!" she replied.

"Naw, but you don't get it, though. A nigga really down and around. It ain't on me, it's *in* me, you feel me?" he chopped sounding like an old school pimp as he puffed on his blunt lightly.

"I feel you, daddy," Betty Wap yelled back from the other room smiling to herself as she finger-combed her bang over her eye.

Betty Wap leaned over to peek through the doorway to make sure he was still sitting down, then pulled out her list and secretly wrote something on it quickly before folding it up and placing it back. Rarri was still clowning, but his voice fell on deaf ears as she gathered the rest of her things, simultaneously fantasizing about the vacation he was taking her on and all the things she was going to do to him, sexually.

A couple minutes had passed and Rarri was still going, feeling himself as usual on some cocky shit. Betty Wap was just standing over him looking in admiration at all the diamonds dancing on him like he was related to a Sierra Leon mine owner. Just hours ago, he was looking like a normal nigga who had been knocked for everything he had; furious, upset, broken and trippin'. People laughin', cameras flashin', postin' pictures with captions readin': **hoe less pimpin.** Unknowingly, got the competition promotin' him, live streamin' fuckin' niggas over, road rage high beamin' rushin' bitches over. Game in a different lane, too confusin' to explain. But it's guaranteed Betty Wap was in the presence of the most intriguing being she had ever seen; got her panties washing machine wet.

Betty Wap tossed a small bag on his lap, snapping him out of his mode for a minute. “I’m ready,” she said with her luggage in hand.

“What’s this?” he asked with a confused expression. “Yo fee, duh,” she replied like he should have already known. Rarri opened the bag and started thumbing through the bills in surprise.

“What the fuck,” his mouth moved, but no words came out. “What, that ain’t enough?” Betty Wap asked sadly and finger-combed her bang again.

“Naw... I mean yea . . . like... damn how much is this shit, Wap?” he replied looking up at her.

“Like eighty-four bandz,” she replied and started smelling her lip wondering what it smelled like.

“Eighty-four bandz? Where you get eighty-four bandz from Wap?” Rarri couldn’t help but ask.

“I been savin’ it. And shid, I don’t really be buyin’ nothin’ like that. So, I just been stackin’ it up,” she replied like it was nothing, then hit him with his shit again.

“Now is you goin’ to give a bitch some directions or ask a million questions?”

“Fuck you, Wap, you always turnin’ some shit around on a nigga,” he joked as he got up and went to the front door so they could leave.

Being the gentlemen that he was, he let her out first, then closed the door behind them.

“Ima go tell Mr. Lee Ima be gone for a minute,” Betty Wap said.

"I already took care of all that . . . paid yo room up for the year so you good," Rarri replied as he texted.

"For the year?" she asked. "Why so long?" "Ain't no tellin'... plus yo shit so damn cheap, might as well had paid it up. My shoes cost more than what he be chargin' yo lucky ass," Rarri joked as they walked through the hotel.

"So . . . you already had all this planned out since earlier?" she asked.

"Somethin' like that," he replied bluntly, still texting. Both of them stopped dead in their tracks as soon as they hit the parking lot.

King Doe, T Mack, Ricky-Rick and Peso was all standing by the Bentley they seen him leave The Show in, turnt all the way up.

"Look at my nigga, tho!" Peso yelled loudly as Rarri and Betty Wap made their way through the crowd, which seemed to part like the sea when Moses walked through it. Everyone they passed went mute and stared in awe at the nigga trendin' in pimpin' like never before. He was going viral in a new way, giving the game a new look. It was plenty of people who had been in it longer than him fa'sho, but they wasn't doing it like he was doing it.

Nobody knew what to expect next from Rarri. Making yo name known in the Pit was like gold around there, especially getting respect when you from out of town. Plenty of people tried popping up like him before only to get beat up, shot, robbed, but most of all knocked for their bitches and sent running off with no toes. On top of all that, he was the little nigga who the Bentley Bitches called daddy and broke bread for.

"What's the deal 'P'?" T Mack asked giving Rarri a 'P' shake as he approached. "Why you doin' niggas so cold, bruh?" he joked.

"I'm just doin' me, Mack . . . you seen how they was treatin' a nigga when I pulled up. Brushin' a nigga off; whisperin' when I leave. Said they even had the hoes chucklin' and all that," Rarri joked back.

"You held that shit down though bruh... I ain't goin' to lie, I thought you was losin' yo damn mind 'P'," King Doe added in. "Check these out," he said and handed him some all-black shades. "Put them on and tell me what you see 'P'."

Rarri slid the shades on and took them off quickly. "I can't see shit nigga," he said examining the lenses. "P' you got black tape on the lenses."

They all started busting up laughing. "Them the glasses my bitches better be rocking when I hear you in town, 'P'," Peso clowned.

"Y'all niggas is crazy," he replied handing the glasses back to King Doe. "I'm still tryna figure out why you ain't come shut shit down from the start with them badd ass bitches. Like why you even fuck wit the Pit in the first place?" King Doe asked, straightening his Gucci belt buckle. "And who is you really bruh?"

"I'm Rarri nigga! The same muthafucka I always been," he responded, slightly offended.

"That ain't what he mean, 'P'," said T Mack. He sayin' like . . ." Peso touched Rarri's jewelry as he spoke but looked him directly in the eye with a more serious face.

"Who . . . is . . . you... really? 'Cause you ain't come here like this, bruh."

Rarri matched his expression. "Like I said . . . I'm the same nigga. This shit that's on me don't define what's in me 'P' . . . I had to make that known. Most of these niggas only knockin' bitches cause of what they got, not what they bout. Hearin' all the fucked up stories about the Pit from G-Man and how muthafuckas gotta be hard body wit the IZM to breathe around here only let me know if I could make it here, I could make it anywhere. To keep it all the way 100, I'm new to this shit. I grew up gang bangin', shootin' at niggas and getting shot at. Then I started learnin' shit about my family and bein' on some money shit, so now I'm just on my Dulas."

The four of them looked at each other for a moment then nodded in approval, feeling the real shit Rarri just kicked at them.

"Real recognize real," Ricky-Rick said, breaking the silence and giving Rarri a 'P' shake, then embraced him with a hug.

"I thought y'all was bout to try and rob a nigga 'P'. Got this crazy-ass Mexican lookin' at a nigga all funny and shit," Rarri joked and they all started laughing again.

"Fuck you 'P', I keep tellin' y'all I ain't no Mexican… I'm—Puerto Rican, Black, and Creole!" All of them said at the same time and laughed some more.

"Y'all muthafuckas ain't shit, bruh," Peso joked as he lit a cigarette. "Who is this?" he asked pointing to the Lincoln pulling in with the Limo tint on some high-class shit.

"Oh shit… yea this yo ride Wap," Rarri told Betty Wap who was still standing there with her luggage in hand.

"My ride? You not goin' wit me?" she asked. "Naw, I got some shit to handle, but Ima meet up wit you later," he instructed as he took one of her bags, led her to the backseat and opened the door for her to get in, but Betty Wap just stood there looking sad with her head down.

Rarri sighed deeply, put her bags in for her then turned back around and stood right in front of her. He put his index finger under her chin and gently lifted her head up so he could look her right in the eye.

"My bitches stand tall Wap. Don't ever put yo head down again, you hear me?"

"Mmmhmm," said Betty Wap. "Do you trust me?" he asked.

"Duh I do," she replied with a smile.

"Ight... don't ask no questions. Just get in and know that wherever you land is where I want you to be," Rarri said and gave her a kiss on her forehead, which seemed to give her all the love in the world.

"K," was all Betty Wap said and jumped in the backseat with a quickness.

"Oh yea, here," he said and tossed her back the bag of money she had just gave him." "Blow all that shit on *you,* Wap... all of it," Rarri added then closed the door.

Betty Wap rolled down her window and waved good-bye to everyone as the Lincoln pulled away. You would think she thought she was Megan Markle on her way to meet the rest of the royals by how she was looking. In all, it was good to see her happy, especially after the Big Tommy incident.

Rarri went to the driver's side of Bird's Bentley and opened the door. Y'all tryna move this party or what?"

"Hell yea. Where we at wit it?" Peso asked before taking a big sip from his bottle of Remy.

"The Chopp Shop!" Rarri yelled like a maniac then jumped in the car. Peso damn near spit all of his drink out as he laughed. "You's a foo bruh!"

The crowd went crazy and everybody rushed to their cars making sure not to get left behind.

The ride there was something like the takeover in L.A. Muthafuckas was zig zaggin' in and out of different lanes, hanging out of windows, turning up shaking dreads out the sunroof, chopping at square bitches in traffic with or without a nigga. You even had some hoes shaking ass and twerking in they shit going all the way up. The scene was lit.

"I'm feelin' rich today, I'm feelin' rich today, might take yo bitch today, might take yo bitch today, I'm rich I'm rich, I'm rich, I'm rich."

"You hear that shit?" Money-Mike asked Twin, who looked at Pay Day and Dolla.

They had been sitting in the living room quiet the entire time since The Show ended, looking baffled as fuck.

"Yea, that's that Sauce Walka I—" Pay Day said, but before he could finish NeNe was running down the stairs followed by Lae Lae, Kandi and all the other bitches in the house.

"Rarri just pulled up and he got a gang of muthafuckas wit him!" NeNe shouted in a panic.

"Bitch get yo happy ass back upstairs!" Money-Mitch shouted, noticing Lae Lae tighten her lips to break her smile like she always did. "You heard em!" Twin barked at Kandi not knowing what else to say or how lame he sounded saying what he just said. "*Fuck*," he thought to himself as soon as Pay Day and Dolla looked at him for saying that dumb ass shit.

"A chuckle here and a chuckle there… bitches laughin' at niggas and shit," Dolla mumbled to himself, but loud enough for the trio to hear.

"BAM! BAM! BAM! BAM! BAM!"

"Open this muthafucka up, 'P'," Rarri laughed dramatically, shaking the doorknob up and down before using both hands to cuff around his eyes so he could see through the screen door.

"Lae Lae, baby open the door for daddy and stop playin'." Lae Lae turned around to run down the stairs. "Move!" she yelled as she snatched away from Kandi.

"You stupid," she replied. "Wow," NeNe, Kayla and the rest of the bitches said at the same time shaking their heads in disgust and smacking lips.

Lae Lae had been hitting him up all day, so she knew he was coming to snatch his bitch back. Rarri gave her a one-arm hug around her waist, slid his hand down to her fat ass and grabbed a cheek as he grinned at Twin.

"I'm just fuckin' wit you," he whispered in Lae Lae's ear and started laughing.

"What the fuck, Rarri!" she shouted as she pushed him away and swung at his shoulder.

She felt played. Real played, and by the look on Money-Mitch's face she could see that things would be hard for her is she stayed, so she ran out the door as people close enough to see what happened laughed and booed her dumb ass like no talent at the Apollo. Little dumb Lae Lae . . . always doing some dumb shit.

"Man, I told these niggas it was somethin' about you 'P' . . . don't fuck wit him, he cold 'P'. He cold man, the bitches ain't worth it. I was tryna tell this nigga Twin. Niggas don't listen to Pay Day though, niggas don't listen to Pay Day."

Pay Day was talking fast than a muthafucka tryna exclude himself like he wasn't the main nigga clowning him, too.

"Ain't nobody worried about none of that shit," Rarri replied giving Pay Day a 'P' shake then extended his hand to Money-Mitch.

"We turnin' up or what?" Money-Mitch looked at Twin, Pay Day, Dolla then at J-Money who just walked in from the backyard, sliding off his Beats by Dre headphones in confusion.

"This nigga up to somethin'," the twins thought at the same time...Not wanting to seem sour, Money-Mitch stood and gave him what seemed like a genuine embrace on the outside, but it was far from it on the inside, and Rarri felt it.

"You already got the party here, might as well," Money-Mitch said with a smile as he pulled away.

"Yea, what better place to turn up at than the Chopp Shop?" Rarri asked looking at his cousin like he could see right through him, then turned to embrace the rest of them getting the same vibe.

"I mean… shit, niggas can't make it around here, right?" he added sarcastically.

Peso and King Doe made their way in like they were invited. Peso poured about thirty Molly's on the table, grabbed two and chased them down with a swig of Remy.

King Doe sat down next to Twin as he threw a bag of weed in his lap and a pack of White Owl blunts next to him. "Roll up bruh."

Twin looked at him like he was out of his fucking mind. He couldn't stand niggas like King Doe running around like they some real pimpin'. He looked down at niggas like him, rocking 10k gold like it was the thing to do, wearing designers that's not even in season or only on special occasions like The Show. "*These niggas ain't got no class,*" he thought but said, "Don't do it to yo'self ,'P'," as he tossed the weed and blunts back.

"Oh, you a bougie blood?" Peso asked and started laughing, causing Rarri and King Doe to start laughing too.

"Bougie? 'P', you niggas is part timin'…pimp yo way out the Pit, then come holla at me nigga," Twin replied and laughed as him and Pay Day slapped fives.

"Maaa'n, you niggas will get robbed in the Pit, that's why y'all talk all that high power shit like y'all really—"

"Ight, ight, ight," Rarri said stopping what was about to become something more than what it was.

"Fuck who doin' what and all that . . . both you niggas funny lookin' than a muthafucka," Rarri added.

"No disrespect cuzzo," he added talking to Money-Mike. Everybody started busting up laughing and just that fast, the elephant in the room was gone.

They all went to the backyard talking like nothing ever happened and J-Money led the people in front of the shop around back. Dolla had all the fly music blasting from the speakers outside as more people kept coming. Everybody was posting videos on social media with the location, telling more and more people to show up cause it was popping. Muthafuckas was bringing bottles, weed, pills and everything else to keep the party lit. Bitches flocked in groups wearing close to nothing. Ass cheeks was everywhere.

Dolla seen that the bitches was feeling themselves, so he threw some Cardi B on and them hoes went crazy, song after song, singing word for word. Twerking was at an all-time high and bitches was choosing and getting knocked all night. The 'P' circle was so vicious, if you wasn't pimping, you wouldn't dare get within five feet of it. Those who did, immediately felt out of place, got clowned, ignored or pointed to other circles.

"Wrong circle, 'P'… the dope dealin' niggas over there . . . the niggas robbin' shit over there . . . the square niggas still in the front … Aye 'P'! no bummy niggas allowed bruh," Pay Day would say, cause as far as he was concerned, it was his place to let everybody know where they should be, especially the females.

"Ugly bitches in the front with the squares …This ain't no strip club bitch, stop square dancin' … say… itty bitty, pretty, lil bitch, come stand next to Pay Day…fuck you then bitch, that's yo loss wit yo ugly ass. I wasn't bout to let you stand by a 'P' anyway… Aye hoe you wanna lose? Follow the bitch who just walked past me."

"I ain't no hoe," the girl said stopping in her tracks to set him straight.

"I can't tell," he replied causing the 'P' circle to laugh.

"Yea that's cause you too busy out here playin' to buss a bitch, goofy-ass nigga," she shot back as she turned to leave.

The circle went crazy with side comments and chuckles. "Bitch I will slap the shit out yo dumb ass," Pay Day barked as he grabbed her by the wrist, instantly noticing she wasn't the slightest bit scared.

"POW!" Everything happened so fast, but it moved in slow motion at the same time.

Pay Day then seen all the red flags about her that he quickly missed just seconds ago, like her cold light brown eyes, neck tats, black hoodie stretched almost past her ass, gold rings on her fingers and the link around her neck that she had purposely tucked. '*Damn! Them real gold hoops,*' Pay Day thought as he fell backward, looking at her the entire time.

"PlayDay!"

He couldn't hear her, but he knew what she said by the way her mouth moved. Rarri knew it too. He wasn't close enough to grab her before she stuck out her tongue at his cousin on the ground then ran off.

"*Damn that's a bad bitch,*" Rarri thought to himself standing there lost in his thoughts as people ran, ducked and screamed in a panic. He probably would have been on the ground or running like everybody else, but he was too loaded to react, and before he could she was gone.

J-Money and Dolla ran over to Pay Day who was now on the ground holding his stomach and crying as the blood pooled in the back of him.

"I'm dyin' 'P' . . . don't let me die…I don't wanna die, I'm sorry...tell her I'm sorry 'P'… tell her I said I'm sorry. I ain't goin' to play no mo... I ain't goin' to play no mo."

Pay Day was sobbing so serious it was low-key sad. You see who a person really is on two occasions; when they drunk or dying.

Rarri and the twins were now by his side, as well. "Turn the fuckin' camera off!" Money-Mike screamed at the people who somehow found time to start recording what was going on. They all picked him up and took him in the house until the ambulance came.

The Next Morning

"Ima kill that bitch 'P' . . . I swear to God, Ima kill that bitch," Pay Day cried.

Everybody sat in silence not knowing what to say. Pay Day would forever wear a shit bag from now on. Literally! Wasn't nothing fly about that shit.

"They got all the new technology Pay Day. They fucc around and make somethin' for shit like, I mean stuff like this," Rarri's grandpa said to his nephew.

"Fuck that! Ima show that bitch some gangsta shit" Pay Day screamed with so much force that spittle flew from his mouth and gathered in the corner as he groaned in pain. Rarri & his boys started cryin laughin.

"This shit ain't funny Rarri! Pay Day could have died my nigga," Money-Mitch yelled hoping up like he was about to do something, but they only laughed harder. After a brief moment of crying into tears and catching his breath Rarri calmed down, but he couldn't dare look at Pay Day without laughing, so he looked away.

"Naw it ain't funny… it's just... never mind," Rarri replied trying his hardest not to laugh again.

"Just what?" Money-Mike asked a little too hostile for his own good. "We wanna laugh too, nigga!"

"Fuck it! The nigga just was cryin' about how he ain't goin' to play no mo, now he talkin' bout he goin' to show her some gangsta shit . . . so, so, so now he playin' again?" Rarri started dying laughing. "This shit funny...Pay Day can't stop playin' . . . I know y'all seen the video."

Rarri pressed play on his phone and turned the screen towards them to see Pay Day crying talking about he sorry and how he wasn't going to play no more. At the time it wasn't funny, but now knowing he wasn't about to die, and he was going to be alright, Rarri thought it was an okay time to laugh at the situation.

"Naw man, I ain't tell nobody they could record me," Pay Day said sounding hurt, which only made Rarri and his friends laugh harder.

"I think you and yo lil friends should bounce 'P'," Rarri's grandpa said with a disappointing look.

"G-Man you serious?" he asked in disbelief. "Y'all niggas serious?"

Nobody said nothing but that said everything. "Ight," Rarri said as he got up to leave. "I see y'all all emotional and Shhh-stuff . . . I'm out."

"I could have died Rarri!" Pay Day shouted.

Rarri stopped, turned around so Pay Day could see how serious he was. "Bitches live and die every day 'P' . . . I ain't JAP," he replied then left with his boys.

The only person who understood him was G-Man. All he could do was shake his head.

"Never do for a bitch more than she do for you, you hear me? You can't be soft out here either, especially not on the blade. Bitches live and die every day, that's what the blade mean to me. I gots no love for these hoes or a JAP."

"What's a JAP?" God asked kicking an empty soda can out of his way as he walked with his dad.

"You see that nigga over there?" he asked pointing to what looked like the flyest nigga on the blade. He had everything pimps pimped for; nice clothes, jewelry, cars, and hoes.

"Uh-huh," God replied. "That's a JAP. Without his hoes, he would starve in these streets cause he's

Just.A.Pimp. Don't ever be no JAP lil man. Never!" he said to his son.

"Okay pop," God replied, soaking up game early on.

G-Man shook his head again thinking about his son and missing him more than ever. Deep down he couldn't help but feel like he played a big part in his son's death. Especially teaching him all the things that went against the rules of society. God was a fire gone wild, creating flames that grew larger than he even noticed. Rarri was ten times worse, Hell on two feet, burning the world as he walked by scorching his footprint on the gravel beneath him with each step. He was becoming everything his father wanted him to be and more.

Chapter 20

"I don't see what the problem is!" Rarri's grandma shouted at G- Man.

"The boy don't listen, that's the muthafuckin' problem," he shouted back at his wife who was now folding the clothes she just took out the dryer.

"Don't listen?" she asked sarcastically and tossed the shirt aside angrily. "He ain't no hoe! Who he supposed to be listenin' to— You?"

"You damn right he supposed to be listening to me. I'm his grandfather he sh—"

"He shouldn't do a muthafuckin' thing but what he wanna do . . . You fucked up! Not him," she yelled cutting him off.

"What's that supposed to mean?" he asked, but when she didn't respond he got the point.

She would always blame the death of their son on him when she was mad but he knew that was just some sort of defense mechanism she used to hide the guilt on her behalf. In reality, it was neither of their faults. God's destiny was written in stone before he was born. Even he knew he would die at a young age. The times he would talk about it, both parents would say it was nonsense. It wasn't until finding his book collection after his death that they found complete understanding despite what they thought they were teaching him. A lot of the books he wrote crushed them both because it was brutally true. A lot of the books also made them laugh, smile and brought warmth in their hearts as he talked about all the good times he had with his parents. He even wrote a book dedicated to them titled 'The Best of Friends'. In it he talked about how having parents who were the best friends he ever had was the greatest thing to ever have.

"Most kids couldn't talk to their parents about certain shit, so they were easily manipulated or misguided by others. Not me tho, bruh. Hell naw! My pops never hit me and I can't think of a time when my moms ever did, either. Really when I think about it, they ain't ever even yell at me or none of that. When I would catch them arguing, they would instantly stop and start talkin' to me. They would even laugh with each other like nothing had just happened. I remember asking them why they would do that and expressin' how fake I thought it was. That's when my pops told me that respectin' each other in my presence was about respectin' 'me' more than anything. I love them for that. Yea, I knew what it was between them; never would I get that twisted, but the way they went about it only made me respect them even more and I knew what type of bitch I would have. As complicated as it may seem or sound, I never seen true love in this lifestyle outside of my house, especially not like theirs. Pure, genuine, sincere, platonic, intellectual and spiritual. Creatin' me made us three, The Best of Friends."

G-Man wiped the tears from his wife's face and gave her a loving kiss on the lips after reciting the words written by their son. That was something they would always do for each other when one of them was on edge so they could feel him in the room.

"Come on," he said grabbing her hand and leading her out of the washroom down the hall and into God's room.

Being in his room was meditation for them both. They would hang out in there and enjoy each other's company, tell stories reminiscing on all the good times they could remember with their son. G-Man walked over to the dresser, opened the drawer at the bottom and grabbed one of the jars of weed. He laughed to himself and shook his head as he examined the emptiness of it. Then he grabbed a pack of papers, an ashtray, and lighter and closed it back. He went and sat next to his wife who was already sprawled across the bed with her shoes off like always twirling her hair, smiling in deep thought.

G-Man rolled four joints, each one fatter than a cigarette, lit one, took his shoes off and laid next to his wife, putting the ashtray between them. They were on the second joint smoking in silence, looking at the ceiling like a T.V. screen, high as fuck.

"You know I was thinkin'," G-Man said passing the blunt.

"Me too," she said as she grabbed it.

"Bout what?" G-Man asked looking over at her.

She took a big pull of the joint. "Niggas always wanna get high and start thinkin' and shit."

They both started laughing hard as hell, which went all bad for her 'cause she still had smoke in her lungs, so she was coughing and laughing feeling like she was about to have a heart attack.

G-Man grabbed the joint that fell out of her hand before it burned the bed, put it in the ashtray then went to his wife's aid, patting her back but still talking shit.

"That's what yo ass get," he chuckled.

She couldn't even get a word out, all she could do was point at the mini-fridge.

"You lucky I love yo ass," G-Man said as he got up to get her a bottled water. He took the top off then handed it to her.

She downed it like a fish out of water, then sat up straight in the bed putting her back against the headboard as she caught her breath. G-Man gave her a kiss on the cheek, lifted her legs, sat down and put her feet in his lap so he could massage them. They joked and laughed so much that it hurt, making good fun of each other.

"Why you skip the part about gettin' shot in the ass?" she asked laughing.

"Oh, that's funny? That's funny huh?" G-Man put both feet under his armpit, locked on them just enough to make sure she couldn't kick free and started tickling her.

"Ok! Ok! It ain't funny. It ain't funny," she cried out laughing uncontrollably, but he kept tickling.

"Stop laughing then if it ain't funny," he chuckled and kept tickling.

"Ok! Ok! Ok," she replied. He stopped for 'almost' a split second.

"You still laughin'."

"I'm not, I'm not," she cried out. "Ok! Ok! Babe I gotta pee! I gotta pee."

"Go on and pee then… I done seen you pee before," G-Man laughed. "Pissy ass . . . yea we goin' to tell Rarri that, too."

Rarri was crying laughing quietly to himself with his ear to the door. "Tell me what?" he asked pushing the door open, damn near giving both of them a real heart attack. G-Man was the one to scream out loud though, causing Rarri and his grandma to laugh even harder. She used that time to slip from his grip and ran into the bedroom bathroom so fast, she only cracked the door when trying to push it closed.

"G-Man you too old to be screaming like that," Rarri laughed.

"Supreme Scream!" his grandma screamed, and they all started laughing some more.

Rarri grabbed one of the joints, lit it and sat down next to G- Man. "So… you goin' to apologize or what?"

G-Man gave him that *nigga please* look, grabbed the joint and hit it hard like four times before blowing the smoke out. "You know Pay Day ain't built like that . . ." he said then exhaled and passed it back. "That's still my nephew, tho."

"I'm already knowin' G-Man, and that's still my cuzzin'. The shit was just funny. I was tryin' my hardest not to laugh on some real shit, he just wouldn't shut the fuck up and stop sayin' stupid shit." Rarri hit the joint. "Then y'all wanna get mad at a nigga for tryna cheer muthafuckas up. That's what was crazy to me."

"You know these niggas be in they feelins," his grandma said as she came out the bathroom. She took the joint from him and pulled on it then passed it back. She went to the closet and pulled out a container that she hadn't opened in years. It had all the combs, grease, rubber bands and necessities she used when doing his father's hair when he was young.

His grandma put a pillow on the floor next to the bed then sat down. "Come on… let me twist you up."

Rarri went and sat between her legs on the pillow. The three of them laughed as they swapped life stories catching up on the things they missed. He told them about things he would never tell nobody else but Heaven and asked every question he could think of about his dad. When they shied away from certain questions, he knew it was something God wanted him to find out on his own.

"Why did he call himself God?" he asked his grandma.

"God named him God," she replied bluntly as she parted his hair neatly. "You should have seen the nurse's faces when I wrote God down on his birth certificate. Them muthafuckas tried everything they could to get me to change it, but I wasn't hearin' that shit," she laughed.

"I was mad when I found out, too. She lucky I was in jail, cause I specifically remember tellin' her to name him after me," his grandpa threw in as he rolled some more weed.

"What you do when you found out?" Rarri asked him.

"Wasn't nothin' he could do but respect it…before we went to visit him, I wrote him a short letter explainin' myself, tho cause I knew he was mad at me," she chuckled.

"What did it say," he asked.

"Somethin' I will never forget and always respect," he said seriously. "It said this word for word:

Do you believe Jesus died for our sins? Do you believe God created Lucifer to be the God of Hell and ruler of all evil? Why do people hate the devil if he's exactly who God created him to be? I don't know either, but what I do 'know' is that he created our child to be the God of game. Not the great I am but the flesh of the great I am. Born God but not 'the' God. We are his prophets and you will bow down to him just as I do. His legacy will be long-lived, misunderstood by most and proudly hated by fakes. Everything but a saint the great ***I am*** *made him great at being him for a purpose and everyone else knowing all the bad we might do, someday. No matter how good or bad, he created us to live out our deeds, knowing them and loving us all the same, using the two of us as vessels. A pimp and a whore to bore something more, whose granddaughter's name will be "Ora Galore" cause everything around her will be plentiful. Our seed, seeds will strive to be the successors of their successor. Elevating more and more each generation. Our beliefs will delineate our ethnicity, not our ancestors. God will create our people to call our own. People segregated from disloyalty, jealousy, envy and hate instead of race. Brought together by loyalty and love. Believe and behold everything.*

Rarri was amazed at how much faith his grandma had in his father. "Damn that's deep."

"Too deep to speak to outsiders, so don't," his grandma said firmly.

"Never," he replied just as firm. "G-Man, how you remember all that by heart though?"

"Boy you don't listen or what?" his grandma asked yanking one of his dreads hard making him groan in pain and regret asking what he just did.

"I am my son's prophet," G-Man replied so sincere that Rarri believed him without the slightest bit of doubt.

"Grandma don't pull my hair can I ask one more question, tho?" Rarri asked.

"The world is yours, ask as many as you want," she replied kindly.

"Don't prophets teach people shit about shit?" he asked tensing up, waiting on her to yank one of his dreads out.

She laughed and hit him softly, twice on the shoulder. "That's two for flinchin' . . . the definition of a prophet is one whose revelations are divinely inspired, and a revelation is somethin' that is revealed... the only person we have to reveal anything to is you until *You* need us to do more."

"More like what?" he asked them screamed out in pain again after she yanked another dread. "Shit… grandma that hurt."

"Good! Maybe you might start listening more closely now when grown folks talkin'," she replied with humor.

G-Man passed him another joint he had just lit. "You *will* be your father's successor. Believe and behold everything. That's the real meaning of BABE St: Believin' and Beholdin' Everything you can possibly imagine for yourself, those around and most importantly those who will be here when you are gone. You might fall. Anything is possible, and as fucked up as it hurt me to even think about, it hurts, even more, to speak but . . . you *could* die just like yo father did, but know if you die, fall or not, whatever it is, it's what you were born to do... selfishly selfish while being selfless is hard to fathom any person balancin', but it's what you *gotta* do. Believe and Behold Everything. "

"Go ahead," his grandma said when he looked at her knowing he wanted to ask another question.

"I thought you said *you* came up with BABE Street and it stood for Break a Bitch Easy?" he asked with a sour expression towards his grandpa.

"I did," he replied proudly.

"So, what's all this 'Believe and Behold Everything' shit y'all keep talkin' about?" Rarri asked still looking sour.

"Rarri . . ." his grandma said as she put down the comb and took a minute choosing the best words to put simply.

"BABE Street means anything positive for *you* and anyone else welcomed in this lifestyle to mean. As long as it's motivation to be somethin' *worth* cherishin'. Break a Bitch Easy means more than takin' her money. You can Break a Bitch Easy out of bad habits and send her to school to get a degree so she could have a career to fall back on.

Breakin' someone ain't just a bad thing, but even if it was, as long as it's for the cause it's good. It's goin' to be some good people against everything you stand for, simply 'cause they don't understand it, hate it or just 'cause they can't be a part of somethin' that's not for everybody. Whatever reason it is, never wait to break nothin' or nobody who against this shit, Rarri. Break the world into pieces if need be, just have meanin' behind it. You are your father's successor. Now put yo head back so I could finish the front before my hands cramp up."

Rarri did as his grandma said and thought deeply about what they were telling him. Never did he think of having to think this far ahead, but he had to admit it felt good to do so.

In Compton, everybody just thinking about surviving to see the next day. Ain't nobody worried about life after theirs. Ain't too many trust fund babies in the hood like that. You even gotta watch the ones who supposed to have yo back cause it's so cutthroat. You even gotta watch out for niggas with known reputables cause it ain't unknown for a banged out gangsta to get on the stand, point you out, go back banging harder than ever and start fucking with one of your homegirls who always talking about how stupid you is for shooting him in the first place, knowing people was outside looking, that was fa'sho going to say something regardless of her nigga coming to court or not. Everything else don't even matter cause you put him in a situation to have to tell cause getting shot while on probation is a violation so you the bitch nigga for making scenes, busting on shit in the daytime instead of at night like you should've done to begin with.

The fuckery! Rarri got up and brushed the loose hairs off of his clothes then walked to the mirror. "Damn!" he said looking at his dreads thoroughly. "These low-key better than when I got em," Rarri admitted.

"That's cause grandma love you boy," she said grabbing his face like a baby and giving him a big kiss on the cheek. His grandpa was just watching the two of them with absolute joy.

"I love you too G-Ma . . ." he replied, still looking at himself in the mirror glad as hell he wasn't born nobody else. "Oh yea, I'm bout to go back home for a minute… I cracked the cheat code I need the next one."

His grandma opened the drawer and handed him the one under The Cheat Code. She noticed he brought it back a couple days ago but didn't grab the next one. "These yo books Rarri, you ain't gotta ask us to grab them for you," she assured him as she was handing it to him but snatched it back quickly. "You never told me how you cracked the code."

"We goin' to need another joint," Rarri replied, then told them the long version of how he was able to crack the code on some fluke shit. After talking more about other shit, his grandma gave him a chain from his dad's drawer. It was a diamond-encrusted link with a 24k Ferrari Medallion that had *'The best son ever'* engraved on the back. Rarri was lost for words.

"You earned this one," she told him then proudly placed it around his neck, smiling as she admired the way it fit him so perfectly. "Ight, kick rocks nigga before I start cryin'," his grandma added taking the joint out of his hand

and replaced it with The Book, then sprawled back on the bed.

"Breathe," he read out loud with a smile. "Ight G-Man I'll be back in a minute," he added giving his grandpa a 'P' shake, then walked out the bedroom closing the door behind him knowing they would more than likely stay in there all night.

His grandma hit the joint then passed it to G-Man. "Blind Bill huh?" she asked herself out loud then exhaled.

Chapter 21

Lil Dink was talking non-stop, telling Rarri about everything that was going on. Trigg and the Flocks came through as soon as they heard he was at Lil Dink's house. Macky popped up with his boy Kill Kill without letting Lil Dink know he was bringing somebody with him. He wasn't really tripping cause this was just the spot he kept a couple bricks at. The only people ever to come to his house was Trigg cause that's his boy and Heaven cause she's the one who purchased it and basically told him that's where he had to keep the work she gave him.

All of them was getting fucked up off weed and drank. Macky and Kill Kill kept going to Macky's car to bump lines on the low. Trigg kept pointing out how they was high off powder every time they left. *He would know*. The flocks all agreed they didn't trust Kill Kill for nothing at all. Especially Infant.

"Blood keep lookin' some type of way when I blood, blood but on Piru I'ma blood 'em til he leave Rarri on Ru's."

Infant was loaded. "What up Kill Kill blood!" he yelled as Macky and Kill Kill came back in.

Macky could feel the bullshit from a mile away, so he shook told them he had some shit to do. Kill Kill shook Rarri, Lil Dink and Trigg's hand but he wasn't fucking with the Flocks.

They all did the blood call at the same time before Kill Kill walked out the door and started crying laughing. Kill Kill turned around about to do Lord knows what, but Macky grabbed him before he could and the two was gone.

"What's wrong wit him, Trigg?" Lil Flock asked still laughing. "Super cuh don't like super bloods. You know how that shit go foo," Trigg admitted truthfully.

"Who Super Bloods?" Flock asked with a smile and his hands out like he really didn't know.

"Y'all… the Flocks. All y'all some Super Bloods," he replied pointing at them all. "I fuck wit y'all tho."

"Fuck it! Whatever! So, what if Ima Super Blood. Trigg, I don't see how you talk about super nothin'. You and Lil Dink YAAH everybody and they momma," he said matter of factly. "And since we on the subject *Trigg,* my momma *been* told me to tell you to stop YAAH'n her." Rarri and Lil Dink was in tears.

"Stop lyin' foo! Bang that," he chuckled.

"On Bompton," he swore still laughing and everybody started laughing harder.

" And stop playin' wit my sister, blood. Ain't nothin' happenin'," he added playfully but so serious at the same time.

"Aye, we bout to go west tho... niggas gon link up tomorrow or what?"

"Mando," Lil Dink said, giving them all shakes, so did Trigg and Rarri.

"So, what's the plan now?" Trigg asked Rarri once everybody was gone. Besides telling them about everything that happened in the Bay, Rarri was quiet most of the time.

"You tell me, "Rarri replied with a smile and took another sip of his drink.

"How he goin' to tell you foo?" Lil Dink butted in.

"Just as easy as you said that," he replied bluntly. "What you wanna Trigg? Whatever you wanna do is what we goin' to do."

Trigg didn't know what to say. As far as he was concerned, he was doing what he wanted to do. The shit with Spank's mom had him all fucked up. Rarri still didn't know what really happened to her and Lil Dink was on that *when the time is right,* shit, so he just went with that.

"Man, I'm bout to crash out. We goin' to talk when we sober up foo," Rarri said as he got up and went into the guest room almost passing out soon as he hit the bed.

"Wassup wit him?" Trigg asked. Lil Dink just shrugged his shoulders, lit a blunt and turned the T.V. up.

"*I know what I'm doin'*," Trigg thought to himself as he grabbed his .45 and left.

Chapter 22

"Kilo after Kilo I give you, and what do I get in return, huh?" Tony asked slipping on his loafers, custom made by John Lobb to go with his Lanvin suit. "I'll tell you what I get; nothing! Not a single dime! Not even a penny!

Tony stood up and walked to the mirror to adjust his clothing. Still rambling, he grabbed his watch by Richard Millie he loved so much and put it on angrily.

"I give you everything! Everything!" he barked. Heaven threw the magazine she was looking at on the floor and stormed out of the room. You could hear the aggression coming from her Ferragamo heels almost devouring the wooden floors of his massive yacht.

"Where are you going?" Tony asked, power walking after her. "Away from you! I'm done Tony, I can't do this anymore, keep yo money and all this shit," she replied still walking fast, but not *too* fast. Heaven was more calculated than anyone could see. She never did something for nothing. She didn't love Tony. Not because she didn't want to but because she couldn't. Love another, her heart wouldn't.

"One . . . two . . . three," she counted down in her mind, and like clockwork, Tony came running full speed grabbing her by the wrist apologizing like he always did when she threatened to leave.

"I'm sorry," he admitted, trying to kiss her lips as she dodged him continuously each time.

Heaven placed her hand on his stomach right under his navel moving her thumb up and down only twice purposely, seemingly unintentionally, soft but firm, her voice low yet demanding and sensual. Making sure her lips were close to his. Not too close, but close enough to feel the warmth of her sweet breath. Close enough to make him relive every time she put him to sleep with her mouth that seemed to never stop watering. Close enough for him to miss something that has never left. Close enough to control him.

"Move," was the only word she needed to use. Tony wrapped both hands around her waist to keep her from leaving again, not knowing he was better off jacking off a wild bobcat in a phone booth.

"Never again," he said softly kissing her neck that smelled so good it made his dick hard.

"You said that last time Tony," Heaven replied pretending to try and break free of his grip.

"I promise you... this time was the last. Never again," he swore with confidence.

She believed him. Tony was everything but a liar. Heaven could feel his love radiating from him to her from miles away. He truly loved her and she knew it.

"I don't believe you," she lied almost upsetting him again, but he calmed himself.

Tony hated being called a liar. He contemplated smacking her, but the last time he did that she smacked him back harder, even threw in a couple punches. It took two of his guards to get her off of him, so he didn't want them problems, especially not today. Most of his clientele seemed to only want to do business with her around now, for some odd reason.

"Heaven I would give my life for you. I love you more than anything and anyone here on earth," he replied genuinely.

She let out a sarcastic laugh. "Not more than your little boats." "Which boat? Pick any boat I have and it's yours," Tony replied in his heavy accent. "Any boat," he added before lifting up her 'Married to The Mob' skirt and going down on her like it was his favorite thing to do. Heaven leaned against the rails bracing herself with both arms and put both legs on Tony's shoulders while he ate her pussy.

The feeling of controlling someone as powerful as him was enough to make her cum instantly. Breaking a rich nigga was a high she chased and craved for, daily.

Heaven was twirling her pussy in a circular motion enjoying every bit of Tony's pleasuring. He was never in a rush to stop tasting what she could let out for him. He was in fact, more addicted to her more than the people strung out on the drugs he put out on the streets.

Tony put her down after satisfying her, stood up kissing her passionately while he undid his pants quickly. Heaven took off her top and turned around so he could hit it from the back. Tony couldn't help but let out a manly moan as he slid into her already wet pussy. He fucked her and she fucked back, neither of them noticing the man snapping pictures of them while they sexed each other on the deck of Tony's yacht. No one ever noticed him.

Chapter 23

Pretty Me da P was making a name for himself in San Bernardino. He had four bad bitches in his stable and they was going hard for him on G street. His bottom was a Pilipino named Daphne. She was about 5'8", petite body with big breasts and a pretty face. Her skin was naturally tanned giving her an exotic sexy look, and her attitude could be seen from a mile away. Her mouthpiece made up for the ass she didn't have, and the pussy was so good, most of her tricks became regulars after the first fuck. Daphne could make the trick with the smallest dick feel like he just beat that thang up. Bout time she was done with him, he would be feeling like Superman doing the Daddy Dick dance like Jodi in Baby Boy. Yeah, she was that good.

Then there was Foxy. She was dark-skinned, short; not too petite but her body made her bad. You could literally sit a cup on her ass while she was standing up without it falling. Foxy was a little rough around the edges but that was kind of cool because she could handle her own in sticky situations. Unlike other bitches, Foxy dated black tricks because she felt able to communicate with them better than whites and Mexicans. Most of the black men she fucked with were squares. The others were wanna-be pimps and thugs. Foxy could spot a fake 'P' with a quickness, or so she thought.

His other two bitches were Trisha and Lisa. Both of them was white hoes from up north and was way more ghetto than Foxy. Both pretty with blue eyes, red hair and was tatted the fuck up. Trisha and Lisa were almost identical cousins. Trisha was just a little thicker than Lisa but Lisa's ass looked better than Trisha's. They was bad as fuck; their only flaw was they was too got damn loud. You couldn't take them, bitches, nowhere and be low-key. Everywhere they went they made a scene. Pretty Me da P hated going out to eat with them cause they always found some reason to curse the waitresses out no matter how good the service was.

"Damn 'P', you ain't been playin' out here," Amazin' said as he passed the blunt to his cousin.

"A nigga can't be playin' when bitches payin' ya dig?" Pretty Me da P responded after he pulled on the blunt.

"Hell yea, I could dig that. I'm bout to step my shit up . . . I just cracked a new piece," he told him.

Pretty Me da P started busting up laughing. "P', who you playin' wit? You know damn well Ebony ain't lettin' you bring no new toe's around."

Ebony was Amazin's baby momma and his only hoe. She didn't allow him to bring no other bitches into the picture, and every time he tried she ran them off.

Ebony was huge like them Samoan girls, so most bitches didn't want no problems. She was known to fight a nigga if he pissed her off. Ebony once went to jail for beating a trick up in her motel room for trying to rob her. She beat him so bad, the police kept asking him where were the rest of them, assuming he had been jumped by her pimp and his friends from how fucked up he was. Muthafuckas swear she be fucking Amazin' up, on the low cause she was running the show, fa'sho, fa'sho.

"She gon get wit this program or get the fuck on 'P' . . . I'm not bout to be stuck on the same level my whole life cause she don't want me to shine . . . I been out here longer than you and you already passed me up by far. Fuck all that," Amazin' replied angrily.

"It sound good 'P', but uh... what's the hold-up? You scared or somethin'?"

Pretty Me da P knew how to pump Amazin' up. He had been doing that since they were kids.

"Ain't nobody scared of that bitch. She already know what's up," Amazin' said smoothly then put the blunt to his lips.

"What bitch?" Ebony asked from the side window scaring the shit out of Amazin', causing him to drop the blunt in his lap and fumble around for it.

Pretty Me da P janky ass seen her walking up through the rearview mirror, but instead of saying something he let him keep talking.

"Yea, what bitch," he chuckled.

Amazin' handed Pretty Me da P the piece of blunt and when he looked at him, he mouthed "shut the fuck up" quietly.

"You play pimpin' 'P'," Pretty Me da P said with a sour expression as he relit the blunt. His words shot Amazin' right in the heart. Amazin' wanted to be taken seriously, not looked at as no play pimp. Ebony was fucking his name and game up and he was tired of it. Either she was going to get with his program or get lost cause he was ready to get on his cousin's level.

“What bitch?” Ebony barked.

“You!” he shot back. “You ain’t bout to keep runnin’ my program, that’s out. I need more than what you bringin’, so I got some new toes on the way. She goin’ to be here by tomorrow, so be ready to lace her up.”

“We already talked about this. I’m not fuckin’ wit no other bitches, so it’s either me or her Darnell. Why I gotta share my man? You know what, go ahead and fuck wit her then if that’s what you want. I don’t need no nigga to control my money, anyway. I do all the work while you just spend, spend, spend like you got it like that. Yo lazy ass don’t even flip the money like a real nigga would be doin’ and got the nerve to call yo’self Amazin’. Ain’t nothin’ Amazin’ about you Darnell. Nothin’! I hate I even got pregnant by yo stupid ass,” Ebony cried.

“If you hate it so much, then get the fuck on,” Amazin’ yelled.

Ebony wiped the tears from her eyes. “That’s exactly what I’m bout to do,” she said and turned to walk away.

“Bye bitch,” Amazin’ said dismissing her.

Ebony stormed back up to the car and pushed him in the head with her index finger a few times as she went off. “Don’t disrespect me. You tryna show out cause you in front of yo cousin right now thinkin’ you look cool, but you ain’t nothin’ but a dumb ass nigga. You a fuckin’ joke.”

When Amazin’ looked at Pretty Me da P, he started laughing. Amazin’ was mad as fuck. Wasn’t nothing going right, and Pretty Me da P wasn’t making shit any better.

Amazin' looked forward with a straight face and a knot in his lips. He had his cousin on one side laughing and his angry baby mother on the other, testing him. Not wanting to look at either of them, he kept his eyes looking out the front window and did what he thought was right. "Like I said . . . bye bitch."

Before he could say another word, Ebony was pulling him through the window with one hand and punching him with the other. Ebony had beat bitches up bigger than Amazin'. He wasn't even half her size. Amazin' was at max a hundred thirty five pounds, soaking wet. Ebony had a fist full of his hair as she dragged him around like a little ass kid, whooping his ass. All Amazin' could do was try to block his face while she punched and kicked him. She had so much of his hair in her hand, he couldn't break free for shit. He was met with a punch every time he tried to stop himself from falling on the ground. On top of that, every time she hit him, she said a word.

"You— wanna—talk— like a—bitch— Ima— beat you— like a—bitch . . . I— told— you don't— fuckin'— dis— respect— me— muthafucka."

Luckily nobody else was around cause this shit would have been on World Star too.

Ebony tried to kick Amazin' in the stomach but slipped and fell her big ass on top of him.

Amazin' screamed out in pain. It felt like she broke one of his ribs when she landed on him. He tried to squirm from under her and get up, but she grabbed him by the collar of his shirt and pulled him back to the ground with her. Even though his lip and nose were busted, Ebony wasn't nowhere near done with him yet. He was about to learn not to disrespect her like that.

"Naw, don't run... don't run," she said out of breath as she climbed back on top of him and pinned him down.

"Alright, baby I'm sorry!" Amazin' pleaded as he tried to get from under her.

"No, you ain't… you ain't sorry… not yet," Ebony replied as she put a knee on each of his arms leaving his face exposed between her legs. Her dress was up to her stomach and one of her titties was out. Amazin' could see her pussy cause she, like most hoes didn't work with panties. Ebony smelled like condoms, dick, balls, pussy, and ass all mixed together. Her weave was somewhere around there, so all she had on her head was a stocking cap.

Ebony started throwing punch after punch at his face without the slightest bit of sympathy.

"Who, the, bitch, now? Huh? Who, the, bitch, now?"

Amazin' was relieved when she stopped punching him, but that was short-lived when he felt her stubby hands tighten around his neck. Ebony started choking the life out of him. He knew she was choking the life out of him cause he could feel his life leaving out of him. His eyes damn near popped out of his head and his mouth was stuck open. Never had he seen this look on Ebony's face before. It was like looking at a serial killer. It seemed like she was looking through him.

When their eyes met, Amazin' seen her come back. He saw sadness and sorrow in her eyes. He saw love. The love that kept them together all this time. He seen the tears she shed for him falling down her face. Amazin', despite his current situation, started to feel bad about what he did. He knew how much she had been through growing up in a verbally abusive household. He knew the pain both of her parents put her through when she was a kid. He knew how many bitches her dad would call her on a daily basis when he would beat her. He knew about her bouncing from foster home to foster home after she killed him too, so Amazin' promised to never call her a bitch or put his hands on her. After a split second, he knew that Ebony wasn't looking at him, she was looking at her father.

Pretty Me da P looked in his rearview mirror and seen Ebony on top of Amazin', then turned off the street. He had pulled off as soon as Amazin' was through the window and watched from a distance. Wasn't no way in Hell he was about to fight that big ass bitch and get his ass beat with Amazin'. Amazin' shouldn't have had been fucking with that crazy bitch in the first place. Pretty Me da P didn't know it was going to go this far, he was just playing with his cousin cause he didn't think he would actually stand up to Ebony, and damn sure didn't think he was stupid enough to call her a bitch. He felt bad about leaving Amazin' like that, but he did this to himself. Who is he to get in they business? Amazin' needed to learn how to hold his own. Pretty Me da P wasn't about to put his pimping on a limb for *nobody*. Especially not for a nigga who can't control his bitches. That's all the way out.

"I'm too pretty for this shit," Pretty Me da P said to himself. He bent a couple more blocks and pulled up on his hoes who were standing on the corner.

"Y'all come on, the police hot, we bout to call it a night… where Trisha and Lisa?"

“They up the street,” Daphne replied as she and Foxy got in the car. “We split up to cover more streets,” Foxy added as she took her heels off.

“Bitch, didn’t I tell y’all to start informin’ me before y’all do shit? How the fuck y’all know I ain’t got nothin’ goin’ hoe? I should slap the shit out yo punk ass right now, bitch. Y’all lucky the police hot around this muthafucka, but when we get back to the room it’s goin’ to be consequences and repercussions for all y’all hoe’s,” Pretty Me da P barked as he pulled off.

One hour and thirty minutes later…

“So, y’all bitches think this shit a game. I tell y’all shit for a reason. I don’t just be talkin’ for nothin’ hoe. Y’all wanna make a ‘P’ waste his breath, tho. I swear to God I’ma bea—”

“There they go right there, daddy,” Foxy said pointing across the street anxiously from the back seat. She knew if they didn’t find them soon, Pretty Me da P would have blamed her and Daphne for losing his SNOW. Niggas go crazy over them white hoes.

“I think . . . I think they standing there wit yo cousin and Ebony.” “Fuck!” Pretty Me da P swore to himself and kept driving right past them.

“Daddy they right there, you not goin’ to get them?” Daphne asked looking out the back window then back at him.

“Shut the fuck up and let me think bitch! Fuck!” he shouted in frustration.

"The police hot, I can't make no illegal U-turn wit this weed in the car and put y'all seat belts on before y'all hoes get us pulled over." Daphne and Foxy hurried to do as instructed as Pretty Me da P got into the proper turning lane and turned around. The crazy part is this nigga didn't even have his seat belt on.

Pretty Me da P pulled up and rolled down the passenger window and seen Trisha and Lisa sitting on the steps behind Ebony and Amazin' with their heads down looking scared as fuck.

"Why y'all bitches ain't been answering y'all phones? Come on, we out of here," he instructed.

"I got they phones," Ebony replied holding them back in the air for him to see.

"What?" Pretty Me da P asked angrily. He had enough of this silly shit for one night. He put the car in park and hopped out like muthafuckin gangsta.

"What the fuck you mean you got they phones? Check this out, I ain't Amazin'. You don't touch nothin' that belong to me, ya understand me? I ain't gonna disrespect you cause you his baby momma, but I ain't bout to be out here playin' wit you either."

"So, what you wanna do then? " Ebony asked bluntly.

"What?" he asked in disbelief with his most toughest face on and stepped forward hoping to intimidate her, but she walked all the way up, on him.

"*Damn*," he thought to himself but kept his mug on.

"I said… what, you, wanna, do, then... cause you actin' like you wanna do somethin'," she replied leaning towards him putting her face close to his.

Pretty Me da P wanted to call this bitch a bitch, but he knew better, so he just looked over at Amazin'.

"Aye come get yo girl, my nigga."

"Bro, you just left *me*. How you goin' to ask me to do somethin' now?" Amazin' asked in disbelief.

"Cause he a clown," Ebony said and pushed him in his face with so much force he damn near fell. That nigga was looking like Kevin Hart when the Rock hit him on Jumanji. He couldn't believe this bitch, is what his expression was saying and his jaw was on dumb swivel. He shook his head.

Chapter 24

Shawn was paranoid as fuck. He couldn't stop looking out the window to make sure nobody knew where he was.

After running into Trina at Lil Trouble's spot-on accident, he was low-key spooked. That shit was too coincidental, but he lucked up, on a lick in the process, so fuck it.

"*Gotta keep clutchin'*," he thought to himself then bumped another line. Still on his sheisty shit up to no good, he was running out of places to hide and going back to Jersey was not an option. *Hell naw.* He burnt that out before leaving when he decided to rob his own cousin, thinking he was bout to be gone and had to shoot him when he wasn't. The shit went all bad from there cause he ain't kill him, not that he wanted to, but shooting him and not killing him ended up being worse than doing so. He knew his cousin. He wouldn't tell, but he would want his get back fa'sho and had a lot of people who would help see it through.

Shawn was too scandalous and had crossed too many muthafuckas to trust anyone back home. Relatives and all. They all already was thinking he had something to do with his grandma's death, cause she just so happen to of had an accident after Shawn found out he had something coming if she died. So many people wanted a piece of Shawn, wasn't nothing else left to claim. Laying up under a cougar was easier than he had thought. Especially in Cali.

The one he had now was spoiling him rotten but that still wasn't enough. He *was* about to marry her in a couple of months, but that wasn't fast enough, so he talked her into agreeing to do it, next week. This was his chance to come up big and he wasn't going to fuck it up. Shawn didn't know how much he was getting for the scheme he pulled on his granny. He rolled the dice on that one and crapped out. Just like he did every other time, none of them was worth it in the end cause he never got what he assumed he would get. This time he knew what he was working with. Shawn was doing so much homework on this bitches finances, he almost knew the exact amount he would drain from her.

Everything was going perfectly. He was on point. He even made sure to do everything his fiancé liked on time and all that, so he couldn't understand why she hadn't been home in a couple of days.

On top of that, he could see that she'd been sending him to voicemail, so that had him mad, too.

Thinking a nice warm shower would get his mind right ended up being his biggest mistake. The police had let themselves in demanding he leave the premises immediately. Protesting that was even more of a mistake cause they found the powder he was sniffing on lined up all neatly on a plate awaiting his scabbed up nostrils and took him out in cuffs.

It wasn't long before walking out the door that his fiancé stormed in, walking right past him, ignoring his demands for an explanation. They even hit him with a sells charge on top of possession of a loaded firearm, disturbing the peace and a verbal assault. WTF is a verbal assault?

Shawn saw everything but karma catching up to him. He couldn't outrun that shit and "*I knew she was going to come back around,*" was what he was thinking as he unfolded the paper he just took out the envelope:

Dear Shawn,

I know you're pissed off at me. I know you probably hate me right now for not returning your letters or answering your calls. I know I swore that if times like these ever came, I would hold you down. I know I promised to never turn my back on you no matter what, and I know for a fact, I kept that promise. I know you're wondering what the fuck is going on with me. Oh, and yea, I ended up going through your phone the day you were arrested, so I even know about the times you cheated. I know everything I need to know about your sorry ass, and I know not to waste too much time on this letter. I know I'm going to be alright because God has a plan for us all, even yo dirty dick ass. Shawn, I don't know why you didn't tell me you had that shit. SMH.

"Fuck!" Shawn and his celly said at the same time, thinking of the day they got arrested. They always seem to say the same thing around the same time. That's something else they both almost had in common.

"Don't tell me you down there stressin' on that bitch again . . . man, bust some chips open 'P'."

Shawn snapped and punched Darshawn out before he could get his shoes on unknowingly asking "bust some chips open?" over and over and over before every punch. Shawn treated him just like he did Trina the first day they met. *Exactly like Trina.* Well, at least that's what they both was just thinking.

****

Pretty Me da 'P' wasn't feeling too pretty at the moment, especially after last night. You damn right he told on Shawn. Fuck you thought? Wasn't no way in hell he was getting away with this one. No Sir. The only thing wrong was that telling on Shawn wasn't getting him out no time sooner. The police didn't give a fuck about his booty burning. They actually found humor in this situation.

"Did he get you, good mate?" One of them asked in between laughs him and his partner had sounding like Crocodile Dundee. The two detectives cracked jokes as Pretty Me da P scrolled through a stack of pictures of other pimps they'd been trying to catch, to no avail. The eye that he *could* see through came across a familiar face and lit up like a light bulb. The female detective instantly went mute when he pushed the pictures towards them. By how serious they just became, Pretty Me da 'P' knew he was getting out. It was Amazing. He could finally get his revenge on him.

*****

"His name is Rarri," was all Maria heard as she picked the picture up off the desk and examined it a bit more than intended. Then she tossed it back down and walked out casually.

Three Months Later

Rarri was now playing most blades around the way. He was mashing harder now on familiar ground and it was easier pimping in L.A. Muthafuckas in the Bay would finesse the shit out of your hoe on a daily. In L.A., it was more territorial. You had to worry about gangs pressing you and your bitch for being on *they* blade. Some even just banged on you because that's just what they do. Others just so they can mark you out in front of your bitch if you let them. Niggas tatted all over their faces, gang sliding on the blade was the norm that's when Rarri noticed how gang-infested pimping was, and he loved every bit of it. He didn't want to, but damn he couldn't help it. He got a rush from living this life. Carpooling with Macky didn't make it any better because they always ended up fighting with some muthafuckas or shooting some shit.

Macky had hoes, though. Like some real stomp down bitches ready to do whatever for that nigga. Besides all his tripping on shit, he was actually a fun person to be around. Trigg started hanging with Kill Kill a little more than he did with Rarri and Lil Dink. Them two niggas was buddy-buddy on some trigger-happy shit. They stayed in the cut watching Rarri and Macky, waiting on somebody to trip, slip and fall on some bullets, the two finally getting paid to do what they love doing.

"Luke ain't never fuckin' wit Dark Vader, cuh," Macky said before pulling on his blunt.

"What you sayin'?" Rarri asked pulling on his, looking at Macky like he was stupid.

"Nigga, you already know what I'm sayin'," he responded as hostile as he could, then blew the smoke in Rarri's face.

Rarri immediately put his blunt out on the ground and set it on the hood of his Benz. Macky didn't waste no time in smacking it off, sending it flying under the other car next to his.

"Fuck this shit," Rarri thought to himself and hit Macky with a left, right two-piece slap, he backed up then tucked his chains.

"Oh shit," Trigg said and hopped out the car with a quickness, as did Kill Kill. The two looked at each other. The split second was tense. "Wassup?" Trigg asked.

Kill Kill didn't waste no time digging in his hoody trying to beat Trigg to the punch. Everybody in the parking lot had toes running around somewhere and a couple dollars to put up on the action.

Rarri and Macky was going at it. Strategically though, neither of them wanting to get bruised too bad knowing the other would be up one. Macky dipped in low, dodging one of Rarri's swings and hit him with a three-piece. ***"Slap! Slap! Slap!"*** Rarri backed up, then rushed back in with the same three-piece he just got force-fed, only with a little more force and the perfect timing on the last slap, sending Macky falling over to the ground. He stepped over Macky like he was a beast.

"Slid 'em!" Rarri shouted and started busting up laughing, running around slapping fives with the other 'P's in the parking lot. He knew Macky really tripped over the curb he backed him in to cause he did it on purpose.

Every time Macky tried to explain the slip, Rarri over talked him loudly so he couldn't be heard. Macky hated when he did that shit. Always manipulating his wins knowing he lost. No shame. Macky was hot. Real hot.

"I'm poppin' the trunk on yo ass," he said pointing to at Rarri as he walked to his car.

Muthafuckas thought he was playing for a minute, but when he opened his car door and they heard his trunk open, everybody started running. Everybody except Rarri.

"Don't nobody care bout you poppin' that lil muthafucka," he replied calmly looking under cars. "Where my blunt go foo?"

"Fuck yo blunt!" Macky said and lifted his trunk open.

"Like that?" Rarri asked standing up in front of Macky's car. Macky lifted the trunk down a little bit so Rarri could see his face, then put it back down.

"Bet," was all Rarri said after seeing Macky's expression and walked to his car which was parked next to his.

Macky whipped out and hit Rarri in the back of the head with his lightsaber. Next thing you know, these niggas rolling again. The parking lot playing Star Wars on their motion boards having the time of their life.

"Give me my money nigga," Trigg said snatching the hundred dollar bill out of Kill Kill's hand. He knew they was going to end up pulling the lightsabers out. Them two niggas had a Star Wars bond or some crazy shit like that. It was nothing to see them running around battling it out, making sound effects and all.

Ten minutes later, Rarri and Macky was sitting on the curb out of breath. Why were they smoking again? I don't know; you'd have to tell me.

"What you think about that Kanye West shit?" Macky asked after exhaling a big cloud of smoke.

"That nigga stupid 'P'," Rarri replied instantly then added, "talkin' bout being a slave was a choice," and shook his head in disgust.

"What's stupid about that?" Macky asked straight-faced.

"We was brought here on boat, cuh! They stole us, nigga!" he said like Macky should know this shit then added, "nigga you older than me, how you don't know this shit?"

"Yea they did all that shit, but what cuh tryna say is that after four hundred years, muthafuckas could have came up wit a plan before what happened to Emmett Till and Harriet Tubman and all the other niggas after them. They tryna make it look like he crazy, but he ain't. Cuh really smart as fuck, and if you think about it, these people kill all the smart niggas we get. It's like I want him to shut up but then again, I don't cause I feel what cuh be sayin'. It's deeper than that slave shit he was talkin' bout, but the media know how to feed information in pieces, so they get the reactions they want. They even got niggas like ol boy on TMZ who called himself speakin' up against him type shit. Now if he genuinely did that cool, but we all know about the house niggas who sold out after niggas was tryna run free. If that ain't a slave by choice, I don't know what is. Not all of them was there by choice tho, but by him sayin' it how he did they used it against cuh. Then they even put on that bullshit ass nigga Daz video talkin' bout the Crips lookin' for Kanye West, like we all beefin' wit him now . . . fuck Daz! He don't call no shots like that and

I'm rockin' wit Kanye anyway. Cuh will die for some shit he believe in; that's what I respect. The world just too damn sensitive right now. I'm tryna find out when they goin' to bring up *the new Jim Crow* book."

"Who is Jim Crow?" Rarri asked.

"Not who, but what... that shit is basically a law that was set up to keep niggas slavin' and in order at all times, like some of these hoes be... we wasn't never set free. Not like the free, they lied about in schoolbooks we *had* to read... These muthafuckas mastered slavery to the point where we are mentally enslaved, still. That's all cuh was tryna say my nigga," Macky schooled as he got up.

"I still think somethin' wrong wit him," Rarri admitted holding his hand out to Macky.

Macky pulled him up and looked him in the eyes and said, "yea . . . it's somethin' wrong wit all of us." The way he drifted into somewhere else, Rarri knew he was thinking about something serious.

Macky was one of them *Black Lives Matter, matter of fact, I'm bout to kill a nigga tonight* ass nigga. Rarri wouldn't be so surprised if Macky saved a nigga just so he could kill him himself, but he did know Macky could talk about some shit that will have you thinking deep. Sometimes he even thought about seeing what Macky thought about his pop's book, or just having a conversation about some of its topics, but he always changed his mind right when he was about to. Rarri didn't talk too much about that yet to none of his friends, and when he did it wasn't much they'd get out of it anyway.

"You tryna hit fig or what?" Rarri asked as he opened his car door and sat in with one foot out.

Macky bumped a fat line then put his head back to catch the drip. "You still tryna be funny my nig—"

"Boom! Boom! Boom! Boom! Boom! Boom! Boom! Boom! Boom! Boom! Boom! Boom! Boom! Pat! Pat! Pat! Pat! Pat! Pat! Pat! Pat! Pat! Pat! Pow! Pow! Pow! Pow! Pow! Pow! Boom! Boom! Boom! Boom! Boom! Boom! Pat! Pat! Pat! Pat! Pat!"

Niggas hit the corner busting hard as fuck, non-stop. It looked like an entire hood pouring in; niggas just kept coming. Rarri looked over at Macky just in time to catch the white ring around his nose turn red. After that, the sharp pain he felt in his leg was overcoming his whole body. Cooking him in the inside, mixing organs with different organs. Chewing through him with no strain, relentlessly piercing his lungs, not leaving much left to 'breathe' on had him pleading for air. Begging for it. Rarri wanted to run or react anyway he could but his body wasn't working. All he ended up doing was leaning to the side, getting caught between seats. The only things stopping him from falling more was the middle console and his arm.

The passenger door opened and Rarri knew who it was without seeing his face. "Scoot yo bitch ass over," Tana Jay said as he swatted Rarri's hand away from the passenger seat and seated himself. Tana Jay then went into the middle console, pulled out a bag of weed and stuffed it into his hoodie. After that he pocket checked him taking his money, then relieved him of his jewelry as rough as he possibly could without breaking any of the pieces.

The moment was over quick, but it seemed like hours for Rarri who couldn't die fast enough. Well, as fast as he wanted.

" These screw out?" he asked referring to his earrings and really looked at Rarri for an answer.

"Fuck it, I was tryna be nice to yo weird-ass," Tana Jay said and snatched Rarri's earrings out one at a time. He didn't mind getting a little blood on him; he actually enjoyed it.

Tana Jay was crazy, like real crazy, and he had money, like real money. See, Rarri was like Steph Curry in the game . . . Tana Jay; that nigga was LeBron. He been doing this shit. Pimping, selling dope, banging, all that shit. He couldn't wait to get his hands on Rarri little ass. They had been beefing ever since Rarri got back from the Bay, non-stop. Tana Jay really didn't like the shine and money Rarri had been taking out his pockets. Then he got niggas taking his hoes hostage, chasing them all around the city and shit. It was funny at first, but now it was the perfect time to end this vendetta cause it was touching his pockets at the wrong time and he had shit to do.

Tana Jay pulled out his phone and recorded using his front camera.

"Get it together my nigga got damn. Look at yo self 'P'. slippin' on yo pimpin' and slackin' on yo muthafuckin' mackin'... Compton's finest slacker."

He laughed with the camera still on Rarri. He wanted to talk so bad, but he couldn't say shit. All he could do was look at the phone and see how fucked up he was. Rarri didn't want to go out like this but wasn't shit he could do. He used all his strength and spit out as much blood as he could on Tana Jay's screen.

Tana Jay looked at Rarri like he was out of his mind. "This a iPhone 8, I just got it!" he screamed wiping his phone on his sweatpants and then put it in his pocket. "You just turned some business shit personal." Tana Jay pulled his .357 out and pointed it at Rarri's face. " bye nigga." ***"Boom!"***

Chapter 25

Rarri jumped up for air like someone splashed him with some water.

"What the fuck, how you just goin' to leave me on stuck like that," Stacey yelled then threw the plastic cup at him.

"*Did this bitch just throw water on me*?" Rarri thought to himself then asked in disbelief wiping his face. "Did you just throw water on me?" "Yes, I just threw water on you," she replied sounding out every word dramatically like she was talking to someone who didn't speak English. Then she sat hopelessly on the bed feeling defeated. "God, Rarri you got me out here lookin' stupid."

"My bad bae, come here," he said as if he was talking to a baby using that smile to soften her up as he pulled her closer.

"No, it's not my bad… my bad not goin' to get business handled Rarri... my bad not go—"

"Alright, fuck!" Rarri barked in frustration and got out of the bed. "Ain't nobody tryna hear you bitchin' early in the mornin'."

"It's three o'clock in the afternoon. If you stop poppin' Xanax every night, you might be aware of that," Stacey shot back as she followed him to the bathroom.

"You don't think I wanna pop pills, smoke weed, drink and all that, too?"

Rarri didn't even answer. He just squeezed the Colgate on his toothbrush and started brushing his teeth like she wasn't even there. He drifted off thinking about that dream he was just having while Stacey kept rambling on and on like he was listening. The dream felt too real. Usually, he could distinguish his dreams from reality, but lately, his dreams were more vivid. Xanax was known to do that, though. Them bars will give you some bomb ass dreams or some scary nightmares.

Rarri and Tana Jay had been going at it so hard, both of them was having nightmares of the other, something neither of them would ever admit to anybody. Terrorizing each other was somewhat of a ritual and breaking even was impossible because both of them sought get back. The weird thing is they were obsessed with each other and low-key looked forward to seeing how the other would react. They even caught themselves laughing at each other a couple of times. Tana Jay had to laugh when Rarri and his crew came through shooting up specific cars in his hood because wasn't nobody slipping. He even had him on surveillance tape riding past his spot, up and down the block all night in frustration. Seeing how determined he was to get him made it funnier. Tana Jay even paid the neighbors for the tape so they didn't put him in jail by giving it to the police. He would often put it on and watch it like a movie when he wanted a laugh or two.

Rarri had to laugh every time he saw a group of young niggas running for their lives in his hood without hearing any gunshots. Tana Jay would catch niggas slipping, break a body part and tell them to let Rarri know he had some bullets for him.

One time, Bird called him crying talking about Tana Jay was following her. All she could think about was his gorilla looking ass breaking her fingers or some crazy shit like that, and went into pure panic mode, then went the fucc off on Rarri for laughing like the shit was funny. They were each other's nemesis.

"I quit my job, Rarri."

"Ain't nobody tell you to do that shit," he replied with a mouthful of toothpaste looking at her crazy.

"What are you talkin' bout? That's exactly what you told me to do," she shot back in frustration.

"Oh yea," Rarri laughed thinking back on the day he told her to quit her job. It was that day he popped those Mollys with Peso and them and ended up fucking on Ms. post a lot, Tasha.

Stacey let out a frustrated sigh. "All for that dumb ass label you kept talkin' bout in jail but forgot about when you got out."

Rarri rinsed his mouth then spit out the water as she shook his toothbrush. "Don't call it stupid and it's not just a label it's—"

"A lifestyle and a brand," Stacey said along with him already knowing what he was going to say. "I know what it is but if you don't start takin' this more serious it's not goin' to be shit."

Rarri dried his mouth with a towel and pushed out to the living room with Stacey still behind him and saw the funniest shit.

Bird, Mia, Tia, Fia and Dria was suiting the fuck up. Putting each other's hair in ponytails; taking earrings out. It almost looked like they was about to go to the gym, but he knew that wasn't the case when he saw they all had on their 'tap out' gloves and by how quiet they got when he and Stacey walked in. The four of them looked at her like they were vultures, then at Rarri for an answer, then back at her, then back at Rarri. Tia gave him the 'what's up?' gesture with her hands not giving a fuck about Stacey seeing or not. Her jaw instantly dropped in disbelief when Rarri chuckled "*chill out*" and gave them each a kiss then sat on the couch.

"Wow! So y'all was just goin' to jump me?" Stacey asked looking at Bird.

"Aaayyyee!" Mia, Tia, Fia, and Dria all cheered at the same time. Stacey just shook her head at Bird in disappointment. "I expected better out of you," she said then sat down next to Rarri.

Stacey used to look out for Bird when she was in the halls a few years before she met Rarri, so she always assumed they shared some type of connection, but Bird felt like she was fake for fucking with Rarri cause 'Ms. Brown' used to talk all this square shit about only messing with niggas who got degrees and all that bullshit. Mia, Tia, Fia and Dria didn't like Stacey cause she always talked to them differently than she talked to Heaven. like they were kids or like she was better than them or something. On top of that, they just didn't like Stacey.

"You the one popped up throwin' water on papi like you got it like that," Dria said butting herself in.

"Bitch! I do got it like that!" Stacey barked back and that's all it took for the arguing to start.

The five of them yelling at Stacey; Stacey yelling at the five of them. It was too many egos, too much emotion, too much pride. To put it simply; too many bad bitches in one room. They laughed at her cause to them she was broke; she laughed at them cause to her they were ignorant. They was mad cause she fucked up the surprise meal they were putting together for him. She was mad cause they let him sleep in and miss a business appointment. They don't tell him what to do; she going to tell him what she want. They was playing ping pong with an agreement. Five against one. All this bitching would drive a nigga crazy.

"Nobody said pimpin' was easy," Heaven said as she walked in the door with some thick bitch behind her who was carrying Heaven's Juicy Couture Leopard Velour backpack. She had on a Melissa Odabash swimsuit, Christian Soriano denim shorts, Prada sandals with the matching sunglasses and a Giuseppe Zanetti choker. Her hair was dyed light brown which seemed to go well with everything she had on. She walked almost identical to Heaven, demanding attention with every step. For a minute it almost seemed like they came in in slow motion. Rarri watched her walk all the way to the couch and couldn't help staring at her feet. She had some real pretty feet. He instantly started thinking of some shit to say but forgot as soon as the thought entered his mind.

"Damn," he said out loud on accident causing everyone to stop arguing and the girl to laugh to herself.

"Anyways," Stacey said rolling her eyes at the girl then turned to Heaven. "Heaven, tell them they should have woke him up this morning."

" yall should have woke him up," Heaven told them seriously. "Thank you," Stacey said throwing up her hands and sitting back on the couch, happy Heaven agreed.

"Tell her she shouldn't be waking him up by throwin' water in papi face," Dria said with attitude in her neck, looking directly at Stacey and leaned closer to her with her handcuffing her ear that was pointed at Heaven.

"Hold on!" Heaven said finally looking up from her phone. "Y'all didn't beat this bitch ass?"

"Thank you," they all said at the same time, Dria pointing her finger in her face moving it like she was scribbling.

"Whatever," Stacey said pushing her hand away. Bird, Mia, Tia, fia and Dria was laughing and clowning. They knew she wasn't going to argue with Heaven and it always felt good to make her feel wrong about anything they could.

"Next time we goin' to beat that ass like bing! Bow! Boom! Smack! Smack!" Mia said grabbing a pillow off of the couch demonstrating with sound effects how she was going to do Stacey.

Then, Tia, Fia and Bird jumped in throwing punches too, talking shit. "Naw, don't run! Don't run bitch." Bird said punching the pillow.

"Hold her hands down," Mia said, then her and Fia stopped hitting imaginary Stacey and pretended to hold her arms down while Bird, Tia, and Dria punched, kneed, elbowed and threw a few kicks in before getting up and stomping the pillow out.

"Get her," Heaven cheered.

"I said don't run bitch," Bird laughed as she and the rest of them chased the pillow they were kicking around.

Everybody was laughing, even ole girl. The only person who wasn't was Stacey, but she wanted to though. Stacey knew this was one of them serious jokes like if there *was* a next time, she would really be looking like that pillow for real. She knew they didn't play about Rarri. Low-key, that made her want to go even harder for him, seeing how devoted *they* were, but all he wanted her to do was worry about other shit.

"Ok ok," Heaven chuckled gesturing her hands for them to stop and quiet down. "On some real shit, y'all should have woke him up, tho. That was an important meetin'. We need this so we could move up another notch… like on some legal stuff."

Stacey gave them that look again.

"I already told y'all who I wanted to fuck wit first. Ain't nobody else important like that; not like her. I'm not goin' to wake up for no other muthafuckas cause they not in my vision... what, y'all don't feel my vision no more? My game weak?" Rarri said.

Stacey, Mia, Tia, Fia, Dria and Bird all immediately catered to his side, rubbing through his hair, rubbing on him, kissing him and telling him how strong his game was, boosting up his ego.

"I *feel* that vision papi, I *feeeel* that vision," Fia said like she caught the holy ghost and they all started shaking and laughing.

"Y'all could get up off me," Rarri laughed as he got up, struggling to break free of their grip. They all was holding him playfully.

Despite the random arguing here and there, everybody always had a good time. They might not like business Stacey, but they *loved* late nights in the bed Stacey. They would get off a Molly sometimes and fuck the shit out of Stacey. They turned her all the way out in the bedroom, sometimes with or without Rarri. It was always liable to go down at any moment.

Like for instance; you know how Dria was talking all that shit? Well, right now she got her hand between her legs hoping she don't move cause it's making her pussy wet thinking about how good hers taste and look. Stacey opened her legs a little, then closed them back once Dria's hand fell in deeper, thinking about her lips on her other lips. The whole time everybody talking about what they need to be doing and putting a plan together. They could be the perfect team when doing some shit together.

One blunt a piece and a hour later, the plan was solid. See, when you know the positions of every player on *yo* team it's easier to score points, but when the players on *y'all* team know *their* positions, *y'all* win games. Always play to win unless losing for a greater purpose. Sometimes you could win by losing if you know how to lose right. Most of us been doing it our entire lives without noticing until sitting in a jail cell wondering what the fuck happened. Fast money got a lot of us **failing up**.

The plan was A B C simple. All they had to do was do that shit. Money will walk you through doors broke people couldn't turn the knob on. Literally! All it took was one night in a five-thousand-dollar suite in Tony's Hotel for DJ Janky to sign her life away.

DJ Janky made the best beats in L.A., though nobody really knew. Not yet. Rarri heard her shit when Bird and them was bullshitting on Sound Cloud listening to instrumentals. They stayed in that suite for two weeks. Dumb bangers was the only thing being made in there. Mia, Tia, Fia, and Dria was like magic on the mic. Bird had all the catchy adlibs; she made shit sound even hotter.

DJ Janky was a bad Kreesha Turner looking, bitch. Green eyes, full lips, kinky hair and all. The only thing was she acted like a nigga too much and that shit be throwing a nigga off. Rarri could see she wanted to loosen up though, by how she had been eyeing him and Bird. Especially how she be looking when they all chilling and she be solo. One night she called her girlfriend over which ended up being a mistake cause all she was worried about was fucking with one of the Bentley bitches, so DJ Janky got mad and made her leave. That made her want to really be down when they told DJ Janky about her bitch and didn't fuck her like everybody used to do. DJ Janky was green, so she didn't see the game being ran on her.

Mia and Tia was sending DMs from DJ Janky's girlfriend's phone to Bird, and Bird was, of course, showing them to DJ Janky, after getting her to swear on God she wouldn't say anything that night cause they weren't trying to get kicked out of the luxury Hotel for making a scene. The shit was just too easy. They could make the biggest scene and still not get kicked out; nobody came out of pocket for the room or for her contract. Thanks to Heaven everything was on Tony.

Rarri was feeling good about the songs his bitches made with DJ Janky. All eight of them. They was on some uncut hoe music, no filters or none of that watered-down bullshit. Everything was raw, nasty, explicit and probably too graphic for people not in that lifestyle. The streets was going to love it and that's all that mattered at the moment. They all already had money, so nobody was worried about anything outside of making good music to listen to. Rarri had a gold ear for music, but he didn't know how to rap. He just knew the type of sounds that grabbed people's attention, especially ratchet music and trap shit, but this was a different game. A different topic that was going to be having strip clubs going crazy. I'm talking about making Uncle Luke and Lil Kim sound square, shitting on Pink Dollaz and them. They were talking all hoe shit, most and foremost for the hoes. Nobody was making music for them cause bitches didn't want to be known as hoes. Bird, Mia, Tia, fia, and Dria didn't give a fuck. They been popping and doing trending shit, making it *look* cool. They was "**304 Lit**."

The Flocks were making their way into somebody's backyard again, about to flock some shit they'd been scoping out on their own. You know Infant always triple checked to make sure no dogs was back there, after the incident in the turtle costume. Every time he did his little doggy call, the other flocks would laugh. The muthafuckas whose house it was had the whole thing on camera, but the coldest part was that the owners gave the video to the police, who then put it on the news, which made it's way to YouTube and World Star.

Infant went viral; the whole country was laughing at the Turtle Burglar. Really damn near the whole world.

Luckily, they didn't know who he was but the ones closest to him did, and that was bad enough. Especially Heaven and all them. Every time they saw him, they yelled "what up T.B.!" or "T.B. blood what it doooo!" deepening their voices to manly impersonations. It was an inside joke that he hated and loved at the same time. He hated it because he knew it stood for 'Turtle Burglar', but he loved it cause Bird, Mia, Tia, Fia and Dria was saying it and they didn't even really fuck with the other flocks like they did with him. Sometimes Infant would even go kick it with them by himself and Rarri didn't trip. He was really like everybody's badass little brother they wish they had.

"I'm out here," Lil Flock grabbed him before he could walk off.

"You a cry baby blood," Baby Flock whispered harshly and pushed Infant's shoulder, all of them forcing their smiles off so he would calm down. Every time Infant knew they *needed* him to be the one to go in first, he would be waiting on them to crack a joke or even the slightest smile. Matter of fact, if he even thought they was thinking about laughing he would threaten about not doing it, but always ended up doing it anyway.

That's why he was scaling the wall right now, making his way up to the cracked window while the other Flocks kept lookout. The good thing about Infant was that he wasn't too heavy or too big, so he could always get in or to the hardest places. The wood diamond structured posts held him with ease. Infant was a Pro Flocker, so he knew how to shift his weight properly to make himself even lighter. When he made it to the window, he paused for a minute and listened close because he heard voices. The

Flocks all went mute, still looking up at Infant who was looking down, but not at them.

"We good," Infant whispered after a tense ten seconds. It was the T.V. He knew that All-State commercial almost by heart. That nigga with the deep voice was funny to him.

Infant pushed the window open slowly with his free hand, braced himself on the ledge with his forearm then climbed up and halfway in, quickly.

The first thing he saw was his momma, then his granny, that time the teacher kicked him out of class for flexing on him, his big homies, the flocks, all the good times and hard times they had, all the bitches he fucked at Centennial, The Turtle Burglar shit and the day it happened, all the times he slapped Heaven on the ass and would run, especially that time on his birthday when she tried to chase him and fell in the pool and fucked up her phone, hair, and Dolce and Gabbana dress, then he thought about earlier today cause today was a day nobody would forget. A day he wished he could unsee; not that he was hating or nothing like that but today was *the* day. The day Juice got plugged the way he's been waiting on.

Rarri called a meeting and only the real niggas were invited. The niggas who been down stayed loyal and the ones he trusted most. (Which is not many.)

The meeting was held on one of Tony's yachts. The one he gave to Heaven a few months ago after having it redesigned and named after her of course. Everything from the blankets, pillows, towels, tables, chairs; even the shot glasses and cups they were drinking from had either

Heaven's name or the letter 'H' on it. It was beautiful, but this was no vacation.

Rarri, Lil Dink, Trigg, Macky, B-Dog and the flocks were at the rear of the yacht smoking weed, drinking and chopping it up, clowning, having a good time. All of them fly as fuck, but you know Rarri and Macky gotta try and out dress the world, plus each other.

Macky was low-key on some casual shit, but his Versace swim shorts and Versace beach shirt slightly exposing his Versace briefs let Rarri know he was still trying to flex on the low. Rarri, already ahead of the game wasn't worried about it. He had some custom-made MCM shorts out of this world with the matching loafers and a slim fit fur hoodie all created by the same designer that you would never see again unless he wore it twice. (More than likely, unlikely.)

The older niggas was posted at the front part of the yacht, basically doing the same shit. Everybody was feeling themselves off the liquor and having a good time. Rock, Crow, June, and Studd was clowning on Juice and Brick.

"Nigga I got more money than all four of y'all niggas put together muthafucka," Brick joked, but was serious at the same time. Everybody knew Brick been balling. Out of all of them, he was the only one who actually owned property in his hood. Brick was from Westside Piru. Even though he was a Piru, he been cool with *some* Compton Crips since he was a kid. Really all of them go way back, and Brick plugged Juice with his connect on some real nigga shit before Rarri got popping.

Juice and Brick laughed and gave each other dap. "You two fat cheeseburger, bean bag lookin' muthafuckas ain't got shit," Studd clowned. "First off Brick, yo bitch run yo shit. Cuz . . . and Juice, you this nigga minion, what the fuck you laughin' at?"

"You got me fucked all the way up, I ain't no nigga minion . . . you ole crusty round the mouth, ass nigga," Juice cracked back. "You too old to be forgettin' to wash yo face cuz."

Everybody started laughing at that one, even Studd, cause his face stayed ashy sometimes.

"Dad come look at this, hurry!" Juice Jr. said excitedly as he ran up and pulled on his dad's arm. "Hurry! You goin' to miss it."

Juice didn't want to bring his son with him, but he couldn't find a babysitter on such short notice. "*It's cool. I'm with the homies,*" he told himself. This ain't no place for a nine-year-old to be but wasn't no way in hell he was missing this meeting.

When they made it to the side of the yacht, Juice Jr. stuck his head through one of the rails and pointed down at the water.

"Look dad, sharks."

Juice looked down and saw the sharks too. "Yea son, those is sharks."

"Can we feed them? Please dad," Juice Jr. asked looking up at his father.

"Not right now Jr.," Juice said looking out in the distance of the ocean. He couldn't see anything but water. He hadn't noticed how far out they came until now. *"Where are we goin'?"* he thought.

"Aww," Juice Jr. Cried in frustration. "We're goin' to miss them, dad."

"Arrgh!"

Juice felt a push at his back shoulder and was startled . He jumped hard and quickly turned around.

"I couldn't help it, I had to get you," Heaven laughed.

"Got damn girl, you almost gave a nigga a heart attack," he said with his hand on his chest.

"My bad Juice, you know I love you, boy," Heaven said and planted a kiss on his cheek leaving her lip print.

"*Got damn*," he thought as he inhaled her Gucci perfume. "*This probably what her pussy smell like.*"

She had on a classy black dress that covered her breast, but you could still see that ass from the front. Her hair was in a perfect bun, giving her a sophisticated look. Her pearl necklace and diamond earrings brought out her beautiful eyes that looked so innocent and slightly vulnerable. Everything about her screamed money.

Juice couldn't even respond, but he couldn't take his eyes off of her either, causing Heaven to blush. She loved the way she could make a man forget how to talk just by standing there.

Heaven noticed the sad look on Juice Jr's face. "What's wrong Jr, you not havin' fun?" she asked as she squatted down next to him.

"Yea but dad won't let me feed the sharks," he replied sadly.

"*He's just like his dad*," she thought as a smile spread across her face. "You're so cute," she said as she pinched his cheek. "I'll tell you what. We could feed the sharks before we head back, I promise."

Juice Jr. gave her a hug, so fast, he almost made her fall backward. "Thanks, Heaven."

"You welcome, baby," Heaven said as she hugged him back. "You wanna play the game?"

"You got a game on this boat?" Juice Jr. asked as he pulled back from the hug to look into her eyes.

"Yup! I sure do. I got a PlayStation 4 wit a lot of games too," Heaven replied.

"Can I dad?" he asked looking at his father.

"Go head lil man,"

Heaven stood up with Juice Jr.'s hand in hers.

"Enzi!" she called out loud.

A moment later, a tall black well-built young man came out from inside the bar section of the yacht. His all-black pants and shirt made him look like a bartender or a security guard. He had strong African features, but boyish in the face and the kindest eyes God has ever placed on a person. "Yes, ma'am?" Enzi asked.

"Enzi take Jr. here to the game room and you guys play whatever he wants," Heaven instructed.

Enzi's face lit up with joy. "Yes ma'am," he replied proudly. "Come on Jr. I'll race you there."

The both of them ran back inside and into the game room. Juice shook his head and smiled as he watched his son disappear with Enzi.

"Thanks, Heaven, you know ever since Balinda died, it's been kind of hard for him, without a mom and all."

Heaven put her arm between his and rested her head on his shoulder as they looked into the sea. "You don't have to thank me Juice, you know me and Balinda was close. "

"Yea I know," he replied feeling bad. As he should. I mean how would you feel if you served yo baby momma and she died off yo product?

"What about you, tho, how you been holdin' up?" Heaven asked. Juice sighed deeply. "I been coo, just takin' it one day at a time," he replied. "You know how it is."

Heaven sighed too. "Yea, unfortunately, I do," she said thinking about Angel and God.

"My bad, I ain't mean to br—"

"No, it's ok… it's not a day that goes by I don't think about them," Heaven said then took her arm from around his, grabbed his hands, locked her fingers with his and looked him in his eyes. "You know you could talk to me bout anything right?"

"Yea I know… you been tellin' me that since high school," he replied as his palms started to moist. "*If it wasn't for that bitch ass pimp nigga, I woulda been had her on my team*," he thought to himself.

"So, you ain't gotta tell me nothin'?" Heaven asked searching his eyes with hers.

"*It's like she could see through me... like she lookin' at my soul or somethin'... do I tell her that I always been in love wit her? Even though she stood me up at prom? Or that I hate lookin' at her nephew because he remind me of that bitch ass pimp nigga from Oakland? That I cried in my room when I found out she was hoe'n for cuz? Rarri lucky I ain't pop his lil ass. I should have been killed cuz, but I got somethin' for all these niggas, then it's just goin' to be me and Heaven. Damn that sound good. Me and Heaven. Yup! Just us and us only. Fuck everybody else*," Juice thought to himself.

"I'm good right now, but when I do I'll get at you," is all he said though.

"Ooohh," Rocc, Crow, June, Studd, and Brick all said at the same time. "Y'all cute," Rocc teased.

Juice turned around to look at the crew. "Don't this remind yall of high school?" he asked as he turned back to face her with a smile on his face, but that quickly faded when he saw her hurt watery eyes drop a tear as she stared at him. "What's wrong?"

"Nothin'," Heaven said releasing her hands from his and walking off to the back of the yacht where Rarri was. She stopped and dried her eyes before she stepped insight, then put on her game face. The last thing she needed right now was for muthafuckas to think she was weak.

"Aayyee!" they all cheered when she stepped back there. Heaven couldn't help but laugh and blush a bit. She loved these little niggas. All of them was with the shitz and loyal.

"Y'all come to the front so we could get this shit over wit and head back," Heaven instructed before walking off.

Before she got to the front, she grabbed two of her henchmen to come with her on the deck. When everybody made it to the front, Rarri started the meeting.

"I set this meeting up today so everybody could hear from me personally. It's a few other muthafuckas that could have been here, but we don't need a big ass crowd to get a point across… I'ma always be from where I'm from, I can't change that, and at the end of the day I'ma always rock wit my section, from getting' money to saggin' on shit, whatever; but I'm done wit this gang bangin' bullshit… I'm done wit beefin' wit niggas because of where they grew up at or what they homies done did. If I got a problem with a nigga, it's wit that nigga and that nigga only, but if a muthafucka wanna trip, I'll kill him off, too. If a nigga come between my money or my homies money, he getting killed off. Ain't no way around that. It's a lot of ways to get paid. Some of us sell dope, flock, credit card scams; all type of shit. Me! I'm getting money out of a bitch. That's what I'm good at. That what I like to do. It's in my blood."

Heaven smiled. "Whatever you do best or whatever you feel you could do best, that's what you need to do, and we all need to support each other in whatever that is. If you wanna go back to school, do that shit. You wanna open up a business, do that shit. However you choose to get money is on you, but getting money is a must. Ain't goin' to be no broke niggas in our circle. That's out! Those of us who choose to get ours out the mud, on our gutta shit, we the ones who really puttin' on for the cause. Fuck tryna put on more gangstas, everybody ain't a thug; but you got niggas imitatin' cause they feel like that's the only way to be accepted. Then when shit get real they tell on niggas. It's more muthafuckas nowadays that claim to be bangin' getting' on the stand pointin' at the niggas that shot him than ever before. And niggas is lettin' them live, but wanna kill a real nigga? What part of the game is that? If I ever snitch, y'all muthafuckas better give me a painful death, cause if the shoe is on the other foot, I swear I won't hesitate. If a nigga wit the shit, that's great, but if he ain't that's even better."

"We need to put on muthafuckas who wanna be lawyers, DA's, Cops, Doctors, Athletes, and business-oriented muthafuckas so we could make power moves. Everybody don't gotta be hard. The most important rule we push is no snitchin'. Zero tolerance for snitches no matter who it is. Snitches on a no live policy. We need a circle of trigger-happy niggas to take care of that. That's goin' to be their job; to catch 'em and kill'em. That's it! From them to the squares we goin' to fund them all. Success is the goal. If a homie got a bail, ain't no reason he should be in jail cause that make us look bad. If a nigga goin' to trial, it ain't wit no public defender. One thing we goin' to do is look out and support each other to the fullest. Families and all. If one of us have a home, we all got a home . . . if I'm on, you on."

Rarri stopped and took a sip of his drink, then put the cup down. "So… who ain't wit it?" he asked looking at all of them. Nobody said nothing. Everybody just looked at one another.

Brick stood up and starred at Rarri for a minute with a serious mean mug, then smiled. "So, what y'all goin' to call that shit?"

Rarri smiled back and said, "**BABE STREET**."

"What 'BABE' stand for?" Lil flock asked.

"It stand for whatever you want it to stand for," Rarri replied. "For me, it stand for **Break a Bitch Easy** cause I break bitches . . . for a nigga who sell dope, **Break a Brick Easy... Believe And Behold Everything** , it stand for whatever you want it to Flock. *You* run this shit. *We all* run this shit.

Everybody was just nodding in approval soaking it in. "And I ain't askin' y'all to stop bangin', that's just a decision I'm makin' for me and for the movement… I gotta give this shit my all," Rarri added.

"So, what's up wit the product. How that's goin' to work out?" Rocc asked.

"*That's what the fuck I been waitin' on,*" Juice said to himself.

"Lil Dink, yo ass is out of my way. Won't be goin' through you no more."

Rarri looked over at Heaven. She took a sip of her drink and happily stood before speaking.

"Ok, Ima keep this short cause I got shit to do, unlike y'all muthafuckas," Heaven joked.

Everybody laughed.

"It's goin' to be business as usual, same shit just a better price . . . I found some more places to open up shop for those of y'all who want to expand to some more money . . . . . . umm, the flocks; y'all already know how we do, I got some shit for y'all. We bout to start gettin' rid of competition and turnin' them into customers… let me see, umm . . . what else? What else? I think that's it," Heaven said as she was thinking deeply.

"*What the fuck?*" Juice thought.

"Oh yea, I almost forgot. Juice come here," Heaven said with her hands extended out to him and a seductive look in her eyes.

"*Yes! I knew it . . . she bout to put me on . . . she want a nigga,*" Juice told himself as he quickly got up, walked to her and put his hands in hers.

"Juice, we go way back . . . shid, really I've known you longer than everybody on this yacht…I can't explain the connection between us, but I know it's real," Heaven explained looking him in his eyes so he could feel her words. The whole time Juice looked like a bitch who knows the man she loves most is about to ask her to marry him. I'm surprised he didn't say *I do*.

Heaven leaned in to kiss him and you know he met her halfway. Both of them closed their eyes as they locked lips. The electricity between them was so strong, Juice felt like he would bust a nut standing up, right then and there.

Heaven pulled back keeping her eyes on his and biting her lip like she was in the middle of cumming.

"Carlos! Jose!" Heaven called the two men standing next to her, never taking her eyes off Juice.

"Yes?" they both asked standing at attention. "Chain this nigga up," she said coldly.

Carlos grabbed him while Jose simultaneously locked the 250-pound ball weight chain around his ankle. It looked like the same ones slaves used to have on back in the day. All the older niggas hopped up at the same time about to move in on her henchmen.

"What the fuck!" Juice yelled at Heaven.

"Sit down," she told them ignoring Juice, but they all still stood.

"What you doin' Heaven?" Crow asked. "Take that shit off the homie leg, cuz."

Juice was trying to yank it free, but the lock was on solid. "What the fuck Hea—" Juice started.

"Shut yo fat ass up!" Heaven yelled. Now her eyes didn't seem so loving anymore. "Carlos play that shit."

Carlos pulled out a remote from his pocket and pointed it at the stereo that was connected to the speakers on the yacht then pressed play.

"You know we could charge you for murder on top of the drugs we found in your car, right? Everybody knows you gave your baby mother the drugs that killed her you piece of shit, but I don't want you; I want the person that's supplyin' you and the others you work with," the detective said.

"I can't testify on nobody man, if I do I'm dead," Juice replied.

"You don't have to testify. I just need names and phone numbers you know, that type of shit," the detective said.

"If I give you the names, I walk?" Juice asked. "Today?"

"Hell, if you give me the names, you can run, skip, jog, whatever pleases your fat ass the most, but if you bullshit me, I swear to God, I will fuck your life up," the detective threatened.

It was a brief pause then you could hear Juice sigh deeply.

"Rarri and Lil Dink…them two niggas been floodin' the city wit this shit . . . everybody movin' packs for them, now. Me, June, Rocc, Crow, Studd, and Brick. They frontin' everybody for the low wit good work. I could give you all of they phone numbers."

"Where are they gettin' all of these drugs?" Whose supplyin' them?" the detective asked.

"Nobody knows, but it has to be someone big cause they ain't ever ran out. It's always around—"

Heaven signaled for Carlos to turn it off. Juice looked up from the ground at the niggas he just sold out.

"Brick it ain't even like that I sw—"

"Shut the fuck up blood," Brick barked. "You snitchin', it's like that."

"June! Cuz I—"

"Keep cuz out yo mouth homie, you a imposter, nigga," June said with a look of disgust on his face.

"Rocc! Crow! Studd! Come on y'all… w-w-w-we grew up together," Juice trembled. You could see his bottom lip shaking from a mile away. He didn't dare look over at Rarri or Lil Dink cause he already knew how they got down.

"You made yo bed homie, now you gotta lay in it," Rocc said as he sat down and casually drank from his cup.

Juice looked to Crow and Studd, but they just shook their heads and sat down, too.

"Heaven please!" Juice cried as he fell to the ground and grabbed on to one of her legs. "Please don't do this."

All of the young niggas started laughing hard as fuck. Juice looked like a kid holding on to his momma crying cause he didn't want her to leave the house. Carlos and Jose had to pry his hands from around her. Juice balled up and sobbed like a mark, which made the little niggas laugh harder and harder.

"Can y'all believe this nigga thought I was goin' to give him some pussy?" Heaven joked then turned back and looked down at him. "Juice did you really think I would fuck you?"

Juice was in such a shocked and panicked state of mind, that everything around sounded far away and muffled as he kept crying. Juice had never been this scared in his life. Back in his days when he was coming up, killers would kill you with mean mugs and hardened faces, like they was mad or something. Everything would be more serious. But as he lay there and sobbed, these new little niggas find it funny; hilarious that he about to die. "*These lil muthafuckas goin' to laugh as they shoot me in front of my son. Oh, shit my son!*" he thought.

He felt someone pulling at his arm. When Juice looked up it was Lil Dink.

"Get yo bitch ass up," Lil Dink said smiling as he helped Juice to his feet. Lil Dink shook his head with that same smirk on his face as he looked him over one last time and went back to sit down.

Juice looked over at Brick and the other older niggas he grew up with. None of them was laughing or smiling. They kind of looked sad and mad at the same time. Yeah, Juice was obviously a snitch, but deep down it hurt them to see him begging for his life and crying like a little bitch in front of Heaven and these little niggas. When somebody knows they are about to die, you see the real them, not the image they portray. When it's somebody you grew up with, it's more fucked up because you feel like you've been lied to, played, deceived and tricked your whole life. It's like your parents waiting until you turn thirty-five to let you know you were really adopted as a child. Yeah, it's that bad, but a person only understands the feeling when it happens to them.

"Y'all goin' to let them shoot me in front of my son?" Juice asked. "We better than this my nigg—"

"Ain't nobody goin' to shoot you," Rarri said cutting him off, coldly.

"Aye! Carlos! Jose! Strap the tank to this nigga."

Carlos and Jose strapped an oxygen tank to Juice's back and forced him to put on an oxygen mask. Rarri walked over to the side and unlatched one of the rails and swung it open. Carlos and Jose both grabbed the 500-pound metal ball that Juice was chained to and walked it to where Rarri was, pulling Juice with them. They sat the ball right at the edge of the opening.

"Come on Rarri my son is g—"

"You's a scandalous ass nigga, Juice," Rarri said cutting him off and loud enough for everybody to hear him. "You greedy, selfish and jealous . . . You sold out niggas you grew up wit and told on young niggas that used to look up to you . . . ain't a loyal bone in yo body. You all for yo'self. We would all be in jail right now… lucky for us, the one thing you never knew was that we been gettin' police on payroll."

Juice's eyes grew wide at the last part. "Yup! Everybody passed but you. That shit was just a test my nigga. Honestly, I ain't expect you to go out like that. 'Naw! Not Juice' . . . *not the loccsta . . . Mr. Get Dough."*

Rarri laughed at the last part and continued. "I waited to get everybody together before I put you on blast so they could hear it personally . . . you ain't give us choices. You just tried to down us and drown us the first chance you got. But I'ma fair nigga; Ima give you two choices.

Carlos and Jose both placed a foot on the ball's weight.

"You could either drown or sink to the bottom and get crushed by pressure," Rarri said and looked over at Lil Dink who was texting on his phone.

"Aye Dink! What's that word called again?"
"Implode, it's like explodin' but it explode *in,* tho," Lil

Dink replied using his hands as examples as he emphasized the different meaning of the two words.

"Yea, so they call it implode, cuz."

"That shit confusin'," Rarri thought.

"Yea, implode or drown nigga... that's it. Them yo two choices," he told Juice.

How could someone choose between two horrible ways to die; drown or sink to the bottom? Really, getting crushed before you make it to the bottom. Damn, that shit would hurt. I don't know which is worst.

Juice was lost in his thoughts trying to figure out what to do. The last two choices he would ever have to make would both be painful. Getting shot doesn't seem so bad right now. At least it would be over faster than this.

Rarri leaned in close to Juice so that he could only hear him and nobody else. "Don't think I'ma slip up like you did, my nigga … you shoulda killed me a long time ago. This for settin' my pops up, bitch. My momma killed herself cause of that shit."

"How did he find out about that? The only people that knew was me and- . . . fuck ... Sir Master!" Juice thought.

When Rarri stepped back, Carlos and Jose kicked the ball weight over the ledge. The force of the ball weight pulled at his ankle so hard that his foot yanked outwards and he fell back, hitting his head hard on the deck before sliding off.

"Dad!" Juice Jr. screamed as he saw his father slide over the edge of the yacht.

Juice Jr. ran to the edge and looked down at the water screaming for his dad. "Dad! Dad! Dad! Dad! Dad!"

This was more than a sad sight to see. It was horrible; no child should ever have to witness their parents' murder.

Rarri just walked off leaving the little nigga screaming cause he honestly didn't give a fuck about no son of a snitch, especially not Juice or Juice Jr. *"I fuck around and don't even drink no more got damn juice,"* he thought as he hit the blunt Macky passed him and sat down. *"Damn I forgot to tell him I'm the one who gave Balinda the hot-shot . . . fuck it."*

Enzi walked over to Juice Jr. and stood next to him. "Enzi my dad is in the water," Juice Jr. cried pointing down.

"You want your pops little man?" Enzi asked in his heavy accent.

"Yes! Please, Enzi, please!" Juice Jr. begged still looking into the water hoping his dad would come back up.

Enzi grabbed the back of his collar with his left hand and the top belt part in the back of his pants with his right hand. "Go find him," he said as he threw Juice Jr. as hard as he could into the air, sending him flying off the yacht.

Juice was sinking fast. He didn't want to keep going down alive, but he couldn't bring himself to remove the mask either. He could still hear Rarri's voice in his head.

"Don't think I'ma slip up like you did my nigga . . . you shoulda killed me a long time ago."

"He said he's not goin' to slip up like I did. What did he mean by that? How did I sl—"

It hit him like a ton of bricks right in the middle of his thoughts.

"Jr!" Juice screamed as he looked up to the top of the ocean, then something fell in. He couldn't make out what it was, but he was sure it had to be Juice Jr.

"Junior-rrrrr!" Juice Jr. instinctively tried to swim back towards the yacht, but he wasn't fast enough. The harder he tried, the more tired he became, eventually giving up and going under.

Heaven watched the whole struggle while sipping an apple martini and cheering on Juice Jr.

"Faster! Faster! Come on you could make it Jr. You could make it." "Aww! Poor thing" is all she said when he gave up.

When she turned around everybody was staring at her like she was crazy.

"What? I promised him we'd feed the sharks . . . the fuck!" Heaven barked with more attitude than a little bit and stormed off.

"You still in love, my nigga?" Flock asked his lil homie

Infant saw all that flash before his eyes after he heard the BANG! It seemed like the world stopped spinning soon as the other flocks heard the shot. It was like somebody pressed pause as they looked up at Infant who was still in the window, then slid him out in slow motion, only so he could fall in fast forward. He hit the concrete porch hard and lifeless.

Flock and Lil Flock took off running. Wasn't nothing they could do. Sometimes all you got is a split second to make a decision that could be life changing. Baby Flock couldn't move; he was stuck. But even if he wasn't, he couldn't leave Infant. That was his nigga and Infant wouldn't leave him. Baby Flock sat next to his little brother until the cops came.

***

Rarri wiped the sweat from his face with the towel halfway around his neck as he came out of the fitness room and walked down the hallway back to his suite listening to some shit DJ Janky put together with *304 Lit*, while he was gone earlier. The drops on her beats were crazy and the symphonies were really the jankiest shit he had ever heard. It's like her sound would escalate each time, pushing them to go even harder. Their vocals were so perfect it blended in with her instrumentals. They related to each other's sound like they shared the same DNA, musically entwined in each other's style, feeding on the other vibe and energy, seizing the moment.

Rarri nodded at Jose who was walking towards him like nothing happened earlier. He always smiled at people like one of those Mexicans who never stopped smiling and said *yea* to everything cause they didn't know English.

Jose held his hand out to give Rarri a handshake, nodding his head up and down extra hyper like he thought all cool Mexicans did. Rarri always chuckled to himself, cause he thought Jose probably watched the movie Grease too many times by how he walked trying to look cool, slicking the hair back and all that.

As soon as they shook hands, Jose's grip tightened hard as hell and he pushed him to the left with all his might. Rarri was taken by surprise and quickly braced himself with his free hand preparing to hit the door, but it swung open before he even touched it and both of them fell in.

Carlos closed the door just as fast as he opened it. The timing was so precise and professional; it didn't even look like nothing just happened.

Rarri was trying to wrestle Jose off of him and they ended up halfway in the front bathroom. He paused in shock at all the bloody body parts in the bathtub and instantly thought about the movie Scarface looking at Enzi in there all chopped up.

"*How Tony find out about Chu Chu,*" Rarri asked himself, but Carlos injected him in the side with something before he could come up with an answer. Rarri stumbled out of the bathroom and into almost everything in the living room of the suite, until finally falling to the floor. "Aunty?" he mumbled reaching for the blurry woman figure who was fading away.

TERRANCE CASH
THE UNDERDOG

AZJAH
PRINCESS OF
Compton
AVAILABLE 4/26

Please
excuse me
for being
antisocial

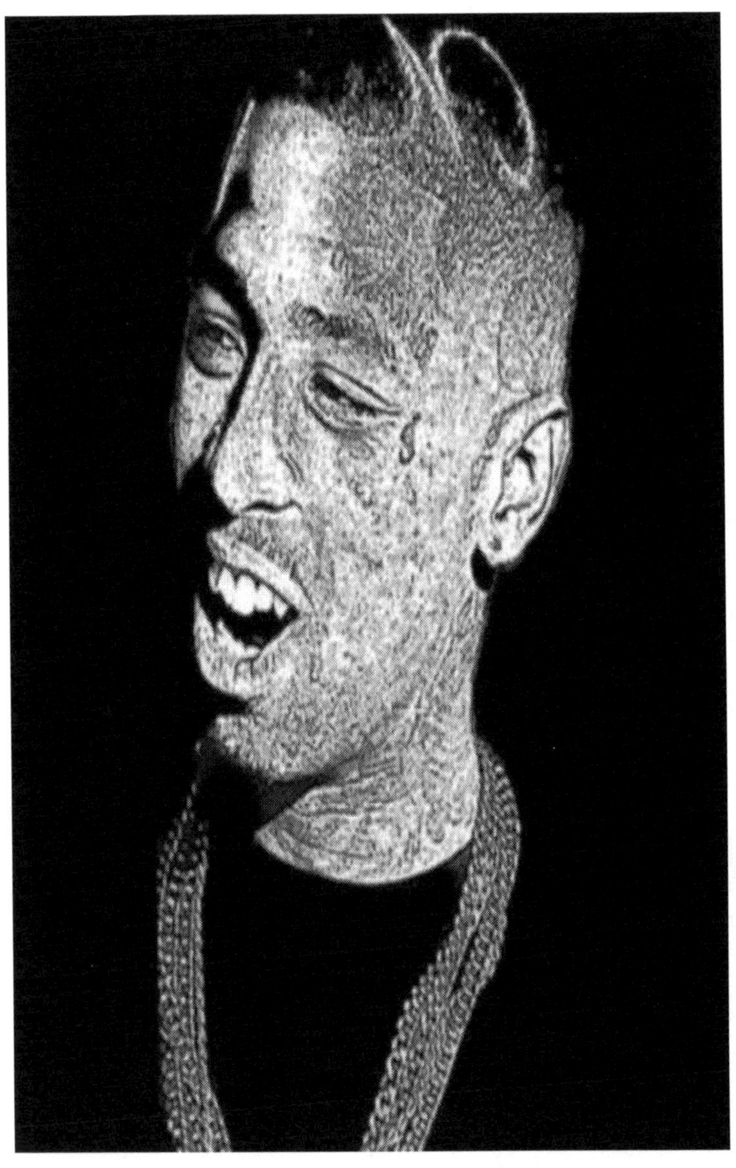

Keep askin for it ✌️ ?

Asanibandz88@gmail.com

Facebook : Studd dula

Instagram : Asani Bandz

Send a picture of you holding my book and I will post on my pages.

Cover designed by :

Facebook: iesha bree

www.ieshabree.com/covers-my-way

Made in the USA
Columbia, SC
31 July 2024